Flaxfields

by

Deirdre Bates

◇

Flaxfields

by

Deirdre Bates

◇

Hodgson Press

First published in Great Britain by Hodgson Press 2011

Hodgson Press
PO Box 903[A]
Kingston upon Thames
Surrey
KT1 9LY
United Kingdom
enquiries@hodgsonpress.co.uk
www.hodgsonpress.co.uk

A CIP catalogue record for this book is available from the
British Library.

ISBN: 978-1-906164-14-0

Printed in Great Britain by Lightning Source Ltd.

Contents

Part I

Dublin: Reunion and severance

◇

The Prologue

Summer 1937

In a cramped room at the far end of the top floor corridor of St Hilda's Convent School, Dublin, a kimono-clad woman twisted and turned listlessly in front of a full length mirror on the inside of a wardrobe door. At her feet lay a large, liberally-labelled, partially-unpacked, black tin trunk with a mish-mash of stuff on the floor around it. A warm breeze stirred the curtains at the open casement window and carried the smell of new mown grass into the room. In the Chapel beneath the window, Evensong was underway. A blackbird fluted on the Chapel roof.

As the woman – mid-thirties – looked at her reflection, shafts of low sunlight highlighted strands in her unmanageable, albeit chin-length auburn hair; played on the turquoise silk of her kimono and on the resplendent gold-embroidered dragon on its back. Her workaday shoes spoiled the image so she took them off and put on the kimono's matching mules.

Vaguely cheered (a nice dressing-gown and slippers for the summer months! she thought. Why hadn't she thought of it sooner?), the woman scanned the clutter on the floor, not quite accepting its uselessness. There were little pieces of silver – baptismal mostly – Apostle spoons, napkin-rings, egg-cups; bamboo canes of various lengths (why on earth had she kept those?) and knick-knacks in rattan, ebony and ivory… many finely carved. Letters and photographs galore (she hadn't dared start on those!) were there too, as were numerous well-read books, a few school magazines and a couple of white, silk garments.

Specifically the woman had come in search of a remnant. With a sigh, she knelt down and turned her attention to the remaining contents of the trunk. She unearthed a piece of pale pink silk, held it up, smiled wanly and placed it on a nearby chair. Then she dug out a rectangular, satin-lined basket, tentatively undid the ribbon with which its lid was secured and gingerly extracted a thin strip of cream lace to put with the piece of silk on the chair. Forlornly she fingered the rest of the basket's contents – further strips of lace, an exquisitely carved, dark brown necklace, a pure linen hand towel monogrammed with her father's initials, a well-thumbed nature project – before carefully rewrapping them. As she replaced the basket in the trunk, a flat parcel on the trunk's base caught her eye. She frowned, and with nothing short of unseemly haste, repacked everything on the floor, took her kimono and mules off and repacked them too.

Evensong came to an end. The blackbird fell silent.

Agonised, the woman heaved her heavy trunk under her bed. Slumping against the covers she thought: my God, how could it have come to this – ashes to ashes? How could so much love have become so blighted, so much beauty so tarnished? And so quickly! And when, if ever, will the purpose and equilibrium that once pervaded my life be restored?

Chapter One

September 1926

Inniscone Station, County Cavan – a County in the Free State, the southern part of recently partitioned Ireland – was busier than usual; there was a horse fair on in the town that day and any fair or market in the land was apt to increase trade. The weather too was favourable, it being that lovely between-season time of year when migratory birds prepared for long flights, fading green leaves gave way to russet, limp September blooms to autumn berries; when farmers took stock of their harvest and the pace slackened on the land. And when lamps were once again trimmed early in the evening, and morning mists lingered longer over Cavan's hills, lakes, woods, marsh-meadow lands and bogs.

The train due in, a southbound one, was running late, something the station guard – a spindly old fellow, clinging as tenaciously to his beard as his job, took in his stride, whistling his way through his day's work with spasmodic renderings of 'Are Ye Right There, Michael?' Though more numerous than usual, his waiting passengers were not unfamiliar to him. He could put names to most of them: to the blanched priest at the head of the platform, the scattered farmers, the small clusters of black-clad, brimmed-hatted elderly women whose heaped shopping baskets bore witness to their early-morning, mist-laden start to the day.

The mist had lifted now – it was about ten am – and the September air was fresh and clear; and peaceful. More peaceful than anyone could have anticipated five years ago when, as 'the Troubles' climaxed, Cavan had been wrested from Ulster and the United Kingdom and assigned to the Free State. 'Out, out!' the IRA had cried to the County's Protestant Establishment – its British army and RIC (Royal Irish Constabulary) personnel in particular. The Establishment had dug in, confident to the last, right down to the wire, that when the crunch came the Unionist leader, Edward Carson, and his Ulster Volunteers, would not let them down. Their confidence – with some exceptions – had been badly misplaced.

Notwithstanding – five years on from Partition, Cavanites (Protestants as well as Catholics) were settling down in the Free State, making the best of things, especially the peace.

A distant toot heralded the train's approach. Waiting fares – inured like the guard to erratic time-keeping – waited patiently. When they were all aboard, doors slammed, and the guard poised to wave his green flag, a young woman rushed on to the platform followed by a hefty man making light of a heavy suitcase. Smiling at the guard – I know them, he was thinking, unable quite to place them – the woman made for the rearmost, the nearest carriage and climbed in. Her companion lifted her case up after her and, with a quick good-bye to her and grateful wave at the guard, hurried off. Puzzled, the guard dispatched the train. Then he smiled; he had remembered who the latecomers were – Allens from 'Shandoran', the big Protestant flax estate in the parish of Kilbeg, over Ballymun way. It was a long time since he'd seen them but the hair was unmistakeable. Good folk, he thought, and very lucky to have survived the Troubles in Cavan. Whistling, he went on his way.

Relieved to have caught the train, if mildly angry with her brother, Henry, for cutting the trap ride from their home, Shandoran, so fine, Amy Allen – a practical, level-headed girl with a balanced view of all things – straightened her cloche and coat and sat back. She was twenty-three years old, shapely and of moderate height – about five foot seven – with hazel eyes in a neat-featured, freckled face. What distinguished her above all else was her hair – an unbiddable shoulder-length mass of auburn curls that made wearing hats, something she liked doing, very difficult. Today she was returning to Dublin for the start of another year at 'Glenarkle' – the boys' preparatory school where she taught. Normally she caught a train from her home town, Ballymun, but because there was a horse fair on in Inniscone and her brother, Henry, was on the look out for a new shire it had been Inniscone today.

Even as she chided Henry, Amy knew in her heart she could never really be angry with him: he had suffered so much in his youth, and there was a vulnerability about him that would always give her concern, especially when they were apart. But at least she could bid farewell to him nowadays without the anguish that had accompanied their earlier partings. It was marvellous to see him so happy taking leave of her: master (de facto as well as de jure!) of Shandoran – the estate they both loved; with a wife and daughter he adored. It was enough to make Amy's heart burst with pride.

Heartened, and with Inniscone and Cavan receding by the minute, Amy allowed Shandoran and her brother, Henry to slip to the back of her mind. Something else was demanding her attention; another man she loved. Hankering after him was pretty stupid, she knew. You've had two short outings with him, Amy, a long time ago, her practical, down-to-earth nature said; he's probably married now or engaged; you've no idea where he is. Her forthright mother thought the same: 'Where's your common sense, girl? – The man's a wastrel – here today and gone tomorrow – with no land or heritage behind him or a good profession ahead; no provenance or prospects, Amy!' For Amy's mother, a good profession for a man was the Church, medicine or law. But hanker Amy did. Because overriding the negatives were two, for her, huge positives: the two short outings with the man of her dreams were unforgettable; and although she had no idea where he was now, she knew where he might be – Dublin, the very place she was headed for.

Lulled by fatigue – the trap ride from Shandoran had been long as well as fraught – and the train's rocking, Amy did a little recollecting.

Meantime, in the train's foremost carriage, the blanched priest who had boarded at Inniscone was studying his breviary. In the opposite corner of the compartment a young man looked up from his book – books were his life-blood, he devoured them – and threw a cynical glance in the priest's direction. Inhaling deeply on the last of his cigarette, the young man wondered if

7

the priest knew his breviary by heart, and if he was happy. No women! And prescribed books only! Not much fun in that, he thought, stubbing his cigarette and lighting another.

The young man's name was Phil Handy. Twenty-seven years old, six feet tall and slim, with brushed-back straight fair hair, he was travelling to Dublin from his home town, Fermanagh, in Northern Ireland. Six years previously his home had been in County Cavan – a county directly to the south of Fermanagh – in a small market town called Ballycool on the opposite side of the parish of Kilbeg to Ballymun.

Picking up his book – Aristotle's *Ethics* – Phil started reading where he had left off, the part where the author considers what the chief good at which all men aspire is – Pleasure, Wealth or Honour. After a few more pages he put the book down again. Wealth and honour seemed distant dreams to him; but pleasure, happiness? That was different.

Looked at rationally – and he did try to look at things rationally – Phil knew he should have been happy. For after years of teaching in Wales he was heading back to Dublin to his old school 'Poynings' where he had always wanted to teach. That said – and with Phil there had to be qualifiers – Dublin was no longer in the Union, and the job he'd accepted at Poynings was not exactly the one he'd envisaged, and the prospect of having to rub shoulders with a certain person at the school irked him.

Whatever have I done to deserve it? He asked himself unable to think of a single thing. Happiness is illusory. There's no justice in life. If there is, where was it when my law-abiding, Bible-loving, hard-working parents were driven from their home in Cavan, and my lovely sister, June, scarred for life. The IRA ruined everything. Damn them.

Aggrieved, Phil reflected on his family's lot.

Pretty much destitute, his parents had come into Ballycool, Cavan, at the start of the century and owed what little they'd accrued there to the RIC. His father had risen to the rank of Sergeant, a position enabling him, his wife and their burgeoning offspring to reside gratis in the town's spacious Barracks. They had never known such luxury. Sadly, a shoot out with law breakers on the eve of the Great War led to the loss of the Sergeant's lower left arm and his pensioning from the force. Stoically he'd bought a small terrace house on the edge of town, thanked God for his remaining blessings and even, in time, detected advantages in his adversities. For when the Troubles had begun and the IRA set their sights on Cavan's Establishment – its British Army and RIC personnel in particular – Mr Handy told his family not to be alarmed. His long absence from the RIC, he said, and unsuitability for the British army (an amputee was not wanted there either) would persuade the IRA to pass the Handys by in much the same way as the Lord had passed over the houses of the Israelites when He smote the first born in Egypt. The IRA had had other ideas – Get-out warnings; stones; incendiaries.

Phil's reflections saddened and angered him.

At the back of the train Amy Allen's were having the opposite effect on her despite them coinciding with the arrival, April 1920, of the IRA's first Get-out-of-Cavan warning to the Handys.

On nodding terms with Mrs Handy at local markets, fairs etc. Amy's mother, Eleanor Linnaker, was moved to help the stricken family. 'They've been through so much in the past, Amy, and now this!' she'd said, handing her daughter a basket of fresh farm produce – eggs, butter and so on. Acts of charity like this were second nature to the mistress of Shandoran.

No mission could have begun more auspiciously, as Amy – sweet sixteen for another month, her spirits as high as the pennoned purple ribbon on her panama – cycled westwards out of Shandoran towards Kilbeg and Ballycool; secretly she was hoping to meet Phil whom she'd heard a lot about from his brother, Al, at the ceilidhs; Phil was never at the ceilidhs. April sun glinted on Shandoran Lake to her left. A swallow – the first she'd seen that year, a good luck sign – dipped low round Shandoran Hill to her right to skim across the water. Thanks to a lull in the fighting, the guns weren't cracking. Two hours later – dripping, bedraggled and mud-spattered, not so much a Sister of Mercy as an unsold sheep on a wet market day in Ballymun – she was standing in the Handys' small hallway holding out her now sodden gifts. A sudden break in the weather, a speeding Crossley lorry, and a rough search ('Mind the eggs!' she'd cried, too late) by a 'Tan', British army auxiliary, at a checkpoint had confounded the good omens. Adding to her ignominy, a glance through the Handys' ajar parlour door revealed Phil (it could not have been anyone else) looking up from his book to give her a cynical once over. The rest of the family made her very welcome though, especially June – Phil's second sister, a frail, tall-for-her-age-girl with long, straight blonde hair and a magical touch at the piano. 'Fine for scrambling' June said about the broken eggs; and later – after non-stop rain and the curfew forced Amy to stay the night – she joined in Amy's solo at the family sing-song; Amy didn't have an ear and everyone had to do a solo except Phil who kept out of sight.

The following morning, mightily miffed, Amy rode away from Ballycool. I suppose he thinks I'm a silly little schoolgirl, she thought; I am after all still sixteen and he's a grown man turned twenty-one. A little further on, she heard a voice – 'Aren't we feeling sociable today?' She pulled up, and shuffling her bike round saw Phil reclining on his mack on a bank of primroses, his bicycle on its side nearby. 'I thought you were playing tennis!' she said indignantly, remembering his cursory 'Bye, all! I'm off to play tennis' round the kitchen door at breakfast. 'That was only a ploy,' he replied, smiling, and getting to his feet to stuff his mack in his carrier and join her on the road. She liked his smile – a winning, heart-stopping one – and the word ploy; she could only think of good words after the event. She liked his accent too: soft, and more-Dublin-than-Cavan, it smacked of sophistication. Her own accent, despite as many years at boarding-school in the capital as him, was still broad Cavan; she put it down to her lack of an ear. And something about Phil's eyes…

They rode along together; circumventing hazards (ruts, potholes and hastily filled in trenches dug by the IRA to ensnare the Crossleys), chatting and laughing in the fresh morning air, bending low into the wind on the ups, leaning back on the downs. Mostly they chatted about their families. And Amy told Phil she was hoping to go to Trinity College, Dublin when she left her Convent boarding-school, St. Hilda's that year. She knew Phil was already at Trinity – his brother, Al, had told her that at the ceilidhs too – and that he was teaching Maths in Wales to pay for it. Lots of students worked their way through the College like that, taking advantage of the war-related shortage of teachers on the other side of the Irish Sea and seven instead of the usual four years to qualify. 'Do you know what they call us?' Phil asked apropos his nautical to-ing and fro-ing. Amy shook her head. "'Steamboaters'", he said, making her laugh and tell him she was planning to offset some of the costs of her own university studies by having digs and helping out at St. Hilda's. The time flew by.

Coming up to Shandoran Amy didn't want the journey to end. 'Have you ever been up to the fort?' she asked indicating the ruined ramparts on top of Shandoran Hill. Phil hadn't. 'Well come on then,' she said, ditching her bike and haring up the hill. 'Hold your horses,' he cried in hot pursuit.

At the top of the hill she pointed out the sights: flax fields to the north; her maternal grandparents' home, 'The Mill', to the south; Kilbeg and Ballycool – the direction from which they had just come – to the west; her own home, Shandoran, to the east, and beyond it Ballymun – end of the Dublin line. The River Lisanne held all together, twisting and turning on its north-south axis, swallowing tributaries, powering mills, discernible even when out of sight by lines of lordly poplars. 'Would you like a wish?' Amy asked then, and took off around the ramparts with Phil close behind. She almost toppled at the last, but he caught her arm and steadied her. His touch, his voice, his everything – thrilled her. As they stood in the centre of the ring to make their wish, their eyes held; Phil's were grey-blue, and searching.

They sat down on the ramparts and looked out over the flax fields – acres and acres of them. 'It's a picture in summer,' Amy said. 'I bet,' Phil replied – 'God, how I love Cavan!' Detecting a note of wistfulness, and not unmindful of Shandoran's survival in the Troubles so far, Amy asked kindly – 'Do you think you'll be able to hold on in Ballycool?' It was a moment before Phil answered. Then, 'Sure we will!' he said buoyantly – 'Carson and his Volunteers won't let us down!' He stood up. 'Now let's be off!' he added, 'or your mother'll be sending a posse out to look for you.' Amy savoured the word 'posse'. They raced down the hill and parted where they'd left their bikes.

Recollections like these, at a time like this, on the train to Dublin, kept Amy's hopes alive.

By now, Phil Handy's humour had improved slightly. For happiness, he'd concluded, had not been entirely illusory – certainly not in the pursuit of carnal knowledge. A pitiful glance at the priest, who had switched his breviary for his beads – fifty-five, the lesser number, Phil noted cynically – accompanied this thought. Despite his parents' Godliness, Phil was an avowed atheist: 'Churchmen, all Churchmen, are hypocrites,' he would say. 'They give me the pip.' At the same time, he felt mildly sorry for the priest missing out on so much that came natural to a fellow.

Mulling over his past catches, Phil wondered what the capital held in store for him. A fling was what he liked, nothing permanent, definitely not marriage. So strongly did he feel on the subject of marriage he had a little way of warding off clingy girlfriends; it hadn't failed him yet. One girl in particular – not a catch, a girl he'd met in passing – came to mind. A fling with her might be nice! But maybe she had left the capital; gone back to Cavan to teach. Her family, as much a part of the Protestant Establishment there as his, had survived the Troubles. Why? And why was he even thinking about her? Wherever she was, she was probably spoken for, and even if she wasn't wouldn't be interested in a loser like him. She must have changed a lot since he'd seen her. Had she had the hair cut? My God, what hair!

For a moment or two mixed visions of Amy Allen's hair preoccupied Phil. The sopping waist-length mass of auburn curls pasted to her neck and freckled face when she'd pitched up at his parents' home in Ballycool with her basket of charity – As if the Handys needed charity from anyone! And the breathtaking beauty of the same curls when he and she had ridden back to Shandoran next day: glinting in the bright spring sunshine at the top of Shandoran Hill, they'd mesmerised him; and done the same at the end of the summer hols on their second outing, another bike ride instigated by him. A bike ride whose original goal, a wide sweep of the locality's lakes and hills, had been reduced, as these things often are – he'd inquired about her ancestors and she'd suggested a gander at their memorials – to the mile separating Shandoran from Kilbeg Church. Trailing over her lace-trimmed, lime-green silk blouse and pert breasts as she'd sat on the tiny triangle of pebbled shore, Lake Gar-na-Ree's, behind Kilbeg's old graveyard, her hair'd put him in mind of deep-red ivy trailing a mossy bank. Wonderful!

The train was nearing Dundalk where passengers for Dublin had to change. Realising his cigarettes were running low, Phil left it quickly to find a kiosk.

Chapter Two

Some ten minutes later he walked on to the Dublin platform and couldn't believe his eyes.

'Well I'll be damned,' he said jauntily, 'if it isn't Amy Allen!'

Amy — she had her back to him — nearly fell over. She recognised his voice immediately; she would have recognised it anywhere. She just wasn't expecting to hear it now.

Turning to face him she said, as calmly as she could — 'Hello, Phil, How lovely to see you again!' Seeing him in the flesh — all six feet plus of him, with his unforgettable eyes focussed on hers and his winning heart-stopping smile was too good to be true. But she didn't want to appear too eager especially given the length of time he'd ignored her: wherever he'd been it couldn't have been that far from Cavan!

They shook hands and told each other where they were living and headed.

'You got the job at Poynings then?' Amy said, a little too eagerly for her liking.

'Not *the* job, Amy, *a* job,' Phil replied, suddenly shuffling uncomfortably and welcoming the noisy arrival of their train — on time for a change. Picking up Amy's heavy suitcase, he carried it and his own much smaller one with no little difficulty to an empty compartment; though tall, Phil was not robust.

'I see you've had the hair cut,' he said when they were settled by the window.

'Do you like it?' Amy asked, blushing under his searching gaze and self-consciously adjusting her cloche over her shoulder-length, wayward curls. Cloches were in vogue and Amy had bought this one the previous year. Her coat — she had taken that off — and fitted costume were old faithfuls.

Phil smiled, and said he did; in truth, he missed the trails of ivy. And remembering them, on top of Amy's current embarrassment, reminded him of an earlier confusion behind

Kilbeg's old Churchyard. In a moment of quiet at the lakeside there, so quiet you could hear lapping in the reeds, Amy had looked up at him, and he'd known at once what she'd been thinking. He hadn't kissed her; to have done that to a starry-eyed, barely-out-of-gymslips girl would have been caddish. So, flustered, she'd said it was time they were going and beetled up the pebbled shore to a hedge-gap leading through to the Churchyard. In the gap her hair'd got caught up. Yanking at it made things worse. 'Let me do it,' he'd said, and she'd let him; and he'd enjoyed her nearness and fluster, and the turfy, hayey, flaxy smell of her hair as he'd untangled it.

Faced with a similar embarrassment now, he handed Amy a cigarette, and when she leaned forward for a light, smelled her perfume, and was intrigued by her necklace – a dark-brown, beaded one set off beautifully by the ebbing flush on her white throat. He decided against commenting on it for fear of embarrassing her again.

'I suppose you're wondering what exactly I'm doing at the old alma mater,' he volunteered, having recovered his composure on the matter of his job and rightly guessing Amy would want to know more about it. 'Well the Beard's not ready to let go of the Maths Department yet! I'm to teach French as well as Maths! Second in command in both, I'm afraid. But the man can't hold on forever! Being Headmaster and Head of Maths at his age must be taxing! And he's as good as promised me the Department when he goes – maybe as early as the end of this year.' A nonchalant flick of his cigarette accompanied this last remark.

Amy's expression registered relief. She didn't need to inquire about the Beard (Poynings' Headmaster's nickname) or about Phil's love of Maths: their exchanges in the past had covered both. After qualifying, Phil had continued teaching Maths in Wales. 'I'm really pleased for you,' she said, overjoyed he was back in Dublin.

'And what about you,' Phil asked, 'Wasn't it History you liked at school and wanted to study at Trinity? Are you teaching it at St. Hilda's?'

It was Amy's turn to look uncomfortable. Abashed, she told Phil she'd failed 'Little-go' – a multiple exam all students had to take to get on the Honours course at Trinity – and, unwilling to face the multiple re-sit, had settled for 'Pass Arts'. Her undoing, she said, had been her French oral – 'I don't have an ear.'

'Never mind,' Phil consoled smilingly. 'Plenty of people have done very well for themselves out of Pass Arts. I'm sure we'll be no different – now we're both in the same boat that is!'

'What do you mean, 'both in the same boat'?'

'Steamboat, silly; didn't you know steamboaters aren't allowed to do Honours?'

Amy didn't know. She laughed – the first time she had laughed about her failure – and told Phil how much she enjoyed working at Glenarkle where she taught a variety of subjects to the younger boys and helped with Latin throughout the school. Next to History, Latin was her favourite subject; and she'd had enough, she said, of her old school St. Hilda's where she'd had digs and helped out at while at Trinity.

Listening and talking to Phil reminded Amy, just as he was being reminded, of this or that incident from their earlier outings, and brought home to her all the old features and mannerisms that had first attracted her to him. Aside from his voice, eyes and winning smile, were his kindness and wit; his shyness and aplomb; the way he listened to what she said; so many men only wanted to talk about themselves. With his swept back straight fair hair, and smart suit – the first she'd seen him in – and his Trinity tie tucked into his waistcoat, he looked a regular swank. Not everything about him was so appealing of course. Like, for example, things never being quite right for him; his cup for ever being half-empty. But Amy dealt with these in her own way which seemed to work.

Having established their current occupations, they caught up on family news as people do after long periods apart. Already

Phil knew that Amy's father had died when she was young, that her mother had remarried and that four of her seven siblings were half-siblings. Now she told him about the departure of the Linnakers – her mother, step-father and half-siblings – from Shandoran, and about her brother, Henry's marriage to Harriet and the birth of their daughter, Lottie. Also about two further departures from the estate – those of her younger brother, Benjie and sister, Lucy. Out of loyalty to her mother and Henry, she spared Phil the sordid details of all the departures.

Compared with the upheavals at Shandoran, life in Fermanagh for the Handys – considering all they'd been through – appeared positively rosy to Amy. Phil's parents had settled into their new home and his oldest brother, Al, was progressing in the local bank. Rose, his oldest sister, was doing well in the Civil Service in London, and younger sister, June, and the rest of the siblings – like Amy he had seven in all – were coming along nicely too.

'You like it up there then,' Amy said confidently.

'It's all right,' Phil conceded grudgingly, 'better than the stones and incendiaries.' Bitterly, and with undisguised disdain he added – 'What gave people like that, Amy, the right to hound law-abiding people like us from our home?'

A number of things went through Amy's balanced mind not least the houndings of a different kind from Cavan in years gone by; in the seventeenth century, that is, when a predominantly Catholic Cavan had been planted and transferred to an overwhelmingly Protestant Ulster. Cavan's Catholics had been bundled out: 'To Hell or Connaught' the Lord Protector, Oliver Cromwell, had said to them. Over the years their descendants had crept back – to fill a hole in Cavan's labour market – and eventually they'd reclaimed what they considered was rightfully theirs. So the rights and wrongs of houndings in Ireland depended on perspectives. That said, Amy knew this was no time for moralizing – something she did not go in much for anyway; people knew the difference between right and wrong. Also, Phil had more cause for his gripes than most, especially when families like hers that had been expected to go under in the Troubles had not. What did he make of that! Down-to-earthly but understandingly she said – 'I'm not sure right came into it, Phil. It was much more a question of might. The British were up against it after the war and their enemies everywhere took advantage. I'm sorry the last few months in Cavan were so awful for you, especially for June. We heard she was nearly blinded by flying glass.'

'That she was,' Phil owned – his sadness at the memory of his sister's suffering palpable. 'They stitched her up as best they could; the scarring's bad. Not that it stops her playing her piano, mind! And she's still a beautiful girl.'

A little silence ensued. During it, Amy looked out of the window – at the fleeting hills, fields, houses and glimpses of Irish Sea – and remembered her one and only meeting with June; June's tactfulness above all – her 'fine for scrambling', her joining in in the solo – and her magical touch at the piano.

And while Amy was remembering this, Phil was observing her closely, wondering how he could have let so much time elapse without looking her up. In his heart he knew. By Christmas 1920 – some three months after his and Amy's second outing, the one where they'd ended up beside Gar-na-Ree Lake – his family had left Cavan and the distance between his and her homes increased greatly; even more marked had been the distance between their workplaces – Wales and Dublin. Significant too, were the differences in their ages and backgrounds, the demands of his family, apathy, and, last but by no means least, unless he was very much mistaken, Amy was a one-man-woman and one-man-women were not for him.

All that said, Amy was here now, within touching distance, and marvellously transformed from schoolgirl to young woman. Her fitted costume and lace-collared primrose blouse suited her; from pert, her breasts had become fulsome; all in all she was crushingly desirable. And the physical thing aside, a certain something about her – something that had struck him on both their previous outings but was as hard to nail down now as then, captivated him anew.

Handing her another cigarette, he smelled her perfume again and looked again at her necklace. Noting his interest she let him examine it, something she would not have volunteered earlier, he knew.

'Umm, acorns!' he said admiringly, 'and beautifully carved at that!'

'It's made of bog oak,' Amy told him, blushing when his fingers brushed her skin. 'Grandmother Sad gave it to me for my twenty-first.'

'Sad?' Phil queried.

'My Grandmother's initials,' Amy explained. 'Sarah Ann Daker is her full name. You remember I showed you her house, The Mill, from the top of Shandoran Hill?'

Phil nodded. He remembered it well, and wondered as he'd wondered on the Hill's ramparts what she'd wished for. His own wish – to remain in Cavan – made him smile wryly now. So did Amy's final comment on her necklace: 'It's a bit like a family heirloom,' she said. 'I love it.'

Conscious of the absence of heirlooms in his family (Amy, it seemed, had them on both sides of hers for Shandoran must be stuffed with them if the memorials in Kilbeg's old and new Churches and Churchyards were anything to go by) he asked – 'Why did Shandoran survive the Troubles?'

Sensing some resentment in his tone (she couldn't blame him for that) Amy took her time before replying. Then speaking candidly and seriously – she owed him that – she said: 'Well I've thought about it a lot, Phil – we all have – and come to the conclusion we were very, very, lucky. But there was much more to it than that. Unlike yours, no one in our family – not at Shandoran anyway – was connected with the military or police. We were searched for guns of course. Who wasn't! But nothing was ever found – except the old double-barrelled thing we use for shooting the wild duck and the rabbits an' that, or putting the odd animal out of its misery. The truth was – we couldn't afford to get involved in the fighting. Shandoran has always been Unionist, Phil, but flax is more important to us than any Union. Labour as you know is hard to come by and we need a lot of it for harvesting the crop. Catholics have been working on the estate alongside Protestants for donkey's years – at least since the days of my Great Uncle Joshua. He was a doctor, and treated all manner of patients in his surgery – Catholic as well as Protestant. My father inherited the estate from him and had no quarrel with Catholics either; nor had or have my mother, stepfather, or Henry. Most of the Catholics are seasonals, it's true, but some have tied cottages on the estate and are no less liable to be let off their rents in bad times than Protestants. So you see, we've always treated our workers fairly, and they've known that if they got involved in fighting they'd lose their jobs. Somehow we've survived.'

Throughout all this Phil listened attentively. Amy wondered what he was making of it, and if his resentment had increased or lessened as a result of it.

'Well I'm very glad you did,' he said, smiling kindly. Amy's candour and sincerity had disarmed him. His smile lingered: that certain something was there again – clearer now than before. It was a kind of inner surety, he thought; a stillness and calm – notwithstanding the odd fluster or embarrassment – that gave an impression of great solidity; of unshakeability even. There was pride in it, but no conceit; confidence but no smugness. Amy was at one with herself and her surroundings in a way that was markedly at odds with his restless nature. What, he wondered, lay behind such surety? And what if anything could shake it? Food for thought, he mused – a mite perversely.

They were closing on the capital and had had their compartment to themselves the entire ride. As the train slowed for Amiens Street Station, Amy wondered if Phil would arrange another meeting; he needed pinning down though not pushing. Phil had a couple more gripes to air.

'I hope to God,' he said, 'being outside the Union hasn't altered Poynings.'

'Of course it hasn't,' Amy rejoined encouragingly. 'Well not if Glenarkle's anything to go by! Or Dublin for that matter! Nelson is still on his Pillar in O'Connell Street, you know; and King Billy on his horse in College Green! And Poynings is where you've always wanted to be, isn't it?'

'I suppose,' Phil conceded grudgingly. Frowning he added – 'It's just a great pity Neil Crotchley has to be there.'

'Who's he?' Amy asked when they'd left the train to cross to the Kingstown platform; Glenarkle was in Kingstown, on the south, or posh side of the capital; Poynings was on the north, the downmarket side. Phil told her Neil was Poynings' Games Master and disdainfully tagged on – 'he was a games mad creep at school and is probably worse now.'

Amy despaired – time was running out. 'Sure every school has its games master,' she said, unable to see what all the fuss was about, 'and as far as I'm concerned they're all much of a muchness. I remember ours at St Hilda's...' She stopped talking: unusually for him, Phil wasn't listening. Minutes later, after a nonchalant – 'We must go to a show sometime,' from him 'and maybe have a walk around Howth Head. I'll write' – he waved her off.

Chapter Three

After Amy had gone, Phil considered taking a taxi to Poynings then decided against. Compared with Amy's, his case was feather light, and Poynings was not all that far from the station. Also, there would be no pay cheque till the end of term, and although he had saved as much as possible from his job in Wales, handouts to his mother – there'd be no freeloaders in her house! – and his own day to day needs were quickly eroding the savings. As he left the station he felt happy. Returning to Dublin had always given him a lift. He was back at Poynings. Amy was in town.

Crossing Talbot Street, he negotiated a short cut gauntlet of tattered tenements that made him wonder if the country's poor would fare any better under its current rulers – Cosgrave and Co. as he disparagingly thought of them – than under the British. He doubted it. Cosgrave and Co. were a bunch of shysters in his opinion; at the first whiff of power they'd abandoned their partners in struggle and caved in to the British government. In many ways Phil had more respect for DeValera's lot – men of principle! Republicans to the end! But they were all upstarts, mountebanks, Charlatans, Papist puppets. And if you asked him, it was a great pity they hadn't annihilated each other in the Civil War that had followed Partition, and left 'all-Ireland' in the Union. Before long, Rome would be dictating what one could and could not do. Worse – what one could and could not read!

Emerging from the tenements, Phil arrived in a once-posh Georgian Square one side of which was mostly occupied by Poynings. That the school was on the north side of the capital didn't bother him. Neither did the fact that some people found it odd he was working in the Free State. But the IRA had another think coming if they thought they could deflect him from his chosen career at Poynings (with or without Neil Crotchley's presence there) as easily as they'd driven him out of Cavan.

Having picked up his key from the school porter, Phil made

his way across the fenced-in area of neglected trees, shrubs, paths and grass in the centre of the Square to the staff residence on the other side. The residence, a basemented, three-storey building, was in keeping with its surroundings: its classic façade and interior had seen better days. Phil's room was on the ground floor. He went straight to it, knowing the rest of the staff, all of whom lived in the Dublin area, would not be returning till the next day, when the boys came back as well. Coming from Fermanagh, Phil had the option of returning a day early and, anxious to get to Dublin (the holidays had begun to pall), he'd taken it.

Glancing round his sparsely furnished room, he took in its peeling paint and crumbling stucco, bruised skirting-boards and friezes, and knocked about bits of furniture. So what! Repairs were not his problem. And the room, no worse than the one he'd had in Wales, was his own space, something in short supply at home. He wondered where Neil Crotchley's room was and hoped it wasn't anywhere near his.

After unpacking and changing out of his suit, Phil wondered what to do next. He'd been told there was a kitchen in the basement with necessities like tea, milk, sugar and bread in it; he did not feel hungry. Too restless to read (seeing Amy had unsettled as well as cheered him) he collected his wallet and went out.

◇

Meantime, Amy was chugging through the capital's salubrious south side suburbs towards Kingstown. Much of the journey skirted the coast. The tide was out, and miles and miles of Sandymount's smooth and ruckled sand gave the illusion of a walkway to Howth Head on the other side of Dublin Bay. From time to time, an isolated cockle-picker, a child waving, a solitary walker, flocks of seabirds lifting off or landing, a Martello, caught Amy's eye and held it. It was a real daydreamer of a ride, though she only really used it on her way to and from Cavan, normally she used the tram in Dublin. And as the coast slid past, her thoughts ranged as widely as its wide sandy stretches, over good times and bad, the way back and the nearer to. In the light of her recent catching up on family news with Phil, and being the kind of person she was – a person of sound faith – she prayed her younger brother and sister, Benjie and Lucy, would come to no harm. Despite pre-marital promises to the contrary, Henry's wife Harriet had rudely ousted them from Shandoran soon after she became mistress of the estate. Harriet was a dab hand at ousting and though the exit of the Linnakers from Shandoran, mostly at her instigation too, had not overly displeased Amy, the exits of Benjie and Lucy had. Benjie had gone to America; there had been no word from him since. Lucy had taken up residence in Aikens' – the little drapers in Ballymun where she already helped out in her spare time and the owners of which, two octogenarian sisters, welcomed a live-in assistant.

Promises, promises! Amy thought. And would Phil keep his to get in touch? Or was that merely a ploy to fob her off? On his own admission he was good at ploys.

As the south side's sandy beaches gave way to the rocks and deep water round Kingstown Harbour, Amy convinced herself her wish at the top of Shandoran Hill – that one day Phil would love her as much as she loved him – had not been fanciful.

On alighting from the train, she accepted a helping hand from a porter, parted with a tanner and took a taxi to Glenarkle where she parted with two bob.

The Headmaster, Mr Appleby, and his wife who doubled as matron, greeted her warmly in the hallway, a large one with a polished, parquet floor and marble-topped, semicircular table. Amy regarded the Applebys as friends as well as employers, and admired them greatly for their work at Glenarkle. In their early forties now, they'd inherited the premises – a large Edwardian house in spacious grounds about a mile from Kingstown's sea front – after the war, quickly converted them and, barring some jitters when the Free State emerged, gone from strength to strength. Already the school had acquired an enviable *esprit de corps*. Rules were made to be kept, and goals – admission to the big public schools in England or their nearest equivalent in Ireland – achieved. Englishness pervaded Glenarkle. Not the chauvinistic or bigoted variety one so often encountered in Ireland but a mild, well-mannered Englishness that accepted the Free State as a fact of life while being quietly confident, once the jitters had subsided, of its right to exist within it. Gratitude didn't come into it; still less, a desire to participate – beyond the purchase of postage stamps and payment of income tax – with its new political masters. For whatever the niceties of its Englishness, Glenarkle was viewed – like every other pocket of Englishness in the Free State, depending on one's perspective and with varying degrees of enthusiasm – as an unwanted mole hill on a newly cut lawn, or a pearl in a pile of dung.

After she had taken leave of Mr and Mrs Appleby, Amy dumped her suitcase in her room, hung up the clothes she did not want to get creased and hurried downstairs to the staffroom. On the way, she had three little bets with herself. There would be no new faces in the room. Mr Appleby's three stalwarts – William Dodson, the English master; Max Stone, Classics; Peter Pagley, History – would be sitting in 'their' chairs, each with his copy of the *Irish Times*. Before she left the room, the same three would be sounding off about their favourite bugbears.

The staffroom, parquet-floored like the hall and with a big bay window overlooking the front garden, was welcoming. Everyone smiled and shook Amy's hand, including the games master – a fit, breezy fellow, typical of his kind, who made her wonder anew why Phil was so against Neil Crotchley. There were no new faces among the staff and, sure enough, William Dodson, Max Stone and Peter Pagley – each with his copy of the *Irish Times* – were sitting where Amy expected them to be. Dodson – a kindly English teacher, oldest of the three, comfortably slumped in the room's one and only arm-chair, a fireside leather one. Max Stone – dubbed 'Caesar' by the boys on account of his subject, Roman nose, and imperious bearing – bolt upright in the leather-backed carver at one end of the large, centrally-placed, oak table which was normally obliterated by piles of exercise books but today bore only tea things. Peter Pagley – a readaholic, like Phil, and keen hiker – splayed out in a ladder-backed chair half way along one side of the table.

Two down, one to go, Amy thought, helping herself to tea, scones and a slice of fruitcake before sitting down on the bay banquette. She enjoyed the view of the garden through the bay window – dahlias at this time of year – and by avoiding the chairs she avoided showing any preference for this or that occupant of the room. As the only woman (apart from Mrs Appleby) on Glenarkle's staff, Amy sensed a little rivalry – nothing acrimonious, for gentlemanliness was as much a part of the school's make up as Englishness – among the masters for her attentions, especially between Max Stone and Peter Pagley. The former wanted her to take up bridge; he and his wife were addicts, he said, and would welcome her into their circle. The latter, unmarried, to join him on a mountain hike; he'd been up the 'Big Sugarloaf' more times than he could remember. Amy liked Peter the best, but physically (podgy hands, impossible hair) he wasn't her type; Max was married. With Phil back in Dublin, neither bridge nor hiking with her work colleagues appealed to Amy.

'What can they hope to gain by it?' Pagley was saying, running his podgy fingers through his dun, half-hackled hair, and picking up on the subject under discussion before Amy's arrival – the remit of the recently established Commission on Evil Literature. Ostensibly the remit was to clean up newspapers and magazines in the Free State, but many were predicting it would soon be extended to books as well. 'Sure if the IRA could run guns to Howth, what's to stop the rest of us running books to Kingstown?'

'Talking of which,' William Dodson said as the laughter produced by Pagley's comment died down, 'has anyone read the rumour here…' (Dodson tapped his *Irish Times* on the arm of his fireside chair) '…that they're thinking of renaming Kingstown?'

'Not 'Dun Leary' again?' Amy said, indignantly. Dun Leary – English version of the old Gaelic name for 'Fort of Leary' – had been Kingstown's previous name.

'Yes,' replied Dodson, even more indignantly, 'but they want the pure Gaelic version of it. Don't ask me how you spell it, though, Miss Allen!'

'I won't,' Amy said, already two thirds of the way to winning her final bet.

'And I won't ask you what Healy thinks about it either!' More laughter followed this.

John Healy, an ultra Anglophile, was the editor of the *Irish Times*.

'Sure the whole idea's an affront to the English language,' Dodson went on. 'Correct me if I'm wrong, Pagley, but wasn't it King George IV himself who named the town Kingstown when he embarked from it in 1820?'

'Twenty-one,' corrected Pagley.

'Why change it?' said an exasperated Dodson.

'Beats me,' put in Max Stone imperiously. 'But then, what else can you expect from a government whose henchmen refer to Trinity College, Dublin as an "Elizabethan rat-pit"! Sure there's no finer institution in the country!' Max Stone, fiercely loyal to his alma mater, was incapable of comprehending the constant carping by republicans about the Union Jack over its West Front, and the singing of *God Save the King* at College Races and the conclusion of graduation.

Listening to the banter, Amy – she had won all her bets – wondered if attitudes at the school would ever change. Not that it mattered much. The Free State had come to stay and, as Amy saw it, her colleagues were not being seriously discommoded by it; it was only their noses that were out of joint. She understood their concerns though, and found it easy to indulge them. Anything else would only have made her unpopular and the attitudes harder. Moulded by experience, these would only be changed in the same way; airing them to justify them merely entrenched them – like too much sunlight on the newly washed linen at Shandoran made it doubly difficult to eradicate the creases. Besides, she liked her work colleagues and their banter, and as she and they waited for the Headmaster, she wondered yet again what Phil could possibly have against Neil Crotchley.

Before long, Mr Appleby (he had a bugbear too) came into the room and gave them all a little pep talk and wished everyone well for the new term. More than ever, Amy was looking forward to it. She couldn't wait to hear from Phil.

Chapter Four

For the next few days, and despite innate uncertainties where Phil was concerned, nothing was too much trouble for Amy. Rain or sunshine, she greeted every morning with a freckled smile, and fairly floated down the stairs to Glenarkle's parqueted hall to check the mail on its semicircular, marble-topped table. If her boiled egg was too hard she didn't frown. If the boys forgot their Latin subjunctive, or construed without parsing – cardinal sin in the eyes of Abbott, his *Via Latina* was Amy's classical Bible – her patience was inexhaustible; she had never had any trouble with discipline. Autumn's coppers, golds, yellows, browns and greens were more colourful than usual to her. The west wind was softer than usual, the east tangier. And Kingstown itself had *never* seemed so hospitable.

Asylum port, Mail Boat terminus and pleasure resort, Kingstown had seen better and worse days. From a 'shabby' state of 'undress' in Thackeray's time, it had blossomed in the wake of a mid-nineteenth-century face-lift into a beautiful spa where the cream of Dublin's late-Victorian and Edwardian society piled in to take the air. By the mid-nineteen twenties, much of the glitz was gone. But the overall impression of the place – wide promenades and tree-lined roads, zigzag cliff paths, bandstands and a municipally pretty People's Park, pastel-shaded terraced hotels, like Ross' and the Royal Marine, and everywhere bounded by white, black and pale-blue railings, many of ornate design – was still pleasing. So, too, was its buzzing main thoroughfare, George's Street – named, like its Yacht Club, after George IV.

For Amy, the best part of Kingstown – no question! – was its East pier, most popular of its promenades and a good enough reason on its own for living there; she traversed it regularly with the boys as part of her duties at Glenarkle, less regularly on her own. At the end of it she would inhale deeply. 'To help the apple keep the doctor away,' her favourite nun at St. Hilda's, used to say, 'take ten fresh air breaths a day.' Amy had got into the habit. Now, in anticipation of a letter from Phil, her inhalations were accompanied by longing looks across the Bay to Howth, and imaginings of herself there with him; ambling round the headland with him; getting close – though not of course *too* close. Such thoughts swelled Amy's chest to bursting, like the full-blown spinnakers in the Bay, running home before a stiff easterly.

A week of euphoria went by. No letter arrived from Phil. Slowly Amy's happiness dissolved like snow in a steady drizzle.

I should have known better, she told herself crossly, unable to believe it was over before it had begun. Uncharacteristically she snapped at the boys on the smallest pretext, and struggled to be polite to her work colleagues. 'Is anything the matter, Miss Allen?' kind William Dodson, the English master, asked her concernedly. 'No. Why should there be?' she replied abruptly. Max Stone offered again to teach her bridge; Peter Pagley suggested a mountain hike; she declined them both. Outdoors, she prayed for a bird, any bird, to shit on her; her common sense did not preclude the odd superstition. Not a single feathered beast obliged, not even on the East Pier which she traversed more often than usual to relieve her frustration. Browned off, she went to see her best friend, Catherine Townley, who had digs at St. Hilda's and had been to the Convent school; if she couldn't help her, no one could.

She arrived at the Convent – it was in Ballsbridge, about two thirds of the way into the capital – just after the evening meal. Artichoke soup, again! she thought, pulling a face as the smell of St. Hilda's culinary special hit her; mixed with Jeyes Fluid and incense (the nuns were 'high' Anglican), it was odious. The girls were heading for the prep room and all but the youngest of them waved or smiled at her; in her diploma year as well as an undergraduate, she'd had digs and some duties at the school.

Catching sight of Sister Martha (her favourite nun) and Sister Cecilia in the Refectory, Amy asked them if Catherine was in; it would have been unusual for her not to be. The nuns, who were rushing to Vespers, said she was. Despite a heavy schedule – *ora et labora* – they remained remarkably cheerful. Sister Cecilia, aptly named on account of her beautiful soprano voice, smiled at Amy beatifically. Sister Martha – rosy-cheeked and green-fingered – offered her some apples from the pannier of windfalls on her arm. Amy took two – one for herself and one for Catherine – and popping them into her bag – a commodious leather one stuffed with stationery, cosmetics and sundries – went upstairs to see her friend whose room was on the top floor. A late Victorian red-brick fortress – massive oak front door, high encircling wall, heavy black-tarpaulined metal gates – the Convent had three floors.

'What's up, Amy?' Catherine asked, as soon as she saw her visitor. Years of companionship had made it easy for each to detect signs of trouble in the other.

'Long story,' Amy replied plonking herself and her commodious bag on Catherine's bed, which had been hers when she'd had digs at the Convent. When she went to Glenarkle, Catherine commandeered it as Amy's room was bigger than hers and had a window overlooking the Chapel roof.

The two women had been friends since the age of eleven – the age at which Amy had gone to St Hilda's and by which Catherine had already spent eight years there. [Catherine's mother had died when she was three, and her father instantly seized on a suggestion by his sister, Catherine's Aunt Agatha, that he send Catherine to St Hilda's.] The school had some thirty pupils, mostly from orphaned or otherwise stricken families; a handful were under eight – boys as well as girls to that age. They were looked after by a Mother Superior, half a dozen nuns and novices, and a couple of lay teachers. On leaving, Catherine, like Amy, had taken digs at the Convent. Following a secretarial course, she got a job in a solicitor's office in Dublin. She was still in it.

'Let's have a cigarette,' said Catherine, glancing at her watch and heading for the window. Amy double-checked the time, and the two of them climbed out on the Chapel roof and crouched down behind its low parapet to light up. At

St. Hilda's, 'canonical hours' had acquired an extra dimension for Amy and Catherine. Below them, Evensong had just started and Sister Cecilia's sweet soprano voice was leading, without dominating, the voices of her Mother Superior and fellow nuns and postulants in the *Magnifiat – Song of the Blessed Virgin Mary*. As the paean ended, to be followed by a lesson, Amy told Catherine what had happened.

'Men,' said Catherine, disgustedly, smoothing back her crimson-braided hair. 'What else can you expect, Amy?' Catherine had very fixed ideas about men, as about most other things in life.

Catherine was petite, and had a moon-shaped face with huge, round, Wedgewood-blue eyes. Her hair was long, pencil-straight and mousy (her word), and she was for ever twiddling and fiddling with it so that you never knew from one day to the next how she would have it done up – pig-tailed, pony-tailed or hanging limply down her back. The only constant was a brightly coloured slide or ribbon. To suggest that she have it cut, in line with current fashion, was to invite the retort: 'Certainly not. Mummy liked my hair long.' Similar evocations of her Mummy – 'Mummy didn't like drinking,' 'Mummy said you shouldn't swear' – supported all Catherine's moral preferences. Not because of anything her mother had done or said, but solely because her Aunt Agatha had instilled in her a dislike of all the things Catherine's father – inveterate drinker, gambler and womaniser – had done, and which Agatha was convinced had 'done' for Catherine's mother. Smoking was Catherine's only vice, if vice it was, and Amy had introduced her to it.

Catherine never spoke about her father, and had a pretty poor opinion of men generally. She regarded them as one might a basket of windfalls: most were blemished, but somewhere among the dross there might be one just right for her. Her response to Amy's next comment – 'I do love him, Catherine' – was in keeping.

'Don't be ridiculous, Amy,' she retorted, tucking her hair well back behind her ears, 'you can't possibly say that.' Though no scholar, Catherine could add; and two plus one times to see a fella, with a six year gap in the middle, were nowhere near sufficient in her book to get to know him, never mind to love him.

'But I do,' persisted Amy as the reading in the Chapel gave way to the *Song of Simeon* (*Nunc Dimittis*) and Sister Cecilia rose once more to the challenge. She did so, so melodiously that Catherine and Amy listened to the singing for a bit. Then Amy returned to Phil. 'I simply can't believe it,' she said. 'I've been hanging around all these years waiting for him. And now, just when I feel I'm getting somewhere, he bugge…'

'Amy!' Catherine said. 'Swearing won't get you anywhere!' Amy shrugged, and Catherine, who had never met Phil but had heard all about him and disliked him more now than before, wracked her brains for a lifeline for her friend. In desperation she suggested Amy drop Phil altogether and think again about Peter Pagley, or Andy McPhearson – an unrequited suitor in Kilbeg – both of whom she had also heard about and vaguely approved of.

'Do give over about them,' Amy said crossly. Sneaped, Catherine removed her crimson hair-band and shook out her straight, mousy hair before clipping it back again, this time with two bright blue slides from her pocket. 'I was only trying to help, Amy,' she said. 'You're jolly lucky, you know, to have so many men who fancy you. I've yet to meet *one* that I fancy.'

'If you weren't so darned picky, you might,' Amy said.

Catherine let the 'darned' go. She thought on, then suggested Amy write to Phil, asking him how his term was going and telling him a bit about hers. 'No,' Amy said dismissively, 'he'd see through it at once.' Eventually, if reluctantly though, she gave way: the closing prayers of Vespers, excluding now the one for the Chief Governor of Ireland, were coming to an end and Catherine's 'What have you got to lose, Amy?' seemed worth a try.

Back inside, Catherine collected up her writing materials

and plonked them in front of her friend. After nearly as many restarts as Catherine had sheets of paper, a letter was penned, sealed, addressed and stamped. Then Amy had second thoughts. 'I don't think I'll post it,' she said, waving it in the air. 'Oh yes you will!' Catherine insisted, whipping it out of her hand, fed up with her dithering, and the waste of paper and postage. And before you could say 'penny post', she was out of the room, and haring down the top floor corridor to the Convent's three flights of stairs. 'Stop, Catherine, Stop!' shouted Amy, no slouch, in hot pursuit; 'it's mine. Give it back to me.' Catherine laughed. A race was on but the winner was never in doubt. Fastest left-winger ever on St. Hilda's hockey field, Catherine tore down the stairs, and made for the front door, almost bowling Sisters Martha and Cecilia over in the process. Amy followed, headlong, causing the nuns to start again. But by the time she got through the Convent's big black tarpaulined gates, Catherine was legging it down the road to the letter-box. The missive disappeared.

Huffily Amy stomped back to the Convent where the nuns, still in the hall in a state of shock, asked no questions. Both Amy and Catherine had acquired most-favoured ex-pupil status at St Hilda's – Catherine, because she had been so good at hockey there and because her mother had died when she was three; Amy, because she had got to Trinity and not many of the school's pupils did that.

Later, Amy calmed down; she hated rows, and what was done was done. 'What the heck,' she said, 'maybe the letter will do the trick.' 'And sure if it doesn't,' Catherine rejoined, 'it's not the end of the world. Mummy always said – "Men aren't worth the candle".' Amy disagreed, but didn't say so. Instead, she offered Catherine an apple from her commodious bag. Predictably, Catherine refused it, saying it was too scabby. Amy ate hers then left, hopeful her letter would work.

Had she known it was about as relevant at that moment to the likelihood of Phil's contacting her again as were timetables to the punctuality of Ireland's trains, she might have felt a deal less hopeful.

◇

While Amy was opening her heart to Catherine on St Hilda's chapel roof, a very different upstairs-downstairs scenario was unfolding in Poynings staff residence.

Returning to his ground-floor room from a pub, a disgruntled Phil stabbed life into his banked-down coal fire, lit a cigarette and sat down with a book in his one and only armchair. The chair, an uncomfortable winged one, made him wonder cynically if a pair of 'Gumbril's pneumatic trousers' might not come amiss. The book, a racy little one the English master at the school in Wales had given him – 'There's one to watch, Handy!' he'd said, indicating the author's name – would, he hoped, help him forget the quandary that pint after pint of warm, smooth Guinness had failed to resolve.

Since seeing Amy on the train, Phil's need for her – for all of her – had become unbearable; that she was mad about him was obvious. At the same time, the knowledge that, having had her, he would, sooner or later, abandon her was immobilizing him. Given the kind of woman she was, he was certain of it now, a trusting, one-man woman (Oh God! he thought, marriage! and children!), it seemed heelish to treat her so.

'Damn it,' Phil muttered, opening his book. He had read it on the Mail Boat coming home but, a firm believer that good books – like good symphonies, paintings or sculptures – did not reveal all their secrets first time round, often reread them.

Scarcely had he finished a page when clattering in the room above distracted him. 'Bloody, hell – That's all I need!' he thought, scowling at the ceiling. Seconds later, the clattering gave way to thumping and thudding. Poynings' Games Master, Neil Crotchley, had begun his exercises. He did them nightly, at length.

Irritably, Phil listened to the noise and, as an extra loud thud threatened to precipitate its perpetrator through the ceiling, began churning over – yet again! – all the things about Neil that narked him.

The Games Master's fixation with sport topped the list ('The man must have amassed enough swimming and rugby trophies to anchor a bloody battle ship!') and with no other evidence to the contrary, accounted for Phil's conviction that Neil was a philistine. ('Had the boor ever read a book in his life! Head of Department! – My God.') Neil's sanctimony came next. The Games Master never drank or smoked; frowned when Phil mentioned women in the staff-room, or complained about the residence armchairs; averred Cosgrave and Co deserved a chance. ('Only an arse-licker like *him* could get away with a thing like *that* at a school like Poynings!') Phil put the piety down to the Salvation Army. Neil's parents – shopkeepers from the north side who had recently moved across the Liffey, the capital's great divider, to a better class of greengrocery in the Terenure-Rathmines area – were 'soldiers'; '*nouveau riches* soldiers!' Indeed, as Phil saw it, the Crotchleys were doing annoyingly well for themselves, including Neil's brother in the Hong Kong police to which he had wisely transferred, rumour had it, in advance of Partition. Finally, Phil regarded Neil as untrustworthy. The mistrust went back to their schooldays when Neil had reported Phil's brother, Al, for teasing. At the time Phil had not been privy to the worst of the teasing; if he had he'd have stopped it. Even so, reporting Al was mean, Phil thought: everyone got teased at school; in time the raggers moved on to someone else; it had nearly got Al expelled – something that would have brought shame on all the Handys. And since his return to Poynings Phil's mistrust of Neil had increased – not on any substantive grounds but merely because of Neil's coyness about where he went on Thursday evenings, the only evening in the week he went out. ('Where *did* he go? Hardly to a pub or library! Definitely not to meet a woman! – Who'd want a bloke with a name like that anyway, or such an unsightly hairy mole, poor sod?')

As silence resumed in the Games Master's room, Phil looked

scathingly at the ceiling and thought – Praying now, I suppose! But what in God's name for! More cups!

Tired, he looked at his watch. Eleven thirty – too late to add more coals to the fire. He got up and got ready for bed, and propped himself on his pillow with his book. After a few pages he halted at a salubrious little bit about a character called Rosie. 'Damn and blast,' he muttered, closing the book and putting it away, his mind a confusion of Rosie and Amy; and of Neil Crotchley's prudery, and holier-than-thouity. What a sap! he thought, proud of his own manliness. I'll write to Amy in the morning. She's not in gymslips now!

Chapter Five

On receipt of Phil's letter, the gloss was restored to Amy's life – much to the relief of her work colleagues and Catherine. She regretted having written to him, not that it mattered, he never referred to the note; neither did she.

Slow to start, their relationship ripened quickly and before September was out Phil invited Amy for a walk round Howth Head, fully intent on seducing her; and this despite them having had nothing more than a few strolls in the capital, tea at the Metropole and a variety show (Edwardian variety was clinging on) in the interim. In the wake of the show, it's true, they'd had their first kiss – a kiss that should have been a warning to Amy, but wasn't. 'You're not going to take me all the way back to Glenarkle in that, are you!' she'd said, amazed to see Phil hailing a taxi when they left the theatre; trains and trams were still running. He'd shrugged, taken hold of her arm and guided her to the vehicle – geeing her up in the process; till now, he'd scarcely laid a finger on her in public as public displays of affection embarrassed him. In the back of the taxi, he'd put his arm round her, pulled her gently towards him and kissed her lightly but lingeringly on the lips, as though he were sampling a rare, delicate wine. For an impetuous fellow like him, this was quite something. Then easing his tongue into her mouth, he'd relished her sweetness, marvelled at her pliancy and snuck his hand inside her coat and blouse to explore her breasts through her satin undies. Gone, long gone, Amy had wanted the kiss to last forever; she'd gulped it down; and come close to fainting when Phil felt her breasts. For a level-headed, down-to-earth woman like her this was also quite something.

A kiss though, however passionate, was still a kiss. Seduction, Phil knew, was different; and in fairness to Amy, he decided to tell her in advance of it how he felt about marriage. Then if she enjoyed the act as much as he did – he'd make sure she did! – there could be no harm in it.

Saturday afternoon, they met at the Pillar, otherwise known

as Nelson's Column. It was the number one meeting place in the capital, and viewed – depending on one's perspective, and with varying degrees of enthusiasm – as the symbol of a hundred glorious years of British naval supremacy in the world or eight hundred years of accursed British rule in Ireland.

Phil was late. He blamed Neil Crotchley who, he said, had deliberately kept the boys late at rugby practice – a pre-match warm-up – making him, Phil, on duty till they got back, late getting away. 'Did he apologise for his lateness?' Amy asked, as bewildered as ever by Phil's attitude to Neil. 'He did,' Phil owned reluctantly. Truth to tell he had been genuinely surprised by Neil's friendliness since his return to Poynings. He chuntered on though, only stopping when he and Amy climbed on to a tram for Howth.

From a front seat on its upper deck, they had a grand view of the coast. Amy sat next to the window, in a madness of an orange coat – her common sense no more precluding the odd madness than the odd superstition – whose only redeeming features at the time of purchase (Cleary's sale the previous January) had been its price and sable collar. 'You'll never wear it!' Catherine had said, knowing Amy's preference for soft colours with her pale skin. Amy had worn it, but only once. Today it felt just right – a little *risqué*. That said, she was more determined than ever to keep a tight grip on her emotions; she should *never* have let Phil go as far as he had in the taxi. Beside her – in flannels, and a leather-elbowed, tweed sports jacket over a pullover and white shirt, and with his mackintosh tucked in at his feet – Phil was wondering how he could steer the conversation round to marriage or, rather, his abhorrence of it. Alert for an opening, he asked Amy what kind of a morning she'd had.

'A good one,' she said, 'except for Hopley two's tears.' She went on to explain: Hopley had been made to sit with the 'scrubblies' – nickname for new boys at Glenarkle – for eating with his mouth open; scrubblies sat at the bottom table in the dining-room for a year where manners, if lacking, were instilled; a popular punishment for backsliders was being made to sit with them. 'Mr Appleby's a stickler for good manners,' she concluded. 'They're "not exclusive to Winchester!" he says.'

'And what about the other masters?' Phil asked, laughing at Amy's bad take off of her Headmaster's posh accent. 'I suppose they've all got their quirks too. Ours certainly have!' Amy smiled, and told him to his further amusement a little about William Dodson (English), Max Stone (Classics) and Peter Pagley (History) and their bugbears.

'Men after my own heart,' Phil said. Not quite, Amy thought, there being none of Phil's bitterness about the Free State among Glenarkle's staff.

'I suppose they're all married?' Phil went on seizing the chance he'd been waiting for. 'All but Pagley,' Amy replied. 'Wise man,' Phil said. 'I'd have to be stotious, Amy, before anyone led me to the altar. And three sheets in the wind to have children!'

Amy heard what he said, but was not unduly upset by it: cynical young men like him were always talking that way, and she had no immediate plans for marriage, still less for children, herself. 'Best stay sober then!' she quipped, pleased to have thought up the retort. Phil appreciated it. *'Touché,'* he said, pleased she had taken his remarks so well. Clearly, she was as happy to be where she was as he was. Her hazel eyes sparkled, her freckled face was eager, and she wasn't pulling away when he pressed his thigh hard into hers. In her orange coat, with its sable collar ruffling her hair whenever she turned her head, she looked and smelt absolutely delicious; apple blossom, she'd told him was her favourite perfume. Remembering her kiss in the taxi, and the fullness of her breasts, he couldn't wait to explore more of her. He imagined her naked under her coat except for her bog-oak necklace and, embarrassed by his thoughts, shifted his position. How, he wondered, would she react to his advances? How far could he persuade her to go?

Sensing his desire for her, aware of her need for him, Amy told herself she must not go too far.

Jocosely they swayed along – past Clontarf, Dollymount and

the other north side strands. White horses rode high in the Bay. Silvery clouds scurried across a bright blue sky. The firmness of Phil's thigh against her's, excited Amy.

She'd been excited since Thursday afternoon when she'd found his letter on the hall table at Glenarkle. 'In case you are doubtful,' he'd written after a few pleasantries and his invitation for today, 'let me remind you that it is quite *comme il faut* to walk around the headland. Terenure and Rathmines people do it regularly.' Amy had smiled at that: it was all very well for Phil to poke fun at the *nouveaux riches* of those suburbs, but what wouldn't he have given for a slice of *nouveau* money; she could have done with some of it herself. Phil's postscript had made her smile too: 'It is now Thursday and is not the weather awful? I hope it picks up by Saturday. Do try to come out. P.' Try! Amy had thought, unable to think of a single more pleasurable request.

At the tiny town of Howth they alighted from the tram, along with one or two other passengers who were soon lost from sight – easy enough, despite there being little in the way of obvious cover except a few scattered cottages and liberal outcrops of rhododendrons and heather.

Choosing the Bay side of the peninsula, they set out along the coast path, outwardly calm, inwardly turbulent. Amy kept telling herself not to let things get out of hand; the risk of pregnancy aside, she believed no man respected a woman who threw herself at him at the first opportunity. Phil, on the look out for a secluded place, reminded himself not to rush things. A little surprisingly for a man, he thought of seduction in terms of unpicking stitching – something he had often observed his mother doing. Tacking represented an easy lay; hemming, moderate resistance; seams, major resistance. Seducing Amy – a tightish seam (he guessed she was a virgin) in a delicate silk blouse – would require a mixture of firmness, gentleness and coaxing at the corners.

At the far end of the headland they found a sheltered nook: a crumbling stone wall behind, banked heathers on either side, tantalising sunshine from the scurrying cloud-swept sky. Spreading their coats on the warm, mossy ground, Phil's mackintosh first, Amy's orange one next, they sat down.

'Isn't it glorious,' Amy said, inhaling the salty-sharp air and telling Phil, between breaths, about Sister Martha's adaptation of the old adage. 'Take some,' she added, as though instructing him to swallow medicine. He smiled, and took a couple of deep breaths to please her. She completed her quota of ten; being alone with him like this made her panicky. Bemused, he watched her.

At the base of the cliffs, waves sluiced the narrow, deep-sided gullies that cut into the rocks. Overhead, and above the Bay's inshore waters, seabirds wheeled and mewed. In the distance, in the deep channel that linked Dublin's docks with the outside world and was the graveyard to many a wreck, two cargo vessels slowly plied their opposite ways through the choppy seas. On this side of the Bay, there was no illusion of a walkway to the other.

'I can't think of anywhere I'd rather be,' Phil said, putting his arm round Amy when she'd finished her deep breathing, 'I'm so glad you could come.' The scent of apple blossom and an onrush of passion made him pull her closer to him. She looked at him and, as their eyes met, the sun escaped into a wide patch of blue. Amy felt the tips of Phil's fingers on her ear lobes and at the nape of her neck. They kissed. She crumpled. Phil eased her back on her orange coat on the mossy ground. Her hat was askew. He removed it and put it to one side, and kissed her again, and traced a line with his finger round her necklace and the lacy collar of her lilac blouse. She trembled a little. Then he undid the buttons of her darker-shaded lilac cardigan, and the buttons of her blouse, and caressed her through and under her satin underwear. She let him. He removed her cardigan and blouse, and, tense with excitement pushed down the straps of her underwear, and feasted his eyes on her white skin, and fondled her breasts whose aureoles were nearly as dark as her necklace. Him looking at her, feeling and pinching her taut nipples – excited Amy. So did the breeze on her skin. 'Somebody'll come,' she said. 'Nobody'll come', he replied, picking her up in his arms and burying his head in her neck, her hair and her breasts. Her head was thrown back over his arm, and the sight of her like that quickened his desire for her. Reaching under her skirt, he stroked the silky smooth skin above her stocking tops; her knickers were moist between her thighs. 'Stop it, Phil!' she said, but didn't sound as if she meant it. Reassuringly then – 'It'll be OK, Amy' (sheaths hadn't let him down yet) – Phil teased and tormented her under her skirt – he'd got the seam just right – and encouraged her to feel him though he was nearly as shy about that as she was. In the back of Amy's mind a small voice cautioned; but like the cry of a hobbled beast in a stampede, it went unheeded. 'Do it now, Phil!' she murmured, ready for the taking. 'Hold on, Amy, it gets better' he murmured back, which it did.

In the gullies below, waves surged, swirled and fell away. All around, gulls screamed. Far away among the white horses, two cargo vessels closed on each other, became one, moved on.

Afterwards they got dressed, and when Amy fumbled with the buttons on her blouse, twice mismatching them, Phil helped her straighten them out; she liked the way he did that. Then they lay back, saying nothing, physically and emotionally replete. The afternoon was well advanced and the late September air that penetrated their little nook was just starting to chill. They found it soothing.

Then doubts set in for Amy. Would everything really be all right? And whether it was or wasn't, would Phil want to see her again? Maybe he'd got all he wanted from her. 'If anything happens, Phil,' she said, sitting up and wrapping her arms round her bent up knees, 'you'll find me floating on Shandoran Lake. You know that, don't you?'

Phil almost laughed out loud. For despite what was on her mind, Amy's demeanour was more composed than he'd ever seen it; her surety more marked; by now he was beginning to understand what lay behind the surety. 'Nothing's going to happen,' he said confidently, 'haven't I given you my word?' He smiled as he spoke, but could see Amy remained doubtful. Convincing her, he could further see, would take commitment, something he was not prepared to give. He decided to distract her; if possible get her going about something. Her surety would do the rest.

Catching sight of a Mail Boat approaching Kingstown Harbour, he offered Amy a cigarette and said nonchalantly – 'I suppose you could say, "Howth missed the boat!"' 'What do you mean?' Amy asked, aware he was dodging the issue, reluctant to press him on it, and recalling his quip about steamboaters though no wiser for that. Phil explained about Howth's bid to become the country's main mail terminus long before Kingstown's, and about the silting at Howth, and the advent of larger packet boats that enabled Kingstown to pick up the tab. 'And what a lucrative tab it was, Amy!' he concluded, pleased to see her smiling. He carried on – uncertain where: getting Amy going about something wasn't easy; she was always so measured. 'They can keep their Bay of Naples,' he said, 'this for me is as good as it gets.'

'Yes, it's timeless, isn't it?' Amy said.

'Poppycock,' Phil retorted provocatively. 'Nothing's for ever!'

'Nothing! Not even God'? Amy questioned, knowing that whatever her choice Phil would rubbish it in his present mood.

'Ah! You've got Him on your side, have you?' he mocked. 'Well that explains a lot!' He paused for a moment, reflectively. 'For the rest of us, Amy,' he went on cynically, 'time and erosion will put paid to all. Look around you if you don't believe me at the state of flux in the world! New brooms everywhere – not just in Ireland! Empires collapsing on all sides! And how much better is the new than the old; nationalism, communism and republicanism than good old fashioned imperialism? It puts *me* in mind of the barbarian hordes descending on Rome. Had no use for its monuments, so left them to decay.'

Amy countered. 'Now you're being ridiculous,' she said,

genuinely caught up in the exchange, 'You know that's not the real picture.' The real picture, she went on to point out was indeed all around them, not least in the capital they both loved, a capital five years of Free-State rule had scarcely changed. 'Yes,' she owned, 'parts of the new order irk me as much as you. I wouldn't like to see the Catholic Church increasing its influence on government – Or Gaelic taking hold!' Like Phil, Amy had little time for Gaelic or the current 'Revival' in it. Her formal education like his had been entirely English in character; for her as well as him, poetry had stopped at Tennyson. But even here Amy found something to substantiate her point. 'Mind you,' she said, 'if Yeats is part of the Revival it can't be that bad!' Everyone knew something of Yeats. She finished strongly – 'And Trinity, Poynings and Glenarkle are as English as ever they've been and I don't doubt the best of Protestant and Catholic Ireland will win through in the end.'

'God, Amy, you're beginning to sound like Neil!' Phil said, as exasperated now with his ploy as pleased. 'Sometimes I wonder if I oughtn't to join the emigrants and head for the Raj. A fresh start…' He broke off. Something was telling him he'd be seeing Amy again, and again and… 'I'm famished,' he said tetchily. 'Tea at the Metropole would be nice.'

As they retraced their steps on the Headland, the sun sank into the mountains across the Bay through a gloriously streaked apricot and duck-egg blue sky; seagulls worked themselves into a frenzy over a splurge of effluent on the outgoing tide; the Bay emptied of traffic. It was a not unfamiliar scene in this part of Howth.

Similarly recurring patterns were shaping Phil and Amy's lives, but with outcomes far less predictable – even less, wished for – than those of the streaked sky.

A waiting tram – trolley-heads and seats reversed – took them back to the Pillar and the Metropole tea-room hard by it.

Chapter Six

Later that evening, on his way into his room in Poynings staff residence, Phil bumped into Neil Crotchley. The Games Master was carrying a big sports bag and wearing his navy and yellow school scarf. He looked pleased with himself, prompting Phil to comment sarcastically – 'They won then?' He found it hard to address Neil without sarcasm. 'We did,' Neil replied, with neither his voice nor the self-satisfied grin on his big square face giving the slightest hint as to whether or not he had noticed the sarcasm, 'an' if we go on improving like this we might even hold on to the Cup.' 'I'm glad to hear it,' Phil said. 'You'll be off up to your exercises now? Mustn't keep you from those, must we? I've had all the exercise I want on Howth Head. You should try it some time, preferably with a woman!' 'There's a time and a place for everything,' Neil responded, seemingly unoffended. Turning his back, he bounded up the stairs two at a time leaving Phil thinking what a thick-skinned boor he was and how much more fulfilling his own day had been than Neil's.

On entering his room, Neil closed his door then stood for a minute with his back to it, easing his muscles the better to relax. A long session of exercising awaited him for, if not the be-all and end-all of his life that Phil assumed them to be, sport and keeping fit were a major part of it. After the work out, he would write to his brother in Hong Kong, the real reason for whose departure there was a closely guarded secret. Like Napoleon the Third's, Neil's nature was clandestine. Secrets – where he went on Thursday evenings was another – made him feel one up.

Before starting his exercises – a mixture of stretch-bends, press-ups, and running on the spot – Neil put his sports kit away tidily and hung his scarf on the back of the door. Though his room was much the same as Phil's size- and decorwise, it differed from Phil's in that there were no books – read or unread – in it, and no ashtrays, full or empty. A big bowl of oranges, courtesy of Neil's parents' greengrocery shop, and a

Salvation Army collection box lay on a small table beside his comfortable-enough-for-anything, winged armchair.

Next, Neil undressed down to his underwear and pulled on a pair of black shorts. He was about five foot ten, and broad. Not fat in the Billy Bunter sense, just broad. Broad-necked, broad-chested, broad-beamed; a great steam-roller of a man, whose big, square head and cropped hair accentuated his close-set eyes, small mouth, and the hairy mole on his lower lip. All in all, Neil reckoned himself a fine figure of a man and better equipped than most to fulfil his chosen career in life; he gave thanks to God nightly for this. Also in his prayers he remembered his brother, and his parents, who had worked so hard to give him and his brother a good start in life. People like Phil Handy scoffed at people like the Crotchleys, labelling them *nouveaux riches*; scoffed at their morality too – their moderation and restraint in all things. People like that, in Neil's opinion, were all talk and no substance.

It was a matter of some concern to Neil, that despite his moral rectitude, fine physique and undoubted ability at sport, he had failed as yet to attract a woman. How was it, he wondered, pushing back the sparse furniture in his room and starting his stretch-bends, that someone like Phil Handy – that weedy braggart…that unprincipled snob – could get any woman he wanted whenever he wanted her? That, at any rate, was Phil's staff-room boast, and Neil had a sneaking suspicion it was not a hollow one. He thought it unfair, a gross miscarriage of justice by the Almighty. Why should the brother of the boy who had made his first year at secondary school so miserable, find life so easy?

Moving on to press-ups (one, two, three, four…) to flexing and relaxing his huge biceps and dorsal muscles, Neil thought some more about Phil and his brother, Al, and the grudge he bore the Handys – a huge grudge, that lesser-proportioned men than he, he was sure, would have caved in under long ago. He had not caved in. To have done that would have been to forgo reprisal – something that had seemed a distant dream till Phil's return to Poynings.

Keeping tabs on the press-ups (seventeen, eighteen, nineteen…) Neil remembered how, as a new boy at Poynings, he had instantly acquired the nickname 'Crotch', and been slow to make friends; his only friend till then had been his brother, who was not due to start at the school for another year. Loners at Poynings made perfect targets for bullies, and Neil – just into his teens, with a prominent labial mole, more perfect than most. The first to draw attention to the disfigurement had been Al Handy. 'You'll never get a girl with that, Crotch,' he'd said, shoving his face into Neil's, pursing his lips kissy-kissily and encouraging his bully-boy mates to join in. How Neil had hated it! One day I'll grow a beard, a big bushy one like the Head's, he used to tell his lonely self. With not so much as a whisker in sight, that day had seemed a long way off. Notwithstanding, if the bullies had stopped at the nickname and mole, he might have been able to ride out their jeers.

Crimson-faced and sweaty (forty-eight, forty-nine, fifty) Neil got to his feet to complete the final stages of his routine – slow deliberate stretch-bends, brisk running on the spot, more stretch-bends. Aside from strengthening his muscles, the workout had a cleansing effect on him: like an exorcism, it helped to expel the worst effects of his early experiences at school; make them bearable. Reaching for his stretch-bends, he remembered how they had become unbearable. How the most promising under-fifteen at games when he'd arrived at Poynings had been Al Handy. Being overtaken by Neil had upset Al greatly; he and his poisonous pals set out to reverse the newcomer's progress. (Running on the spot kicked in here.) On match or competition days they'd hidden or damaged his games gear. Not every such day, of course; that would have aroused suspicion; also, keeping Neil guessing had been part of the fun. A sock, plimsoll or rugby boot might be missing; his laces, shorts or shirt. The clothes might be torn or dirtied, the elastic cut in his shorts. He'd scrabble around in the changing-room for a replacement – something, anything, however ill-suited. As often as not he'd be late for the session in hand and punished accordingly: told off in front of everyone, with Al and his mates sniggering; kept in at free time, or even – like when he couldn't find a replacement and missed an entire match – caned. On someone like Neil (final round of stretch-bends), to whom sport and good behaviour meant so much, and telling on the bullies had appeared unthinkable, the effects had been devastating. Along with the never-ending jibes about his mole ('Shame it isn't on your arse, Crotch,' was another one) they'd wreaked havoc with his insides. Particularly hard to endure had been his soldier-parents' perplexity over the reputation he'd acquired for slovenliness; the irony here being – for his mother and father's sake, he could never not give of his best on the games field. He'd been at breaking-point when he'd eventually spilt the beans. His parents had told the Head.

After his workout, Neil selected the biggest, juiciest orange from the bowl on his table and sat down to ponder – God, how he'd suffered! – how best to effect reprisal; how best an unsophisticated man like himself could tackle a brainbox like Phil. For it mattered not to Neil that Phil had not been party to the bullying at Poynings. Phil was Al's older brother; he must have known what was going on and had done nothing to stop it; he, Al, their whole stinking family were equally culpable.

Biting into his orange – with difficulty, his mouth being so small – Neil hit on a way forward. Hitting on it caused his close-set eyes to narrow cruelly, his hirsute lip to curl nastily. The key was in the word tackle. He would tackle Phil just as he would the opposition in a game of rugby. Look for the weak spots, needling where necessary to find them though he had a fair idea already where they lay; sell him the dummy; strike when he fell for it and tripped up; press home his attack when he had him at his mercy. Careful planning would be needed, of course. But planning was second nature to Neil – he considered himself a great strategist – as much a part of his success on the games field as fitness. Meanwhile, no trace of what was afoot must be revealed. He would remain genial to everyone, especially Phil; hiding his feelings from the world had become second nature to him.

The last orange segment disappeared into Neil's mouth. Refreshed, he wondered again about the merits of growing a beard. Maybe the protuberance *was* frightening women away. He decided to leave things as they were. He didn't like beards – they were out of keeping with his line of work, he thought – and no-one was teasing him now! His sporting prowess had guaranteed Al's cruelty, once exposed and stamped on, would never recur. Al's promise had quickly faded.

Before turning in for the night, Neil wrote to his brother, a brother whose hasty departure to Hong Kong had been caused not, as Neil had led everyone to believe, by forebodings about the fate of the RIC in the Free State, but by an adulterous liaison and pregnant woman. It was some time since Neil had written to him, and he knew he would be as pleased as he was about Phil's return to Poynings and the plans he had for him. If the Crotchley brothers had a mission in life, it was to do down a Handy where- and whenever they met one.

Chapter Seven

In the weeks following their trip to Howth, Phil and Amy couldn't get enough of each other. The disobedient times encouraged them. For these were the 1920s – a decade when change came not so much to be frowned on as marvelled at, when strait-laced succumbed to laxity, buttoned up to exposure, sedate to frenzied. When hem- and hair-lines kept on rising and hat-brims contracted to zero; when dance-halls were overrun by the pixilated rhythm of the Charleston, and popular theatre by a fresh 'Rose-Marie' genre of musical that knocked old style variety for six.

Weather and time permitting, Phil and Amy lay in each other's arms on Howth Head, or in the capital's mountainous hinterland; sat close on trams and buses, in taxis and pubs, in the theatre and newly emergent picture houses. Swanked through Dublin's parks and streets, ogled at the latest vogue models from Paris, sipped coffee in Bewleys, took tea at the Metropole, aped their betters. A kind of routine was established. On Wednesday, their half-day, Amy would catch the seventeen minutes past two tram from Kingstown, and meet Phil in the capital to savour the delights of the city they both loved. When their weekends off coincided, Phil might travel to Kingstown for a blast on the East pier, followed by a cosy tea in Ross's or the Royal Marine. Or, lured by the hinterland, the lovers would head for the Dublin and Wicklow Mountains, where, once arrived, they'd climb till they could climb no higher. Leap over streams and boggy bits, pull up sharp on the brink of tarns, circumvent prickly gorse, make love and daydream in the heather, dibble hot toes in icy water, feel the silence, drink the air, soak up the stunning vistas. When Amy's period – or the 'gift' as she called it – was late, they were in turmoil till it started. If a pre-arranged outing was scotched, they were desolated and wrote to each other to ease their desolation. Besotted, Phil no longer pondered the nature of happiness; to be with Amy was happiness plus. Amy's life was complete. So ignorant were they of Neil Crotchley's scheming, they played right into his hands.

◇

Coming up to the end of term, a damp evening drove Phil and Amy into the 'Cock and Bull' – one of Dublin's numerous watering holes where the crack was side-splitting and the yarns as long and improbable as Pinocchio's nose. Feeling more relaxed than they'd done for a fortnight – the length of time Amy's period, which had started that morning, was late – they sat down with their drinks in a quiet corner. 'Would you mind telling me,' Phil said, 'why you call it the gift?' Amy laughed. 'Blame Sister Martha for that,' she replied. 'Once, she gave Catherine and me a dressing down for calling it the "curse". At the time, we were studying the gifts of the Holy Spirit in RE and at the risk of being accused of sacrilege we came up with the new name.' 'Number eight, as it were?' Phil said. Amy smiled, and told him that for a godless person he knew his Bible very well. 'Blame my mother for that,' he quipped, 'she taught us all to read from it by the age of five.'

An old joxer joined them and asked if they'd heard the one about the freak and the floozie. They hadn't, which was just as well as the joxer was bent on telling it. 'Straight from the horse's mouth' he'd had it, the horse in question being the aforesaid floozie – a young filly by the name of Mazie behind the bar who, when not serving drinks to customers was servicing clients of another kind in her domestic quarters. 'One o' them – the clients, I mane,' the joxer said, warming to his tale – 'liked a walk with her in the capital – "No knickers mind! Just the high heels and stockins, and that nice frock you're wearin"' – before gettin' down to the brass tacks at her place.' Then a few weeks into the acquaintance, the client invited Mazie straight back to *his* place. She accepted – 'Double rates!' the joxer explained, 'an' a change from the knickerless perambulations, don't you know!' – but ere long wished she hadn't. For after a few tots in his kitchen, the client steered her through to his parlour – 'where the fun really started!' Colourfully the joxer expanded –

"Glory be to God!" Mazie yelled, "What's that?" In the middle of the parlour floor – God's truth – plain as a pikestaff, big enough for a sumo wrestler, and lined with the lovliest crame satin y'ever saw, lay a coffin.'

'A coffin,' Phil and Amy exclaimed in unison.

'A coffin,' the joxer affirmed, delighted with their response. 'Now hold on to yer sates,' he went on, kindling their incredulity. 'One look at her client's eyes, locked on in turn to the stately box an' herself, told Mazie to be off; another at the bait – triple rates now! – induced her to stay. She did what the fella asked, then took fright again – "Holy Mary, will ye let me out o' here" – at the climax. Yer man relased her at once, an' fast as light – with or without the knickers and cash I couldn't say, mind – she got the hell out o' the place. Now did y'ever hear the like o' that?'

Even if Phil and Amy had, they would not have capped the tale. Amy was a little unsure as to whether she liked it, but absolutely sure she wouldn't tell it to Catherine. When Phil asked her why not, she told him about Catherine's prudishness. 'Sounds like another Neil!' Phil scoffed. His words gave Amy an idea.

'You know that dance we're going to at the Rotun… ?'

'Oh no, Amy, you're not thinking what I think you're…'

'Why not, Phil, what harm can it do? Catherine's no dancer, mind, but I could teach her the rudiments between now and then.'

Phil laughed. 'I wouldn't worry too much about that!' he said. 'I doubt Neil can tell a waltz from a two-step!'

Sensing no major obstacles, Amy warmed to her idea: Neil might be just the windfall Catherine was waiting for; and whether he was or wasn't it would be nice to repay some of Catherine's magnanimity towards her own happiness with Phil despite her friend's known reservations about him. 'Yes, it's got to be worth a try, Phil,' she said, and pointed out that at the very least Neil and Catherine would have a love of sport in common. Phil promised to put it to Neil. 'I can do no more,' he added, 'but don't blame me if your friend takes flight when she sees the fipple hairy mole.'

'The what?'

Phil explained about the obtrusion on Neil's lower lip. Grimacing, Amy stuck to her guns; one man's meat and all that. Phil remembered the joxer's tale, and laughed as he pictured the look on Neil and Catherine's faces if he told it to them.

◇

He wasn't laughing, though, the following week when Neil stepped confidently on to the Rotunda dance-floor, and pausing a moment to take his stance with Catherine, and feel the beat, glided smoothly into a waltz. Catherine stumbled once. If she did so again no one noticed as, deftly Neil took control and guided her – he could just as easily have carried her – through the steps.

'Well I'll be damned!' Phil remarked on the sidelines where he and Amy were hanging back to see the sport. 'Wherever did the fellow learn to dance like that?'

'Don't ask me!' Amy said. 'But maybe you'll see him differently now!'

Phil doubted that. 'Mind you, it's only a waltz!' he scoffed, leading Amy on to the floor. 'Sure anyone can do a waltz!'

When the dance ended, the four of them returned to their table, Catherine and Neil patently delighted. Each had initially turned down their invitation, and even after accepting it, was sure they'd done the wrong thing. The prospect of having to spend the evening with someone they might not like had been daunting enough; of having to spend most of it on a dance floor made it doubly so. And not just for Catherine, as only too well did Neil know the difference between practice, of which he'd had plenty, and performance on the day; he had never been to a dance before. A few seconds waltzing had reassured him.

Even less time was needed to dispel Neil and Catherine's

concerns about each other: they'd clicked on sight; taken to each other like Dubliners to the pictures. To Catherine, Neil was everything and more than a man should be: strong, muscular, protective; courteous and attentive, and *the* best dancer in the room; his hairy mole had no more effect on her than an eye on a potato had. Catherine's petite but athletic figure was just right for Neil. So were her moon-shaped face, chirpy voice, and big, round Wedgewood blue eyes. Her sky-blue frock and matching Alice band were lovely on her, he thought, and it was 'ever so refreshing' he told her, to meet a girl who didn't feel obliged to have her hair cut short.

The next dance was a foxtrot – Phil's favourite; waiting fruitlessly for Neil to falter quite spoiled it for him. Sensing his irritation, Amy wished he'd forget about Neil. He couldn't. 'Let's see him do the Charleston!' he said, continuing to refute what his eyes were telling him. And no matter how hard he tried to avert his gaze, it kept gravitating back to Neil, or to other people's looking at Neil.

There was no let up with the Charleston, or with anything else – even reels and jigs, which Phil loathed and sat out with Amy. Fast and slow rhythms; turns, twists and twiddles; walks and demi-veultas; chassis, toddles and shimmeys – were all the same to Neil. Irrefutably he was a master of the dance floor.

'Well I'll be damned!' Phil iterated perplexedly as the interval came round, 'Where did the fellow learn to caper like that?' Seconds later he had it. 'I know, Amy! I bet that's what he does on Thursday evenings! – Has lessons, I mean. I'll challenge him.'

'For God's sake, give over about him,' Amy pleaded, before heading off to the powder room with Catherine. Already Phil had had more than enough to drink and she didn't want him making an ass of himself, which he was quite capable of doing.

'You kept that a close secret, Neil,' he said, when the four of them were once again seated round their table. 'What?' Neil questioned politely. For Neil, the evening was going splendidly:

he was dancing with the girl of his dreams while surreptitiously needling Phil; maybe he'd even get a dummy out of it. 'Your dancing,' Phil said, irritably – 'You never said you could dance like that.' 'Sure I had no occasion to, man,' Neil countered pleasantly. 'Anyway, I don't consider myself any better than you or anyone else.' Neil's self-effacement went down well with Catherine and Amy but cut no ice with Phil. 'You've had lessons, I take it,' he said, in the kind of tone that implied deviousness on Neil's part. 'Yes,' Neil owned, innocently looking at Catherine and Amy as much as to say – What is he making such a fuss about? 'There's a dance school near my home in Rathmines. I go there Thursday evenings and take the opportunity to see my parents afterwards. They keep me topped up with fruit! It was their idea I have the lessons, and the only reason I didn't mention them was because I was worried about the real thing.'

Amused by the reference to fruit, Catherine and Amy nodded kindly. Unkindly, Phil said, 'Is that so? I can't say I've ever had much time for lessons!'

'Ah, but you're one of the lucky ones,' Neil came back agreeably. 'You're a natural.' Natural bastard too, he thought.

Rudely Phil shrugged, and deliberately ignored Catherine when, self-consciously adjusting her sky-blue Alice band, she said she wished she'd had the foresight to have dancing lessons. Amy frowned at Phil. She didn't take to Neil – he wasn't her type – and found his niceness to Phil in the face of such provocation vaguely unnerving. But his love of sport was harmless and if she, Amy, could be pleasant to him for Catherine's sake why couldn't Phil? Gratuitous nastiness was incomprehensible to her. [Amy knew nothing about the teasing at Poynings; but if she had, it would only have strengthened her opinion; she didn't see Neil as a threat.] In an effort to undo Phil's rudeness, she drew attention to Neil's rugby and swimming prowess: 'I gather Poynings is on line for the Cup again this year!' she said. 'And you're one of the Forty-foot brigade I'm told!' (The Forty-foot was a place near Kingstown where good swimmers like Neil swam.) Her efforts backfired.

Bored with the talk about sport, cross with Amy for being so nice to Neil, and in a mood to shock, Phil launched into the tale about the freak and the floozie, holding back on nothing. Amy tried to shush him up then helped him out in the vain hope of toning the story down. Horrified by it, Catherine and Neil reverted quickly to talking about sport, and when Catherine announced she couldn't swim at all, Neil offered to teach her. 'Killiney's nice,' he said. 'You'll learn there in no time. We could start in the summer term and carry on in the holidays.'

At the mention of holidays, all Phil could see was the yawning gap about to open up between him and Amy: Christmas was round the corner and the recent spate of inclement weather had made intimacy between them impossible; no such thoughts troubled Catherine and Neil! Overcome with another urge to shock, he said – 'It's a blasted nuisance, isn't it, Neil, being unable to bring women into the residence?'

'That's enough, Phil!' Amy said, sternly. No school in the country would tolerate such behaviour; Phil knew that perfectly well. Unbowed he went on – 'Well it's not as if we wanted to turn the place into a brothel!' Amy glowered at him, and to ease the atmosphere offered round her cigarettes including, inadvertently, to Neil. He refused of course. 'In deference to the healthy body,' Phil sniped. 'Ignore him,' Amy said, 'there's nothing wrong with a healthy body.' Neil smiled at her. 'I've nothing against books and learning, mind!' he said; 'it's just that I think books are overrated. Remember the old saying! "Those who can – do. Those who can't – read".' '"Teach,"' Phil rebuked, incurring another glower from Amy. To her relief, the orchestra struck up and Neil and Catherine returned to the dance floor.

After they'd gone, she had another go at Phil. 'Why do you provoke him so?' she asked, 'it's not as if he went out of his way to upset you!'

'That's just the point, Amy, he's a creep.'

It never occurred to Phil to tell Amy what had happened in the past; if it had he would have kept silent from embarrassment; also, as far as he was concerned the teasing at Poynings was irrelevant; teasing or no teasing, he didn't like Neil and saw no harm in poking a bit of fun at him. 'Who does he think he is anyway!' he added truculently now – 'Bloody Valentino!'

Amy gave one of her eyes-up-mouth-down head jerks – a little mannerism, adaptable to all sorts of occasions, she had acquired from her Grandmother Sad. This one showed hopelessness and humour; Phil could always get round her. The rhythm of a soft knee toddle lured them on to the dance floor.

On the other side of the room, Neil was positively levitating. Weak spots had piled up – together the product of such arrogance, tetchiness and depravity, he thought, as couldn't fail to suffice his needs. Crucially, he had his dummy. Selling it would not be easy. For that he would need time and luck. He had all the time in the world and, in his, a winner's experience luck was always on the winning side.

Chapter Eight

Clueless as ever about Neil's plotting, Phil and Amy rollercoasted on; Christmas was upon them before they knew it, when each returned home. It never occurred to them to go anywhere else for holidays – Amy spending the bulk of hers with her brother, Henry, and his wife, Harriet, at Shandoran in Cavan; the remainder, a few days, a week at most, with her mother at Knockmore in Louth. She and Phil wrote frequently – about anything and everything, except love; they only *did* that. About people and events locally, their families, the odd moan. Living in a teetotal household, especially at Christmas, bugged Phil: 'Bacchus should always be master of the revels at the feast of the nativity, Amy.' Space in Fermanagh was at a premium: 'Everyone has come home and there is no room to move.' And his sisters were driving him up the wall mastering the latest steps in the Charleston: 'Everything goes to *Bye Bye Blackbird*.' Al (oldest brother) had a new girlfriend – 'a pasty-faced piece from the Bank' – and Rose (oldest sister) was full of the Civil Service, and had her hair shingled; he didn't like it – 'too short.' June (second sister) looked up to Rose and was talking about following her into the Service: 'I'd rather she stuck to her piano.' At Shandoran, Amy's main concerns were the price of flax, and Harriet's laziness – something Phil knew all about by now despite Amy's loyalty to Henry. On the former: 'They seemed to want it for everything during the war, Phil, even down to wrapping linen round the aeroplane wings. When peace came, prices fell – from £5 to 5/- a stone, almost overnight. They haven't recovered since.' On Harriet: 'She can't or won't get stuck in to chores, hates animals and the fields, and finds any and every excuse – backache and child bearing mostly – to avoid them; she's pregnant again, five months gone, her last miscarried. The men have started calling her "Shoo Shoo". They spotted her in the yard once, shooing off a drake she assumed was harassing the ducks. It was treading, of course! For peace and Henry's sake we all indulge her, but wonder how long it can go on. Thank goodness she appreciates Maggie. I think I told you about Maggie – our long time albino maid; she had feared Harriet would take a dislike to her and send her packing like Lucy and Benjie.' For the rest – Amy's old schoolteacher, Master Gamble's rheumatism was playing up badly. ('He still holds sway in Kilbeg's schoolroom but struggles terribly in his schoolhouse garden.') Dr McPhearson – another Kilbeg worthy – still hoped she and his doctor-to-be son, Andy, would get together one day. ('If he knew what you and I got up to in Dublin, Phil, he might be a deal less optimistic.') And the Doctor, one time Home Ruler, and his long time sparring partner in Kilbeg, the dyed-in-the-wool Unionist, Reverend Badell, still argued incessantly about their political beliefs but remained the best of friends. 'Who was it,' she asked, 'who wrote – "nothing is more conducive to arguments than disagreement over semi-abstract themes"?' Phil's reply to that made her smile – 'Tolstoy's *Anna Karenina* is the source of your quotation; have you read it? If ever I feel myself sliding into marriage, I'll reread it.' Phil could no more resist a dig at marriage than at Neil; jibes at the Games Master's expense peppered his letters. And he had a cold. 'My mother puts it down to a "weak chest", Amy. People like me, she says, who survive childhood diphtheria, are left with a weakness; maybe so; I thought my main weaknesses were for drinks, fags and the other.' From Knockmore, Amy wrote that her mother thought she had got thin. 'If I have, I'll be even thinner when I leave here. The well is over a mile away – up a big hill behind the house and down the other side. The hill, by the way, is the only one in the vicinity; hence the name of the house – Anglicised Gaelic for "big hill".' And as in Fermanagh, space was at a premium at Knockmore. 'We have two and a bit bedrooms to Shandoran's four. I share one with my half-sisters – Iris (11), Lydia (9) and Naomie (5). Vincent, he's seven, has the bit. It's off Mama and Tom's room and still smells of cider from the apples that used to be stored in it.' The Linnakers had no maid. 'There's no money to pay one, but thankfully everybody pulls together – including Tom; at Shandoran he never lifted a finger. Thankfully too, the land here is rich – a hundred-acre mix of everything *but* flax and pigs. Mama's had enough of flax; my stepfather of pigs. I can't say I blame them.'

With Christmas behind them and a new term underway, Phil and Amy resumed their rollercoasting. Occasionally Catherine and Neil joined them on an outing as, left to themselves, they would have had no invitations to parties and dances; Phil and Amy were the natural socialisers. Phil huffed and puffed about their presence but always gave way – for Amy's sake: he loved her so much, and Catherine was her best friend. For the same reasons he tried not to spoil the outings. Everyone seemed happy to put the Rotunda episode in the past; recalling it embarrassed Phil.

So galloping days and weeks became galloping months, and spring when it came had an added zing. Amy's new hat was in keeping. 'Do you think it's too outlandish?' she wrote when she and Phil had returned home for Easter. 'Outlandish? Yes,' he wrote back, 'but I liked it. The asymmetrical high crown, with lateral tracery in red, harmonised the restraint of Athenian art with the more luxuriant Assyrian. How's that for a sales pitch? Maybe I should have gone into marketing.' That same holiday, Al was talking about getting engaged ('I told him he was mad'), June was definitely going to follow Rose into the Civil Service ('It's her life') and he had just finished reading *The Great Gatsby* – 'the best thing to come out of America, since Mark Twain.' 'I'm lucky my mother likes to see me reading, Amy' he added. 'She says it's the only way to get on – or "to the top" as she calls it. Mind you, at the rate I'm going it will be a miracle if I ever get to the top of anything! But then, I don't read to get on. I read because I have to. It's a compulsion, and the best antidote to boredom I know.' For Amy, rheumatic Master Gamble was getting 'more like "the crooked man" each day' and Shoo Shoo was 'milking her pregnancy.' 'Par for the married course,' Phil wrote back cynically on the latter. 'I wonder how things will pan out for Neil and Catherine. The swimming lessons at Killiney might be fun to watch!'

Meantime, Neil waited – patiently. His plan was working – its immediate objective now being to win Phil's confidence, without which the dummy could not be sold. Amy was the key to success. Unwittingly she was fulfilling her role.

◇

In the course of the summer term shared outings became, if not the norm, more usual. Though never enamoured with them, Phil became less and less obstructive about them and, occasionally, even enjoyed them. This was especially the case with their expeditions to Killiney, where watching Catherine learn to swim was not only entertaining but enlightening. With a mixture of firmness and tenderness that surprised Phil as much as Neil's nimbleness on the dance floor had, Neil put Catherine through her paces. First, he would demonstrate with a strong, fluid breaststroke. Then he'd show her the strokes on dry land and get her to practise them before leading her into the sea by the hand and coaxing her to duck down. When she was wet up to her neck he'd hold her under the chin for her swim. She'd struggle and struggle, spitting and spluttering, with her hair pinned high under a firmly strapped on cap – white, with a pink aster over each ear – and the frilly skirt of her togs, the only buoyant part of her, billowing round her like a giant jelly fish. 'Oh bother,' she'd say, after yet another flounder, 'I'll never learn.' 'Yes you will,' Neil would insist kindly, 'everyone finds it hard at first. I certainly did!'

'Did you hear that?' commented Phil to Amy the first time he heard it – 'Whatever next!' Amy smiled; pleased his antagonism towards Neil was waning. When the antagonism waxed, as it did from time to time, she still found Neil's 'niceness' curious but with everything else going so well was not about to question it.

As the term advanced, things got better and better, leading Phil to conclude that Neil was a changed man. His mistrust of him fizzled out; even his hairy mole seemed less repellent.

On the last outing to Killiney before breaking up for the summer holidays,

Phil's conclusions received a big boost.

It was a sultry kind of day – flat sea, thin sunshine, fuzzy horizon. Phil got out of the water first – he generally did – and got dressed immediately, which he always did, from shyness and the cold. Catherine excelled herself in the water, managing six strokes unaided. She wanted to do more, so Amy volunteered to stay with her while Neil went up the beach to Phil. Normally he swam out to sea and back after his stint with Catherine, but today he said he'd had enough swimming at the Forty-foot the previous evening to last him a week. Phil welcomed his company. He'd been feeling a little down of late: there was no sign of the Maths Department, and a refresher course in France was looming to take him further away from Amy than ever. He had actually wanted to spend today in the mountains on his own with her and was regretting not having done so when Neil joined him.

Without bothering even to dry himself, Neil sat down. Covertly scheming (he had not been swimming at the Forty-foot the day before, and Phil's current bout of the blues had not gone unnoticed) he leaned back on his elbows to let whatever sun there was get at his broad, bronzed, athletic body. Casually he said – 'Aren't we lucky to have such nice girlfriends, Phil?'

'You can say that again,' Phil replied, overtly wistful and vulnerable.

The two men watched Catherine and Amy cavorting in the sea – Catherine, with her cap still firmly emplaced; Amy, with hers about to squirt off. Phil thought she looked beautiful. This kind of weather, he knew, suited her perfectly: she didn't like hot sun, not because it brought out more freckles but because she wilted in it. He wondered if she minded him going to France; she didn't seem to. Then he wondered if Neil had ever been abroad (he didn't think so) and was about to ask him when Neil spoke – confidentially, and a little hesitantly, giving an impression of great sincerity. 'I..I know you think I'm an awful prude, Phil', he said, 'I..I'm not really. It..it's just that I haven't got your way with women. I wish I had! An' though I'd never have the courage to voice my opinions on the matter in public, I..I'm beginning to understand...

Within the next few minutes the dummy was sold.

◇

When the term ended, a deeply disappointed Phil – the Maths Department had not come up – left Dublin for the continent – the College Mariette in Boulogne.

By the time he got back, he was fluent in French: 'A miniature cosmos, Amy,' he'd written about the College, 'where Czechs, Germans and Italians, Chinese and Americans, English and Norwegians rub shoulders in a common endeavour.' Disenchanted with Boulogne and its environs: 'rather flat and dull; the French people are the same as ourselves, only dirtier.' But enraptured with Paris where he'd spent a weekend with a party of Americans and procured a copy of *Ulysses*: 'I'll lend it to you on the qt if it's not too impure.' On Paris he wrote: 'It's like another world, Amy – a fairy tale one where anything's possible. Vistas, palaces, monuments and galleries litter it. Maybe you and I could visit it together one day. It's light years away from Dublin, never mind Kilbeg.' This particular letter was rather long, but 'you, not I, have the fag of reading it,' was tagged unapologetically on at the end. Overall, the trip to France inspired Phil. He was a new man when he got home – intent on leading a healthier life style; on drinking and smoking less, taking more exercise. If the Maths Department didn't come up (though he was sure it would) at the end of the coming school year, he would definitely look for another job – and on the south side, which was where Amy wanted to be. Desperate to see her, he thanked his lucky stars she'd returned to Dublin before him and could meet him on Wednesday – the day before his own term started.

Straining at the leash and sporting a walking-stick he'd

bought in Paris, he made his way jauntily (with the weather set fair, Howth beckoned) to the Pillar at the appointed time – three pm. An hour later he was still there – champing at the bit, feeling more and more conspicuous, more and more edgy. What the blazes can have happened to her? he wondered, mashing his umpteenth cigarette into the ground. He would have one more: if she hadn't shown up by then he'd go. She hadn't.

Unable to face his room, he decided on a walk to settle his nerves.

Crossing to the GPO, he remembered the note home in his pocket telling his family he'd arrived safely in the capital and to be sure and let him know if June got worse. Bronchitis had laid his sister low – like him she had a weak chest – and it was doubly worrying as she was due to start in the Civil Service that autumn; they were holding the post, but for how long? Having bought a stamp and posted his letter – thinking as he always did inside the GPO, the building was far too grand for its function – he re-emerged in O'Connell Street. Glancing at the Pillar, he saw Amy: in her mad orange coat, it could not have been anyone else. He dashed over to her, missing by a hair's breadth a Lipton's messenger-boy careering along on his over-loaded bicycle. Some Hafner's sausages bit the dust.

'Hello, Phil,' Amy said, overjoyed to see him. 'Thank Heavens you're late too!' Phil laughed, explained that he wasn't and, desperate to take her into his arms, held back from innate reserve. When she got over *her* embarrassment, Amy explained she'd been helping with the laundry at Glenarkle, as Mrs Appleby had a headache; headaches were the bane of Mrs Appleby's life.

It was too late for Howth – and inadvisable now given the darkening skies from the west – so, swallowing their disappointment they opted for a stroll in the capital, a capital whose age-old sights and sounds another year now of Free-State rule had barely dented. Phil in particular took comfort from this.

In O'Connell Street, the voices of the Moor Street hawkers swelled the traffic's din; as did the clatter of Guinness drays on the cobbled quays. A Guinness barge crew waved and blasted a siren, before being gobbled by O'Connell Bridge.

In Westmoreland Street, the familiar face of the clock over the *Irish Times* office prompted Phil to say, 'Only paper worth reading in Dublin. Thank God it's still under Healy!' Amy smiled. Despite his words, she felt Phil was coming round to the Free State; hopefully he would come round to marriage in the same way; he and she were so at one, time was moving on. Then on they went to College Green, where King Billy was still holding out on his horse despite frequent attempts to unseat him; and Trinity's West Front still played host to the Union Jack.

In fashionable Grafton Street, a Matelasse suit caught Amy's eye. 'Phew – seven guineas!' she exclaimed. Minutes later they were in St Stephen's Green, sitting close on a bench; chatting, laughing, reminiscing; observing ducks, pigeons and passers-by; feeling good. Both regretted not being in Howth – the more so as the incoming clouds on the warm west wind seemed less threatening.

'Don't forget your stick,' Amy said, when they eventually got up to go; she'd noticed it at the Pillar but didn't like to comment on it. Self-consciously Phil thanked her and, lifting the stick from the back of the seat, told her where he'd bought it. 'I call it my "ashplant",' he added, giving it a little shake. 'Like "Daedalus" in *Ulysses*!' Amy asked what he thought of the book. 'Second to none,' he replied. 'Sure the man's a genius, breaks new ground with every word!'

From somewhere in the back of Amy's mind the words 'barbarian hordes' came to the fore. She couldn't resist a little jibe. 'This Joyce wouldn't be a Catholic?' she said cheekily. 'Yes,' Phil replied more seriously, 'but his own disowned him!'

'No matter,' Amy came back, 'they spawned him!' Phil appreciated that. A little guiltily then, as he imagined parts of the book might shock her – he asked her if she'd like to borrow it. She said she'd love to.

Exiting the Green (high tea at the Metropole beckoned) they returned to the city centre via Kildare Street wondering *en route* what the long dead Duke of Leinster was making of the current use of his earthly home, Leinster House. In the eighteenth century, the Duke had been ridiculed for building the house on the then unfashionable south side of the City. Time had proved his choice a good one but never in his imaginings could he have foreseen the day when his beloved home would house 'Dail Eireann'. Yet even here, a statue of Queen Victoria, plump and complacent, gave comfort to the old brigade.

The Metropole tea room was warm and plushy. Phil and Amy ordered an omelette followed by apple tart and custard. As they waited for the food, an advertisement in an abandoned copy of *Good Housekeeping* made them laugh. 'Give her pleasure – Give her leisure', its caption read, beside a dancing cherub with the plug end of a flex in one hand, a suction pipe in the other. A rapt housewife, and an Electrolux travelling salesman and his wares occupied the rest of the space.

When the waitress approached, Phil and Amy sobered. When she'd gone, Phil expanded a little on *Ulysses* – the bit about the 'one-handled adulterer' – making Amy laugh again. The sight of her – flushed and excited after their walk – coupled with so much hilarity, increased his longing for her.

As the meal advanced, and they lingered, so near and yet so far apart, over a pot, two pots, of tea... and talked some more... and looked out on the moving city, lit up now and heaving with rush-hour traffic... swaying, lurching trams, whose trolley-heads spat sparks... ships of the night rolling on a seething sea of weaving, dodging, hurrying pedestrians, cyclists, taxis and horse-drawn carts in the midst of which Dublin Metropolitan Policemen (unarmed now, but not yet integrated in the new 'Garda Siochana') kept a kind of order – Phil's longing reached breaking-point. 'There's no one in the residence but me, Amy,' he said, picturing his empty room in the empty residence. 'Come back with me for a few hours.'

'Are you out of your mind, Phil? I couldn't poss…'

'Just the once, A…'

'No. It'd be complete and utter madness.'

Phil agreed with that but continued to implore – 'The rest of the staff don't come back till tomorrow, Amy. It's dark now' – and the look of pleading and longing and roguishness in his grey-blue eyes eventually paid off. A rush of emotion – he'd been so good about her late arrival (and to think she'd been worried about the French trip!), she wanted him as much as he wanted her – overcame Amy's guard.

Chapter Nine

If Phil's absence in France was having the proverbial effect on his and Amy's relationship, nearness was not producing a dissimilar one on Neil and Catherine's. The summer holidays had gone swimmingly for them in every sense of the word. At Killiney, where Catherine was losing her fear of the water; at Neil's home in Rathmines, which Catherine visited most weekends and where his parents thought the world of her; on the romantic front, where not once had Neil's advances, tentative it's true, been repulsed. All in all things could not have been better, they thought. But about that Neil was wrong.

A few days before his term started he received a letter from the Head asking him to return to Poynings a day early to unpack and check out some new equipment for the gym; dutifully the Games Master obliged. Then a stroke of that luck he believed was always on his, a winner's, side came into play: he was in his room over Phil's in the residence – he could just as easily have been knocking about – when Phil returned from Fermanagh. After which – on the off chance, it being Wednesday, that Phil was meeting Amy – Neil clandestinely followed him to the Pillar (What a fop! he thought when he saw the walking stick) and loitered (Would she never come!) in a secluded shop doorway to catch sight of Amy's arrival. The rest was in the lap of the Gods. Would the dummy ('If you e..ever wa..nted to bring Amy into your room, Phil, I..I'd turn a blind eye') work?

That it had worked so quickly really surprised Neil: he didn't think Amy would break this particular school rule. Some other woman might, however, and if Phil's staffroom boasts were anything to go by there would be other women.

When Phil and Amy came into the residence Neil was actually doing his exercises – in the dark of course. Quickly and quietly he sat down in his winged armchair. Listening to the sounds from below – hushed voices, girlish giggles, creaking bed springs, moans – fired his imagination, and in a moment of guilt he reached for an orange from his piled-high fruit bowl and knocked a second one on to the floor. He sat even stiller after that, with only an occasional tweak about his face or body, a cat anticipating a pounce, belying mortality.

As the lovers left the residence Neil smiled smugly behind his window. 'Now I've got him,' he said meanly to himself. Moving away from the window, he replaced the orange he was holding in his fruit bowl and rescued the one on the floor. 'And the best is yet to come,' he thought, launching into the exercises he had earlier broken off; he had just finished his press-ups. After his stretch-bends and running on the spot, he embarked – his energy barely dented – on his dance practice and had no sooner started the Black Bottom, latest thing in the dance halls, than he heard Phil come back from seeing Amy off; he carried on, knowing it would only be a matter of minutes before his victim came up the stairs.

'Come in,' he said curtly, when he heard the knock on his door.

Neil's tone struck Phil as odd, making him wonder if something had happened at home to upset him and send him back to Poynings a day earlier than usual. Perhaps Catherine had dumped him? And who could blame her! Though if she had, Amy would probably have mentioned it. 'You came back early?' he said amicably – no point upsetting the fellow further! – and noticing the fruit bowl and Salvation Army box on the table. Rattle if forever, he thought. You'll not get a penny out of me! (It was Neil's practice to do the rounds in the staffroom a couple of times a term; everyone but Phil contributed.) Self-importantly – that too seemed odd to Phil – Neil explained about the new equipment for the gym. Then, with a deep intake of breath, he folded his arms on his broad chest and said – 'And if you're asking me did I hear anything, Handy, I did.'

There was no mistaking the inference here – not so much from the use of Phil's surname as from the snide way Neil had spoken; surnames were the norm at Poynings, just like at Glenarkle, even though Phil and Neil mostly used each other's Christian names now when off duty. Bloody earwig! Phil thought, less sanguine than before about what lay behind the Games Master's tone. 'You wouldn't snitch on us, would you?' he said, holding to his friendly approach, unhappy at having to ask the question at all.

Neil took his time about replying. He had noticed the uncertainty creeping into Phil's voice, was thoroughly enjoying it, and looking forward to prolonging it. He would reveal his plans – the end game, as he thought of it – step by step, watching his enemy squirm. 'Well now,' he said, slowly unfolding his arms and walking over to the table to perch on the edge of it with one of his thick legs dangling from his black shorts, 'I'd say that was for me to know, Handy, and you to find out.'

'Come off it, man!' Phil said, unwilling still, despite being sober – in keeping with his recent resolution, he had only had two pints after seeing Amy off – to believe his ears. 'Sure you as good as told me you'd say nothing!' So convinced had Phil been of Neil's good faith in this matter, he had used it to reassure Amy when the sound of Neil's dropped orange had alerted her to danger above.

Neil was having none of it. 'Did I?' he said gleefully and watching puzzlement replace the smile on Phil's face. 'Well if I did I'm unsaying it now! I don't like you, Handy. Never have! Not you or any of your nasty tribe. You haven't forgotten what that brother, Al, of yours did to me at school have you? No, I can see guilt in your face…'

'Bu…'

'Don't but me, Handy boy! I know what you're going to say.' Neil assumed a mincing tone – 'I didn't know what Al was doing.'

'I didn't,' Phil said – honestly, and shame-faced at being reminded about it like this. So ashamed – getting a fellow caned like that was out of order – he wanted to apologise on his own and his brother's behalf and was on the point of doing so when Neil vengefully told him he didn't care whether he knew or not. 'You Handys are all the same,' he added. 'Snobs. I wonder what the Beard will make of it if I…'

'You bastard,' Phil flared, stepping forward with frustration. He had noted the 'if', but that Neil was bent on trouble had sunk in at last. 'You're an even bigger fucker than I…'

'Temper, temper,' taunted Neil, getting down from the table and squaring up; 'go on, hit me if you dare.' The self-satisfied smirk on his big face made Phil want to smash his fist into it and send the blood spurting from its hairy mole – suddenly repellent again. Had he had a blackboard rubber in his hand he would have undoubtedly let fly with it – something he not infrequently did in the classroom; but fisticuffs with Neil was a non-starter: aside from boxing his brothers' ears, Phil had never hit anyone in his life; compared with Neil he was a stripling. 'I wasn't going to hit you,' he said, lamely stepping back, kicking himself for being duped. 'I bet you weren't,' Neil sneered. His vindictiveness scared Phil. From being the happiest man in town, with everything to live for, he had become the most got at; and all in the space of a few minutes. In the next few minutes, the hours just spent with Amy flashed through his mind: their walk in the capital, their meal at the Metropole, the excitement of entering the residence, like children scaling a forbidden orchard wall; their lovemaking. In his room at the outset he'd sensed a little constraint on Amy's part, so he'd attended to the curtains and fire while she'd looked around and examined the contents of his bookcase. 'You won't find it there,' he'd said, joining her by the books, 'I keep it under wraps.' She'd leaned back into him, her constraint gone, and in the fireside glow had given herself to him as never before. When they'd left the residence, she with his copy of *Ulysses*, 'Molly's monologue' was no longer an issue. How different it all seemed now! At his feet his dreams were splintering. If Neil reported him, it would be good-bye to Poynings, maybe even to Amy, and his copybook would be blotted for ever. The thought terrified him. In a desperate effort to get through to Neil, he clutched at the only straw – the 'if' – to hand, and said, trying not to antagonise –

'You do know Amy's career as well as mine will be threatened if you report us? I wonder what Catherine will make of that!'

'Leave Catherine to me,' Neil retorted, determined to keep Phil guessing; he had thought through his game plan well. 'As for Amy,' he added, 'Catherine and I will say nothing to her. *You* can say what you like.'

Desperate now to get away, Phil couldn't bring himself to go without pinning Neil down about his intentions. 'So what's the score?' he asked, hopeful humility and a lighter touch might yet sway the Games Master.

'About twenty-one nothing,' Neil said implacably, 'and if I were you, Handy, I wouldn't count on a comeback.' Far from being moved by Phil's meekness, Neil was wallowing in having the upper hand, and jubilant at the prospect of tormenting him some more while keeping him guessing; in his own time, he had every intention of reporting him and Amy. Coldly, he said, 'You can go now, Handy. As far as *I'm* concerned, the game's in the bag. I'll let you know when it's over.'

Feeling sick in his stomach and in his heart, Phil turned to the door. As he gripped the handle, he heard Neil say – 'Oh! And by the way, you couldn't lend me a quid, could you? I missed the bank today and need something to tide me over.'

Stunned, Phil turned round. Gloating, Neil stretched out his hand.

'That's blackmail,' Phil said, openly dumbfounded.

'You don't say,' Neil sneered, tweaking his fingers.

Dazed, Phil reached for his wallet. He felt as if he'd been knocked down by a taxi and kicked by a passer-by. Giving a pound to Neil, he left the room.

Chapter Ten

Somewhere in the small hours, Phil fell into a restless sleep. When he woke, wherever he looked, whichever way he turned, the road ahead was murky. Should he tell Amy? – two heads were better than one – or drop her altogether so as to spare her when the storm broke and she would inevitably be caught up in the scandal? Better still, should he tell the Beard and take the consequences, or give in his notice, which would probably amount to the same thing? Asking the questions was easy. Finding answers much harder: all routes imperilled his relationship with Amy and his hopes of the Maths Department. Unable to clear his mind, he decided to confide in Amy at the first opportunity – the following week, Wednesday.

As usual they met at the Pillar – Amy having caught the seventeen minutes past two tram from Kingstown. It was a non-stop rainy day, so they went to the pictures then straight to the Metropole restaurant for tea. Here goes, thought Phil, and even before their food arrived, he told Amy what had happened. He was a little embarrassed about the teasing part in case she thought he'd been involved in it. Her attitude reassured him; she was absolutely outraged by Neil's behaviour; it was inexcusable, even allowing for what Al had done.

No other response would have made sense to Amy given her enjoyment of the evening in question: even now she thrilled at the memory. Entering Phil's room had felt like being offered a loved one's diary to read and being unsure about opening it. Looking around, she'd noticed the shoddy décor, Phil's partially unpacked suitcase on the floor, and a photograph on his bedside table of his sister, June – his favourite sibling she suspected if only because of a little story he'd told her about pocket money he used to dole out, eightpence for a quarter of Mackintoshes toffees; when the price fell to sixpence, the siblings kept it from him till conscience prevailed and they elected June to confess knowing he could never get angry with her. Then, her reservations gone, Amy couldn't believe the things she was

79

doing in the fireside glow. Though not wholly convinced by Phil's reassurance about the one-off noise overhead (a niceness too far, she'd thought) she'd easily let it go.

Matter-of-factly in the Metropole tea room, and with a minimum of weighing up, she told Phil he must go straight to the Beard. 'There are no two ways about it,' she said. 'Tell him what we did. I'm as much to blame as you are. We'll face the music together. It's the right thing to do.' Notwithstanding their transgression, Amy knew how much being on the right side of the law, including school rules, had always meant to Phil. 'And tell him about Neil's blackmailing,' she added, equally forthrightly. 'I can't see him treating that more lightly than our shenanigans. Come to think of it, having to get rid of two staff might make him think twice about sacking anyone!'

'Especially not Neil,' Phil said, smiling and hugely relieved by Amy's support. 'Who'd bring the cups in then?'

Their food arrived. As they ate it, they wondered whether to put Catherine in the picture, and decided against: Neil might not tell her anything, if only on account of his blackmailing, and the fewer people who knew about the affair the better. 'Now let's not talk about it any more,' Amy said. 'You go to the Beard tomorrow. We'll take it from there.' Wholeheartedly Phil agreed with her. 'Thanks, Amy,' he said, 'you're a trooper.'

What seemed obvious with Amy in the plush, softly lit Metropole tea room, however, seemed far less so to Phil next morning – alone in his room in the blare light of day. Summoning the courage to face the Beard (Neil would deny the blackmailing, he reckoned) was altogether too daunting for him; too final. The happiest moments in his life had been with Amy; trying to define them would have been a waste of time; that was, if he could define them: happiness had a way of vaporising under analysis. And more than anything, he wanted his and Amy's relationship to go on – just as it was, indefinitely – and couldn't bear to risk losing her. So – I'll go this evening, he said to himself; and when evening came, I'll go tomorrow. It was the same the next day, and without Amy to stiffen his resolve at the weekend (both were on duty) at the start of the following week. On Wednesday she had another go at him, stressing that even if Neil denied blackmailing him and the Beard took his word against Phil's, he must still do the right thing. He agreed with her; but didn't do it. After that, bolstered by some good news from home – his sister, June was on the mend – he let things slide, taking comfort from this or that thought. Neil's demands (there had been no more yet) might not be crippling; ignominious, yes; but bearable. Also, great or small, their yield might persuade Neil to hold fire indefinitely on reporting him and, in time, making much of something that had happened so long ago might appear pointless. Failing all that, there was an outside chance Neil would drop dead – drown at the Forty-foot, or swim so far out to sea at Killiney he couldn't get back.

It was the line of least resistance, Phil knew; the coward's way. He didn't care. Amy continued to press him to own up but eventually, unable to shift him, she let things slide too. They talked about it less and less – it got drowned out in the 'twenties roar' – and, with one or two adjustments, carried on as before.

◇

Maybe there was a moment when Neil hesitated about reporting Phil; if there was it was extremely short lived. For pleasing though blackmailing was – having Phil at his mercy, just as he, Neil, had been at the mercy of his tormentors at school – and useful though extra income proved, extracting money by menaces seemed somehow demeaning to Neil. It was a bit like begging; the Crotchleys had never begged. That said, driving Phil from Poynings now would be far less satisfying than when the Maths Department materialised – something that looked increasingly likely at the end of the current academic year if the rumours abounding at present about the Head's relinquishing it were anything to go by. Pending, Neil could stomach the ignominy of occasionally blackmailing Phil, and gloat when he dared not snub his Salvation Army box in the staffroom.

For Neil it was a win win situation.

For Phil – a reckoning deferred. Not that he and Amy dwelt overly on the reckoning; their adjustments, if nothing else saw to that. Some of the adjustments irritated Phil: like fewer handouts to his mother, who misguidedly put the blame on Amy; fewer presents for Amy, like the Box Brownie he'd bought for her last birthday; and less opposition on his part to going Dutch; as a rule, he liked to pay for everything; not doing so unmanned him. Most, however, were welcomed by both of them, not least the little trysts they now embarked on – half-terms and the beginning or end of holidays – in out of the way mainly hitherto unfrequented places. As Mr and Mrs Brown, for example, in the 'North Star Hotel' – a commercial joint in Dublin where the chances of seeing a familiar face were as unlikely as being run over by a hansom; anon in a candlelit dive in Dundalk; as Mr. and Mrs. Jones in the 'Royal Hotel', Snowdonia – an area Phil knew well but where he was not well known.

But there was hollowness to it all – as hollow as the 'twenties roar'.

◇

Half way through the last half of Poynings' summer term, Phil's second at the school, rumours about the Head's partial retirement were suddenly firmed up.

Immediately, Phil sensed the Maths Department within his grasp. Amy dared to savour a proposal, something she had long ago concluded would only, if ever, materialise with Phil's promotion. Neil scented victory.

On the final day of term, staff assembled in the staffroom for their usual send off by the Beard. No one doubted he would use the occasion to offer his Department to Phil. 'Sure you're bound to get it, Handy,' they said. 'He can't possibly go over your head to an outsider.'

Now that the moment had come, Phil was anything but certain of getting it. Half of him – the half that was looking forward to going up into the mountains the next day with Amy and telling her the good news – said the Department would be his, whether or not Neil reported him; a single act of human weakness, so long ago, could surely be pleaded away especially when coupled with Neil's avarice. The other half – the half that saw Neil eying him spitefully across the room – said it would not.

Watching Phil sweat was like an appetiser to Neil. For weeks now, he had thought of little else but shaming him in public; of pressing the button on his stopwatch and blowing the final whistle. (In his 'game' with Phil, he was player and referee.) He had it all worked out. Immediately after the Beard's announcement, he would make his own – like at a wedding when the Vicar referred to 'just cause and impediment.' And if anyone asked why he had not spoken out sooner he would simply say he hadn't wanted to cause trouble at a time when Phil was not in a position of any real responsibility. Head of Department was different: people who broke school rules – and rules of such importance! – should not be trusted with positions like that. If Phil mentioned being blackmailed, Neil would deny it, confident the Head would believe him.

It's perfect, Neil thought, savouring the moment. Not so perfect, though, it couldn't be spiced by a little scrum. Turning to the RE master beside him, he asked, loud enough for Phil to hear – 'Has there been anything from the Commission on Evil Literature lately? I gather *Vanity Fair* is under scrutiny. And none too soon, if you ask me.' To date, Neil had read very few books; *Vanity Fair* just happened to be one of them. On the curriculum at school – where its sexual connotations were ignored, laughed at, or rationalised away – it had made little impact on him. Recently, though, a secretive reading, to find out what all the fuss was about, of a neglected copy at the bottom of his parents' piano stool (part of a job lot, to give greater respectability to the Crotchley's parlour) had proved much more rewarding. And now, along with the latest arguments in the press on censorship, it more than met his needs.

'Yes, indeed,' said the RE master, fully supportive of Neil.

The rest of the staff – supportive or otherwise, mostly the latter – looked at Phil knowing he could never ignore a comment like that by Neil or anyone else. Argie-bargies between him and the Games Master in the room were not uncommon. No one saw any harm in them or in Phil's more extravagant claims about women which were taken with a pinch of salt; he was no less popular than Neil at the school; he too had done it proud; it was in his nature to exaggerate.

'You're not serious,' he said now – true to form, and grateful in a way for the diversion.

'Never been more serious in my life,' came back Neil, digging in for the scrum and speaking casually, playfully almost, so as not to alert Phil; just make him more edgy. 'I take it then you wouldn't agree Becky Sharp is an immoral character'?

'What if she is?' Phil said, amazed Neil could speak so confidently on the content of any book. 'Becky Sharp's a fictional character. But even if she wasn't, her morals would be no concern of mine.'

'So there's nothing wrong with fornication,' Neil pressed, choosing his words, especially the last, carefully. In the room as a whole it raised one or two eyebrows, but more because Neil, not Phil, had come out with it. In Phil, it conjured thoughts of his trysts with Amy, and made him question the wisdom of getting embroiled in such a contentious topic at a time like this: *good* impressions were needed now. 'I didn't say that,' he said, unable not to respond; 'it's just that I think morality's a personal thing, and that censorship of literature *per se* is wrong.' Deliberately then, he stubbed his butt firmly in the big, cut glass ashtray on the table beside him to give the impression he didn't want to pursue the subject.

Neil had other ideas. 'So we just let the filth disseminate, do we – Fictional and otherwise? Mind you – it's not for me to question the wisdom of a worldly-wise womaniser like yourself!'

Everyone noticed the sarcasm. Only Phil was troubled by it.

'And just what do you mean by that?' he asked, unable to let it go.

'Well,' Neil said, resuming his playful tone, while tensing for the big heave ho. 'We all know you don't tolerate numbskulls like me gladly!' Laughter encouraged him to go on. 'And we've all heard your claims in regard to women, haven't we?' More laughter; it wasn't meant to be unkind but that was how it seemed to Phil. Desperate to shut Neil up (the Beard would be along any minute now), he couldn't think of anything to say.

Victory beckoned for Neil. A door banged. Time for one last try, he thought, snatching the ball from the scrum – 'I'm not the only one, Handy, who's heard you boast you could have any woman you wanted' – and heading for the base line.

In vain, Phil searched for words. He was panicking now. All eyes were on him, waiting for a response he couldn't make. Without words he was lost: a belly up tortoise; Samson without his hair. An impending sense of doom swept over him.

Anger welled inside him. 'Mind you,' he heard Neil saying, 'we all know the kind of woman he means. Why else would he be wanting to bring her into his room?'

The nearest thing to Phil's hand was the cut glass ashtray. Without any thought for the consequences, any thought at all, he picked it up and flung it at Neil. Deftly, the Sports master fended, but not before the Beard had appeared in the door-way, witness to the whole incident. In the same split second that the ashtray shattered, Phil knew it was the end for him at Poynings. Neil – he had never seen a better own goal – knew his most heartfelt wish had been granted, albeit in not quite the way he'd planned.

◇

That evening, at home with his parents in Rathmines, Neil unpacked and tidied away his belongings and wrote to his brother in the East. The last time he'd written to him was in the wake of Phil and Amy's visit to the residence. What a sequel! he thought now, settling down with his pen and pad.

Later, having foregone his exercises and dance practice (he had earned a respite from both, he reckoned), he said his prayers, went to bed and slept soundly.

Next day, Saturday, he met Catherine in Ballsbridge as pre-arranged. At Sandymount Station they took a train to Killiney. During the ride, Neil was tempted to tell Catherine about the events of the previous day in Poynings' staffroom. He decided against: Phil was bound to tell Amy everything, and hearing it from her could only enhance him in Catherine's eyes; he would put his own slant on the story then. So he and Catherine talked about other things and wondered, as they got off the train, how long they would have on the beach it being a warm, windy day with iffy looking clouds coming in from the west.

In the event, they had a grand few hours, during which Catherine managed a dozen strokes – the most she'd swum to date – and Neil swam almost to the horizon and back afterwards. Not since the day he'd packed his brother off to the East, had he felt so happy and relaxed. And as he lay on the beach beside Catherine, he wondered how Phil and Amy were getting on. Badly, he hoped.

◇

High in the Dublin Mountains, where a man could be king and conqueror without lifting a finger, Phil and Amy spent their last hours together that term.

Phil, who was due to return home to Fermanagh later in the day, had spent the previous night in the residence, grateful everyone else had moved out. But he'd scarcely slept at all, so worried was he about what had happened and what Amy would make of it. He'd never been so ashamed of anything in his life; a blackboard rubber in the classroom was one thing, a cut glass ashtray – anywhere – quite another. What on earth would he say to her? And to his parents! Like Fitzgerald's Nick Carraway, Phil believed himself to be 'one of the few honest people' he had ever met. Explaining things to his parents would be an occasion, he knew, for half-truths; he could live with that.

No such demi-measures would suffice for Amy, and finding the courage to reveal all to her would be hard. If she had had a vice or two it might have been less so. Why, Phil had wondered sleeplessly, did she have to be so damned blameless? And to have so much – her God, her heritage, her job; things he had long ago concluded (and rightly so) were the bed rock of her surety; of that oneness with herself and her surroundings that made his own restlessness more marked now than ever – when he had so little? Compared with hers, his life had appeared almost superficial to him: whatever happiness he'd had was illusory; love had blinded him; he should have known better than to let it. Yet even as he'd reflected, ashamed of what he'd done, and of envying Amy – if envy it was, he'd never envied her before – he'd known he had only himself to blame. He could have had Amy's faith, shared her heritage, and changed jobs long ago. Instead, he'd rejected God, steered clear of marriage, clung to Poynings; now, he had no idea where to turn.

In pursuit of a way out, his thoughts had gone back and forth relentlessly. He would do this, that or the other; the other, that or this. Eventually he'd arrived at a solution, the first step towards which would be to tell Amy about yesterday's events. Amy would understand; she always did, which was why he could never really envy her. And telling her in the outdoors would make things easier for him.

But despite the fresh mountain air, and few but him and Amy around to breathe it, opening up to her was proving much harder than Phil expected. They'd been walking for the best part of two hours – he with his stick, and a bottle of Guinness in each of his rain-coat pockets; she with her commodious bag which today, as well as the usual clutter of stationery, cosmetics and the rest, contained a mack and some paste sandwiches the extra weight of which had prompted her to omit her Box Brownie – and still he hadn't found the courage to confess. And if he couldn't find it here, where could he find it? For this was a part of Ireland, isolated but nowhere remote, where mystery, surprise and the commonplace were all one. Where black, brooding tarns rose up ahead like cavernous shafts from Hell. Where shadows played tag on the mountain sides, and small, watchful wildlife flitted, stalked and scurried over bog-brown, heathered earth. Where gorse-gold vied with sunlight to dazzle the eyes, and nothing was too great or too small to be encompassed. Even the names on the milestones, familiar to all Dubliners, rang with a peculiar charm: Enniskerry and Powerscourt; Glencree, the Sally Gap and Glenmalure; Lough Tay, Lough Dan and Glendalough; the Big and Little Sugarloafs; Cahygolagher and Lugnaquilla – highest peak in the Wicklow range. Striding out along the open roads, or stretched out on the moors and downs, it was easy for a person here to imagine that the world really was his oyster. And when the wind, like Lochinvar, came 'out of the west', there was no need here for guile or dissembling. Such a day was today, and still Phil couldn't find his tongue for the things that most harried him – not least his plans for the future.

They stopped for lunch by a little brook – by its beached shallows at the base of a steepish incline – spread their macks on the ground and sat down, Phil having first removed the Guinness from his pockets. Two horses – a grey mare and a piebald stallion – grazed lazily nearby. Amy's feet were crying out for release so she took off her shoes, peeled down her flesh-coloured stockings and dibbled her toes in the icy water – Heaven. What little pink was in her skin quickly vanished, making her freckles stand out clearer than ever. 'Glory be to God for dappled things'! Phil thought – the only thought that had made him smile genuinely since the morning of the previous day. He wasn't in a paddling mood. His appetite had deserted him too but he took the paste sandwiches when Amy offered them to him, along with her bottle-opener; he'd been about to use a flat stone.

'A penny for them', she said as they ate and drank, and her refreshed feet dried on the bank, and the westerly blew the clouds across the sky, and the shadows over the mountain sides, and the grey and the piebald grazed. She'd known from the start that something was up – Phil's long silences and forced banter were hopelessly out of character – but couldn't believe he hadn't got the job; only the tiniest doubt had prevented her asking him about it. Much more likely was it, she thought, he'd got the job and was planning to propose to her but couldn't bring himself to do it.

'I've something to tell you, Amy,' he said, offering her a cigarette, taking one himself and lighting both with the second-hand silver lighter, initialled P.H., she'd given him the previous Christmas. Immediately, Amy knew what he had to say was not what she'd imagined had been on his mind. She waited. He told her everything – right down to his loss of control in the staffroom ('letting fly like that, Amy, was unforgivable') and his ignominious one to one with the Beard afterwards, where explanations in full had been demanded and given. 'What a total ass I've been,' he concluded, lying back exhausted on the ground. Though still worried about what he had yet to disclose, he was relieved to have got the sordid bit off his chest.

Amy felt sorry for him. Of course he shouldn't have lost control like that. But nor should Neil have said and done what he had – nasty, spiteful things designed purely to goad and humiliate; visiting a person's sins on his brother was contemptible. Also, Amy being Amy – her practical mind was moving on and, bleak though the scenario was, she was beginning to detect signs of hope in it. The Beard had not only promised to say nothing to Mr. Appleby but further promised – doubts about the blackmailing, Phil's record at Poynings? Phil didn't know – not to refer to the incident in the staffroom in his references about Phil. And there were, as Amy had so often reminded him, other schools – including some near Kingstown. And another job would probably mean more money, more stability, less antipathy to marriage...

'I was thinking of going abroad,' Phil said, casually.

'What?' Amy gasped incredulously; Phil's offhandedness had upset her as much as his words. With a supreme effort, she added more calmly – 'Would you not think of applying to another school in Dublin? There's plenty of excell…'

'No, Amy. If I make a break it'll be a big one. I don't feel I belong here any more.'

'What do you mean you don't belong? Of course you belong.' Despite her best efforts, Amy was beginning to sound angry. Suddenly, from being a straightforward, albeit fraught, affair – a problem to be solved like any other, practically – the situation was becoming complex. A clutch of concerns rushed into her head. Was this Phil's way of ditching her as well as Ireland? she asked herself, turning away from him to face the brook. Or did he intend for her to go with him? – in which case he was presuming an awful lot. They had of course discussed (who hadn't?) emigration in the past, but never seriously, and she'd always assumed Phil's attachment to Ireland was as strong as hers. Now, it appeared, it was not…

'You know what I mean,' he said forcefully, and a little put out by her crossness. 'Being Anglo-Irish, Amy, is neither one thing nor the other. Never has been. The English have always regarded us as Irish – more Irish than the Irish themselves, remember! – and the Irish as English. We're hybrids. No other word for it. British nationality in the Free State is a farce.'

Amy took her time before replying. Equally forcefully – his attitude was really annoying her – she said at last: 'Come off it, Phil. If you'd got the Maths Department at Poynings you'd have settled down like most of the rest of us. Don't make the treatment of your family in the past and your own mistakes now an excuse for emigration. And if it's me you're tired of, just say so. I've no intention of foisting myself on you.' Instinct told Amy she belonged in Ireland. Being Anglo-Irish (born in Ireland, of British parents, and the holder, like Phil, of a British passport) was not a problem for her. What Phil was doing – running away from Ireland, with or without her, was cowardly…

Breaking into her thoughts Phil said, 'Why don't you say what you're really thinking, Amy. You think I'm a funk, don't you? Go on, say it.'

'Well you don't *have* to go.' Amazed by his perspicacity, Amy was unable to deny her thoughts outright. Phil appreciated her honesty. 'I *do* have to,' he said.

'You *must* understand.'

Turning, Amy looked at him, with the intention of impressing on him that he did not have to. But his face and eyes – the latter more grey than blue, something she'd come to recognise when he was up against it – were so serious she couldn't do it. He had let himself, his parents and her – or so he thought – down; ashamed, and boxed in – he just wanted to escape. What right had she to stop him? 'Do you have anywhere special in mind?' she asked, as uncertain as before about his intentions towards her.

Relieved she was mellowing, but reluctant still to ask her to join him – in her present mood she might say 'no' – Phil said, 'Well a fella I was talking to once told me the Colonial Service was a good bet. Malaya's especially nice, he said. Maybe not all that easy to get into straight off, but definitely worth a try! What do you think, Amy?'

What do I think? Amy thought, turning away again to hide her feelings and convinced by now she had slipped to nowhere in his calculations. Not so long ago Boulogne had seemed too far away from her for him; now, the Orient was acceptable. So what does it matter what I think? You've obviously made your decision. 'It sounds wonderful,' she lied.

He noticed the despondency in her voice, and decided to lay his cards on the table. 'Good,' he said, 'you'll come with me then?'

That threw her. Suddenly her thoughts began racing. Did Phil really mean what he was saying? Was a proposal in the offing at last? If it was, she knew she would accept it even if it meant giving up much of what she cherished. If it was not, she saw no reason why she should give up so much for such an uncertain future with him, especially as he probably didn't want her at all: Why else would he not have consulted her before reaching his decision? He was only asking her to join him now to avoid telling her he'd had enough of her. It was another of his ploys, and a pretty cowardly one at that...as cowardly as his decision to go abroad. What an ass I've been! she thought. Well, I'll show him...

'Say something, Amy.'

'No, Phil. I won't go with you.' As she uttered the words, with her back to him and her eyes fixed on the water, Amy felt sick inside. She wondered if he would change his mind about going abroad, or ask her to marry him, which she wasn't at all sure she'd say yes to now as he'd only be proposing to her to hold on to her, which she didn't want at all. He did neither. Let's face it, he thought, ruefully, I'm hardly the best of catches. Unwilling to press her, not wanting to lose her, unable to change tack even though he sensed what he was doing was not in his own best interest, he said again, 'I *have* to go, Amy. You *must* understand.'

'Well go then,' she said, in a mind set much like his.

A long silence followed. Phil continued to lie on his back; Amy, to sit facing the brook, with her arms clasped round her bent up bare legs. The mare and the stallion grazed nearby. A skylark started singing overhead. Amy looked up but couldn't see it for bright sun. She listened to its song, waiting for the drop and the little run around that would follow... Then something nearer too distracted her. Looking across the brook she saw a bearded old man, no more than a few paces up the opposite bank, staring at her and Phil. Loosely tied with frayed string, his grubby, straggling coat reached almost to his ankles; ragged trouser ends hung over his tattered shoes; and a battered, back-tilted hat gave Amy a full view of his blood-shot eyes and wrinkled face, burned black-brown by sea-salty, mountain air. Amy wondered how long he had been there. Conscious of her bare legs, she shrank back.

She missed the drop. The old man made to go, shaking his head and muttering, 'The grey mare is the better horse.' Amy shuddered.

'What is it?' Phil asked.

'Nothing,' she replied, reaching for her stockings, 'an old tramp; he's gone now.' Then putting her stockings on, she added matter-of-factly, 'It's time we were going too, Phil. The clouds are banking up in the west.' She finished dressing. Phil watched her, a little ruefully, then got to his feet and helped her with the macks. They retraced their steps – talking, if at all, about incidentals – downhill to Rathfarnham, then on to Terenure where a number fifteen tram kept them dry when the threatened rain started and took them into the city centre. Foregoing a meal at the Metropole, they said good-bye in the rain at the Pillar, not knowing if they would ever see each other again.

Part II

Cavan: The weakest go to the wall

◇

Chapter Eleven

Before the week was out, Amy was on her way to Shandoran. Right now, there was nowhere else in the world she would have preferred to be.

Waiting for her on his own with the pony and trap at Ballymun Station, was her brother Henry – a big muscular man with hunched shoulders at odds with his twenty-seven years, and a ruddy face at one with his outdoor life. His prominent cheekbones were high, and his chestnut eyes hugely expressive beneath a shock of shallow-waved chestnut hair; physically he took after his father. Seeing Henry on his own pleased Amy; togetherness was something they had always shared. He beamed at her when he saw her, took her heavy, leather suitcase and tossed it into the trap as though it was a brace of pheasants. Then the two of them climbed aboard, and Henry – bursting, it quickly transpired, to tell his sister his wife, Harriet, was pregnant again – picked up the reins in his large, scarred hands and shook them lightly on Stella's back. At Shandoran, the pony was always called Stella.

In Ballymun Main Street, they halted outside Aikens' – the little drapers where their younger sister, Lucy, worked and resided. She and the younger (mid-eighties) Miss Aiken came to the door for a quick hello, the older (late-eighties) Miss Aiken having been bedridden for some time. Amy told Lucy she'd be back in a day or two to catch up on news and check out the shop's remnants. Then Stella carried on down the road, her passengers acknowledged by passersby (everyone in the vicinity recognised the Allens) and the gossipers at the stand pump where she exited the town.

Once through Ballymun, Henry put the pony into a brisk trot. He had a reputation as a 'bloody Jehu' but trying to impress Amy with speed would have been as useless, he knew, as jazzing up a lullaby to induce sleep in a babe.

Before long, Amy told her brother about Phil. Hearing it, made him almost as desolate as she was; big-hearted and gullible, he'd gleaned nothing from her manner. Glad to be there for her, as she had been there for him on so many occasions, he offered what comfort he could – 'Maybe he'll have a change of heart, sis. Sure there's plenty of other fish in the lake' – then fell silent at Amy's wan smile.

As Stella clipclopped rhythmically, picking her way through ruts and potholes – among the worst in the land – as deftly as a cat across a shelf of Victorian bric-a- brac, Amy surrendered herself to the familiar sights, sounds and smells of her homecoming: To the generality of hills and lakes for which Cavan was as famed in Ireland as was the American mid-west world-wide for its prairies and dustbowls; and to the particular little landmarks – some seasonal, some not – that never failed to catch her eye. Here, the lonely ruin of a burned out big house slowly succumbing to ivy; there, an abandoned cottage cannibalising its thatched roof; coming up to this corner, an outcrop of purple heather in a brown bogscape; rounding the next, a meadow ablaze with corn poppies; from the crest of a hill, a lake glinting in the late afternoon sun; silhouetted on the skyline, an electrocuted tree posing bizarrely in the middle of a wild caper.

In due course, Shandoran's perimeters were reached and the estate's oases of blue flax, stitched through by the River Lisanne, skirted.

'It'll not be long now till the pulling,' Henry said, bouncing over a humped back bridge, knowing how much Amy liked to get stuck into harvesting.

'Indeed, yes,' she replied. 'And a grand crop it looks too!'

Henry agreed with that, then added – 'It's a pity prices haven't recovered, sis. Makes paying off the debts near impossible.'

Aware of what debts were being referred to – the ones left over by their mother and step-father when, five years back, they'd left Shandoran – Amy nodded sympathetically. She was also aware of some things which, had they not existed would have made Shandoran's money worries far less problematical.

Saying so, though, would only have upset Henry, caused trouble between him and Harriet, and solved nothing.

Moments later, the towering elm tree at Shandoran's front entrance came into sight.

Someone had opened the gate so Stella swung her load under the elm and up the long avenue to another gate – also open, overhung by a magnificent copper beech and giving access to 'the street.'

This, the street, was a wide, fully-enclosed area in front of the house. Both the back and front doors opened into it as did a second entrance to the estate from the road, a lane entrance. Facing the house was a low, nasturtium-topped wall backed by tall clumps of glossy laurels in which the hens were prone to roost. Behind the glossy laurels, a spacious yard, surrounded by outhouses, stretched all the way back to the road between the avenue and lane. Each of the latter boasted a well.

As Stella came to a halt, the street came alive. Henry's collie, Nancy, barked excitedly. Roosting fowl fluttered in the laurels. Strays from the yard – like Shandoran's two cockerels, Jasper and Sardine, whose names, like the pony's, were passed on from one generation to the next – scattered. The back door was flung open by Harriet who, toddler armed and her pregnancy either forgotten or not troubling her, rushed out to greet her sister-in-law. Lottie skipped beside her mother, and behind them, Shandoran's maid, Maggie Scott, waved, and smiled her warm, shy, welcoming smile. The men came round from the yard. 'Home again, Miss Amy!' Matt Doran, most senior and long-serving of them said, giving Amy a crinkly smile and shaking her hand warmly. A quiet, stolid man – digging words out of him, it was said, was harder than extracting a cow, deep-sunk, from a boghole – Matt's sincerity and dependability were beyond question; Henry was lucky to have him. The other two full-timers, Fleming Young and Paddy Finch, waved to Amy from the lane gate. She lapped it up. Not even the thought of the absentees – her mother and half-siblings, Lucy and Benjie (and still no word from Benjie in America), Henry's dead

99

cocker, Barney – could dampen her spirits. And this, despite the unpleasantness she knew or imagined had surrounded their exits from Shandoran.

In the kitchen, homey with the smell of turf and freshly baked soda bread, the fire glowed brightly in the wide, open hearth. The Aladdin stood ready for lighting on the Pembroke table – the only piece of furniture in the room not made of pine. The hurricane lamps hung on their hooks. The scrubbed, stone-flagged floor bore witness to the maid, Maggie Scott's elbow-grease; the piping pot of tea on the hearth, to her foresight on hearing the trap's approach.

During the days and weeks ahead, Amy planned to throw herself into the life of the estate, not to blot out the memory of Phil – that would have been impossible – but to adjust to life without him. Keeping busy was the best way forward.

At Shandoran, jobs were never ending. Indoors – scouring and scrubbing; polishing, blackening and raddling; washing and ironing; emptying buckets and gazunders; cooking and child-minding; fire-stoking and larder-stocking were the order of the day. Outdoors, the kitchen garden had to be tended, fowl fed, fruit picked, water fetched, the dairy manned, and a helping hand proffered in the fields and meadow bogs at the busiest time of year. And aside from all this, there were shopping trips to Ballymun and other market towns; churchgoing, visiting and visitors; crises – man or beast trapped in a boghole; an escaped horse; illness or injury. A non-stop round of doing in which Amy enveloped herself – as in woollies and muffler on a wintery day; wallowed in – like Lottie in her weekly bath; surrendered herself to – like a willing cart-horse. Others might have tackled a similar bust-up differently. Amy did it the only way she knew – practically.

Reinforcing the endeavour was her love of the estate – the place which, for as long as she could remember, had been her number one bolt hole; succoured her when everything else had failed.

Her love for Shandoran was easily explained.

Amy loved it for what it was, the sturdy, old Tudor house – thick, grey stone walls, windows deep-set – and four hundred-acre flax estate on which she had been born and brought up; whose every tree and flower she could name straight off, every hill she had climbed and rolled down, every pike-, perch-bream-, and rudd-laden lake and river she had circumvented, rowed on or paddled in.

And for what it stood for above all else in her mind: her heritage – nearly three centuries of Allen gentility in Kilbeg, notwithstanding the dispossession of Catholics. Kilbeg Church, with its memorials to her ancestors bore witness to that gentility – a gentility that had survived many tests of time not least her mother, Eleanor's arrival on the estate. For how, Eleanor's folks at The Mill, and many others, had asked, could the twenty-one-year-old daughter of John Humphrey Daker – a God-fearing, puritanical, corn miller of Huguenot decent (Daker was the Anglicised form of the French D'Acre) – tame a red-headed, roistering, rumbustious character like Samuel Allen, twice her age and of no fixed abode till he'd inherited Shandoran from his Uncle, Dr Joshua Allen. Also, though a kind of peace was holding on the land – nothing permanent, more like the hush of nectar-sipping bees as nationalists from all shades of the political spectrum (orange, green, blue) were keeping their heads down in readiness for the next clarion call – these were difficult times on estates. Eleanor and Samuel were married in 1900. Land Acts and economic depression were taking their toll, leading many to conclude with Wilde's Lady Bracknell that land had 'ceased to be a profit or a pleasure…' But the newlyweds had proved the pundits wrong. Marriage and responsibility sobered Samuel; with the aid of a steward, John Fisher, he'd made good husbandry his watchword. Eleanor, a milliner by training – something Amy attributed her love of hats to – but well-schooled in domesticity at The Mill, had presided over kitchen, poultry, dairy and domestics. Had Shandoran's old thatched roof, the reeds for which were becoming scarce and which she didn't like anyway, replaced with slates, and the kitchen furnished with pine. A Catholic nursemaid, Doxey – a childless widow returned to the land of ancestors who'd emigrated to America in the wake of the Famine – had looked after their four children – Henry, Amy, Lucy and Benjie. Rumbustious Allen and puritanical Daker worked. Another test of time at Shandoran had been surmounted.

Above all, though, Amy loved Shandoran and wanted it to prosper for her brother, Henry's sake – not just because he was her brother but because he had suffered so much at his mother's hands in the wake of his father's death. For ten years into Eleanor and Samuel's marriage, a rollicking roister too many had catapulted Samuel from his horse's saddle and broken his neck. He had been a popular master at Shandoran; it was said of his cortege that the last carriage was leaving the estate when the first was arriving, a mile away, at Kilbeg Church. Devastated at the loss of his adored father, a barely nine-years-old Henry had looked to his mother for solace. Instead of that he got loathing – and all because his father had bequeathed the estate to him on his twenty-first birthday instead of to Eleanor for her life time. By some bizarre sleight of mind she blamed Henry for the 'injustice'. Beatings rained down on his head, the one in the wake of the 'turned cart' becoming as embedded in family lore as had an episode from Kilbeg's past – the 'turned stone' – been entrenched in local lore. The arrival, some four years after Samuel's death, of Eleanor's second husband, Tom Linnaker, on the estate aggravated things. Henry despised his step-father – a small, rotund man a few years younger than Eleanor; clean-shaven apart from his tidy, matchbox moustache, he looked more suited to an office stool than the busy life of a flax estate. But the contempt was not based on Tom's age or appearance; or on the fact that he was a struggling pig-farmer from Ballymun. Henry wasn't a snob. He despised his step-father because of his laziness on the estate; hunting, shooting and fishing with his pampered pointer, Jess, were what Tom liked; and because of his accounting. 'I'll keep the books for you, Ellie,' Tom had said as soon as he was entrenched on the estate and leading Eleanor to dismiss the steward, John Fisher, who up to then had kept the books and of whom Henry had grown very fond since his father's death. 'Keeping the books indeed' – Henry used to say, echoing John Fisher's words; 'cooking them more like.' Sally, rod and horsewhip rained down and when Henry was too big to beat, Eleanor lashed him with her tongue; boy or man he was no match for her. Aware of his vulnerability, Amy comforted him when she could. A deep bond of friendship was forged between brother and sister out of the white heat of their mother's rages against him. Eleanor could never understand the bond and dearly wanted Amy to come round to her way of thinking: Henry was a no good wastrel who had deprived her of her rights to Shandoran. Amy stayed even-handed – decrying the beatings, hating her mother on account of them, forgiving her because she was her mother.

Given all this it is easy to see why Amy welcomed her return home. Shandoran would not let her down. It was solid and enduring – like the elm at the avenue entrance, and the thick, grey, stone walls of the house. It was the symbol of a heritage to be justly proud of; something to hold on to in a changing world.

This was not to say it would not face more trials in the future, its debts alone would see it did; or that Amy could insulate herself from them any more than she could forget Phil. Somehow, though, the estate had always proved bigger than its problems. They and people came and went. Shandoran outlived them all. What you expected from it you got – comfort and reassurance, give or take.

◇

What Amy did not expect or foresee on the estate was the emergence of something which, while it undoubtedly helped to take her mind off Phil – more than anything else, it transpired – she would have much preferred to be without. Of something Maggie had feared in the past but been persuaded by Harriet's behaviour and Amy was unlikely to materialize. That it had materialized was revealed to Amy a few days after her return home.

It was a Sunday and the family as was customary was taking tea in the parlour, a still cosily furnished room despite Eleanor's trawl of the whole house before she left it. Nothing but the 'best' had sufficed for Mrs Linnaker; best feather bolsters from the bedrooms; floral gazunders, jugs and hand basins; best china tea and dinner services, silver salvers and cutlery from the dining room; baking utensils and iron pots from the scullery and kitchen; best lamps; best linen. In general, though – Knockmore being nowhere near as big as Shandoran – Eleanor had stuck with the smaller stuff and for that the parlour, an undiluted farrago of Victoriana, had provided rich pickings: its daintiest goblets, ceramic trinket boxes, *cloisonné* vases and porcelain figurines were now at Knockmore. So were its heavy drapes.

But plenty of its old furnishings were still in situ including a beautiful walnut credenza, inlaid with boxwood and ebony (too unwieldy for Eleanor) and a walnut piano she had no time for as none of the Linnakers played. The piano had been Joshua's and was still referred to as his though 'Harriet's piano' was creeping into usage. As for the room's seating – the antimacassared chair in which Henry was plonked had been too bulky for Knockmore, the walnut scroll settee where Amy sat, too worn; and the button backs accommodating Harriet and Lottie too old-fashioned, a quality that actually endeared them to Harriet, their stubby cabriole legs on castors being particularly appealing to her because of their manoeuvrability.

'Dear, dear,' she was saying, handing her toddler, Luke, to Amy, and picking up the delft teapot as though it was made of lead, 'I don't know how I'm going to manage with another baby. I've not been at all well, Amy, these past months, and Dr McPhearson says I must be careful with my back.'

Amy and Henry nodded sympathetically, and remembering one of their mother, Eleanor's unkind remarks about Harriet

– 'Humph. Child-bearing won't come easy with those scrawny hips!' – Amy couldn't but think there was some truth in it: a few years older than Henry, and nearly as tall as him, Harriet was woefully thin.

Thinness, however, did not make her unattractive. She had a natural poise, a long shapely neck, and alluring hooded eyes. Her clothes, flowing black skirt and high-necked, black lace blouse, were just right for her – perfectly disguising her thinness, in keeping with her old-fashioned ways, setting off her copper hair. The latter had a magnificent sheen; she brushed it night and morning. Most beautiful of all, as befitted her musical talents (she was a truly gifted pianist, Joshua would have been proud of her) were her hands. Smooth, nimble-fingered and lovingly manicured, they were the kind of hands that were perfect for piano playing and making soda bread (something else Harriet did very well) but as unsuited for the rough manual work expected of Shandoran's mistress as was parquet to hob nailed boots.

'There's so much to do and organize as it is,' she went on, putting the teapot down heavily and passing round the cups. Some tea slopped into Henry's saucer as he took it, causing her to frown and tut loudly. Tutting and frowning were among her less attractive traits, as were her pouting and wheedling when she wanted something – like now. 'You'll stay for the whole holiday, won't you, Amy?' she said, slicing up her soda bread, knowing perfectly well Amy liked to spend a week in the summer holidays with her mother at Knockmore. Having said as much, Amy looked around appreciatively before adding – 'And as far as I can make out, Harriet, you and Maggie, here, are managing very nicely.' The maid had just come into the room from the scullery with the last pot of last year's blackcurrant jam (she'd been saving it for the occasion knowing how much Amy liked it) and a kettle of boiling water to top up the teapot.

'Indeed, yes,' Henry put in, chomping his wife's soda bread and giving Lottie – she had moved from her buttonback to his knee – a little squeeze. She was incredibly like him, her high cheek bones and chestnut eyes especially; her hair was strawberry blonde and deeper waved than his. Maggie smiled shyly, and having topped up the teapot placed the kettle on the hearth and returned to the scullery. Harriet had completely ignored her. Amy noticed that.

Later – after a comment by Amy on how well Lottie looked, and a shy rejoinder from the child that she'd be four 'in Augt' and her Daddy had 'promit' to buy her a filly – Henry nuzzled his smooth, Sunday best chin into his daughter's curls, and put it to Harriet it would be a birthday indeed for the child to remember if she had her first ride on it.

'No, Henry,' Harriet said, firmly, 'it's still far too dangerous. You know what happened to your father!'

'We'll bide a bit longer, then, if that's what you want,' Henry conceded, not wishing to be reminded of his father's death though unable to see any correlation between it and what he was proposing for Lottie – a gentle introduction to the filly. Disappointed, Lottie looked to Amy for help and, receiving none, made to go off to the scullery to Maggie for comfort. Harriet stopped her. Amy noticed that too.

And later still, after Henry had left for the yard, Harriet stood up and examined her hands. A neglected cuticle caught her eye. Tutting, she pressed back the offending skin, and smoothing down her clothes, said, 'My goodness me, Amy, I feel quite stretched already! It'll be no time till I'm into my smock.' She couldn't wait to get into her smock – proof positive she was pregnant, therefore excused all heavy tasks. Then Maggie returned to the parlour to clear away the dishes. Amy helped her, and noticed as she did the maid's badly bitten fingernails – something that had escaped her eye till now. Nibbled would have been OK, but badly chewed was not. It was another worrying sign that all was not well between the mistress and her maid.

In the wake of her observations, Amy asked herself what lay behind the change in her sister-in-law's attitude to Maggie.

Was it a passing phase – the result of early pregnancy? Or was Harriet up to her old tricks again?

An only child indulged something rotten by a piano tuning father and organ playing mother, Harriet had never had to strive for anything; even her skill at the piano came naturally: a born pianist, folks said of her. Brought up in Wexford, a county in the south-east of the Free State, she had moved to Kilbeg when her widowed mother, Mrs Harper took up residence in the Vicarage there about a year or so before the Linnakers left Shandoran: Mrs Harper was Reverend Badell's sister; he was a bachelor whose aged housekeeper had just died. The arrangement worked, with even parishioners benefitting from it by never being without an organist. Winning Henry had been a cinch for Harriet too, and her wedding day – hard on the heels of the Linnakers' exit from Shandoran – gone just as she wanted. Dressed in a long, cream-satin, Edwardian gown, whose flowing lines and deep-cuffed, puffed sleeves were, however outmoded, a perfect disguise for her thinness – she'd radiated happiness. As she and Henry walked down the aisle – Henry with his hair cut tidily for the occasion, his head held high on his hunched shoulders (hunched, it was said, from cowering beneath the lash) – and later rode home to the estate, a wealth of goodwill and sympathy had gone with them; since when, sympathy for Harriet at Shandoran had diminished.

Her trouble was, she was neither domesticated nor any good at organizing. Had Henry been a better manager this might not have mattered. He wasn't, and nobody expected him to be. Everyone, though, expected Harriet to manage Shandoran like her mother-in-law, Eleanor, had done before her. To begin with they made excuses for her. 'Give her time,' they said, 'how can someone with *her* background be expected to manage a big estate like this straight off? She'll learn.' But Harriet didn't want to learn and quickly discovered that if she left things long enough, someone else – Henry, the men, Maggie, or Amy if she was at home – would do them for her; it was what she had come to expect in life. When things got too hot for her, she came up with scapegoats; Lucy and Benjie had been sitting ducks. 'It's not my job to feed them,' she'd started saying soon after she moved into Shandoran, 'aren't they old enough to stand on their own feet?' – which indeed they were. Benjie helped Henry on the land; he could have done the same sort of thing anywhere; Lucy, lined up for a nursing career in the Adelaide Hospital in Dublin pending the start of which she was doing extra time at Aikens', could have moved out too. As it was, she played right into Harriet's hands by taking up with the local taxi-driver, Jo Heggerty, in Ballymun and foregoing her nursing career on his behalf. It wasn't right, Harriet said, for a young girl like her to be fooling around with an old fella like him. If she wasn't careful she'd be 'up the pole. Then what – another mouth to feed!' Played night and day, Harriet's carping eventually got to the younger Allen siblings. Their treatment had been strongly frowned on but criticism of Harriet over the affair, as over her other shortcomings, was muted – for Henry and Shandoran's sake; Henry, like his father, was hugely popular on and off the estate. Also, no one doubted Harriet's love for her husband; or for Lottie and Luke; or the sincerity of her intent to fill her home with the patter of tiny feet and make Henry happier than anyone else (his mother especially!) had made him. Indeed, it was her desire to please him, and distract him from her own ineptitude that drove her to scapegoat others. But if she were to start on Maggie, to even contemplate driving the maid away from Shandoran, keeping what Amy referred to as her 'sympathy balance' in the black would not be easy. In the event of Maggie's dismissal from the estate the outlook there would be bad; the outlook for Maggie would be dire.

Unable to believe Harriet was up to her old tricks again, and with so much going on around her, Amy decided to watch and wait.

Chapter Twelve

As predicted, keeping busy at Shandoran prevented Amy from brooding over Phil. And whoever she talked to about him, she got, as with Henry, a sympathetic response. 'Forget him, Amy. He's not worth it,' her dimpled, fun-loving sister, Lucy, said, when Amy went into Ballymun to see her. 'But I know a man who is!' she added, spreading a remnant of lemon silk on the counter for Amy to examine and winking at the younger, mid-eighties Miss Aiken beside her. Amy gave one of her eyes-up-mouth-down head jerks: How come everyone but herself thought Andy McPhearson was right for her! She enquired about Jo Heggerty – Lucy's long time taximan boyfriend – and heard in reply that her sister and Jo were engaged and saving up to get married. Then at the risk of another plug for Andy, Amy asked Lucy if she'd call in at the Post Office each day in case there was a letter from Phil. There was a weekly delivery at Shandoran but most people checked the mail in town, as Amy had done on her way to Aikens'; despite (or because of) her common sense, she simply couldn't believe, not yet anyway, Phil had gone out of her life for ever. Under protest – 'You're mad, Amy' – Lucy promised then came up with the perfect remnant.

As Amy turned to go, a bell sounded in the room above, where the older, late-eighties Miss Aiken lay bedridden. The younger Miss Aiken sighed, prompting Lucy to say quickly – 'I'll go' – and off she went.

Having collected her bike outside, Amy reflected on what she had just seen and heard. Left to Jo (a mummy's boy, who gambled his earnings away) it would be a long time, she reckoned, before he and Lucy were wed, never mind could afford a home of their own. But if Lucy played her cards right at Aikens'…

On her way back to Shandoran, Amy called in at The Mill to drop off her remnant and confide in old Mrs Mullins – her Grandmother Sad's dressmaker. In the past, Mrs Mullins had worked for many people in the vicinity, including Eleanor at Shandoran, but latterly, as age took its toll, she worked mainly for and at The Mill and if Amy wanted something done she took it over there. Harriet had no use for dressmakers; she liked off-the-peg.

'Now don't be fretting, dear,' Mrs Mullins said, negotiating a tricky bit on her treadle, as Amy unburdened her woes. 'Sure if my first fella hadn't dropped me, I'd never 'a met my husband; an' a finer man I could not 'a met.' Amy's smile reflected the qualified comfort she took from these words. Words apart, she found just watching Mrs Mullins soothing. A tiny woman, to whom tucking and tacking, pleats, gussets and reveres were child's play, the seamstress was worth watching; for the sheer speed and dexterity with which she wound the bobbin, threaded the needle and manipulated the material at the corners was nothing short of spellbinding. Bristling with pins, with an inch tape round her neck and a pair of spidery glasses on the end of her nose, she reminded Amy of nothing so much as the fifth little leprechaun in Stephen's 'Crock of Gold'.

Spellbound, Amy watched her finishing off the tricky bit. Then having handed over her remnant and selected a pattern for her new blouse, she left.

At Church on Sunday, it was much the same – comfort and sympathy on all sides, including, of course, from Andy McPhearson. [For Amy to have tried hiding what had happened between her and Phil would have been pointless. Her relationship with him was well known in Kilbeg and there might be the odd person around, particularly from the Ballycool area, who was still in touch with the Handys.] Andy had just qualified as a doctor, so Amy congratulated him. Brownly – brown hair, brown eyes, brown suit, brown shoes, even a brown tie – he said he was sorry she and Phil had broken up. She thanked him. She hated brown as much, if not more than, the deferential way – 'I'd be ever so grateful, Amy' – Andy prefaced his invitations to her to walk out with him. To his credit now, he made no attempt to muscle in on her affections, just commiserated and pushed off; she appreciated that.

Needless to say, the imbalance between so much understanding for her own plight and so little for the maid, Maggie Scott's – temporary or more serious she still didn't know – did not escape Amy for long. Sometimes Harriet's nastiness was no more than an insinuation, like when Amy, Maggie and Lottie returned home cheerily one afternoon with canfuls of fruit for jam making. The fruit picking had been particularly enjoyable, coming as it did after a morning of scrubbing and tidying in the larder – a big one, on the north side of the kitchen, and at its emptiest at this time of year; by Christmas it would be chock-a-block, most of it Maggie's handiwork. 'My goodness me, Lottie,' Harriet said, tutting loudly, 'wherever did you get that stain on your frock? And I don't think Maggie has your others ironed yet. It's not good enough.' 'Never mind,' Amy put in quickly as the maid began to apologise, 'a spot of boiling water will soon shift that!' Unimpressed, Harriet continued to tut, ignored Maggie's apologies, and Lottie's. 'Ony a litte tain, Mummy,' the child said, remembering the fun she'd had, not just fruit picking, but with her Grandmother's hats that morning when Maggie had opened up the big oak chest on the landing for her. Lottie loved the hats (too *passé* for Eleanor to take to Knockmore) and every time she'd appeared at the larder door in one of them, Maggie and her Aunt Amy had laughed; her Mummy had been happy too, playing the piano. Eventually and grudgingly, Harriet settled for Amy's promise not only to shift the stain but to get the tea while Maggie did the ironing and Harriet had a rest in the parlour. Other times, the nastiness was downright offensive. Like when Amy and Maggie were sitting in the scullery once with a bucket of scalding water and a half-plucked goose between their legs. Harriet stuck her head round the door, and holding her nose tightly, said pointedly – 'Could you not leave that filthy, smelly job to Maggie, Amy, and help me turn the corner on this sock for Henry?' Knitting socks for

Henry appealed to her but she hadn't yet mastered the corners. Amy went to her aid when the goose was plucked and gutted.

Faced with such nastiness, Amy was desperate to help Maggie; a quiet word with Harriet, with the maid's consent of course, was what she had in mind. Helping Maggie though was easier said than done, not least because of Maggie herself.

Unlike Harriet's, Maggie's childhood and young adulthood had been a trail of woe. Abandoned by her parents at birth – neither wanted to be saddled with an albino – she had spent her early years in an orphanage and workhouses. Abused and exploited there, she'd been further maltreated as she moved, offering herself for hire at local fairs, from one heartless employer to the next. Stoically she endured it, and vented whatever emotion she couldn't hide on her red-raw, gnawed-to-the-quick fingernails. A lucky break in her early thirties led her to Shandoran. At the time, she was working for a couple of ingrates, her only respite from whom was posting the mistress' letters in Ballymun. A regular caller at the post office was an old pensioner named Mr Scott. He and Maggie got talking, and in time got hitched, and offered their services at Shandoran where Eleanor, struggling in the wake of her first husband's death, and the death of her children's nursemaid, Doxey, soon after it, agreed to take them on. She gave them a tied cottage, and with that, and their wages, and the 'Lloyd George', Mr and Mrs Scott managed very nicely. Maggie – maid and nursemaid at Shandoran ever since – couldn't believe her good fortune.

The splicing of one so young – particularly one like Maggie (in Kilbeg, albinos were rarer even than tap water) – to one so old, was a constant source of merriment to the men. Paddy Finch (himself the object of much sport on account of his sticky out feet – 'One foot going to Ballymun and the other to Ballycool') dubbed Maggie 'the old man's darlin'. Flemming Young, a coarse, burly fellow, for ever cadging cigarettes off Paddy, composed a ditty for her. Its last two lines – 'to tickle her toes and wipe her nose, and keep her diddies in order' – drew attention to her pensioner husband's age and her huge breasts, and along with Flemming's greeting – 'Hello, there, Maggie, how are yer cramery cans?' – explained her ducking and diving whenever she caught sight of him. But neither workman wished her any harm, and for the first time in her life Maggie felt secure and happy. She eased off her nails (an occasional nibble sufficed) and treasured the little locket (she wore it round her neck at all times) her husband gave her with a picture of his long-dead parents inside it. Even when the old man died, a few years into wedlock, Maggie continued to feel safe at Shandoran. To the end of her days she would be the butt of rustic humour. So what! she thought. I'm a respectable widow now with a home of my own. 'Sure look at me, Miss Amy,' she once said, fingering her locket lovingly and giving one of her shy smiles, 'Who'd a thought an oddity like me would ever 'a got married a'tall?'

And there, of course, was where Amy's problem lay. Shandoran was the only home Maggie had ever known or was likely to know. Initially, Harriet's arrival at the estate had caused her grave concern, but when a working relationship was formed between the two, making her, Maggie, appear more useful than ever, she'd stopped worrying. The recent change in Harriet's attitude perplexed her. She blamed the pregnancy, and the nastier Harriet was to her, the harder she tried to please her. Loyalty to her employers, good or bad, still made it unthinkable for her to criticise them. 'Oh, no, Miss Amy,' she said, anxiously chewing her nails, when Amy made her suggestion, 'I wouldn't like that a'tall. Say nothing, please.'

So Amy pulled back again – hopeful the nastiness would peter out as Harriet's pregnancy advanced. The bottom line for Amy was – Maggie Scott was indispensible at Shandoran; it was impossible to fault her. Reassured by such thinking, Amy threw herself into the harvest.

The vivid but fleeting blue flax flowering gave no hint of the gruelling labour involved in the plant's harvesting. Nor did the joking and laughter among the motley workforce – young and old, male and female, full-timers, part-timers and seasonals, high-born and low-born, Protestant and Catholic – who toiled ceaselessly till the job was done. First the pullers moved slowly down their lines – hand-pulling to prevent damaging the fibres – then later retraced their steps for the binding, binding with reeds and rushes, picked and plaited by the children to further safeguard the fibres. When ready, the bundles were carted to the pits, packed down in water, and weighted with stones and sods for the long retting, the pungent (putrid to some) smell of which suffused the whole vicinity for its duration, and in the wake of which – further rounds of carting and drying preceded scutching. Other tasks on the estate – turf-cutting, hay-making and the rest – were fitted in, as and when, weather and time permitting. Flax took priority. It was what Shandoran was about; topping up the world's linen cupboards – past, present and future. And although prices had not recovered markedly since the war, nobody, least of all Henry, suggested switching to anything else. Flax was in Henry's blood; and he in his element out among the harvesters. Bending and stretching with them, laughing and joking; pausing for lunch and tea from wicker hampers, in the shade of the poplar-lined River Lisanne – the river that held the estate and much else together, that twisted and turned on its north-south axis, swallowed tributaries, powered mills. In the evening, overloaded carts homeward bound swayed precariously to hearty renderings of *Paddy Reilley* or *Ballyjamesduff*.

Observing her brother in the flax fields, Amy felt happy for him but wished to God he had chosen a more practical wife: even at the height of the harvest, Harriet found time to cosset her hair and hands. The hectic activity around her, though, persuaded her to lay off Maggie, leading Amy to conclude the nastiness was fizzling out. Sadly, it wasn't.

◇

'There's something I want to talk to you about, Amy' Harriet said, just after she'd announced she was going to bake a soda cake and a couple of days before Amy was due to leave Shandoran for Knockmore.

Harriet's tone (like a lot of inadequate people she could be quite bossy) and the extra self-importance she attached to donning her apron, stoking the fire and amassing utensils and ingredients on the kitchen's large pine table (everything involved in the baking had to be done by her), set alarm bells off in Amy's head. Harriet's timing was telling too. Henry and the men were in the meadow bogs, seizing a moment of quiet in the flax fields to get in a bit of turf, and Maggie had just gone out to the dairy; Luke was napping, while Lottie, struggling with her scales in the parlour – so much better for her, Harriet said, than horse-riding – was unlikely to come out till her mummy went in.

'It's about Maggie,' Harriet went on, carefully sifting flour, salt, sugar and baking-powder into her bowl, evenness of distribution being essential.

'She's not in any trouble, is she?' Amy asked, instinctively showing concern for the maid.

Harriet tutted, shook her head irritably, and tutted again when she accidently added a zilch too much of a fluid ounce of butter-milk to her well. Her attitude worried Amy. 'What then?' she pressed, unwilling to contemplate what she most feared, and a little annoyed at being held up; she'd been about to go over to The Mill to collect her blouse. 'Are you not happy with her work?'

'Well being as you ask,' Harriet said, pouncing on her words as though they implied deficiency on Maggie's part, 'I'm not.' With that, she slapped her dough on a floured board, and began kneading it lovingly with her beautiful hands; then in answer to Amy's disbelieving – 'In what way, Harriet?' – recited a string of complaints that would have made perfect sense if levied against herself but made none at all when directed at Maggie. 'She's too old, Amy,' she concluded, callously. 'Sure a younger person would do the job in half the time.'

Disgusted by what she was hearing, Amy sat down at the Pembroke table beside the room's small, deep-set window, and picking up a *matinée* coat she was knitting for the new baby, started a row of purl. Patiently (getting angry would only inflame the situation) she countered each and every one of her sister-in-law's criticisms, pointing out that Maggie, a strong, muscular woman, albeit rising fifty, was far from over the hill and would be *extremely* hard to replace. 'Sure nobody knows the ropes round here like she does, Harriet!' Above all, Maggie would be lost without her tied cottage and would find it near impossible to get another job.

Harriet would have none of it. 'Of course she'll find another job,' she said, heartlessly. 'Hadn't she a job before she came here! *And* a roof over her head! She's nought but an embarrassment to us, Amy. Besides, it's not good for Lottie having someone like *that* around her all the time. I'm sure Henry feels the same. He's just too soft to say so. You'll speak to him for me about it, won't you, Amy?' A slick brush over with milk and her job was done. 'There,' she said, flipping back her shiny, copper hair, and backward stepping to admire her work, and dust the flour from her hands and apron, 'I'm depending on you, Amy! Now promise me you'll speak to him!'

Slowly Amy put down the *matinée* coat – it had advanced hardly at all – and stood up. An embarrassment! she thought – to you maybe, Harriet, but to everyone else at Shandoran a treasure more precious than a decade of bumper harvests. 'Henry won't like it,' she said, not expecting (why else would Harriet be asking her to do her dirty work?) or getting (Harriet tutted sharply) more than a hap'orth of change. 'Neither will the men!' *That* had more effect. Harriet looked up from the hearth, where she was adjusting her cake on the griddle. 'I'm not talking about today, Amy,' she said, testily. 'Or even next week! But *you* know what I mean.'

Without further comment Amy went out, and instead of going over to The Mill, went to the dairy to give Maggie a hand. An embarrassment! She thought again sadly. A bee, once lodged in Harriet's bonnet, was not easily dislodged.

Chapter Thirteen

The following day, Amy went over to The Mill.

She went on foot by the Middle Gap trail, eponymously named after its halfway point and running alongside the River Lisanne. The morning – a mild, late August one – was purpose-made for a dawdle; for picturing her parents on the trail in their courting days, something she often did: her mother, Eleanor – tall, erect and slender; a sallow-skinned, dark-eyed beauty with jet-black plaits curving upwards round her fine-featured face; a Daker to her fingertips; and her father, Samuel – a full-blooded Allen. And purpose-made too for sorting out in her head what Harriet had asked her to do. Why she'd asked her was easily explained, even if it did not make the job any easier: Harriet knew how much Amy loved Henry, and that she would never do anything to cause trouble between him and his wife and would put the best possible gloss on each of their viewpoints if they differed. Also, unpleasant though the job was, Amy preferred to be doing it than that Harriet should do it herself. Left to Harriet, the thing would assume crisis proportions within seconds. Left to Amy, harsh edges could be smoothed and, hopefully – especially in the light of Harriet's concerns about the men's reaction – time bought for a rethink. That Harriet was never overtly nasty to Maggie in front of anyone other than her, Amy, had not escaped Amy's notice.

On arriving at The Mill, where three generations of puritanical Dakers lived in perfect harmony (something that never ceased to amaze her) Amy was let in by her Grandmother Sad – a buttoned up, dumpy woman who, though kind, was hard of hearing and difficult to converse with. After a few words with her, Amy went into a little back room where Mrs Mullins was putting the finishing touches to her blouse; not once in Amy's life – not that it bothered her – had a garment been ready on time. When the last button had been sewn on, the blouse – duck-egg blue, with just enough lace for day or evening wear – was held up for Amy to admire. She loved a touch of lace and had accumulated numerous strips from her Grandmother Sad for Mrs Mullins to choose from for the blouses. Lovely! she thought, knowing this one would fit perfectly. What a pity Phil wasn't around to see it. His actual whereabouts were a mystery to her; there had been no word from or about him.

Back on the Middle Gap trail – with her blouse in a brown paper bag – she was soon reassailed by Harriet's request. What *would* Henry make of it! Not only did he feel responsible for Maggie; he was also, Amy knew, genuinely fond of her and had not forgotten her kindness to him, with his boils especially, over the years.

Coming up to the Middle Gap, Amy remembered the big, angry boil on her brother's neck at the time of what had gone down in family lore as the 'turned cart'; one of her saddest memories, it seemed even sadder now in the light of what she had to tell him. When she reached the Gap she sat down on an old stump, the very one that had upended the cart, and recalled the unhappy incident.

◇

Henry and his cousin George from The Mill, both in early teens, had been careering across the Middle Gap trail in their Grandfather Daker's horse and cart. 'Faster, faster,' cried George, as Henry 'Jehued' the horse. At the Middle Gap, the wheel of the cart caught the stump, the cart tipped over, pinning Henry to the ground. From nowhere, Grandfather Daker – 'the old Covenanter' as he liked to be called – appeared. 'Which of ye was at the helm?' he roared, convinced it was Henry as Eleanor had predisposed her parents at The Mill into always thinking the worst of him. Never one to shirk the blame, Henry owned up. 'Well let that be a lesson to you,' his Grandfather roared; 'and that. Jesus Christ, boy, will ye never learn!'

More concerned about a hugely inflamed boil on the back of his neck – Maggie had promised to poultice it that evening – than the toe of the old Covenanter's boot, Henry took his punishment resignedly, then hobbled away like a wounded

118

animal when his Grandfather and George righted the cart and released his leg.

News of the incident reached home well in advance of him as, fearing further reprisal, he'd delayed his return. With a little diversionary help from Maggie, he nipped upstairs and hid under his and his brother's bed hoping time would soften their mother's blows. Late that night she got wind of his whereabouts – tucked up with Benjie and both of them fast asleep. Amy, awake anticipating the worst, heard her mother coming up the stairs, and Henry hauled out of bed; then the muffled sounds as they passed her door and went down to the kitchen. *Do* something! she said, recalling Sister Martha's advice – 'A little help is worth a lot of sympathy, Amy.' She made the sign of the Cross. 'Satan fears the Cross,' the Sister had added, imparting an aide memoire – 'Top to toe and left to right, the Cross will put old Nick to flight.' Shored up by the Cross, Amy got out of bed, and tip toed downstairs in the dark.

The kitchen door was pushed to. Behind it, Henry was crying – 'No, Mama. No more, pleeese. I'm sorry, Mama. Ouch.' Amy cringed at the crack. Then, terrified of making things worse for Henry (she'd witnessed many a beating but *never* intervened in one), she nudged the door open. A hurricane, and moonlight through a chink in the curtain lit up the scene. Eleanor – swollen with rage and pregnancy, embryonic Iris, Amy's first half-sibling – had Henry bent over the table. His face was contorted with pain and he was trying to protect his boil, visible above the collar of his nightshirt; Maggie had been unable to poultice it earlier for fear of alerting her mistress to his hideaway. As Eleanor lifted the sally again, Amy wrenched her feet from the floor and rushed across the room. 'Stop it, Mama! Stop it!' she cried, grabbing her mother's arm. Taken aback, Eleanor tried to shake her off. Amy clung on, dangling. It was enough. Her mother let go of Henry, who was so surprised he did not immediately straighten up. 'Go back to bed at once, Amy,' Eleanor said sternly. 'As for you,' she added, with a disgusted look at her son, 'maybe you'll drive more carefully in future.' The steam had all gone out of her.

Next morning, Henry rose earlier than usual and asked Amy to go for a walk with him. They walked and walked in the crisp air – Amy, thoughtfully; Henry, with his head thrust forward, his eyes fixed on the ground, his large hands plugged in his trouser-pockets; neither sibling dared to speak for fear of rekindling the previous night's passions. Henry's cocker, Barney, frisked at their heels, and every so often Henry booted a clod of earth into the air.

Circuitously, brother and sister ended up in the dell, where they invariably ended up on these occasions. A childhood haunt, in the wood behind the kitchen-garden and orchard at the back of the house, it was first happened upon by the Allen children with their Catholic nursemaid, Doxey. The 'Little Lisanne' – Doxey's fun name for this otherwise anonymous tributary of the mother river – meandered through it, wild flowers carpeted it, and the spreading arms of a gnarled oak gave refuge to whatever winged and flightless creatures were compatible with its half-dead trunk, branches and foliage.

Amy and Henry stood for a few minutes beside the stream which hereabouts widened into a little pool. Barney lapped at the water. Around the dog was a scattering of tiny glass bottles, whose original colours though faded were still recognisable – scarlet, maroon, orange, yellow, purple, mauve, turquoise and green. 'The Doctor's phials,' Doxey had said of them (there had been many more then) 'immersed for cleansing, and left there when he died.' From habit, Amy and Henry counted the bottles, and two colourless stoppers.

Leaving Barney to rummage by the river, brother and sister sat down under the oak. Henry began playing with some acorns – placing them in ever increasing numbers on the back of his hand, bouncing them in the air and catching them on the way down. It was a game he excelled at. Amy noticed the scars on his hands – caused by scutching, the process whereby flax's fibre and woody bark were separated; and the sticky mess on his neck and shirt-collar, where his boil had burst in the night and was no longer troubling him. Henry spoke first.

'Why does Mama hate me, Amy?' he asked, when he got to five acorns; he liked to get to ten without a muff.

'She doesn't,' Amy replied, searching for the healing word, which she had become quite adept at finding where her brother was concerned. 'Her beating you is like a sickness, Henry. Sister Martha told me about it when I first went to St. Hilda's and got teased by the other girls in my cla…'

'Well I hate her,' Henry broke in, 'and I *always* will.'

Amy sighed; being torn between her love for her mother and Henry was hard. 'Don't be like that,' she said, in her big-little-sisterly way, then finished what she'd been about to say earlier. 'Sister Martha says it's like a worm. Hate, I mean. She calls it a hate-worm, and says it wriggles around inside you, eating you up – *so slowly*, Henry, you don't even know what's happening.' Henry laughed.

'It's not funny,' Amy said, miffed at her favourite nun's advice being treated so lightly. She was about to add that things hadn't been all that easy for Eleanor either but on second thoughts (Henry's backside must have been very raw, and might be rawer after the next beating on account of her intervention in the most recent) decided against. Instead, she said – 'Always is a long time, Henry.'

'Humph,' her brother snorted, triumphantly catching ten acorns. Barney came and lay down beside him. How he loved the dog – the last gift to him from his adored father. 'He's for you, son, for your birthday,' his father had said, 'we'll train him to the gun and when you're old enough I'll teach you to shoot.' Henry had felt so proud that day but no sooner had the birthday – his ninth – come round than Samuel had died leaving Shandoran's steward, John Fisher to train the cocker to the gun and later teach Henry to shoot.

Strongly Henry stroked the dog. Then mindful of Amy's last words and knowing how much she loved the mother he hated, he said – truthfully, making it easy – 'I wish her no harm, sis. I just hate her. Now will you tell me this,' he added – 'Why did they tease you?'

Surprised that her reference to teasing had sunk in, Amy answered his question: it was her Cavan accent, she said, that had amused her classmates, most of whom were Dubliners. Say 'moon', Amy, they'd commanded, or 'mince'; and when she'd come out with 'meun' and 'manse', they'd mocked her words cruelly. 'You had to do it, Henry, or they made it worse for you. Gob in your face; or head down the lav.' Henry grimaced; though he had never used a flush toilet, he knew what it was. 'And do they still do it?' he asked, angry that anyone should give Amy a hard time.

'No,' she said, and told him why. 'You remember the nature project I did last summer hols?' Henry looked bewildered. 'Yes you do, Henry. The one you helped me with!' Henry looked even more bewildered; to the best of his knowledge he had never helped Amy with any of her schoolwork. 'You did, Henry. You brought me some bog rosemary and asphodel, which no one at school had heard of before. Sister Martha said mine was the best nature project she'd ever seen. I got first prize for it – thanks to you!' Henry looked pleased. He'd forgotten all about the project, and what with so much going on at Shandoran, Amy had forgotten to tell him she'd won.

'But what's that got to do with you being teased?' he asked. 'I'd 'a' thought winning would have made you even more unpopular.'

'And that's what I thought too, Henry, at the time. I was wrong. Winning had the opposite effect; suddenly everyone wanted to be my friend.'

Henry expressed relief at that, and told his sister if he'd been there he'd have given the teasers what for.

'I don't doubt it,' Amy said, amused at the thought of her hefty brother sorting out her classmates, and happy to see him happy again. Neither he nor she knew that Eleanor had thrashed him for the last time. But nor did they know the depths to which Eleanor's cruelty towards Henry – without the thrashings – would one day sink.

◇

As Amy got up from the stump at the Middle Gap with her blouse in a brown paper bag she wondered, not for the first time, how Barney – so frisky all those years ago, so pitiable in later years as Henry clung to him irrationally – had met his end. When she'd come home one Christmas holidays, the one immediately after the Linnakers left Shandoran, the dog, on his last legs when she'd last seen him, was not in his usual place in the street – curled up on a bed of dry laurel leaves beneath the low nasturtium-topped wall. No one – including Henry, the men and Maggie – had volunteered information about his demise, which made Amy suspect foul play. She'd decided to let sleeping dogs lie but found it sad that Henry could never bring himself to talk about the cocker. Along with the memory of the dog, Henry seemed to have buried the memory of his father, Samuel, and of the childhood he'd shared with his father – the happiest part of his childhood she knew.

No sooner had Amy set off for home than Henry, flushed from his morning's work (he'd been at the farrier's on the other side of The Mill) came galloping along the Middle Gap trail behind her. She turned round, and just for a second, saw – not her brother – but their father, Samuel. Samuel galloping into the street on a summer's evening, and leaping from his horse to pick her and Lucy up in his arms, and swirl them round, before ruffling Henry's hair and going off with him to the stable. The memory dissolved.

Henry and Amy walked home together. On the way, Henry told his sister he was sorry she was leaving the next day. Amy steeled herself. Then picking her words carefully, she told her brother what Harriet had in mind for Maggie.

'You're not serious!' he said incredulously. 'Over my dead body!' he added angrily, booting a clod of earth into the river

– splat. 'What in God's name can have got into her, Amy? Do you think it's the pregnancy? Pregnancy does that kind of…'

'Oh I'm sure…'

'Well I won't have it, Amy. And that's that.' Another clod took off – splosh.

Predictable, Amy thought. 'Now will you stop going on like this, and listen to me, Henry' she said, prepared for the long haul. Though pleased by her brother's loyalty to Maggie, Amy knew his attitude would inflame the situation in the same way as if Harriet had done her own dirty work. He must be made to see some sort of sense. Not an easy thing to do, she knew, but essential if her carefully thought out response to the problem was to have any chance of success. Slowly and patiently, then, she pointed out to Henry, as Harriet knew she would, that there were two sides to everything, and that Harriet was entitled to her opinions. 'Humph,' Henry snorted, 'what kind of opinions could lead anyone to think ill of poor Maggie!' 'She doesn't think ill of Maggie,' Amy said, 'just feels she's getting too old for the job. Yes, her pregnancy probably is clouding her vision, but that's only to be expected. She's doing her best, Henry, under *very difficult* circumstances. It wasn't easy for her coming to a big estate like this, and she *is* wonderful with the children.' 'I know, Amy.' 'So the best thing you can do, Henry – I've given the matter a lot of thought – is do and say nothing at all. I'll tell Harriet I've spoken to you. Tomorrow I'll be going and unless I'm very much mistaken, she'll come to her senses and realise, especially as her pregnancy advances, how dependent on Maggie she is.'

'Of course she will,' Henry concurred. 'She's bound to. Sure no one else could *possibly* take Maggie's place.'

'My own thoughts exactly,' Amy said, pleased to have got her point across and pinning her hopes not just on Maggie's usefulness at Shandoran, but on Harriet's sensitivities about the men – something she, Amy, hadn't mentioned to Henry.

'Right, that's it,' Henry said, putting his arm round his sister and giving her a big squeeze; his faith in her was absolute. 'Whatever would I do without you!' he added. Contemplating life without Amy was not something Henry liked doing. If she would take up with Andy MacPhearson – and he prayed she would though never actually said so – he would never have to do it again.

With what breath she had left in her body, Amy promised herself she would *always* be there for her brother – in spirit if not in the flesh. She could not conceive of a time when she might feel differently about this.

A loud whistle blast from the house caused brother and sister to get a move on, and the horse to neigh loudly. The neighing alerted Nancy – offspring of a collie Henry had acquired in the wake of Barney's death; another cocker would have been too painful. Nancy (her mother died giving birth to her) preferred the yard to the fields, and Matt to her master. Henry didn't mind. The collie was a marvellous guard dog and when she came hurtling down the trail to him now he greeted her warmly.

Brother and sister reached the end of the trail.

Inside, Maggie had cooked a juicy flitch of bacon for dinner; it and Irish stew were her specialities. Though there were no pigs at Shandoran – livestock there being largely confined to horses, fowl and a few milking cows – pig farming came a close second to flax-growing in Cavan and bacon was a popular nutrient throughout the county.

The next day Amy left Shandoran for Knockmore from where, after a week of her mother's 'I told you sos', she was glad to return to Dublin.

Chapter Fourteen

Back in the capital, Amy believed herself ready for whatever life without Phil had in store for her there. Shandoran had cushioned her against his abrupt exit from her life and fortified her against her mother's caustic refrain at Knockmore. Eleanor had never liked Phil, and though Amy had to admit there was some justification in her 'here-today-and-gone-tomorrow' criticism of him, her *ad nauseam* 'And isn't Andy McPhearson still single!' really jarred. Coming from Eleanor it was rich indeed given her rejection in the wake of her first husband's death of not just the advances of Reverend Badell but of his friend and sparring partner in Kilbeg, Andy's widowed father, Dr McPhearson. 'Too old,' she'd said of them, 'once bitten, twice shy.'

But if Amy was expecting a smooth emotional return to the capital she was badly mistaken. Not so much during working hours, as on Wednesdays – her half-day – when the seventeen minutes past two tram went to the Pillar without her; and on her weekends off. At these times, an emptiness such as she had never experienced, possessed her; a flatness, like the flatness of a skimming stone. Increasingly she thought about Phil – something she had tried hard, and with remarkable success, not to do at Shandoran. There had been times, of course, when she had thought about him there. Once, in Kilbeg's old Churchyard, she'd remembered the mixture of cynicism and genuine interest with which he'd reacted to little things she'd told him. Like the exaggerated Scottish accent he'd used to read the inscription on the oldest Allen memorial – a huge slab of a tombstone just inside the graveyard's rusty gate: 'In memory of Colonel Angus Allen, who distinguished himself at the Battle of the Boyne, of Shandoran, Co. Cavan, 1656-1712; and of his wife, Hortense, 1655-1715.' And his tongue-in-cheek response – 'I'll give more credence to local lore in future' – when she'd gone rushing off after he'd untangled her hair in the hedge-gap, and shown him the 'turned stone' – a single large stone jutting out of line at the base of the old Church wall. Roundhead cannon had accidentally dislodged it when a party of the Lord Protector's followers was billeted at a big house – now a ruin – on the opposite side of Gar-na-Ree Lake. Another time, she'd climbed to the top of Shandoran Hill and sat on its ruined ramparts divellicating daisies – he loves me, he loves me not – remembering how they'd raced to the top of the Hill on their first outing together. And as the last petal – he loves me not – of the last daisy within reach had floated to the ground, her wish with Phil on the ramparts, it seemed eons away, that her love for him would be reciprocated, had wilted in her mind like the petalless stalk in her hand. He had loved her – she knew that and was glad of it – but not like she loved him: her love had endured.

Times like these had been rare – what with worry about Maggie, and jobs. Glenarkle was different. For a long time it seemed to Amy that nothing in the capital could take the place of Phil's jaunty air and moans; of the way he made her laugh, and things better for her; of their lovemaking; of his being there.

Further time; friends and work colleagues eased the pain.

Of the friends, Catherine Townley was the least sympathetic, but helpful in her own way. She and Neil had got engaged in the summer – a clear indication to Amy that Catherine didn't blame Neil for Phil's dismissal from Poynings. Amy, being Amy, did not attempt to counter-say whatever Neil had told Catherine about the staff room incident. Like Eleanor, Catherine had never liked Phil and she made it clear now to Amy she was better off without him. Amy appreciated her honesty. Their friendship survived.

In contrast with Catherine, Sister Martha understood everything. Typically, she suggested Amy find a new interest – 'The best antidote for a loss, my dear, is always a find,' she said – and left Amy to take it from there. With the aid of her work colleagues, Amy did just that.

Though not privy to all the facts, Glenarkle's staff knew when a girl had been jilted and, fond of Amy, did everything in their power to pull her through. The Head and his wife (Mr and Mrs Appleby) started inviting her to Sunday tea; she enjoyed their company. The English master, William Dodson, revealed his passion for wild flowers to her; he had a nature project too, he said, going back to his youth. Max Stone (Classics) persuaded her to take up bridge. Peter Pagley (History) renewed his invitation to her to join him on a mountain hike. She still liked Peter – if not his hackled hair and podgy hands – but a hike with him now seemed even less attractive than before; too many good ones with Phil had intervened.

Practical help for a practical woman worked: by the end of term Amy felt confident she had got over Phil, or, at the very least, adjusted to being without him. It was a balanced adjustment, of course. Half of it – the half that responded to her lingering love for him and concerns about his welfare (he had no God or heritage to sustain him; maybe not even a decent job) – in keeping with her one-man-woman side. The other half – the half that responded to a growing conviction that he was perfectly happy without her and had probably met someone else – with her practical side. As such, it enabled her to move on.

Her Christmas holiday clinched the feeling.

Right from the start of the holidays, from the moment she woke at Glenarkle on the final day of term, she felt a sense of renewal. Overnight, a light snowfall had whitened everywhere. Cleansing, she thought, like the host.

As her train neared Ballymun Station, she rubbed the condensation from her window and peered at the Cavan countryside through the clear patch. A dusting of snow was holding, glinting where the sun caught it, making everything crisp and Christmassy; and familiar; familiar as Henry's big smile and warm handshake at the station, and Lucy's fleeting greeting at Aikens'. Everything else – a near deserted Ballymun Main Street, hills and woods draped in white muslin, patchily frozen lakes, hard bumpy roads, the warm breath belching from Stella's nostrils – had a seasonally familiar ring, and along with the keen air, and Amy and Henry's light-heartedness, made for an altogether exhilarating ride. Even the ruined big houses, so hopelessly disfigured by roof slides, crumbling masonry, and gouged black holes where windows used to be, had acquired a kind of mystique in their flimsy, white lace mantles. For the rest, the estate, thinly whitened too, gave no clues – no summer oases of blue carpeting, or stench of autumn's retting – to its real purpose. The noble elm, its leafless branches bluntly studded with glistening winter buds, stood tall, straight, immutable; Shandoran's chief sentinel, rooted in centuries gone by. The avenue's berried hedgerows fairly glowed with thick clusters of red, yellow, orange and white fruit; fat wood pigeons gorged on the holly, oblivious of anything as mundane as a pony and trap. The brittle beech – guardian of the street, the wide, fully-enclosed area in front of the house – was as comfortably stout, satin-smooth, and dependable as ever. Facing the house – separating it and the street from the yard – the tall clumps of laurels where the hens were prone to roost were at their glossiest in the midday December sun. It was all no more or less than Amy had come to expect; habitual and exciting as Christmas should be.

Most heartening of all for her though, was the sight of the maid, Maggie Scott, in the street – waving, and smiling her warm, shy smile.

The run in to the twenty-fifth was fun. Old streamers were dug out and new ones made to replace the torn. Tinsel and baubles were hung on the tree and Henry bought a new fairy for it as the old one's dress was shabby and she'd lost her wand. Lottie was delighted with the new one. Delighted too at the mounting pile of animals that Amy and Maggie constructed for her one wet afternoon on the kitchen table – even the rain couldn't dampen the excitement – from a diminishing pile of matchsticks, corks, ribbons, wool and cottonwool; walnuts and Brazil nuts, stalked and unstalked raisins and whatever else they could lay their hands on. Adding to the fun on this particular occasion, Christmases past were recalled and bygone incidents guaranteed to raise a laugh – like Lucy's mishap with the duck eggs. 'It was my fault really,' Maggie said, putting the finishing touches to a cockerel's comb, and typically taking the blame for the accident, 'I should never have stored the eggs like that.' 'Nonsense,' Amy countered, 'Mama always put them in a hat box; Lucy was just too inquisitive for her own good.' 'Too kistive,' Lottie echoed, loving the story and living every minute of it while trotting her matchstick pony (her favourite among the animals) up and down the table in front of her. 'The eggs broke, didn't they?' she added, looking in turn at Amy, Maggie and her pony with big, brown worried eyes: despite having heard the story umpteen times, she awaited its outcome anxiously. 'They did indeed, darlin'' Maggie said kindly; she adored Lottie; there was never a child at Shandoran she didn't adore. 'And what did Lucy do?' she asked, equally kindly and knowing exactly how Lottie would respond; everyone knew their part. 'She hid,' the child said, trotting her pony faster now. 'And we all know where, don't we?' Amy put in quickly, shushing her finger in front of her lips while nodding at Lottie who nodded too and obediently said nothing till the signal came. Then, raising her hands like a conductor, or a teacher in front of a class for a bit of rote – Amy posed the question – 'What was it Matt said when he found her?' She started to conduct and the three of them chorused, Lottie stumbling a bit at the third word, 'There's an unusual bird in the laurels tonight!' Laughter erupted – as well it might, all being aware that instead of a sound telling off, still less a smack, Lucy had got hugs and kisses in the wake of her mishap. Even Harriet – she had just come into the room with the toddler Luke and knew the story well – joined in the fun.

For Harriet too was doing her bit in these pre-Christmas days, contributing to the festive spirit by not carping at her maid or anyone else; she had even agreed, if reluctantly, to the purchase of a filly for Lottie on her next, her fifth, birthday.

Harriet's condition – the brink of term – made her the centre of attention, excused her idleness (she'd stirred the pudding long enough to have a wish) and accounted for a daily look-in at Shandoran by Drs McPhearson senior and junior.

In the course of the doctors' visits – what with all the excitement and goodwill in the air, and no Christmas greeting from Phil – Amy found herself warming to Andy, a personable enough young man who remained unashamedly fond of her. Since qualifying, he had matured a lot, she thought, in looks as well as manner; that and his healing hands diluted the brownness and deference.

On Boxing Day, the day Harriet gave birth, she warmed to him some more.

Already a pattern had been set for Harriet's deliveries. At the first sign of labour, Henry or one of the men was dispatched to Kilbeg to alert Dr McPhearson – the older of course, Harriet's current confinement being the younger's first at Shandoran. Then knowing as they did the doctor's definition of speed – faster than Shank's pony, slower than a swine special – Amy or Maggie would go haring over the fields (hurricane-armed at night, not that it stopped them falling into a fox-hole) to alert Mrs Cahill, the local midwife – a stout, good-hearted woman who never failed to respond with alacrity. Thereafter, nature and childbirth's pangs (considerable in Harriet's case) dictated the urgency in – swish and pound on the stairs, replenishing water buckets, restoking fires, Henry's pacing.

The delivery in hand adhered to the pattern. When it was over (another boy, they called him Billy) Amy showed Andy and his father into the parlour and went off to make them tea. When she returned they were standing beside the walnut credenza looking at the picture on the wall behind, a picture Eleanor had tried and failed to commandeer for Knockmore. How and why is worth recounting.

Painted by Amy's Great Uncle Joshua, as adept an amateur artist as he was pianist, the picture was called *Flaxfields*. A romantic depiction of Victorian childhood, it was quite beautiful. Commanding the foreground, two pink-cheeked girls, daintily ribboned and bowed, were sitting in a field of flax, the younger holding out a delicate bloom for the older to smell. Behind the girls, a little to one side, the taller of two knickerbockered boys was showing the smaller how to cast a line. For the rest – lake, hills, sky and clouds were all imbued with the same deep-purplish-blue that surrounded the girls.

To Amy, there was a simplicity, timelessness and innocence about the whole that never failed to appeal. For sure, it was an overly rosy representation of childhood at Shandoran; of childhood anywhere. But it wasn't meant to depict the whole of anything, only highlight part of the best. What was wrong with that? Though Great Uncle Joshua had never married, he had the human touch, and Amy truly felt he'd captured something of the essence of Shandoran's spirit and of the heritage that meant so much to her.

Eleanor liked the painting too – it would have been hard not to like it – and included it in a number of items earmarked for Knockmore in a final sweep of the parlour's contents two days before she left the estate for good. Her husband and Amy were helping her pack up the stuff; Tom willingly, Amy reluctantly, though not because of the picture – she didn't know Eleanor had earmarked that – but because of the curtains. It would be impossible to replace the drapes before Harriet moved in to Shandoran as there were no second-best and she, Amy, was returning to Dublin the next day. Also, Amy knew there wasn't a window at Knockmore big enough to warrant them – made not for a small, deep-set window but a comparatively large one installed at that time of 'great improvement', the mid nineteenth century, the same that saw Kilbeg's old church and churchyard replaced with new ones. She said as much to Eleanor, thinking it might have some effect as up to now she'd adopted a policy of non-interference regarding her mother's trawl; Henry had done the same on her advice. Eleanor was having none of it. 'If I took everything in the house, Amy, it would be no more than my due after all the years of toil I've put into it. *She'll* not add much to it I'll warrant. As for *him*, hasn't he enough already with the land.' Eleanor could never bring herself to refer to Henry or Harriet by name; if Harriet had been a saint it would have made no difference. Amy gave way. On her high horse her mother was daunting. Since her first husband Samuel's death she'd replaced the somewhat girlie plaits encircling her head with a harsh, stretched-back bun, and this, and pronounced premature lines on her face, gave her an appearance of severity; her erectness, which forty-four years and eight pregnancies had left intact, reinforced it. Added to which – Eleanor did have a point about the years of toil, and Maggie would think of something for the window.

The first curtain was nearly down – Amy unhooking, Eleanor taking the weight – when Henry returned from the fields, a little earlier than usual but not unexpectedly. Harriet was having a party at the Vicarage, her birthday party, and he needed to spruce himself up for it, shave off his three-day old stubble etc.

Foresighted Maggie had stocked up with water in the scullery.

Having waved to her brother on his way in – the parlour window overlooked the street – Amy prayed he wouldn't come through to that room, at least till the curtains were down; like her he might take umbrage at their removal. 'You'll be coming tonight, Amy,' he said, poking his head round the door, desperate for her to go to the party as Andy McPhearson would be there. 'Of course,' she replied quickly, hoping he would retreat equally so. But stepping into the room he said angrily – 'Put that back!' His command brought the parlour to a standstill; like a quick turn round in a game of 'Grandmother's Footsteps': Henry wasn't in the habit of ordering anyone or anything around at Shandoran except animals, and no one was quite sure what he was referring to. 'Now, Tom, or I'll flatten you,' he said, taking another step forward. The statues held. Tom – reaching over the credenza having just lifted *Flaxfields* off its hook – was waiting for a signal from his wife before obeying her son; it was what he normally did in such circumstances few though they were. Amy, reaching up to the curtain rail, awaited a similar signal; because much as she loved the picture she was prepared to let it go – for peace sake, and for all the years of toil Eleanor had put in at Shandoran, and because the Allen heritage was as much her mother's as hers. As for Eleanor – she simply couldn't understand why Henry was making such a fuss about the picture when he had let so much else go, including, it seemed, the curtains, without a murmur; also, Henry didn't frighten her: 'If I clapped my hands,' she used to say scathingly about him, 'he'd vanish like the fowl that occasionally stray into the street.'

Well not this time. 'Don't make me do it, Tom,' Henry said, closing on his step-father who, arms at full stretch was buckling badly from the weight of his load. His moustache was twitching nervously too on his otherwise clean-shaven face. Plenty of time and water for that! Henry was thinking. He utterly despised Tom, and looked so fearsome now – powerful shoulders braced, fists clenched – that Amy felt constrained to intervene. Her brother wasn't a violent man, but if really pushed – and Amy, unlike her mother, knew he was in earnest – he packed a punch; a single blow from one of his huge hands would send not just his step-father but also the picture flying. 'It's all right, Henry,' she said, 'I don't mind. Really I don't.' 'But I do,' her brother insisted, menacingly moving in for the kill.

Fortunately Eleanor had twigged at last. She nodded to Tom who gratefully rehung the painting. On his way out of the room, a triumphant Henry pointed to the nearly-unhooked curtain. 'And that,' he said sternly.

In silence, Amy and Eleanor rehung the curtain – Amy flushed with pride. Her presence, she knew had emboldened her brother, but without it she believed he would have acted no differently. That he had remembered the painting was hers was most gratifying, it being all of two years since he'd given it to her. 'Is there anything you'd like, Amy, when I come into my own?' he'd asked a little short of his twenty-first birthday.

'*Flaxfields*,' she'd replied, and known at once from his expression he hadn't the faintest idea what she was talking about. She'd told him, and he'd laughed and said the painting was hers. It was typical of him not to give it away till it was his. Eleanor, meantime, was seething.

Two days later the Linnakers left Shandoran for good. In the interim, after Amy had returned to Dublin, Eleanor not only packed the parlour curtains but wreaked her final piece of vengeance on Henry. Many years would elapse before Amy learned about this and when she did, it took the gloss off her brother's bold stand on her behalf.

In the aftermath of Harriet's delivery, however, the gloss was still fresh, and on returning to the parlour to find Drs McPhearson senior and junior looking at *Flaxfields*, Amy felt it again. And how pleased Henry would be now, she thought, putting the tea-tray down and joining the doctors by the credenza if he knew she was softening her attitude to Andy.

'It's beautiful, isn't it?' she said, 'just perfect.'

Andy smiled, implying it was not hard to see why she liked the painting. His father – pot-bellied, beadily blue-eyed, not at all like him – looked dubious. 'Hmm, perfect you say,' he said. 'Now there's a word I think twice about using. Mind you, it's not one we have occasion to use much in our line of business! Wouldn't you agree, Andy?'

A little reluctantly, Andy agreed. Amy appreciated his reluctance. His father went on. 'Here on God's earth,' he said, 'I can't help feeling perfection is an illusion. Strive for it by all means, but don't ever lose touch with reality in the process!'

'We won't,' Amy and Andy said in happy unison. McPhearson senior smiled; the kind of smile that owned it would be hard, despite his caution, to find two people less likely than his son and Amy to confuse the real with the ideal.

Moving away from the credenza, Amy and the doctors sat down: Andy on the walnut scroll settee, his father on the antimacassared armchair, Amy on one of the two buttonbacks that would have been banished to the bedroom long ago in the *beau monde*. Over tea, the chat was about how nice the Church service had been the previous day, especially the anthem; Andy had sung in the choir. Both doctors expressed concern at Amy's old schoolteacher, Master Gamble's deteriorating rheumatism.

Before leaving, Mc Phearson senior made a point of going upstairs to check on Harriet and the baby. In his absence, Andy asked Amy deferentially if she would go out with him some time. She said yes. They settled for the following afternoon.

◇

While Amy's lease of life was being renewed – her first outing with Andy, a walk in the country, was not their last – Maggie's was slowly running out.

The New Year (1929) saw a resumption of Harriet's nastiness to her, and by the time Amy returned to Shandoran for her Easter holidays, maid and mistress were on course for a show down. Harriet's latest cruelties – not allowing Maggie to open the front door to visitors, and referring to her as 'piggy eyes' and 'the white one' – disgusted Amy. It put her in mind of the coots on Shandoran Lake pecking unwanted offspring out of the nest; Maggie was not one of the family, but to Amy it seemed as if she was. Making it sicklier, was the way Harriet continued trying to hide her nastiness from the men and Henry, and sometimes even turned on the charm to Maggie in front of them. The men had been on to her for some time but kept their thoughts on the matter from Henry. He, to his shame, pretended it wasn't happening. All of them wished it would go away. So did Amy, and repeatedly tried to reason with Harriet though increasingly as a lost cause. For by now Amy was convinced her sister-in-law was not so much scapegoating Maggie as getting her out of the house because she couldn't bear living under the same roof as her. Maggie revolted her – probably always had – something she as much as admitted in her next outburst to Amy. 'I don't want her near me any more, Amy,' she said definitively, half way through the holiday. 'She gives me the creeps. Now you'll speak to Henry about it again for me, won't you?'

As reluctantly as before, Amy complied but stopped short of advising Henry to sack Maggie. Whether he would have taken such advice had she offered it, she didn't know. Fiercely loyal to Maggie, he couldn't comprehend his wife's attitude at all.

Meantime the maid clung on – burrlike, with her fingernails gnawed to the quick again. By now, she too knew Harriet wanted her out. Knew also – she would have had to be blind and deaf not to – that Henry and the men, as well as Amy, were aware of the situation. Only the thought (and she had thought about it) of what lay beyond Shandoran stopped her leaving. Pitiable to watch, it could not go on. In the end, it was not so much the 'straw,' as a ribbon that pushed her out.

About a week after Amy had spoken to Henry, a bright spring morning persuaded Harriet to go over to the Vicarage in the pony and trap to see her mother. 'I'll be home in time for dinner,' she said, happy in the knowledge that Henry had promised to take Lottie for a ride, and that Amy as well as Maggie would be looking after the house, Luke and baby, Billy.

No sooner had Harriet gone, than Henry got called away; a harrow had broken down (the restharrow was particularly bad that year) and Matt was considering a replacement – something Henry wanted to avoid at all costs. Inconsolable at first, Lottie soon cheered up when Maggie asked her if she'd like to track the ducks.

At midday, a time when the men – though not Henry, still struggling in the fields with the harrow – were collected up in the street to arrange their afternoon work loads, Harriet returned. Hearing her, Lottie rushed out of the house excitedly to tell her about the tracking. It was cold, so Maggie followed with the child's coat and before putting it on bent down to tie the bow at the back of her frock so that she would look 'her prettiest for her Mammy.'

Furious that Lottie had spent the morning – and such a happy one – with the maid, Harriet got down from the trap. 'Not like that, piggy eyes,' she said, forgetting herself completely, and shoving Maggie to one side. 'We like the bow to stand out, don't we, Lottie? Not all floppy like that!'

Something snapped in Maggie; such a public display of venom by Harriet in front of people she, Maggie, was so fond of, was too much for her. Without a word she went back indoors, carefully not looking at the men: guilt and pity would have been in their faces, and she wanted to see neither.

For the remainder of the day she went about her duties more quietly than usual. Once or twice, Amy – who had not been in the street when Harriet returned – asked her if she was all right. She said she was. In truth, she was preoccupied with what she now knew lay ahead, and was dreading.

Going home that evening, clutching her hurricane and shawl, she failed to notice little things that would normally have thrilled her: the bright gibbous moon, gleaming intermittently on Shandoran Lake; spring blossom whipped up in the wind like snowflakes.

Likewise, opening and closing her cottage door – the novelty of which (her very own home!) had never quite worn off – produced no glow. Although she did feel marginally safer inside than out, the safeness, she knew, was illusory; as illusory as that provided by a bush to a bird with a broken wing. Though less visible than the bird's affliction, Maggie's was no less fatal; her spirit had been broken.

From habit, she lit her fire, which she had laid as usual that morning, boiled a kettle over it and made herself a mug of hot, sweet tea. Still with her coat and shawl on, she sat down heavily in the old rocking chair Eleanor had given her and Mr Scott when they'd moved into the cottage. Eleanor, Maggie remembered, had been unstinting in her generosity – old clothes, furniture, cushions, a clock, utensils, everything. The chair had been Mr Scott's, he being so much older than

Maggie; Maggie had tactfully insisted on it; sitting in it after his death kept her close to him.

Nursing her hot mug in her rough, nail-gnawed hands, Maggie listened to the clock ticking. Company of a kind, it soothed her. So did thinking about Mr Scott. *Mr Scott* – that was how she thought of her dead husband. She had only got round to using his Christian name when he proposed to her, and their engagement as well as their married life had been short-lived; after he died, she had no reason to refer to him as anything other than Mr Scott; no one else did. Her memories of him were all good. Not once had he given her cause to regret marrying him; nobody before or since him had treated her tenderly; loved her. She had never imagined it could be so.

This was not to be disrespectful to Eleanor, or the many at Shandoran who had befriended her. And so quickly! In no time at all there, her 'quareness' had seemed no worse than Paddy Finch's turned out feet; her future as bright as the blooms on the street's low, nasturtium-topped wall. Eleanor had set the tone; the rest followed. Harriet, Maggie thought, was a bad exemplar. Maggie didn't blame her for that; no one understood better than she what lay behind Harriet's cruelty. In a way, Maggie felt sorry for Harriet and wished things could have been different. And she felt sorry for Henry, Amy and the men too, whom Harriet had put in such an impossible position. Harriet would not even agree, she knew, to her staying on in the cottage – something Henry would have had no objection to. Maggie herself, though, didn't want that either.

Thinking about her life at Shandoran, and about Eleanor and Harriet in particular, brought home to Maggie something she had often noticed about humanity – the closeness of cruelty and kindness in a person's make up. It was important, she thought, to be grateful for the one and to understand the other; she had always tried to do that.

As she sipped her tea, the full force of rejection bore in on Maggie. A terrible loneliness beset her; loneliness so terrible it reminded her of the only other occasion she'd felt that way.

About eight years old at the time, and still at the orphanage, she had just managed to make friends with a newcomer – a thin, twisted girl on crutches, 'a cripple' – whose plight, she thought, was much worse than her own. The girl's name was Alice; that Maggie remembered it, proof in itself of the significance to her of the friendship: having a friend – the first she'd had – meant the world to her. Then one day, she overheard an older girl – a girl she knew to be spiteful and whose name she'd forgotten – telling Alice menacingly that she, Maggie, was 'born bad', that God had 'branded' her unfit for Heaven and that ill luck would befall anyone who befriended her. So saying, she kicked one of Alice's crutches aside and left the twisted girl on the floor where she fell. Maggie went to her friend's aid but knew at once she had lost her as a friend. In a life where loneliness was as common as rain, the episode stood out in her mind like a Biblical flood, and magnified tenfold her desolation now. She was back where she'd started out – unwanted. Now, though, the way forward was grimmer. Who would employ a fifty year old albino! Even if they did, it would be like the old days – horrible.

Gripped by panic, Maggie shivered. Putting her empty mug on the hearth, she pulled her chair closer to the fire and wrapped her arms tightly round her chest as though to lock in for ever her locket and the good part of her life, and ward off the cold, empty blackness of night, beyond which further blackness lay. The blackness, though, persisted, making it impossible for her to remain seated. She got up, took off her shawl and coat and methodically cleaned and tidied her cottage whose two small rooms were already spotless. In the process, she burned the few personal papers she and Mr Scott had. No one will be bothered with those, she thought, when I'm gone.

Cruelly, then, the clock struck midnight. For Maggie it was like a death knell.

Grimly, and eschewing last lingering looks around, she put her coat and shawl on again, turned off the hurricane and went out.

Fixing her eyes on the road to Kilbeg, she walked doggedly – praying she would meet no one, thankful the moon and clouds had conspired to envelop her in darkness. As blossom flipped by in the wind, her purposefulness and the chill night air made her feel less alone and fearful.

When she reached Kilbeg – no one had seen her – panic set in again. She hurried into the Church, which she hadn't attended for nearly a year but was anxious to visit one last time. In the past, she and Mr Scott had been regular attenders and when the old man died, Maggie continued to worship there – till Harriet found her presence too embarrassing.

Sitting down in a rear pew, with her clothes dappled in blossom, and a rough circle of blossom on her head, Maggie could feel her heart thumping. Reaching inside her clothes for her locket, she grasped it. Sadness overwhelmed her. She knelt down, closed her tear-filled eyes tightly, and forced herself to say the Lord's Prayer. But the words meant nothing to her. Her mind was everywhere; her heart still thumping. Looking around, she tried, with little success, to focus on the things that had engaged her attention in the past when the service or congregation had failed to: the stained glass windows, at their best in sun- or moonlight; the shiny, eagled lectern; the clean cover on the altar. The memorials to Henry and Amy's ancestors – clergymen, doctors, lawyers, colonels, JPs... gentry to a man – including the most splendid (Mr Scott had pointed them all out to her) – a tablet of black and white marble, surmounted with a cross-bearing *Agnus Dei*, commemorating their great times three Grandfather, the Reverend Alan Allen. The coldness of the marble made Maggie shiver. In the past, she'd found it and the rest awe-inspiring.

Gritting her teeth, for she was trembling all over now, she stood up, and blessed herself hurriedly before leaving the Church. Going round to the old graveyard – her clothes collecting a little more blossom on the way – she picked her steps determinedly through the long, dense undergrowth. Past more Allen memorials, and the 'turned stone', Mr Scott had told her about that too, to the tiny patch of pebbled shore beside Gar-na-Ree Lake. The moon was out again, helping her. Then, slipping her hand once more inside her coat, she felt again for her locket, gripped it tightly, and bravely – so bravely – walked into the water. She had deliberately chosen Gar-na-ree, not Shandoran Lake, as it would be a long time, if ever, before her body was discovered there. She kept walking, knowing that if she stopped she might not be able to start again. The hostile water filled her boots, and crept up her black-stockinged legs to the icy parts above her knees. She looked at the moon and, still clutching her locket, still walking, tried to think of Mr Scott. The cold, and the weight of her woollen clothes, soaking up the water, pulling her down, wouldn't let her. Then suddenly the bottom was gone; she was engulfed. A brief skirmish followed, after which, bobbing blossom marked the spot till wind and currents took them away too.

◇

When Maggie failed to show up at Shandoran the next day, her whereabouts remained a mystery despite Henry scouring the countryside for her; speculation about what had happened to her was rife. Everyone, even Harriet, hoped for the best; many feared the worst.

Needless to say, sympathy for Harriet on the estate plummeted. Most hurtful for her was Lottie's silence – day after day, as condemnatory as a judge's black cap. Henry was livid with his wife and, having initially blown his top, wouldn't speak to her for days and spent more time than usual in the fields. The men – they had long ago stopped calling her Shoo Shoo, it was too good for her – were disgusted with her, even if their comments about the affair in front of Henry remained restrained. 'Mark my words,' Matt Doran said, laconically, 'no good will come of it.' Flemming Young regretted giving Maggie a hard time. Paddy Finch – one foot going to Ballycool – felt more vulnerable. As for Amy – her feelings were best summed up in Sister Martha's favourite example of an oxymoron – 'Oh joyful trouble!' It was good that Maggie was out of Harriet's clutches, but not so good if a fire had replaced the frying pan.

Before the year was out, it seemed as if Matt's predictions were coming true.

Wall Street crashed, with reverberations throughout the world.

At Shandoran – Henry and Amy feared for their brother, Benjie in America (if only he would write); prices fell, maids came and went and everyone blamed Harriet – overtly or secretly – for what was happening.

Christmas and Easter saw no change. A cloud settled over the estate.

For Amy, its shadow was darkest indoors where, as often as not, she returned home to grimy stone floors and besmirched grates. To unreplenished water buckets, and dwindling supplies of turf and wood chippings: 'Where would we be without the chippings, Miss Amy?' Maggie used to say when a fire burned low. Most depressing of all was the larder – a place once stuffed, thanks largely to Maggie, with lovingly labelled bottled fruits and jams, sacked flour and salt, brown paper-bagged sugar, basketed eggs, trayed apples, hung hams, barrelled home-made wines, bunched herbs, and stacked home-made butter, bread, cakes and honeycombs – together creating a perplexity of smells to appetise all but the most ardent ascetic. Now, depleted shelves stared back at her.

Homecomings for Amy, though no less welcoming, became less eagerly anticipated.

◇

Faced with such despondency at Shandoran, Amy rethought her life. Things would get better on the estate, she was sure; they always did. Clouds lifted; the men needed the work; Lottie *was* Harriet's daughter; Harriet *was* Henry's wife; and Maggie was a survivor, she'd survive. Maybe it was time though for her, Amy, to move out. She would be twenty-seven on her next birthday – hardly old enough to be consigned to the shelf; definitely, getting on; a home and family of her own began to beckon.

But, where, and with whom, she wondered, as she returned to Dublin for the start of another summer term? Phil was a lost cause; she'd carried a torch for him long enough. He had treated her badly; dropped her in the meanest way. It would be two years at the end of term since they'd split up, and if he wrote now it would only be to tell her he was married, engaged, or doing quite nicely, thank you, without her. Andy McPhearson wasn't the answer either. He'd kissed her once; nothing moved; he was beginning to bore her. All of which, unless someone else showed up, left Peter Pagley. The History master was already growing on her, if in much the same way as Andy had – like moss on the north side of trees. A mountain walk was worth a try. Yes, definitely a better prospect than Andy, she thought, as her scales tilted firmly towards Pagley.

On the eve of her twenty-seventh birthday and a second mountain hike with Peter to celebrate it, a letter – postmarked Siam – arrived at Glenarkle from Phil.

Part III

The Orient: The grass is greener

◇

Chapter Fifteen

Since his bust up with Amy in the Dublin Mountains, the one certainty in Phil's life was – his decision to go east had been the right one. Indeed, if the most revered and prescient soothsayer in the world had told him not to go he would have ignored the advice so great was his desire to get out of Ireland and as far away as possible from Poynings. Even when the hoped-for job in Malaya did not materialize, forcing him to settle for second best in Siam, his determination remained firm: though not a British colony, Siam had enjoyed good relations with Britain for over a century, and it would be relatively easy, he was told, to transfer from there to Malaya when a suitable vacancy in that country came up. Leaving his family and Amy had been hard of course. Half-truths about his real motives for leaving Poynings had, as he'd predicted, kept his parents sweet; in his mother's eyes, he would still go far. In Amy's case – where he'd been running away from commitment as much as guilt – it had been more complicated; but something told him they had reached a point in their relationship where he must either ask her to marry him or let her go. If she had pressured him or clung on to him it would have been easier. She hadn't, and he'd consoled himself with the thought that he was no longer worthy of her and the sooner he left her to get on with her own life the better. Partly from courtesy, partly from guilt, he'd considered writing to tell her about the job in Siam – for ever second best – and to ask if she would spend a few days in London with him, for old times sake, before he sailed. He had some loose ends to tie up at the Siamese Embassy, after which he and she could check out the last of the Oxford Street summer sales and maybe go to a show. He'd decided against – a clean break was needed – and made do instead with Rose and June's company in London. Taking what time off they could, his sisters had checked out the sales with him, taken tea with him in Lyons' in Piccadilly, and dismissed the idea of a visit to Drury Lane, where *Showboat* was proving hugely popular but would probably have been sold out.

Omissions discovered at the eleventh hour had made the final day one mad rush and his departure on the boat-train from Victoria and, later, the boat from Southampton, little more than a retrospective haze.

The six-week voyage East had been filled with reading, talking, drinking, familiarising himself with the rudiments of Siamese, and learning bridge – a game, he was told, he would find useful in the East. The same occupations filled most of his spare time in Siam. For the rest, teaching Maths in Bangkok, while further wrestling with Siamese – and making a start on Malay – was stimulating. Residing, low-cost, at the Bangkok United Club, something his bachelor status allowed him to do, meant that for the first time in his life money had ceased to be a major problem.

Some things, of course, in Siam irked him. Things like the sweltering heat, made worse by an unreliable fan in his room at the BUC which nobody hurried to fix. Like the derogatory use of the term 'Irish' by some Club members, particularly the English. Like the wealth of other Club members – Americans and Scots mainly, who flaunted their affluence shamelessly; freebooters and bloodsuckers the lot of them, Phil thought. Like the clapped out taxis, fetid klongs, and leaky river craft. Like how to fill time in a place where the climate was conducive in essence to laziness; like learning Siamese and Malay vocabularies.

Nothing, however, was so bad as to get on top of him. His fan always got fixed in the end. Plenty of BUC members – a Scottish tin mine owner by the name of Mackenzie, and an American in tobacco called Hank Borden, were two of them – did not sneer at his Irishness. Siamese and Malay, like French, would soon be mastered.

Drink, talking, idling and bridge were no bad ways to pass the time.

Nothing, that was, till a Christmas letter from his parents set him wondering if Amy would write to him too. There was no earthly reason why she should; she hadn't even got his address. He wanted her to, and when no letter came considered writing to her, but didn't. He became depressed. 'You've reached your "crisis",' Mackenzie told him. 'We've all been there, Phil. Pour yourself another whisky, man!' Hank Borden said it was too soon for the crisis. 'It's just an old fashioned case of the blues, Phil. Join me on another cruise!' The American – big, brash and extortionate; dollar-imperialism personified, Phil thought – was with the British American Tobacco Company. His too-loud voice and shirts, and his too-lavish launch, whose giant-sized drink's cabinet, when open, resembled his mouthful of gold-filled teeth, gave Phil the pip; but his frankness and generosity were hard to resist. He took up Hank's offer.

Coming home on the Menam, with a hired native helmsman at the wheel, and a native girl, whom Hank patted on the bottom and addressed as Honey, topping up their gin-slings, Hank felt constrained to say: 'What gives with you, Phil? I can tell you're straight, but can't understand why you fight shy of women.' 'Women' was a subject Hank reckoned himself an expert on – he changed his lovers as often as his garish, sweat-laden shirts – and Phil's behaviour genuinely mystified him. 'It's complicated,' Phil said, but refrained from elaborating on cramping memories of Amy. Besides, he had not yet met anyone he fancied in the East, a place where single, white women were as rare as winter woollies and tangling with natives and married ones did not appeal. 'It must be,' Hank said, no wiser than before. 'But if you're ever in need of a good screw, Phil – no strings – let me know. I've some time off in the New Year. I generally go down to Penang. Helluva place! Broads to die for! You're welcome to join me.' Phil laughed – Hank's language was as tasteless as his dress – expressed thanks for his offer and said he'd think about it.

With the passing of Christmas, his hopes of a seasonal letter from Amy collapsed; then rose again as New Year (1929) dawned – Nothing. His depression worsened; his New Year resolve to take his lifestyle in hand grounded. Hank pressed him to go to Penang. He went.

After a couple of days on the island, Phil felt refreshed. It would have been hard not to; first-timers were instantly captivated by it – by its contrasting sights and sounds, and serene, minimalist mosques, onion-domed and delicately minaretted; by its fussy pagodas and Buddhist temples reaching to the sky like multi-tiered wedding cakes. By its single, unimposing hill which gave it, in relief, the appearance of a brimmed hat; by its colourful state capital Georgetown, and humming docks and roads.

Waking on the third morning at the luxurious E and O (Eastern and Oriental Hotel), where he and Hank were planning to spend a week (Hank, with friends who were of no interest to Phil), Phil could almost claim to be energetic. He breakfasted early, then went out to explore a little further afield than he had already done. Laughter from nearby tennis courts attracted his attention and when a ball bounced out, feeling livelier than he'd done for months, he chased after it and threw it back. A woman playing on her own against a man and another woman, caught it, and came over to the wire to thank him. In the brief encounter that followed –

'You're new round here?'

'Yes. How did you know?'

'Aha! When you've been in the East as long as I have, you'll be able to spot the rookies too.'

'You're from Yorkshire?'

'Yes. How did *you* know?'

'Aha! When you've been studying languages as long as I have, that's easy.'

Phil noticed the woman's neat, blonde hair, bronzed athletic figure, and wedding ring. He made to move off. She stopped him. 'Do you play?' she asked, indicating her lack of a partner and stepping smartly on to her left foot to sweep an imaginary ball through the air in a smooth forehand drive. Her style was enviable. 'I do,' Phil said. 'Terribly rusty, I'm afraid, but would love a game.' 'Top-hole,' the woman rejoined, and when Phil told her he'd left his racket in Siam, she pointed to her own second one on the side of the court, saying she always carried two. 'I'm Helen Castle, by the way,' she added. 'Phil Handy,' Phil replied; then returned to his room at the E and O to change into his whites, happily not left behind.

On court, they shook hands, and Helen introduced him to the opposition – a Mr and Mrs Ripley, with whom she was staying in Georgetown for a few days; her husband had been too busy to come with her. They tossed for service. Helen won and elected to serve. Quickly it became apparent to Phil her skill at tennis more than matched her enviable style. What with his rustiness, and the Ripleys' mediocrity at best, the sets – punctuated with encouraging cries of 'Played partner!' and 'Splendid shot, Phil!' from Helen – were close-fought, lively and enjoyable.

They played till noon, stopping only for drinks, paid for by Phil, about half way through. Then not wanting to outstay his welcome, or appear at a total loss for company on the island, Phil muttered an untruth about meeting his friend, Borden, for lunch at the E and O. Helen and the Ripleys thanked him again for the drinks and for making the foursome possible. They suggested another encounter. 'Tomorrow morning?' Helen pressed, sweeping the air once more with her racket, this time in a mock backhand drive. Smiling, Phil assented.

Back at the E and O, he showered, changed, lunched on his own, and went to his room for siesta. Though tired, he wanted to do some thinking. Sleep overwhelmed him. Later he had dinner with Borden, and drank himself silly boasting about his catch on the tennis courts. He never did get round to the thinking but, even if he had – to thinking, that is, about Amy, and about all she had meant to him, and still meant to him – it would probably have made little difference to his remaining time in Penang. For he had already convinced himself Amy no longer cared for him. He was obligated to no one; in Penang to enjoy himself.

Next morning, he was pleasantly surprised to find Helen waiting for him on her own at the courts. They played for a couple of hours then packed it in. 'It's a bit one-sided,' Helen said, charmingly.

In the shade of an ylang ylang, they sipped Pimm's, and told each other what they wanted to about their backgrounds. By now, Phil was well practised in avoiding the areas of his that pained him. He had come East, he said, to escape from the Free State, and for adventure. Helen doubted that was the whole truth, but didn't pry: if Phil had things to hide, the East would winkle them out; it always did. As for herself, her father, she said – honestly, and without affectation – had been a Yorkshire shipping merchant. At the start of the century he'd taken a position with the British East Africa Company, and she and her mother had moved to East Africa with him. Holidays were in Zanzibar, and it was there, on the foothills of Kilimanjaro, she'd met her husband, Frank. His parents, missionaries in Kenya, were from the East End of London. Frank had studied medicine and was in practice at the time in Nairobi. 'Both our fathers were killed during the war,' she concluded, 'and our widowed mothers died soon after it. The Ripleys – they were friends of my parents – have been wonderful to us since. He's in shipping in Singapore, and has offshoot interests and a second home here in Georgetown. We moved to Malaya to be near them.'

Listening to and looking at Helen, Phil was increasingly puzzled by her. Part of her – her sculptured face encased in short, sleekly waved, blonde hair; her immaculate whites; her cool sophistication – said, don't touch! The other part – gleaming, dark-brown eyes; glimpses of her tongue through her teeth when she smiled; long, bronzed limbs reaching serpentinely into her whites – I dare you! Don't touch unnerved Phil: he had never made love to a married woman and took a poor view of adultery, whose prevalence in the East reinforced his aversion to wedlock. I dare you excited him: married women weren't looking for commitment.

In an effort to glean why Helen was befriending him, he asked where she lived in Malaya. 'Perlemban,' she said. 'Perlemban,' he repeated after her, 'that has a nice ring to it. And how does it compare with Georgetown?' 'It's quieter and more restrictive,' Helen said, more I dare you than don't touch, but quickly followed with – 'Tell me something about Siam,' which Phil obligingly did. After that, they changed, and returned to the Ripleys for lunch and siesta.

Later, Helen suggested, and Phil happily agreed to a stroll in Georgetown.

Somewhere in the capital's colourful, noisy streets, where metalworkers and weavers, pandan-plaiters and fortune-tellers, food and souvenir merchants made and plied their wares, Helen slipped her arm through Phil's. Flattered, he gave it a little squeeze. At a souvenir stall, Helen admired a charm bracelet. Phil haggled over it and bought it for her. 'A little memento of a bad morning's tennis,' he said, self-deprecatingly, and fastened it on to her wrist. 'You're spoiling me,' she said, rethreading her arm through his when they resumed walking. Phil gave it another squeeze, saying – 'I bet your husband does plenty of that!' 'I want for nothing,' Helen replied in a 'back off' tone of voice. Frank wasn't referred to again.

For supper that evening, Helen wore a slinky, tangerine silk dress that tantalisingly revealed her cleavage. Phil's eyes kept gravitating towards it. As Helen showed off her new bracelet to the Ripleys, he found the contrast between her blonde hair on the one hand and dark brown eyes and bronzed skin on the other, as magnetic as that between her lithe sportiness and cool sophistication. A couple of rubbers of bridge, during which Helen marvelled at Phil's proficiency, followed the meal and preceded the Ripleys' discreet retirement to bed.

When their hosts had gone, Helen sat down on a settee, smoothed her tangerine dress over her crossed, tanned bare legs and invitingly patting the space beside her said she'd really enjoyed the day. 'Me too,' Phil said, sitting down where she'd indicated and taking the cigarette she offered.

As they lit up, a siren blast from the roads reminded Phil uncomfortably about Kingstown and Amy. To quash the memory, he picked up Helen's wrist and examined more closely than before the charms on her bracelet – elephant, turtle, dragon, Chinese lantern, fish, butterfly and snake.

'It's beautiful, Phil,' Helen said, putting her hand on his thigh and thanking him again for the present. Then she leaned into him slinkily, bathed him in the heady scent of jasmine and kissed his cheek. Overcome by her perfume, and the whisky he'd downed, and the glamour of his surroundings, and the novelty of being seduced by a married woman, Phil found himself at a loss. He need not have worried. Taking hold of his hand, Helen stood up, pulled him to his feet, and led him to her bedroom – a lovely double-aspect one with views of land and sea. She began undressing him, running her hands all over his body and kissing him. He blushed; her effrontery temporarily emasculated him. Turning her back, she invited him to unhook her dress. As it fell to the floor, and she pushed her underwear down to her ankles, the serpentine sweep of her lithe, tanned, athletic body saw off Phil's reserve. They made love – vigorously.

During Phil's remaining three days in Penang, his mornings were filled with sightseeing: arm in arm – he and Helen revisited Georgetown's streets, admired the simplicity of the Kling Mosque, and feasted their eyes on sumptuous Kek Lok Si. In the Swiss-built funicular that ascended Penang Hill, they held their breath and gazed, amazed, on emerging from their tiny cable car, at the ever-changing hues and patterns of the island's sky and sea, and throbbing docks and roads. In the evenings they made love in Helen's lovely double-aspect room.

◇

Back in Siam, Phil felt well satisfied with himself. He'd got what he'd gone to Penang for; there was nothing to prevent him going back to recharge his batteries; a free agent, he would stay that way. 'If we ever meet again, Phil,' Helen had said, on their final evening together, 'this never happened. I have a good marriage and want to keep it that way.' 'Fine by me,' he'd replied, and meant it. And as his life resumed at the BUP – iffy fan, clammy clime, fetid klongs, leaky rivercraft, clapped out taxis – not just Helen, but Amy too, faded from his mind.

Why then did Amy come back into it?

◇

One of the more enjoyable of Phil's social activities in Bangkok was wining and dining at the BUC, especially when his Scottish tin-mining friend, Mackenzie, was footing the bill. Unlike many of his compatriots, Mackenzie was generous to a fault. Even when the Depression struck, and tin and tobacco markets reeled, he continued to entertain Phil lavishly, only expecting him to listen to his moans in return. Phil listened, though without any great sympathy. Mackenzie had made a pile in Siam. Also, though he was a pleasant enough man, some of his associates left much to be desired. One – a fellow called Wilson, an engineer, a rough diamond from the Dock Company – was asked on entering the Club's dining room once if he was drunk. 'Drunk? I'm always drunk,' he replied. 'I'm not meself when I'm sober.' Later, after he and his mates had had community singing between courses, he smashed a dish of roast pork on a Chinese boy's head.

Mackenzie excused such behaviour by the Depression which, he said, 'played havoc with nerves already frayed by years in this accursed clime.'

Why not get out of it then? Phil thought but immediately answered his own question: returning to their native land, he'd gleaned by now, was impossible for these people; after a few months leave in the West – where nothing was quite the same as before, where they couldn't get warm, where people and friends had moved on – they longed to be back in the East.

But given that most of Mackenzie's pals were OK, Phil never thought to check on the probity or otherwise of the two the Scot suggested he accompany on a visit to a backwoods mine;

Phil was always going on about how much he'd like to see a works at the face. In the event, the character of his companions – and they were not pleasant – was the least of his worries.

He got a foretaste of their nature when he met up with them for the trip at Mackenzie's 'godown' (yard) in Bangkok. One had a toothache and was in a terrible temper; he sacked the godown keeper on the spot for having a fire in his stove and bundled him and his wife out on to the road. The other took his stick to her when she answered back. Phil was horrified. He'd had his own moments of anger in the East, like verbally giving a native taxi driver hell when his vehicle broke down leaving him, Phil, stranded or worse – late for or altogether missing a meal at the Club. But this was a far cry from physically laying into the natives and, Kipling or no, Phil hoped it wasn't part of his burden in the East.

The mine itself – after a rickety makeshift of a lorry had carried the three of them over ten miles or more of a road that was worse, Phil thought than the worst of the byways round Kilbeg – was certainly interesting; and Phil had never been in the midst of harder men. The journey home, however, left him regretting the trip for months to come. It poured, and unable to share the lorry's tiny cab with the roughnecks – all that could be said in their favour was that they knew their job and Mackenzie could trust them – Phil huddled under a pile of stuff at the back. Soaked through, he fully expected to be laid up with, at best, a cold, at worst, pneumonia.

He got neither, and had just begun to thank his lucky stars when stomach pains started, followed by bouts of diarrhoea and night sweats. Guided by the time lag and wishful thinking, he put it down to a casual bug or his inability to cope as well as others with heat and booze. Aspros eased the pain, and he cut down his drinking, something he was for ever vowing to do but never did. Then his right side began aching and having ruled out appendicitis – he'd had his appendix out as a child – he wondered if he had the clap. His precautions made it unlikely but he preferred the thought of the clap to the contemplation of anything more serious; also, Borden had said precautions were no guarantee against it and that it presented in all sorts of ways; he hadn't specified. Too embarrassed to consult a doctor, or anyone else, Phil stuck with the Aspros. When his symptoms eased, he relaxed, glad he hadn't troubled anyone.

Overall, though, things worsened. His right shoulder started playing up and hurt so much once when he jarred it on a tennis court he packed in the game. His left side began troubling him too, making it hard for him to turn on to it in bed. Disturbed nights became the norm; they made him irritable by day; his energy levels slumped. He lost weight. 'You look bloody awful, man,' Mackenzie and Borden told him. 'Go and see a doctor!' He refused – till necessity made him comply.

He collapsed in the doctor's waiting room, and came round on a couch in the surgery with the doctor, a gruff old Scot called Mercer, standing beside him. Questions and answers preceded an examination. Then frowning, Mercer delivered his diagnosis. 'De ye ken nothin' at all, man, about oriental diseases? The news is bad, I'm bound to say. You've got amoebic dysentey – and an ulcerated liver too, I'll hazard!'

The revelation and its stern delivery stunned Phil. Death loomed; he did not want to die – certainly not on his own in the East. He knew more about illness there than he cared to make out; just never imagined he'd fall victim to one like this.

Faced with his silence, Mercer softened. 'But thank God you came when you did,' he said. 'We wouldne want ye expectorating anchovy. I take it you've heard o' that!' Phil nodded, smiled wanly, then listened as Mercer, in a forthrightly, fatherly way, prescribed treatment. Some man to man advice followed. 'In future, Mr Handy, steer clear of infected water!' (That, on the trip to the mine, had sparked the illness) 'And for your own sake, laddie, if not the Lord's, lay off the booze. I've seen it destroy mare lives in the East than torpor, torridity and bachelorhood put together. Talking of which, a wife wouldne come amiss either. I know – you're not the marrying kind! Well that's as may be. But it's a rare man who can get by hereabouts without the ministrations of a good woman. Finding a suitable one – single and white, I presume? – won't be easy mind. Is there nay wee lassie back home you could inveigle out?'

Amused by Mercer's *sang-froid*, Phil thanked him for his advice and promised to take it on board. The consultation ended.

Healing, complicated by the ulcerated liver, was both protracted and arduous.

During it, in and out of hospital and throughout his long convalescence, Phil's body was wracked with pain; his mind, with soul-searching and self-doubt. He was going nowhere; had achieved nothing. While others – his siblings (Al, Rose, June sprang to mind) – moved on; he was stuck in a rut. His mother's words – 'Phil will go far' – mocked him.

In the midst of his despair, he wondered if he would not, after all, be better off married. It was a giant mental leap for him to make. Avoiding marriage was one of the few sensible things he'd done in his life. Every married couple he knew bore this out, not least his parents, ground down by hard work and children. In the East, adultery made a mockery of marriage. Quickly, he abandoned the idea.

Thinking about it, though, and about Mercer's advice, set him thinking about Amy. The more he thought about her, the more he wanted to contact her. It was perverse, he knew. For in wanting her he was behaving like a spoilt child who, having tired of his Christmas presents, returns to his favourite old, battered toy for comfort; or treating her like one of his good books – to be reread to refresh his soul then put back on the shelf when finished with.

That said, she stood up to rereading.

Turning the pages of their times together, Phil saw Amy clearer than a Bangkok sky. From six thousand miles away, he smelled the turf, hay, and flaxseed in her hair in Cavan, the apple blossom that surrounded her in Dublin, more keenly than any perfume in the East. From six thousand miles away, he felt her suppliance in his arms on Howth Head more truly than the pliancy of his pillows. From six thousand miles away, the thought of her sitting opposite him in Bewley's and the Metropole, in the soft colours she loved and her bog-oak necklace, made his heart beat faster than anything or anyone in Siam. Six thousand miles away from her, he imagined her coming into his room at the BUC, smiling all over her freckled face, delighting him. Then as suddenly as a *fata morgana*, she was gone.

Half-lying, half-sitting in bed one Saturday morning, with his mosquito net fastened round him and a fat brown envelope on the sheet in front of him, it occurred to him that if he wanted to pick up with her again, he must make the first move. I'll write to her for her birthday at the end of May, he thought. Keep the letter low-key – friendly, not forward – to test the waters, not leave me feeling a complete idiot if she doesn't reply or tells me politely where to get off. But he had hardly decided to write when he wondered – To what avail? What have I got to offer her? – nothing. Even if she still loves me, wild horses won't drag her to Siam without a proposal of marriage which I have no intention of making; best to forget her.

He couldn't forget. Reaching for the brown envelope, he emptied out its contents – mementoes of his time with Amy. Lovingly, he examined them – theatre tickets, hotel bills, letters; a tiny, lace-trimmed handkerchief that had found its way into one of his pockets. Picking up the hankie, he sniffed it, and could have sworn it smelled of apple blossom. Then laying it on the sheet in front of him, he wondered if he would ever return it to its owner. What's she doing now? Is she off or on duty? – If off, with friends or alone? Have Pagley, or Andy McPhearson, both well established in their fields – unlike me, in limbo – got through to her at last?

Picturing Amy in the arms of another man made Phil squirm. Yet he knew he had no claim on her; she was a free agent, just like him. Perhaps he should stick to the Helen Castles of the East. That particular thought was no more appealing to him than the one of Amy with another man. The lace hankie beneath his hand said, 'Write, now!' Pushing it and the other mementoes to one side, he got out of bed, collected his writing things, returned to bed and wrote to Amy.

◇

In the course of their communications – letters took six weeks either way – Phil slowly, very slowly, came round to the idea of marriage. What clinched his conversion was the offer of a job in Malaya.

Chapter Sixteen

On receiving Phil's proposal, November 1930, six months and a sackful of letters after the arrival of his first letter to her from the East – Amy read it in disbelief. He doesn't mean it, she thought; he's just throwing it out in a fit of loneliness, the same loneliness that persuaded him to write to me in the first place, convinced I'll turn him down. She had said nothing in her letters to lead him on. Rather, by playing up her friendships – like at Glenarkle where in truth she had grown very fond of Peter Pagley – and her overall contentment with her life, she'd tried to convey an impression of 'I'm all right without you.' She was sympathetic of course about his illness, loneliness and boredom – 'If I was not a reader, Amy, I should go mad from sheer *ennui*,' he'd written – and had sent him books to relieve the latter. Peter Pagley had recommended the books, and Phil appreciated them – especially the Huxleys, the latest of which ('Point Counter Point') Peter fully expected to be on the Free State's recently created Censorship Board's first hit-list. [The Board – representative of the Professions minus the Protestant Church – had the job of vetting all the 'dirty' books coming into the Free State from Britain and the United States.] Sympathy, however, was one thing; intimations of love or need quite another.

But what if he did mean it?

To help answer her question Amy reread the letter in her hand, and the ones that had preceded it.

Scattered throughout them were digs at marriage and children. 'My own opinion,' he'd written after she'd told him a third child, Billy, had been born at Shandoran and that Catherine and Neil were married and hoping to start a family, 'that children are painful to bear, grubby to rear, expensive to educate and serve no useful purpose save the gratification of the same vanity which man displayed in making God in his own image, has not altered.' But Amy had heard such things a thousand times in the past and they paled in significance now when compared with Phil's scattered reminiscences! 'What do you do on your half-days and weekends off?' he'd asked in his very first letter. 'Do you ever instinctively catch the seventeen minutes past two tram from Kingstown to the Pillar?' 'Do you know,' he'd told her in one of his lengthier postscripts (he did like a postscript) – 'I have the bills for all our hotel trysts, even the very first one in the North Star, and the second in Dundalk in the little hotel with tracts about the blessed Virgin on the table? The maddest thing we ever did, Amy, but terribly good to look back on now. God, we had some good times together. The bill for our four night break as Mr and Mrs Jones in the Royal in north Wales, inclusive of breakfast, dinner and drinks came to £5/7/6. How you laughed at my Welsh accent!' Finally, in one of his lengthier letters – after he'd told her about a meal he'd had at the Club with a man whose father had been one-time managing director of 'Ind Coope's Brewery' – he'd asked if she remembered the 'two bottles we had in the little inn in north Wales and the commercial traveller there who told us what stingy beggars the Welsh were? I think it was the day we went to Pwllheli, and later, having run out of cash, spent the night on the roadside. Do you ever, in the safe routine of the year, shiver at the risks we took then? I do, but only because I wish we had taken more.' Amy had forgotten none of these things, rereading about them in the light of Phil's proposal was potent.

Added to the reminiscences were: the way he'd moved in the course of the correspondence from 'Dear Amy' to 'My dearest, Amy.' His undisguised avidity for her letters: 'Write soon, Amy, for your letters to me are like the "silver spring in the wilderness; like the shadow of a great rock in a weary land." Apt, if biblical, don't you think?' And the proposal itself – 'Marry me, Amy. I love you so much and am missing you more than I can say. I'll be on tenterhooks till I hear from you. You'll like Malaya, I'm sure of it. And if you don't, we can always go home after one or two tours – enough anyway to save for a house in Ireland.'

Faced with all this, Amy easily convinced herself the proposal was for real. Phil loved her and wanted to marry her; he had only been waiting for the right job in the right place to come up. She had never stopped loving him.

From that moment, not all the world's most revered and prescient soothsayers could have stopped Amy going East. 'I mun go', she said, smiling at the memory of Hazel Woodus' mental torment on the eve of Hunter's Spinney; she had just finished reading Mary Webb's 'Gone To Earth'; Peter Pagley had lent it to her. Peter often lent her books, just like Phil had done in the past, but despite the books and her fondness for Glenarkle's History master, Amy had never even begun to love him.

In the months preceding her departure East – a hectic, head-spinning time – Amy gave in her notice, exchanged more letters and a few cables with Phil, shopped, packed, labelled and said her good-byes. Everyone – well, not quite; there was one sour note – indulged her happiness. Mr Appleby forwent the usual term's notice, saying she could leave his employ in February. Sister Martha gave her her old room at St Hilda's as a base in the capital in the run up to her departure. The room – vacated by Catherine after her wedding, she and Neil were in a flat in Rathmines – was a godsend, as was the big, black, tin trunk the Sister later came up with. Despite Phil's advice – 'No one wears coats or costumes here' – Amy accumulated loads of stuff. An extended coffee break in Bewley's was perfect for a final get-together with Catherine, and an extended afternoon tea break at Glenarkle for a send off there. During it, Peter Pagley – he'd accepted his fate graciously, gentlemanliness dictated no less – aired his latest concerns about censorship, his earlier ones having been fully vindicated by the inclusion of Point Counter Point on the Censorship Board's first hit list. William Dodson rubbished Gaelic – 'Dun Laoghaire will never catch on' – Max Stone poured scorn on Trinity's critics and mourned the 'wanton' destruction of King Billy in College Green; the equestrian statue, incinerated by republicans, had finally bitten the dust. Would attitudes in the school ever change? Amy wondered yet again.

The biggest wrench for her – notwithstanding her desire to move out – was at Shandoran, where debts were continuing to mount, maids to come and go, Harriet's sympathy balance to stay in the red. For Amy's final visit, however, everyone put their best foot forward. Harriet's desire for another baby meant Henry was enjoying his conjugal rights, the outcome of which was certain to be more grief but the short-term effects of which were pleasing. On Sunday, when Lottie put on her new mauve coat and matching fur-trimmed bonnet, it took no more than a frown from Amy from behind Harriet's back to make Henry refrain from complaining about the purchases. Instead, he complimented his daughter on how lovely she looked, which indeed she did. At Church, the happy family filled the Allen pew. Amy was proud to be part of it, and deeply touched when Reverend Badell wished her well on behalf of his congregation. His next words – he was talking about the East 'where, sadly, so many of our good Protestant sons and daughters have betaken themselves' – made her smile, putting her in mind of a little exchange she and Phil had had in their letters. Phil had been moaning about the high birth rates in the orient and she'd told him that what with so much emigration round Shandoran, and so many people dying – including her Grandmother Sad at The Mill, the older Miss Aiken in Ballymun, and her old school teacher, rheumatic Master Gamble, 'that crooked and bent,' folks said, ''twas a miracle they got him into a coffin' – there'd be no one left in the parish if it wasn't for its high birth rate.

The night before Amy left Shandoran, she and Henry sat up late in the parlour where, earlier, Harriet had played the piano and everyone had sung along. As the turf fire's shadows danced on the room's walls and ceiling, and mingled with fuzzy circles of light thrown up by the Aladdin, brother and sister talked and reminisced about anything and everything so long as it skirted unpleasantness; for there had been plenty of that, much of it all too recent. Some few months back, Maggie Scott's remains – with them was her locket – had been discovered in Gar-na-Ree Lake. People had drawn their own conclusions and to a man turned out in Kilbeg for the maid's funeral. She and her locket were interred beside her husband. But recalling such things was unhelpful, especially as in the aftermath of Maggie's funeral Harriet's stock in the vicinity had only just begun to recover – for Henry and Shandoran's sake.

More appropriate by far for the occasion was Amy's recollection of her and Henry's younger brother, Benjie's close shave in the meadow bogs (he was only six at the time) and of Henry to the rescue – solo – with one of the coiled ropes that were always to hand on the estate. Henry's recollection of leaping about on the flax pits to drive out more noxious gas, till someone – himself like as not – put a match to it and a blinding flash and loud bang sent everyone scampering. Their combined recollections of 'The Twelfth' – from the early morning teasing the men gave Catholic Doxey on that day (they flew a Union Jack from her chimney and belted out 'The Sash' when she invoked 'bad cess to the lot o' them') to the never ending marching. 'Boy what marches we had!' Henry said, recalling the best of them. 'Ay,' was Amy's response, 'fancy dress armies, sounding the last hurrah!' They both smiled wryly at that.

Though tempted, Amy did not refer to diversification nor – though she was as ignorant and curious about it as ever – to Henry's cocker, Barney's demise; her brother would have appreciated neither. Something she appreciated was the front of indifference Henry put up to her going. 'Take your picture with you,' he said. 'That way, you'll not be forgetting us.' 'As if I could', she replied, touched by her brother's words.

In the morning, their Uncle James, whose earlier offer of a lift to Knockmore, source of the only sour note, had been accepted by Amy, arrived in the street in his 'Bullnose'. At The Mill, where the eggs were not all in the one basket, the Depression was biting far less hard than at Shandoran. The bullnose had cost two hundred pounds and – no disrespect to the deceased – attracted more attention at Grandmother Sad's funeral than her hearse.

The whole estate turned out to see Amy off in the street and, one by one, said good-bye as her luggage was loaded up. The last to shake her hand was Henry. 'Good luck now, sis', he said, tightening his grip as he spoke. Thanking him, Amy said it would be no time till she was back. 'I suppose not', he replied, struggling hard now to control his emotions, 'and sure maybe you'll have a babby or two of your own by then!' Amy thought not, but didn't say so as Henry reluctantly let go of her hand: whatever about marrying her, it would be a long time before Phil would agree to a family. 'Good-bye all', she called, as Henry closed the car door and James started up the engine. Everyone waved, and shouted good-bye again, and as James drove out of the street and down the avenue, Amy took a last lingering look at her home. Even if she had left with her eyes closed, every detail of the scene was so ingrained in her mind, it would have been impossible to forget it.

◇

On a bright, sharp, mid-March morning Amy boarded the 'Prins de Nederlands' in Southampton. There were no good-byes at the port. She didn't mind; by the time she reached it every nerve in her body strained east. Sisters Martha and Cecilia had seen her off at Kingstown, with big, cassock-laden embraces pungent of incense, camphor and artichoke soup. Waving to her from the end of the wharf, they resembled, she'd thought, two displaced penguins.

The Prins, a sturdy (it needed to be!) two-funnelled Mail and passenger ship, was Dutch-built, -owned and -crewed. Its passengers were mainly Dutch too – planters and miners from the Dutch East Indies. They spoke loudly and with great intensity. The few Americans, French and English on board were also inclined to be voluble and in the ebb and flow of conversation it seemed to Amy that everyone, not just herself, had reached some kind of marker in their lives. Younger travellers relished the prospect of a golden future – anywhere but at home. Worried planters and tin-miners agonised about falling prices. A number of elderly and middle-aged passengers couldn't believe their good fortune at having sold out before the crash. Hardened civil servants from India bemoaned the state of affairs in their beloved Raj.

Only once did the exchanges dry up.

From nowhere, a violent storm erupted in the Bay of Biscay and word ricocheted round the ship that the 'Highland Mary' had gone down ahead. Terrified passengers took to their cabins and, immured in hers, with two Algeria-bound French nuns who shared it with her, Amy was repeatedly and violently sick. She prayed for deliverance, wishing to God she was on one of the big, three-funnelled liners that plied the Atlantic in pursuit of the 'Blue Ribbon' instead of on the Prins. Later though, when she and the rest re-emerged on deck, like rabbits when the shooting party has passed over, she thanked God, not only for the Prins and its Dutch crew, but for de Lesseps who had enabled them all to short-circuit the Cape.

Thereafter, it was full steam ahead, spiced with exotic stop-overs at far-away picture-book places suddenly come to life. Abandoning herself to the twin novelties of idleness and luxury, Amy lounged in the sun; played deck-quoits, shuffle-board and deck tennis; made up bridge fours; partied and danced, and made friends with some of the younger crew, who nicknamed her Miss Irish. The nickname caught on, and a few of the English passengers used it derogatorily. Amy ignored them. For how were they to know she had a British passport, and that George the Fifth was just as much her King as theirs? or to understand that loving Ireland in no way precluded loyalty to England. She wholeheartedly identified with the sentiments of whoever it was who wrote – 'Never was isle so little, never was sea so lone, But over the scud and palm trees an English flag has flown.' Hopefully no such discrimination awaited her in the East, but if it did she and Phil would overcome it; together, they could overcome anything.

At the Dutch East Indies, most of the passengers disembarked. The rest carried on to Singapore where Phil had said he would meet Amy. They would spend a day or two in the port, sightseeing and shopping – 'You'll pick up a wedding dress there for next to nothing,' he'd written – before going on the Penang to be married and honeymoon. His new job didn't start till July, so they would spend the remaining time in his old one in Bangkok, a city he'd assured Amy she would not like. 'But if I can survive two years here,' he'd added, 'you can manage forty days. Think of it as Lent.'

Closing on Singapore, brightest star in the Far Eastern Empire, lynchpin of the imperial, nautical corset, Amy was not so much Miss Irish, Miss Allen or Miss British as Miss Optimism. Some last minute news that Phil would not be on the dockside to meet her – another bout of illness had beset him – and that she must make her own way to Georgetown and link up with him there at the Eastern and Oriental Hotel, did throw her. But she rallied quickly, and foregoing the wedding dress (there was bound to be something in Georgetown) traversed the world's greatest *entrepot* with an indifference to her surroundings that must have made Raffles turn in his grave, to board a train northbound to Penang.

◇

Rumbling south, a train from Bangkok was heading for the same destination. In one of its compartments Phil smoked his way irritably through a packet of cigarettes. His irritation was threefold. In the first place his train was running late making it impossible for him to be – as he had planned – at the E and O when Amy arrived there. Second, there was a question mark over his appearance, his recent illness – another stomach bug, minor compared with the last – having taken its toll. Would Amy still like him? Finally – a further and even bigger question mark bedevilled him – a question mark that would not have existed at all if his coming posting in Malaya had been anywhere other than where it was – Perlemban; the very place Helen Castle had told him she lived and where, despite his own and her wish for secrecy, their fling was bound to surface. How would Amy react when he told her about that? Not to tell her about it – notwithstanding its triviality in his mind – would be asking for trouble. As much if not more trouble, given the kind of person she was – a trusting one-man-woman – as telling her about it by post, something he had earlier considered, but dismissed on the grounds that she might get the wrong end of the stick and straightening things out on paper might prove impossible. Telling her to her face in Georgetown was the right way forward – whatever her reaction.

Catching sight of himself, a fresh packet and a half of cigarettes later, in one of the large gilt-framed mirrors in the E and O's foyer, Phil momentarily lost his nerve. Lighting up, he inhaled deeply and moved away from the receptionist's desk to a less exposed place from where he could see Amy coming down the hotel stairs before she saw him. When she appeared, in a lime green frock and her bog-oak necklace, and with her hair a little shorter – ear-lobe length – than he'd seen it before, and her eyes shining in her freckled face like mica on a pebbled shore, she took his breath away.

Stubbing his cigarette, he walked over to her.

'Hello, Amy, how are you?' he said, taking her into his arms, his shyness overcome by the moment. 'Jesus, it's good to see you!' He had never meant anything more in his life; never been so certain about what he was proposing to do. His soft Dublin accent – no trace of Cavan now; even the Dublin had mellowed – was music to Amy's ears. Her own accent – the same for which she had been so cruelly teased at school, and the cause of which had also accounted for her failure in her French oral at Little-go, and for Phil's sister June tactfully joining in in her solo when she first visited the Handys' home in Ballycool – had altered little. 'It's marvellous to see you too,' she murmured back, pliant in his embrace, concerned a little by his thinness. The receptionist, touched by such tenderness, looked down at her desk.

The wedding, next morning, was in St Andrews Church.

'Is it really you?' Phil whispered, when Amy joined him at the start of the ceremony; they had spent the night in different hotels. Amy smiled at him, while thinking how frail and handsome he looked in his white tropical suit. Two memories flashed through her mind. The first – she quickly quashed it – of the tramp and his mutterings in the Dublin Mountains; the second, of a remark by Phil about marriage. Well you're not stotious now! she thought. To Phil, Amy had never looked lovelier: fresh and youthful, and wearing the white, Shantung silk frock she'd picked up in Georgetown for next to nothing. Her bog-oak necklace, auburn hair, and ankle-flattering T-strap shoes – she'd bought those in Dublin – complemented the dress to perfection.

Mackenzie and Hank Borden, both of whom had travelled to Penang independently of Phil, witnessed the signatures. One of them gave Amy away, though for the life of her she could not have said which: walking down the aisle had been like a dream – unbelievable.

It was no dream.

Neither was the night of lovemaking that followed it… a night when, like a mighty river that has been diverted from its course is later returned to it, to seep through cracks and crevices, moistening and renewing, all Phil and Amy's holed-up passion found release. In a slow, sensuous, outpouring of emotion, old flash-points were reignited, and savoured anew with new ones. Finger- and tongue-tips traced and retraced lines, swells, curves and grooves…eliciting shudders and jerks here…arousing and slaking there…never quite fulfilling till, in a delirium of love, the newly weds climaxed. Then did it all again before dawn.

Lovemaking apart, the two weeks honeymoon was low key. Phil's health precluded hectic sightseeing, and he felt awkward taking Amy to places he had first visited with Helen. This last surprised him, as his original decision to marry and honeymoon in Penang had been taken on the grounds that it would have been ridiculous not to because of a one off fling there with another woman. Now, visiting places like the little street in Georgetown, where Amy admired an exact replica of the charm bracelet he had bought Helen – 'Sure bracelets like that, Amy, are churned out by the dozen,' he said, 'How about this unusual peacock brooch?' – made him think again. Even Kek Lok Si and the Kling Mosque could wait for another day. 'Sure Malaya's awash with such places of worship,' he said, brushing them aside too.

Amy, who had not yet adjusted to the heat and appreciated Phil's need for a rest, went happily along with his suggestions. In the evenings they went dancing at Runnymede, and to a concert or two. By day they lazed at the E and O, whose plush interior, and beautiful waterfront gardens made the perfect honeymoon setting. One moment would prove particularly memorable for Amy. It was when, shaded by palms, bathed in the scent of jasmine, jacaranda and Bougainvillea, within sight of Georgetown's busy docks and roads, Phil told her, from the depths of his heart, and in the immortal words of the Rubaiyat, '…Here with a Loaf of Bread beneath the Bough, A Flask of Wine, a Book of Verse, and Thou Beside me singing in the Wilderness, And Wilderness is Paradise enow…' – he loved her.

What he did not tell her, in the gardens or anywhere else in Penang, was about Helen Castle. To have done that in such surroundings appeared tantamount to inviting a fall from a merry-go-round by unfastening one's safety belt; or from cloud nine by invoking the rain. He would tell her in Siam.

◇

In Siam, however, his affair with Helen seemed like a total irrelevance and, eight weeks on, delighted to be shot of Bangkok – a little later than expected as their home in Malaya was late being vacated – he and Amy travelled to Perlemban. Maybe, he thought, the Castles will have moved on; people did that in the colonies, some went back to their roots.

Chapter Seventeen

State capital of one of the west coast Federated Malay States, Perlemban had sprung up in the eighteen eighties, like an American frontier town, on the back of tin-mining; much of it was actually built on the levelled sites of worked-out mines. Plenty of mines were in full production though, along with the region's rubber plantations and paddy fields. The colony was well ordered and its DA (District Administrator) rightly proud of it. Recently, a quota system, or cut back policy, had been introduced to offset the worst effects of glutted tin and rubber markets, and falling prices. Some of the planters and miners ('quota busters' they were called) were trying to get round the system, so constant supervision was required by the DA and his right hand man, Major Martin, the Head of Police.

King's, the school to which Phil had been posted – as Head of Maths (head of something at last!) and Assistant Headmaster – was much younger than the town. It catered for Coloureds – the brightest fourteen to fifteen year old boys, selected from the Government English Schools to sit the British Intermediate and Higher Cambridge Examinations. White Perlembans – British public school and army people mostly – had their children educated in the UK. King's headmaster was called Captain Dyson.

On arriving in the town, the Handys were met by Captain Dyson's Malay *syce* (chauffeur). Lazily he drove them in his boss's Chevrolet to their bungalow in Kampong Baru, where most of the whites lived; the natives had their own kampongs. The *syce* unloaded the car, and before leaving, told Phil *'Tuan* Dyson' would be round in the morning to give him a full briefing. A Malay boy, who had already emerged from the house, carried the luggage inside.

A first glance at their home told Phil and Amy it more than came up to expectation. Minimally furnished (they could add to that), its main attractions for Amy (she still found the heat trying) were its sitting room's cool-tiled floor, and a shaded veranda overlooking the garden. As well as the boy, a cook and gardener had been laid on. A *syce* would follow, when a promised car – a small Singer – arrived.

As the Handys settled in, this or that colonist popped in to welcome them; no one stayed more than a few minutes so as not to upstage Captain Dyson. To Phil's relief, the Castles were not among the callers. What he would have done if they had been he didn't know and reckoned the sooner he told Amy about Helen the better. That said, it seemed a pity to risk spoiling their arrival in Perlemban if the Castles no longer lived there. Hopefully Dyson's visit would reveal something. It did, and its brevity ensured the revelation would not be long in coming.

The Headmaster, a bachelor in his late forties, arrived bang on time. Dressed in military khaki – shorts and short-sleeved shirt – his every move and utterance were stamped with parade ground precision. After some perfunctory introductory remarks in the hall, he seated himself in the Handys' cool-tiled sitting room and took instant command of the conversation. Staccato style, and with the odd appraising glance or stretch-band smile at Amy, he gave her and Phil a run down on school and colony. 'I'll be throwing you in at the deep end, Handy,' he said, when he finished his comments on King's. 'Off to the hill-station tomorrow – short break. You'll have full control, old boy, so take no guff from anyone – native or colonial!'

Phil moved to interject: though honoured to be entrusted with full control so early, he was a little concerned about the assumption of so much responsibility in strange surroundings. The Head choked him off. 'Mind you,' he said, almost without a break, 'natives here: a pretty submissive bunch! Nothing like the Indians! Or Irish! Here, they have a sneaking admiration for British values – and exercise their *own* division of labour! Malays – a lazy lot – collar the soft option… minor officials, *syces*, houseboys, *ahmas* [nursemaids]… that sort of thing. Chinese aren't complaining! They're happy in the world of small business. Indians take what's left – hard labour mostly. Makes life relatively easy for us, I'm bound to say. Major

Martin, our Head of Police – deuced fine fellow – would be the first to second that. You'll meet him and everyone else at the Caldwells – the DA and his wife, that is. They're throwing a party for you. I'll be sorry to miss it. We're a friendly lot – Castles particularly so, and more your age than the rest of us. On long leave at present, I'm afraid – back end of August.' The Captain stopped talking.

Anxious to fill the silence – hearing the Castles' name made him more uncomfortable than he'd expected – and still a little concerned about his Headmaster's imminent leave, Phil said: 'You say you're going away, Sir?'

Getting to his feet, Dyson confirmed he was. 'You'll make a top-hole adjutant, Handy!' he added, heading briskly for the door. Amy stifled a snigger.

'What was so funny?' Phil asked when he'd shown the Headmaster out.

'Pompous ass,' Amy said through her titters. Phil smiled – weakly. Dyson's exaggerated Englishness and reference to 'the Irish' had put him in mind of something that had just begun to bug him. 'Maybe it'd be as well, Amy,' he said, 'if you toned down your Cavan accent a bit. The more we can fit in here the better.'

Amazed by the comment, Amy decided to ignore it: she and Phil had only ever joked about her accent in the past; a temporary irritant, she assumed now. 'Well I hope there are no more Dysons in Perlemban,' she said.

'I'm sure there aren't,' Phil rejoined. Helen Castle certainly isn't!, he thought.

But it's a long time – two whole months! – till the end of August!

Over the next few days, what with the novelty of everything, and being kept so busy at King's – being Assistant Headmaster and Head of Maths at the deep end was no doddle – Helen scarcely entered his head.

At the Caldwell's party, however, the name Castle cropped up so often, it was impossible to put her out of his head. Amy, too, heard the name repeatedly.

The party, like all the Caldwells', was hosted in their home – the largest and plushiest in Perlemban. Fountained lawns, jasmine-scented trellised walkways, a balcony and paved patio gave ample space for all – the men, tuxedoed; the women, exotically perfumed, and gorgeously gowned in silk, satin, and chiffon that floated, clung, caressed and revealed delectably. Painted lanterns lit up the scene, and from the not so distant jungle a ceaseless dissonance – cicadas and bullfrogs to the fore – of squawks, squeals, squeaks and screeches went unnoticed by all but the newly-arrived- in-Perlemban Handys.

In the course of the party, the DA, Chester Caldwell – late fifties, with a penchant for cheroots – took Phil to one side of the balcony and gave him a little pep talk; Chester did that to all new male colonists. Solid and important looking, the DA took his work seriously, modelling himself on 'Frank Swettenham' – a man he resembled physically to no mean degree as anyone who had seen him sitting beneath the portrait of his hero in Perlemban's Club House could vouch. Chester's main concern was drink, something he had already noticed Phil's fondness for. Avuncularly tapping his whisky glass with his cheroot, he warned Phil off it – 'In vino veritas, my boy' – just as Phil's Scottish doctor, Mercer had in Bangkok. More seriously he added – 'Your predecessor here fell prey to it. Poor fellow literally drank himself to death. Dr Castle could do nothing for him; first-class man, Castle.'

Meantime, Chester's expansive wife, Mable, showed off her bougainvillea to Amy and promised to teach her mah-jong, a game she excelled at and took almost as seriously as her position as DA's wife. 'The women enjoy it more than the men,' she owned, 'and some of us more than others! Helen Castle plays it on sufferance. She and her husband make a lovely couple, Mrs Handy – rock solid marriage.'

Equally enthusiastic about the Castles was the deuced fine Head of Police, Major Clive Martin. Handsome and ambitious, with a reputation for incorruptibility, the Major was at once officious and entertaining. His anecdotes enlivened every occasion, and he had just embarked on this evening's – based on an incident in the town that morning when a Malay housewife claimed she'd been sold a 'high' chicken by a Chinese trader – when Phil joined the bemused group of guests around him. 'The trader denied the charge of course,' the Major was saying, 'but anxious about his reputation offered the woman a replacement fowl or leg of pork. "No thanks," she said, pushing her half-plucked, putrid bird in his face, "I want my money back!" And who could blame her! Needless to say the fellow stood his ground and defended himself with the leg of pork when the woman laid into him with her bird. Well, you can imagine the rest.' The Major paused – deadpan, watchfully (he was always watchful) with his clingy wife, Miriam, at his side. A listener vocalised his imaginings – 'Passers by became involved, Major? Malays – supporting her? Chinese – him? Indians – undecided?'

'Indeed,' the Police Chief responded deadpan, 'forcing one of our local Malay lads to intervene! Unable to restore calm, however, he carted trader and housewife off to the station where Pincher here…' a disdainful look at his Assistant, Geoffrey Pincher, goosing a guest in the shadows accompanied this '…consigned both of them to the cells. What a good thing none of us was involved! Some of the injuries were quite nasty, I'm told. I'm sure we'll all be very glad when Dr Castle returns from leave. Speaking of whom…I hear you're a keen bridge player, Mr Handy. Well you'll get all the competition you need in that department from Dr Castle. He's an addict.'

By now, Amy had been cornered near one of the Caldwells' fountains by plump, prettily-painted Sonya Pincher, wife of the Assistant Head of Police, and was hearing how she and Geoffrey first met and why, despite Geoffrey's goosing, she remained faithful to him. Mrs Pincher liked to explain her situation to new female colonists before anyone else did. 'On the cliff-tops at Beachy Head, Mrs Handy,' she said, her eyes lighting up at the memory, 'that's where it all began. I was pregnant at the time – some cad I met at my coming out – and suicidal; my parents, you see, had disowned me. Then Geoffrey came by on his roan, heard my story, and offered to marry me. "It would be the first useful thing I've done in my life," he said. Well! Could you have resisted such gallantry, Mrs Handy? Or the prospect of a secure future in the East that followed?' Smiling, Amy shook her head. 'And neither could I,' Mrs Pincher went on, but with the light suddenly gone from her eyes. Lack of promotion in Perlemban, she explained, where a relative had procured Geoffrey the job of Assistant Head of Police, and Geoffrey's failure to give her a child of his own, had made him disillusioned with life and unfaithful to her. 'Helen Castle says I should get myself a boyfriend,' she concluded. 'But much as I like Helen – you'll like her too, Mrs Handy – I couldn't do that! If it wasn't for Geoffrey, goodness alone knows where my baby and I would have ended up – dead or in the gutter!'

Moved by Sonya's candidness, Amy sympathised with her and told Phil her story on the way home. 'They're a rum lot here,' she said at the end, 'but the Castles sound *really* nice – Helen especially!'

Hearing Helen's name on his wife's lips made Phil dreadfully uneasy: it was ridiculous as well as dishonest, he thought, not telling her he'd met Helen. He would do it now, this minute. Bolstered by booze, he stopped the Singer and put his arm round Amy. Looking into her eyes, he asked her if she was happy. 'Yes,' she said, happiness glowing from every pore. 'And you, Phil?' His disclosure died on his lips.

'More than I can say,' he said, and kissed his wife on the mouth. Bugger it, he thought restarting the Singer, it's ages till they return.

◇

August, though, came round quicker than Phil expected and, early that month, a restless night – the result, he knew, of the imminence of the Castles' return – persuaded him anew to make a clean breast of his and Helen's affair. It was now or never, he thought, as he got ready for work; if the denouement went horribly wrong, he could escape to King's and give Amy time to simmer down.

Seated on the veranda in readiness for breakfast, in his white linen trousers (shyness kept him out of shorts) and short-sleeved white shirt, he psyched himself up. Taking his diary – a BATC one Hank Borden had given him – from his pocket, he started thumbing through it. The payment of his servants held his attention: 'Cook, $30; boy, $15; *dhobi*, $3', he mumbled, flicking through the July – 'The liking for "Capstan" comes on when the lid comes off' – entries. (Liberally studded with the names of Company products, the diary also boasted a monthly memo to smokers.) '*Syce*, $25; gardener, $4...' He broke off when Amy appeared on the veranda. 'Did you ever imagine,' he said to her, overjoyed at how well she was taking to Malaya, 'we'd be able to afford servants like this?' A glance at their *syce* lazily polishing the Singer in the drive, and their Tamil gardener – at work since sunrise – weaving slowly among the bright yellow, orange and red cannas, and sweet-scented jacaranda, accompanied the question. 'I did not,' Amy replied, sitting down and doling out two hefty portions of papaya, her favourite fruit and helping herself to lemon juice before passing the jug to Phil. She looked lovely, he thought; this time of day suited her best. Optimum time too, he reckoned, for her to digest unsavoury news. Closing his diary he returned it to his pocket, and took a deep breath. Amy got in first.

'I've another lesson with Mah-jong Mable today,' she said perkily through a mouthful of fruit, 'Says she's going to teach me all the tricks of the trade!'

'Top-hole,' said Phil; already he and Amy – Amy's accent aside – were beginning to look and sound like hardened Perlembans. 'Mah-jong Mable – is that what you call her? I knew she was a whizz kid at the game...'

'Some kid!' Amy laughed. 'She's fifty if she's a day! To get back to the tricks of the trade...trouble is, I'm not so sure I want to know them. A hundred and forty-four pieces – or "tiles" as she insists on calling them – get on your nerves after a while. Give me bridge any day! Miriam Martin says the same. *She's* terribly smug, isn't she? Though I suppose with a husband like Clive – no offence, Phil! – she can afford to be. Unlike poor Sonya Pincher! Do you know what the ladies call Geoffrey?'

'No. What?'

'Pincher-bite-me.'

Phil laughed his head off at that. 'He hasn't tried anything on with you, Amy, has he?'

'Not likely. He'll get more than he bargained for if he does.'

'I can well believe it. And Dyson – has he made any advances since his return from the hill station?'

'No. And he'd better not. Ugh.'

'You do know what they call Dyson, don't you?' Amy shook her head.

'Chief poodle-faker.'

'Chief what?'

Phil explained, and seeing the look of disgust on his wife's face, added, 'Sure what else is a bachelor like him to do in a place like this?'

Amy wasn't amused. 'Adultery's the same by any name,' she said, '...loathsome. I can't wait for those Castles to come back from leave.'

Phil gave up. And as Amy checked her watch – 'Mustn't keep old Mable waiting!' she said, popping the last piece of papaya into her mouth – he knew he would never tell her. Hopefully (he had been thinking about this recently as a last resort) he would be able to have a quiet word with Helen before she and Amy met to remind her of what she'd said to him in Penang about their encounter there never having happened. If the worst came to the worst he would just have to tough it out. Amy would understand. She always did.

Between then and the Castles' return, Phil applied himself to the business of absorption in his adopted country; to becoming more British than the British themselves – something that was greatly facilitated by the nature of his job, the friendliness of other colonists, and the attractiveness of his and Amy's house in Perlemban. Together the Handys were putting their own stamp on the house. A picture or two here, photographs – like Phil's of his sister, June – there, books (English, Siamese and Malay) in every room, along with samples of native craftsmanship – rattan mats, colourful hand-woven carpets, padouk side-tables, hand-painted, tin ash trays, and ebony and ivory knick-knacks. Special prominence was given to Amy's picture, *Flaxfields*, and when visitors commented on it (and most did), Amy told them it reminded her of her home in Cavan. 'It's just like that on the estate,' she would say, not bragging, or trying to convey a false impression, but with a warm glow of pride.

Chapter Eighteen

The evening the Castles came back to Perlemban there was an extra buzz at the Club. Everyone felt it, which, given the nature of the place – the nub of Perlemban's social calendar – was only to be expected. At the Club – planters and miners, civil servants and company agents, doctors and lawyers, straights and odd-balls, whose only common feature was their colour, mingled in convivial, clubby surroundings; card sharps and sporty types, held out, often against desperate odds, for another hand, rubber, round or set. Newspapers and magazines (*The Times, Illustrated London News* etc) kept one up to date, six weeks in arrears, on England and the world as seen through the eyes of Fleet Street. Equally out of date hits from C.B. Cochren's Drury Lane spectaculars, played interminably on the Club's gramophone, kept dancers and party-goers on their toes (Saints' Nights were particularly boisterous) into the small hours. Above all, endlessly wagging, well lubricated tongues exchanged news and views on anything and everything from the depressing situation in Wall Street, and the fight against quota-busters nearer home, to the latest local gossip-gobbets which were latched on to and milked dry like a nipple by a hungry babe.

Tonight was no exception. As tongues wagged, and drinks flowed, a watchful (quota-busters could be anywhere) Head of Police, Major Clive Martin, entertained this or that group with his latest anecdote. His wife, Miriam, clung to him adoringly. The DA, Chester Caldwell, smoked his cheroots in the chair beneath the portrait of his hero Swettenham. His wife, Mable, circulated expansively. Captain Dyson philandered. Geoffrey Pincher goosed and plump, prettily-painted Sonya Pincher wondered if, after all, it might not be a good idea to help herself to a little adultery.

Seated at the bar with Amy, there was nothing Phil wanted more than to be an accepted part of this white Perlemban scene...to be seen as one of the Brits. Not the stiff upper lip, English variety like Dyson; just a British colonist spreading the British way of life in Malaya. Phil had no illusions about wagging tongues in the East and, even now, all this time and distance from Ireland, had the odd panic attack about his past there getting out. He wanted to be rid of it all – his humble origins, his parents' scrimping and scraping, his Irishness, the names Poynings and Crotchley. By and large he felt he had succeeded. Indeed, if the Castles had not been held up in the last part of their journey, forcing them to come straight from Perlemban Station to the Club, and rendering his hoped-for quiet word with Helen before Amy met her impossible, he could reasonably have claimed to be carefree. As it was, he was agitated, drinking more than usual, and pinning his hopes on Helen's sincerity and coolness. Whether or not she knew he was married and in Perlemban, he didn't know.

Amy felt happy. She put Phil's agitation down to the extra work Dyson was heaping on him, in particular – overall responsibility for the Cambridge classes at a time when it was doubly important for the boys to do well in their exams to maximise their chances of employment on leaving school. Also, Phil had volunteered to supervise the relaunch of the School magazine, King's Quarterly, previous efforts to get it off the ground having failed miserably. Seeing her husband so busy highlighted Amy's own lack of a job but neither that nor Phil's reluctance to start a family – she'd agreed with him to leave children till their next tour – caused her any regrets about coming East. Earlier in the day, she had written to Catherine who, unlike Henry and Harriet, wrote back, and unlike Eleanor, did so cheerfully. Writing to her brought home to Amy that she had not yet met anyone like her to befriend in the East: Sonya Pincher was too pitiable; Miriam Martin too smug; Mah-jong Mable too staid. She was pinning her hopes on Helen.

'That's them! Isn't it?' she said excitedly to Phil when the Castles came through the door and a first glimpse of Helen – tall, well-groomed, and wearing a stylish, yellow frock – told her she was nothing if not elegant. Phil swivelled round, the remains of a double whisky in his glass and too slowly to catch sight of the returnees before they were engulfed by other Club members.

Noticing the Handys on a limb, the DA, Chester Caldwell, brandished his cigar to announce above the clamour – 'And we've some newcomers for you to meet!' The hubbub subsided. Like a stage curtain, the crowd around the Castles parted, making them and the Handys visible to each other. Phil got to his feet, feigning ignorance of Helen. Amy took in some more of Helen – short, sleekly-waved, blonde hair; flawless, tanned skin; relaxed manner – and found the prospect of befriending her very pleasant indeed; her husband, too, appeared affable. Chester did the introductions, and as Amy shook hands with Helen, she noticed her charm bracelet and was glad Phil had dissuaded her from buying one like it in Georgetown. Then Helen held out her hand to Phil who, beneath a happy go lucky veneer, was getting more and more worked up. Something about the way Helen looked at him made his muddled mind imagine she was – intentionally or otherwise – about to spill the beans. Not wanting that, he shook her hand and, blushing, said awkwardly, 'Hello, again.' The two words electrified the room. Amy wondered if she'd misheard Phil.

Quickly, Helen took control. 'Hello, Mr Handy', she said, without a trace of embarrassment, 'I hardly recognised you out of whites.' Her manner was a measure of her coolness as the Handys' presence at the Club had been a total surprise to her. Smiling, then, and taking in in turn, her husband, the assembled company, Amy and Phil, she went on – 'He made up a four at tennis once with me and my friends in Penang. It seems a long time ago now – back in his bachelor days, Mrs Handy. I don't think we were ever properly introduced. How nice to meet you again! and to meet your wife!'

Helen could not have chosen her words better. Her tact, along with the rock-solid reputation of her marriage instantly defused the atmosphere; as Castles and Handys shook hands, the tension, if not *all* the speculation, went out of it.

For the remainder of the evening, Perlembans applied themselves to welcoming the Castles back. Though full of their vacation – in Yorkshire first, with Helen's relatives; London next, with friends of the Ripleys – the returnees were not sorry to be back. 'Weather diabolical,' Helen said. 'And bridge evenings,' Frank averred, 'quite spoiled by latest downturns in the stock market.' At the mention of bridge, someone said Dr Castle would have his work cut out to beat Phil at the game – a comment that led to fixtures being arranged between Castles and Handys not only of bridge but of tennis and golf too. [As well as bridge, Max Stone and his wife had introduced Amy to golf; she'd played with them at Killiney. Phil had taken the game up in Siam to prevent him 'having a liver'.]

Throughout all this, Amy found Helen and her husband, Frank, utterly charming, and was annoyed with herself for continuing to suspect foul play. She no longer believed Phil's agitation at the start of the evening was due entirely to pressure of work. Helen's bracelet, and the memory of Phil persuading her, Amy, not to buy one like it, puzzled her. When *exactly* had Phil and Helen met? Was it before or after his first letter to her from Bangkok? – or before, and after! Most crucially – why had he not told her about it when he'd been posted to Perlemban?

Driving home – a short run, ten minutes or so – along Perlemban's main highway, John Street, with only Phil for company, an annoyingly sozzled Phil at that, Amy's suspicions mounted. 'You really must learn to drive, Amy', she heard him say, half in earnest, half-jokingly, struggling to keep the Singer pointed in the right direction. She wasn't amused. The one time he had taken her out for a lesson he'd quickly lost patience when she'd stalled and crunched the gears, and replaced her at the wheel. As they'd left the Club Amy noticed Helen behind the wheel of the Castles' car – a Chevrolet, like Dyson's.

'Why didn't you tell me you'd met her?' she asked.

'It didn't seem important,' Phil replied, taken aback not just by the question but the abruptness of its delivery. As far as he was concerned the evening had been a whopping success. Amy, he felt, had been greatly taken with the Castles, and Helen's assurance to him in a quiet moment that her lips were sealed on the subject of their fling in Penang, had left him confident that episode in his life had been buried for good. An exhumation loomed.

'Well it does to me,' Amy said. 'It was more than a game of tennis, wasn't it?'

'Yes. But if you'd just let me explain...' Tired – he'd had too much to drink, and was beginning to feel threatened – Phil broke off... They had reached their house; he just wanted to get out of the car. Switching the engine off, he climbed out and went round and opened the passenger door. When he held out his hand to Amy she wouldn't take it, and as he followed her along their jacaranda-scented drive, the rigidity in her alarmed him. God, how he wished he'd told her about Helen sooner! It was too late now to go back; too far down the line to avoid disclosure. The jungle cacophony, cicadas and bullfrogs to the fore, roared in his ears; the hot, perfumed air stifled him; he swore under his breath. Ahead of him, Amy, numbed by a gathering sense of betrayal, noticed and heard nothing.

In their sitting room, whose cool-tiled floor did little to cool their rising emotions, Phil offered Amy a drink. She refused it. When he turned round from the cabinet, she was sitting in their cushioned, wicker settee – waiting. He sat down in a chair opposite her, and looked at her not looking at him. A padouk table with a painted, tin ashtray on it lay between them. In her duck-egg blue frock, slipping a little on the shoulders, and with her hair awry and shoes flung off, she looked, he thought, quite beautiful. The very idea that he should prefer Helen to her was sickening; the thought of losing her, terrifying.

Unsure about how and where to start, he offered her a cigarette. Coldly, and keeping her eyes averted from his, she refused it. If only I'd trusted her and told her sooner, he thought again, lighting up with the initialled lighter she'd given him for a long gone Christmas present; any other time would have been better than this. He took a gulp of whisky, and began, and between further gulps, and a refill, told her all he could decently tell her, not forgetting his purchase of the charm bracelet for Helen. Amy sat quietly, listening in disbelief. Phil could see it in her eyes – looking through not at anything; in her stillness, and tightened neck muscles; in her interlocked fingers pressed hard into her knuckles. He had never seen her like this before.

'Say something, Amy,' he said, convinced he had made a good case – the kind of case she would eventually understand and her common sense would lead her to accept – but worried by her looks and silence. 'I'm sorry I didn't tell you sooner…At the time, I thought we'd split up for goo…'

'I wish we had,' Amy broke in flatly.

Hearing her speak was a relief, even if what she said was unpalatable. Emotion, Phil decided, not common sense, lay behind it. She was deeply hurt; the one-man-woman thing was stronger even than he'd imagined. He felt desperately sorry for her. But for the life of him he could not see that he had done anything wrong, except not tell her sooner. He must tread warily, not push her. 'Don't say that, Amy,' he pleaded. 'Look at me and tell me you don't mean it.'

Reluctantly Amy looked at him and found herself, to her annoyance, feeling sorry for him. He had not been unfaithful to her – she knew that now. But he had slept with Helen, and kept it to himself knowing it was bound to come out in Perlemban. How could she live with it when it did? Why hadn't he told her? Not doing so was cowardly; as cowardly as his decision to quit Ireland. In both cases, she, not he, was the one who suffered most. Damn you, she thought, and looked away from him.

In the altercation that followed, Amy mellowed and hardened by turn – irrationally, it seemed to Phil, making it doubly hard for him (every ploy in his armoury was used) to get through to her. That each of them was breaking new ground compounded matters. Both had witnessed their share of domestic strife, but apart from their own bust up in the Dublin Mountains, and some tepid exchanges since, mostly about Phil's drinking, they had scarcely rowed at all and never about another woman or man in their lives.

'You're making something out of nothing', Phil said, clutching at the briefly glimpsed compassion in Amy's eyes. 'What happened between Helen and me was a one-off. I was lonely…she was there…you weren't.'

Hearing Helen's name on his lips set Amy off again. 'I wonder how you'd feel, Phil, if you suddenly found out *I'd* slept with somebody?'

'You didn't, did you?' he said, raising an eyebrow in the hope of raising a smile: past experience told him a touch of humour might not come amiss, and the thought of Amy in bed with Peter Pagley or Andy McPhearson was fanciful.

'Of course I didn't,' she said, crossly, 'but how would you feel if I had?'

'Unhappy.'

'Well, there you are. But *why* didn't you tell me when you knew you'd been posted to Perlemban?'

'I was going to. God knows I wanted to…' Sensing his sincerity was paying off, Phil pressed home his case. 'I was afraid of upsetting you and didn't want to lose you. The time never seemed to be quite right. I didn't think it matt…'

'Of course it matters,' Amy said, cross again. 'What kind of a laughing-stock do you think you've made of me? If I noticed something odd at the Club, others were bound to have done the same. And even if they didn't, *she's* bound to say something…'

'No, Amy. *She*…' deliberately, in another attempt to humour his wife, Phil imitated her tone '…won't say anything. We had a quiet word…'

'Did you now? And I wonder how many more of *those* you'll be hav…?'

'Stop it, Amy. You've got it all wrong.' Phil was beginning to lose patience. Amy's sarcasm was both hurtful and out of character. 'I love you… No other woman means anything to me… Don't let this come between us… It all happened so long ago… You and I weren't even writing to each other…'

At the mention of their letters, Amy's sense of betrayal was rekindled. Phil continued talking, but his words went over her head as touching lines and phrases from his letters (she'd kept every one) flooded into her mind. Lines and phrases that had meant so much to her then, but counted for nothing now. The whole of her married life counted for nothing. It was a sham. It was as if she'd won a major prize only to be told later that the real winner had lost out on a technicality…

'How could you, Phil!' she said, unlocking her hands and glaring at him hatefully, tears collecting in her eyes. The sudden change in her mood mystified him. Angered by it, and unsure how to handle the tears (he had little time for cry babies and had never had Amy down as one) he let her go on. 'It's almost as if you got me out here on false pretences. If you'd told me you'd been having nights of passion…'

'Jesus Christ, Amy!' he exploded – Whatever would she come out with next! – 'It was one short fling…'

'One, two, twenty – What's the difference? God, what an eejit I've been! You didn't by any chance make love to her in our honeymoon bed…?'

'Now you're being ridiculous. Of course I didn't. I told you we were at the Ripleys.' Exasperated, but determined not to lose control – to do that, he knew, would be fatal – Phil got up and refilled his glass, this time with soda water. Taking a deep gulp, he sat down again, and looked at his hurt wife's tearful face, and tried once more to convince her of his love. 'You must believe me, Amy… I love you… No one else… I'm sorry this thing ever happened… Don't let it come between us.'

As Amy continued to glower at him, something told Phil he was losing her. He had tried everything… appealed to every side of her – rational, compassionate, humorous, loving, forgiving; it was no good. Desperate to get through to her, he put his glass down on the padouk table, stubbed his cigarette in the ashtray and stood up with the intention of physically soothing her. But tiredness and too much drink had made him unsteady. As he walked round the table, he caught his leg on it and stumbled into the settee beside her, gripping her to regain his balance. 'Get off me,' she said, furiously, and gave him a hard shove knocking him against the arm of the settee. Badly shaken – he had never known her to resort to any kind of violence – he righted himself. 'Fuck it,' he said, 'if that's the way you want it, Amy, so be it. I've had enough.' Hauling himself to his feet, he gave the table a wide berth and stumbled off to bed.

Not sorry he had gone, Amy sat on – aggrieved, bitter, angry. What was the point of going to bed, she asked herself, when she knew she wouldn't sleep? As it was, she felt penned in. Bed – encased in netting, beside a sozzled Phil – would be suffocating. *Some*how, she must regain control, she thought; make sense of what had happened; decide what to do before calling it a day.

Looking around in search of answers, her eyes lit on a gecko. She followed it up and along the wall till it disappeared behind *Flaxfields*. She looked at the picture, and was struck as never before by its serenity; by the innocence of the little girls' faces among the flax blooms, and the kindness of the taller knickerbockered boy at the lakeside to the smaller. By the floating, bubbling clouds on high; the rolling hills and fish-rich lake – so like the ones that had enfolded her as a child, nurtured her through adolescence, set her free to roam, been there for her when she returned home. The blue, flax flowering at Shandoran would, once again, have come and gone. The harvest would be round the corner. Henry and Harriet, and Lottie, Luke and Billy would reap it, and life would go on on the estate as it had done for centuries…

Looking at the picture soothed and cleared Amy's mind. Phil had not, she reminded herself, been unfaithful to her. In all honesty she had no reason to believe he did not love her. Indeed, their lovemaking had got better, if anything, with time. And the Castles were extremely nice – their marriage was reputedly rock solid. Although a wonderful and unforgettable part of her life, she did not want to go back to Cavan; nor did she wish to return to Dublin. She had not run away to the East like Phil, and would not run away now. She wasn't a quitter. East was East, and West was West. Her home was in Perlemban and, 'for better or worse', with Phil.

Slowly, very slowly, Amy began to weigh things up. A kind of balance was restored in her head. In the smallest hours she went to bed.

Chapter Nineteen

In any other place than Perlemban, any other set of circumstances, Amy's weighing up might well have paid off.

For when all was said and done, she'd concluded, it was unreasonable of her to have expected Phil to remain faithful to her in the wake of their acrimonious parting in Dublin. Of course he could have given it more time. But loneliness had made him impatient, and if she had been similarly cut off from home, friends and family, she might have acted in the same way. He should have told her about the affair – though it was probably unfair to call it that; his own word 'fling' was more appropriate – if not before, then certainly after he'd been posted to Perlemban. Yet here again, his reasons for not doing so were understandable. Besides, even if he had told her, she knew it would not have deterred her from coming East. Underpinning all this, was her desire – she knew Phil felt the same – to make the East work. Thus far, it had worked; never before had she known him to be so content with his lot. Seeing him happy made her happy. Why should a one-off fling – yes, definitely a better word than affair – come between them? She would not allow it to and had every reason to believe, given Phil's love for her (in her heart she felt he loved her) that he would do the same.

But this *was* Perlemban – an isolated, colonial settlement; a closed, interdependent community. Within the colony's narrow confines, wrongs and perceived wrongs were not easily forgotten, they festered; affairs were encouraged, and misfortune more relished than pitied; Helen and Phil were here. Circumstance and chemistry, therefore, combined to thwart Amy and her weighing up.

◇

As everyone had predicted, the Castles – mid-thirties, a little older than the Handys – were indeed the perfect couple for Phil and Amy to make friends with. Golf, tennis and bridge with them was fun, and from such old hands as they, invites for further games, as well as for parties and dances were flattering. The more the four socialised, the more they discovered they had in common, not least their origins – Ireland, Yorkshire, London's East End, and not an English public school or army background between them. Amy found Frank – the oldest of the four – a little wooden on the dance floor and a little too inclined to get carried away by his hobby – Malaya's Minangkabau civilization. But he was kind and solicitous to her, especially on the golf course where he kept a wary eye out for the huge, black scorpions that lurked in the rough and terrified her. As for Helen, she was everything people said of her – witty, charming, friendly – and Amy found her better company than any other woman in the Kampong. OK, so her marriage was not as solid as she liked to make out. But her fling with Phil had been with an unmarried man, and a long way away from home. As far as Amy could tell, the last thing Helen wanted was to rock the Castles' marital boat by committing adultery in Perlemban. That men liked her was not her fault.

Thus reassured, Amy not only enjoyed the Castle-Handy foursome but quickly got into the habit of doing day to day things with Helen: shopping in John Street, Perlemban's main highway; or by mail order from Messrs White, Whitely and Co. Ltd. in Singapore and KL (Kuala Lumpur). Visiting the local library; attending Mable Caldwell's mah-jong sessions, which, thanks to Helen's presence, became less tiresome.

The foursome gelled, and nipped in the bud left-over speculation in the colony about Phil and Helen's encounter in the past.

Gradually, thought, its pattern changed.

On the golf course, where the Castles repeatedly outplayed the Handys, a swap of partners was called for the end result of which paired Helen, the best, with Phil, the worst. A similar pairing emerged at bridge, where Phil excelled and Helen struggled. This was a pity, as it threw Helen and Phil closer together nurturing whatever attraction they had for each other.

Helen had her own agenda, which Amy would discover in time. Phil got swept along. Enjoying and returning Helen's flirtatious glances; ribbing the little that remained of her Yorkshire accent and laughing when she mocked his Irishness. Praising her – 'Ripping drive, Helen,' – when she hit a cracker at golf (and to think he'd been so critical of sporty types in the past!), lapping up her praise – 'Philly, darling, you played that hand like a pro' – when he cleaned up on a daring no-trump bid at bridge. Meantime, Amy got stuck with Frank; kind, bespectacled Frank; the short straw. Scarcely able to detect the Yorkshire in Helen's accent, Amy suddenly became uncomfortably conscious of the Cavan in her own. Phil hadn't referred to it again. The once was enough. Not that she had any intention of toning the accent down; if it was good enough for Glenarkle it was good enough for the East.

Increasingly then, Amy was trapped in a foursome where all her husband's compliments and admiring glances were directed at Helen, making her, his wife, feel like an appendage. Flirting was not a crime; she was not above it herself. But because of what had happened between Phil and Helen in Penang, and the way she, Amy, had found out about it, she could not, no matter how hard she tried, turn a blind eye to their flirting now. More and more she felt, that like a tiny drop of moisture in a bowlful of sugar, Helen's presence in Perlemban was eroding her marriage. Putting the clock back was out of the question. Having gone along with everything in the early stages, pretending, as it were, Penang had never happened (Amy made such a good job of that that Phil, instead of being grateful, took it for granted), trying to reshape the pattern appeared petty. On the one occasion she took Phil to task, he choked her off with, 'Don't be stuffy, Amy! We must have some friends!' which stung her badly and persuaded her to back off.

Whatever line she took, backfired.

St. Andrew's Night – a first for her in the East – saw all of white Perlemban and every Scot in the vicinity – planters and miners mostly – at the Club. Knees, kilts, sporrans, flew high to the skirl of the bagpipes and, as usual, she and Phil were sharing a table with the Castles. A reel was in progress, and Phil, well-lubricated, had his arm draped round Helen's chair; neither he nor she liked Scottish dancing; nor did Dr Castle, to whom dancing of any kind was a chore. Which left Amy, who liked reels and jigs, was bored with Frank and sick of watching Phil and Helen flirting, wishing someone – preferable not Phil's Headmaster, Captain Dyson, or the Assistant Head of Police, Geoffrey Pincher – would invite her on to the floor. She fancied a twirl with Geoffrey's boss, the Major – a man every woman in the room fancied but whose integrity and ambition made him as unlikely to dabble in adultery as a hardened recidivist in an honest living. Not that Amy was looking for adultery; just a mild flirtation to make Phil sit up. Earlier in the day he'd really annoyed her when, hunting for her ball on the golf course, she'd almost trodden on a scorpion. 'It's not a bloody landmine, Amy!' he'd said, irritated when she screamed.

'I'm lucky to be here at all, you know,' he was saying to Helen now. 'The Chinese laundry-man was late returning my tuxedo…'

'Oh you should have seen him,' Amy chipped in, desperate to attract some at least of his attention. '"I'll brain him," he kept saying, prancing up and down the sitting-room drinking more whisky than was good for him.'

'Just as well the laundry-man arrived when he did!' Helen said, tapping his glass in a mild reproof. He smiled at her, making Amy wince: a frown was what she'd have got. Welcoming the intervention of Frank – 'Better at laundering than fighting!' he said, uncharacteristically making everyone smile – she endeavoured to broaden the conversation to distract Phil and Helen from each other. 'Can anyone tell me,' she asked, 'what the Japanese are up to in Manchuria?'

Eager to satisfy her curiosity, and passionate about the rise and fall of all races and civilisations, not just the Minangkabau, Frank answered her. Frank liked Amy, thought he and she got on splendidly and was not at all put out by his wife's flirtations.

'Oh I think it's been on the cards for a long time,' he said. 'The East has always been a good hunting-ground for the West – right back to the days of da Gama and the Portuguese. The Japs are cottoning on now. What's sauce for the goose, you know! It's difficult to say what exactly they're up to, but if it's China as well as Manchuria they want, they'll have their work cut out. I'm not saying they aren't a match for the Chinese. They are. Their war in the eighteen nineties proved that. It's others – ourselves, the French, Russians and Americans they'd have trouble with. Everyone wants his place in the sun now!'

'And none more so than the Land of the Rising Sun!' quipped Phil, to the delight of Helen and amusement of Caldwells and Martins, sharing a table next door. The Head of Police, Major Martin turned round.

'I blame Mahan,' he said, alert as ever for signs of lawbreaking in his patch. Recently, the activities of some upstate planters had aroused his suspicions; the Major always got his man. 'His book – *The Influence of Sea Power upon History 1660-1783* – is as relevant today as it was pre war. 1890, I think, it first appeared. There's a copy in the library for anyone who's interested.' The Major spoke with authority, as well he might, being a not infrequent borrower from Perlemban library's not inconsiderable military and naval section; 'nowadays, every Tom, Dick and Harry feels entitled to naval pre-eminence.'

'Sadly, yes,' agreed the DA, Chester Caldwell. 'If we're not careful we'll be back in the bad old days when Dutch, Spanish, French and ourselves fought it out for supremacy at sea.'

'Long live the Pax Britannica!' said Phil, raising his glass, pleasantly surprised by how genuinely British, English almost! he felt; even Dyson had stopped making digs at him about the Irish. Being on such good terms with the Castles, Phil reckoned, had helped his cause. It was a shame – and so unlike her – Amy was so censorious about his friendship with Helen; everything else in his life was top-hole. 'Palmerston had the right idea,' he went on – 'A top dog that holds the ring fairly!'

'Well said,' said Helen, to an indulgent smile from him, and general laughter. 'God help us if the Nips ever get hold of the reins!'

Unable to think of anything smart to say (watching Phil and Helen flirting put her on the back foot), Amy wished more strongly than before that someone would take her on to the dance floor where a 'Highland Fling' had followed the reel. Chester, meantime, had picked up on Helen's comment. 'Thankfully we have little to fear from them,' he said. 'If they expand a bit in Manchuria, it will be no bad thing. At the very least, keep the Bear at bay!' No one dissented from this and the cross-table exchange dried up.

By now, Phil's arm had moved to Helen's flawless, tanned shoulders. Occasionally he toyed with the strap of her flattering yellow dress; yellow suited her, she wore a lot of it. Or with her sleekly waved, short blonde hair, or double rope of pearls. Nothing improper, but as irritating to Amy as Frank's embarkation on the progress of a Minangkabau Show House in the Public Gardens; its Minangkabau civilization was one of Malaya's most prized, and the authorities in Perlemban had asked him to oversee the project. 'It should be ready for viewing by the end of the year, Amy,' he said. 'Well worth a visit. Did you know the word Minangkabau means buffalo horn...?' Amy shook her head '...That's why the roofs of their houses were turned up at the corners. Just like this!' Unfunnily, Frank demonstrated. Amy forced a smile. The subject, interesting enough in itself, bored the pants off her at a time like this. And when a big, Scottish voice boomed over her shoulder – 'Fancy a twirl, Amy?' – she smiled her apologies to Frank and went off to the dance-floor with Hamish McNaughton, an upstate planter and relative newcomer at the Club, who had taken an instant liking to her.

Two hours later, she was still with him, whooping it up with reels and jigs. Kilted, sporraned and carroty haired, he was not her type, but he was friendly without being pushy, and admired her hair and freckles, and her bog-oak necklace which she hadn't worn for some time but had put on tonight because it felt homey. Out of the corner of her eye she could see Phil looking at her – not enviously, unfortunately, but disapprovingly, as were some others. She didn't care.

As the revels neared their end, she had no one to blame but herself when she missed the last dance with Phil. One of their little rituals, it had held till now. Quietly seething – why couldn't he have waited for her? It was a foxtrot, his favourite! – she allowed herself to be propelled stiffly round the room by Dr Castle whom she couldn't, without rudeness, ignore at this juncture, while Phil danced with Helen.

After the dance, she told Phil he was too drunk to drive, and that she fancied some fresh air. She still hadn't learned to drive. As they walked home along John Street – smiling and waving goodnight to this or that passing carful of revellers – the space between them on the path felt like a mile. Their silence got to Phil first.

'I wish you hadn't made such an ass of yourself with McNaughton,' he said tetchily. 'You do know what they say about him, don't you?'

'No?' Amy's tone was defiant.

'Well for starters – Major Martin suspects him of quota-busting.'

'Is that so? – And for seconds?'

'It's not funny, Amy. Rumour has it he's also touched with the tarbrush…'

'The what?'

Impatiently (the Castles had just driven past, Helen behind the wheel) Phil explained. 'God, Amy, you're such an *ingénue*!' he added.

And Helen's not, I suppose! Amy thought, remembering once more his reaction to hers to the scorpion. She bit her tongue. Silence resumed, to be broken again by Phil. 'And I

wish...' (Amy thought he was going to refer to her accent) '...
you wouldn't wear that *thing*', he said, irritably.

'What?' Amy asked, genuinely puzzled.

'The beads,' Phil said disparagingly.

Amy could hardly believe her ears. Deeply hurt – comparing
her most treasured piece of jewellery to a rosary! – she selected
her pronoun carefully, ignored Martins and Caldwells as they
drove past and said quietly, 'I thought you liked it?'

'Well I don't any more.'

'Why?'

'It's too rustic.'

'And Helen's not!' Amy said, unable this time round to contain
her indignation.

'I'm surprised at you,' Phil snapped. 'Jealousy doesn't become
you.'

Amy smarted. Had she opened her mouth then she knew she
would regret it.

Chapter Twenty

The following morning, after a sound night's sleep, Phil went off to work as though nothing had happened. As he saw it, nothing had happened: he had disburdened himself of a couple of irritants and warned Amy off McNaughton who was unsuitable company for her. What did she think she was doing anyway, cavorting with a bloke like that while criticising *his* friendship with Helen? It wasn't as if he had designs on Helen…though she was damned attractive! Amy was doing herself a disservice behaving the way she was. Maybe she had just reached her crisis in the East? If so it would pass; her surety and resilience would see her through. Or would they?

Not for the first time this question crossed Phil's mind. Not in any wishful-thinking sense; more a perversely curious one. Would Amy's oneness with herself and her surroundings – that oneness which had eluded him for so long but was not so elusive now – hold firm in all circumstances? If he was right about its origins, she was probably missing her job; but with none of the other wives in Perlemban working this couldn't amount to much and, in time, a family would fill the void. More problematical, he reckoned, would be a serious downturn at Shandoran – something that did not seem wildly unlikely – especially in these difficult times – given all that Amy had told him about Henry and Harriet's stewardship of the estate. Maybe she should put less store by it – look less at her picture, *Flaxfields*, from which of late she seemed to be deriving a lot of comfort. But even if things got bad at Shandoran – at this point, not liking the way his thoughts were going, Phil changed tack – they were bound to recover, Amy said they always did; and she still had her God. Yes, her surety would see her through. He certainly had no intention of changing his lifestyle. His work, including the extra responsibilities, was tickety-boo. The school magazine, King's Quarterly, had taken off in a big way, proof positive that a well-read specialist in Maths was more than up to a literary challenge; a few had doubted he could succeed. The Cambridge boys, many of whom contributed to the magazine regularly – their articles on English writers and statesmen; Dickens, Coleridge, Macaulay, Raffles, Cromwell... had impressed him greatly – were working hard for their December exams. No – his lifestyle was perfect. For Phil, Perlemban was the life.

Amy's day began differently. She too had slept soundly, tiredness had seen to that, but as soon as she woke the words 'rustic' and '*ingénue*' came to mind. They were only words, she knew, not sticks or stones, but the more she thought about them – all that morning, the following day, and in the weeks and months ahead – the more significance they accrued. Compared with Helen she was a greenhorn to Phil.

The revelation was a body blow. For right from the start, from the moment she and Phil had set eyes on each other – notwithstanding differences of background, temperament, interests and convoluted fortunes – they'd been entirely compatible; the best things since bicycles for each other. And Helen notwithstanding, Amy had continued, deep down, to feel this; she and Phil loved each other for what they were. Now, as suddenly as the rains came in Perlemban, it was no longer so.

From here, it was but a short step for Amy to ask herself – Does he love me at all? Had she challenged him she knew what he would have said, and probably meant – Of course I do, Amy. He had not slept with Helen (Amy was certain of this) since the Castles return to Perlemban. She was less certain now about whether he would like to sleep with Helen – that was, if Helen would let him! To Amy, Helen remained something of a mystery. She no longer took holidays on her own – a bad sign. Yet while not discouraging Phil, she did not lead him on either – something which, on top of her charming personality, and the still rock-solid reputation of her marriage in Perlemban, made it relatively easy for Amy to remain friends with her.

All that, however, missed the point. The point was – was it possible to love a part of somebody... a part of their real being? Amy did not think so. For her, love was absolute, indivisible.

When she gave herself to Phil, she gave herself totally. If he no longer loved her for what she was, she could no longer do this. Whatever prompted him to make love to her – lust, duty, habit, convenience, or love as he saw it – didn't matter. To the accompaniment of ever-more lurid images of his and Helen's lovemaking in Penang – Amy got the feeling Phil would have preferred to be in bed with Helen than her.

It followed – from being something enjoyable and fulfilling, an essential part of their relationship – sex, for Amy, became a chore; she endured it. She did so not so much to keep the peace, as to avoid making things worse. For spatting between her and Phil (not publicly, neither wanted that) became the norm, with ever uglier words being uttered, which, like footprints set in cement, could not easily be erased.

Had Amy had something meaningful to do, she might not have taken Phil's remarks so much to heart. But teaching was out of the question, there were no opportunities, and Phil was dead against her working anyway. It was a matter of pride to him. None of the white women worked, except on a voluntary basis, like in the library, and the one occasion she mentioned helping out there, his reply – 'It's a bit infra dig, Amy' – made her drop the idea so as not to antagonise him. Gossip, shopping, mah-jong and sport, therefore filled her days; bridge, and carousals in Club or Kampong, her evenings. Never a bookworm, there was a limit to what she could read. The servants did every chore in the house, and Phil's inflexibility on the family front meant that she couldn't even be getting on with that.

Confiding in someone might have helped too. There was no one – least of all Phil. He would have shrugged her off, told her she was jealous of Helen and imagining the rest; they had never discussed sex, just done it. More crucially, Amy could not conceive of a situation where she would risk undermining his happiness by telling him about her own wretchedness. He loved Perlemban so much – his job and the way of life there; the romance of being in the East and able to support her; the Irish thing no longer bothered him, the names Crotchley and

Poynings were distant memories. So although there were times when she wanted nothing more than to put her head on his shoulder and for him to put his arm round her and say – What is it, Amy? Tell me, and let me help you; other times when she wanted to cry out – I loath this place, Phil! Can't you see what it's doing to me? – She couldn't – wouldn't – do either. For the rest – her 'best friend', Helen Castle, was out of the question as a confidante even though the two continued to do day-to-day things together. Miriam, Sonya and Mable were no good either; nor was writing home: Henry and Harriet hadn't answered her letters yet and were unlikely to do so now. Eleanor's response was predictable. ['Don't come crying to me, Amy, when things go wrong!' she'd said on Amy's last visit to Knockmore. Typical, Amy had thought.] Reading about Catherine's fulfilled life with Neil (a baby was on the way), and Lucy's with her taximan, Jo Heggerty (they were still single), only made Amy more dissatisfied with her own and less inclined to confide in them. The three-month gap between writing and receiving a reply didn't help. Pride, too, played its part in Amy's reluctance to share her worries, as did her firm conviction that talking about them would only make things worse, in that people would be pointing the finger. Finally, never one for praying when things went wrong – to Amy that had always seemed like making use of God, who was no more responsible for our ill than our good fortune – Amy found the highway to Heaven as unappealing in her predicament as packet steamers on the high seas.

Thrown back on her own resources, she became resentful, disillusioned and introverted. When alone she moped about, churning over her lot; in company she continued to put up a front; scissored mentally in her slough of despond, she sometimes wondered if she was going mad. Despairingly, she would look at *Flaxfields*. When all else failed, it succoured her…much as pulling the bedclothes over her head during her first terms at St Hilda's to shut out the present and think of home had. Dreamily she would stare at the picture, and let her thoughts meander where they would, slip-slide away to the hills, lakes, and flax fields round Shandoran; to the estate's long buttercupped grass, and shady bluebell glades; to diminutive streams, and cool translucent pools. *Flaxfields* became her escape route… her magic carpet, whisking her away in an instant from her grey, insubstantial life in Perlemban to the vibrancy of what had gone before; above all, to Shandoran, where the ideal was slowly subsuming reality in Amy's mind.

Needless to say, her looking at *Flaxfields* irritated Phil, on top of all the other bits of her that irritated him. 'What is it about that thing that so fascinates you?' he once asked her in the wake of a spat. Her answer – 'Don't you believe in the innocence of youth?' – ignored his use of the word 'thing' for fear of rekindling the spat. 'Believe,' he scoffed. 'Why do we have to believe in anything, Amy? Why can't we just think and do.' Fine for you, she thought, glad she hadn't tried to convey what really drew her to the picture.

But just as her carpet carried her away, so it brought her back. Back to the here and now; the here and now that pressed in, more vacuous than ever; the here and now she longed to be shot of, but could see no way out of. *She* wasn't a quitter.

◇

How much longer can I keep things to myself? she wondered, lying back on her sitting-room's cushioned, bamboo *chaise longue*, a cigarette in one hand, a fan, waved intermittently, in the other. The rains were due. It was St Patrick's Day – her first (she'd spent the previous one on the Prins), Phil's fourth, in the East – and Catherine had sent a letter and card, and a little sprig of shamrock; a nice touch, Amy thought. Along with some good news (Catherine and Neil had a daughter), there was some worrying news about Neil's brother's plans in the East – news Amy decided to keep to herself. Telling Phil would only upset him; he could do nothing about it, but would be quick to point out that had it not been for her, Amy – Catherine, Neil and the brother would have had no idea about his whereabouts in the East. The letter, card and shamrock were beside Amy on a

207

small japanned table that she and Phil had bought during a short break with the Castles in Port Dickson. Also on the table, were a glass of gin and tonic; of late, a morning tipple helped Amy through the day; a prettily painted ashtray; Phil's copy of 'War and Peace' in which, like Tolstoy's armies, Amy had got bogged down, and her scrap-book, in which she intended mounting her shamrock. Though the morning was well advanced, she was still in her kimono. It was a beautiful, turquoise silk one, part of a trio (a fan, and mules made up the rest) she had got by mail order from Messrs White, Whitely and Co. Ltd. in Singapore; tassel-sashed, it had a large, gold-embroidered dragon on the back. There was nothing in particular about the morning to indicate that it would be any different from the previous or following mornings.

Amy sighed. What's happening to me, she wondered, putting her fan down and helping herself to another mouthful of g and t. What in the name of God am I doing here? Let's face it – I never really wanted to come East, never really wanted to give up my job. For what would have been the point of all those years of education if the end result was to be nothing more than this – a limbotic existence in a tittle-tattle society geared to the interests of men. My degree – the one thing that sets me apart from the other women – means nothing here; it's as useful as chopsticks with stirabout. I'm a fish out of water, a bird with clipped wings, a tethered beast.

Then she thought about the other women in the Kampong and wondered if any of them felt like her. They must do. If they could settle here, why couldn't she?

It was no good. Amy felt herself getting hotter and hotter, more and more steamed up. If only the rains would come, she thought, taking another drink and a pull on her cigarette. A burst of fanning tired her wrist. As she rested her fan on her tummy, she looked at *Flaxfields*, and a deep longing filled her soul for the cool, turfy breezes licking in off Cavan's lakes and lapping round its hill sides. For the freshness of changing seasons; for April showers, the scrunch of autumn leaves, the

East Pier's tangy salt-air. For her old life-style – her job and getting involved in what mattered. At Glenarkle, another end of term would be approaching, another holiday be in sight. At Shandoran, planting and sowing would be well advanced; today, the seventeenth of March, was the deadline for potatoes; the flaxseed would not be far behind. Then the beautiful blue flax flowering – so vivid but fleeting... like her and Phil's love for each other.

Saddened by her thoughts, Amy finished her cigarette. Reaching sideways, she stubbed it in the ashtray and picked up her scrapbook – the same prize nature project that had put paid to teasing at St. Hilda's and paved the way for happier schooldays. A whole long summer she'd spent collecting samples for it, and later collating, mounting and labelling them and, wherever possible, listing alternative names and notes on special features. Not a single nook or cranny of Shandoran had escaped her eyes as she'd scoured it for her specimens. Now, page-flipping, she retraced her steps on the estate – through its woods and dells with their wild basil and marjoram, white bryony and straggly herb-bennet (blessed herb or wood-avens). Across its bogs – whose myrtle and nodding water-avens were displayed alongside Henry's dainty sprigs of asphodel and bog rosemary; around its lily-bestrewn lakes, its white ramsons-carpeted hazel coppice, its rough ground ablaze with red poppies. Laden river banks and ditches (forget-me-nots, angelica, ragged robin, red campion and crane's-bill) slowed her progress; as did heavily bedecked roadsides and hedges (pansies and tansy; trefoils, cinquefoils and milfoils – to name but a few). And still the meadows remained – knee-deep in shepherd's purse (pickpocket) and full-bladdered campion; in knapweed, oxeyes and scabious; in goat's beard, meadow saffron (age old curative for gout) and much, much more.

For a brief spell, Amy's troubled nebulous existence was entirely subsumed by an idyllic, idealised past that watered her desiccated soul.

Coming back to the present, though, was as disorientating for her as adjusting to a blinding light: she felt more alone and hard done by than ever.

What right had Phil, she asked herself, to put her in this position? If anyone should have been discommoded it should have been him. Not a charitable thought, she knew, but there in her mind, along with all its concomitants, adding weight to her sense of injustice. She had seen it coming all along; advised against it repeatedly, just as she advised now against his heavy drinking. He wasn't listening then, or now; had gone his own way, expecting her to fall into line. He must have known she wouldn't take kindly to idleness. She'd always been a doer. Inaction on this scale, in this insect-, scandal-ridden hothouse, was slowly driving her crazy. And to think he couldn't see it! Only the other day, she'd again raised the subject of helping in the library; Mable had said there was a vacancy there. Again he'd cold-watered it; she was still thinking about it. But maybe he could see it! If so – how could he be so indifferent! So monumentally selfish! So ineffably callous! So infatuated with Helen or bent on proving his theories about marriage right, he couldn't see how upset this and everything else was making her, his wife! He'd be in any minute now for tiffin; full of himself and his job – a job which, as far as she could see (Dyson wasn't *that* hard a taskmaster!) made light of the white man's burden: playing ring-master in Malaya was a puppet show compared with the mighty Raj circus. All along, he'd implied 'going East' did not have to mean for ever. 'Two tours at most, Amy, if we don't like it.' All along, he'd *known* it *would* be for ever (in the East, spending, not saving, was the order of the day) and that he'd end up like his hardened old mates Hank Borden and Mackenzie in Siam, or like Dyson and the rest in Perlemban. She'd a good mind to tell him what Catherine had told her about Neil Crotchley's brother's plans: having tired of the Hong Kong police, the brother was thinking of transferring to Malaya. Maybe the East would appear less rosy to him then!

The Singer pulled up outside. Amy heard the engine die, and the car door slam. Singing and humming a recent Coward release – 'In Rangoon, where the heat at noon…' – Phil came bounding up the veranda steps into their sitting room. 'Hello there,' he called, heading for the drinks' cabinet. 'How are things? De dum diddle…'

'Bromidic,' Amy replied.

The word, one of his, was apt, but as soon as she uttered it, and saw his back stiffen, she regretted using it. He turned round, with a Pimm's for her and Singapore Sling for himself, and returning to the veranda, said, irritably – 'It's cooler out here.'

Listlessly Amy got up, and slipping her feet into her mules, followed him outside. As she sat down, he wondered what she was wearing under her kimono, and wished the conversation had got off on a different footing. That something was the matter with her was not in doubt. For weeks, months even, he'd been noticing little things – picking at her papaya; tardy dressing; dragging her heels on Club nights; lacklustre sex… not at all like her! But, unwilling (Amy's attitude towards him and Helen was unreasonable) or unable (he was just as trapped as she in the East, albeit more usefully) to do anything about it, kept hoping she would cope. His back stiffening had resulted from his doubts about this. Looking at his wife, he felt both irritated with and desperately sorry for her. Why couldn't she, he wondered, make more effort to fit in? She *would* come round in time. Meantime, a little tact on his part might help. 'Mm… bromidic,' he said, 'I'm sorry you feel that way.'

Amy didn't reply at once. She was examining her fan. It had an ivory handle and gold struts, and when open, displayed a gold dragon – like the one on the back of her kimono; she knew the pattern well. Touched by Phil's sympathy, she said truculently, without taking her eyes off the fan – 'Well I don't always, Phil, but I do now.' It was the sort of Irishism he understood. It made him uncomfortable but gave him the feeling she had definitely reached her crisis and just wanted to unload. He would help her. 'What's at the root of it, Amy?', he asked. 'Are you missing your job? Or is the heat getting to you?'

Surprised and a little embarrassed by his concern (she could hardly have expected him to include Helen or a family) Amy was tempted to make light of the whole thing but decided against. In for a penny, a burden shared...

'Both and more,' she said, looking straight at him, fully intent on opening up. His eyes stopped her: 'Don't do this to me, Amy!' they said, and to have put him on the spot, suddenly became unthinkable to her; hurting him by telling him about Neil's brother's plans, even less thinkable. Robustly she improvised. 'And you needn't ask me if I've tried reading, Phil. I have. I know all there is to know about Malaya, Raffles and Swettenham, and more about the Min-bloody-ankabaus than Frank Castle. I've even re-read *Ulysses*! *And* thoroughly enjoyed it! So there! Put that in your pipe and smoke it.'

Phil laughed at that. 'And one more thing,' Amy said, buoyed by her outburst and his response to it, 'I've decided...' (she had just this minute decided) '...to help out in the library. Mable said there was a vac...'

'You're too late,' Phil broke in, though not spitefully. 'Helen's filled it.'

'Oh.' Amy's disappointment was palpable. 'Maybe something else'll come up,' she said, desperate for him to say something helpful. But thinking the worst was over, and that a return to levity would be best, he took a sip from his Singapore Sling, smiled his heart-stopping smile and said, 'Well thank goodness you're not expecting *me* to bail you out.'

That did it. Amy saw red – flaming canna-red; the kind of red that opened the flood gates – overrode understanding, and made her want to hurt Phil. 'Why not?' she burst out furiously – Who got me into this hell-hole? God, how I hate the place! If only you knew. But you've no idea, have you? You've got your job, and a life tailor made. What have I got? – Nothing. I wish I'd never set foot in the East. And wouldn't if you'd told me about Helen in advance!'

Surprised more by the ferocity than the content of Amy's words, Phil responded quietly to calm her down; the servants were never far away. 'That's what I was afraid of, you idiot,' he said.

Amy didn't want to be calmed; she wanted to empty Phil's sails. 'Don't call me an idiot!' she said, deliberately not lowering her voice. 'I may not be as sophisticated as her bu…'

'Jesus, woman!' Phil broke in (What was she driving at?) 'You're impossible. Why can't you see there's nothing between us. I like her, yes. It isn't a crime. And short of not talking to her or Frank – I don't think even you would like that! – What more can I do? It isn't as if I'd slept with her…' (Amy knitted her eyebrows hatefully) '…Well, you know what I mean…'

'No. I don't. Would you if you could?'

Exasperated, Phil sidestepped. 'I love you, Amy.'

'That's not what I asked. Would you?'

'Not unless you drive me to it.' Anger, and the inability to help his wife was making Phil turn nasty.

Amy was past caring. 'That's right, blame me,' she retorted. 'Not that I care any more *what* you and Helen do. You can do what the Hell you like. It makes no difference to me. God, how I wish I'd stayed in Ireland.'

'Why didn't you then…and rot there with your rotten heritage.' As he uttered these words, Phil regretted them. 'I'm sorry, Amy, he said, 'I shouldn't have said that.' His apology was lost on Amy. 'At least I've *got* a heritage,' she said, 'and nothing in *my* background to be ashamed of! Which reminds me…'

Fake coughing from the sitting room announced the arrival of their lunch. As the boy laid it in front of them – chicken, vegetables, rice, mangosteens – they avoided each other's eyes. When he'd gone, neither could work up the enthusiasm to get going again. Amy thought twice about what she'd been about to say.

They finished their meal in silence. For both – they'd been married less than a year – the sour-sweet mangosteens had lost their edge. Phil wondered if he would not have done better to remain single. With a gathering sense of nausea, Amy recalled what 'Paradise' had been for Phil on their honeymoon in the E and O's shady, waterfront gardens and wondered if she could ever love him again. He never saw her in the kimono again. She had already stopped wearing her bog-oak necklace.

Part IV

Back in Ireland: Facing the facts

Chapter Twenty-one

Three years later – March, 1935.

Out in Shandoran's flax fields, buffeted by a gusty wind, Henry Allen strode longly behind a plough. His big, muscular frame and rugged head were as much a part of the landscape as nearby Shandoran Hill – whose ancient fort crumbled a little more each year – and the nearer River Lisanne, a wide, poplar-lined loop of which encased this part of the flax fields. The coming spring's primroses were already sprouting on the river's banks, and when the sun came out, as it did from time to time, the poplars were reflected in the water. Giving added witness to Henry's affinity with the land was the glow in his high cheek-boned face. Open skies; the wind around his head; working the land his father had worked before him, and his mother had tried to deprive him of – these were the things Henry loved most. Today, though, a frown was stuck fast between his expressive chestnut eyes, and his broad shoulders were more hunched than usual.

Henry was abstracted. Something his brother-in-law, Jo Heggerty, had told him in the pub in Ballymun a few days ago, something Jo had heard from one of his fares and that Henry didn't want to talk about, knew for a fact he shouldn't even be thinking about – was preying on his mind. [By this time, Henry's sister, Lucy, and her long time taximan boyfriend, Jo, were married. The younger Miss Aiken had followed the older to the grave, leaving, as expected, her drapery business to Lucy. She and Jo – they had one child – lived over the shop, and Lucy ran it. Jo, who had got very friendly with Henry since becoming his brother-in-law, still did his taxiing, and still gambled.] All morning it had gripped him as he strode up and down the field, working his horses at a measured pace, taking care not to damage the plough which had broken down yesterday, been fixed by Matt, but might well break down again. The potato drilling was all but done and for that Henry was grateful; barring bad weather, Flemming Young and Paddy Finch would have the potatoes in by the seventeenth. There was a way to go in the flax fields though, and without a full quota of ploughs, three, Henry feared the worst. Back in January he'd ordered a new plough but delivery of it had been refused, pending cash on the nail. It was the first time Henry had been refused credit. He took it badly; no one would have dared question his father or mother's creditworthiness. Compounding things, one of the harrows was playing up; the restharrow was bad again. Henry could see no way out. He was up to his eyes in debt and that despite last year's flax crop having been a good one. Unless prices rose or costs fell the situation could only get worse: seed had to be bought, repairs carried out, the labour force paid.

On reaching the end of his umpteenth drill Henry paused for a moment, mopped his forehead on his sleeve and rubbed his three day old reddish-brown stubble. As he rested, his debts felt like a millstone round his neck. Harriet had no idea. How could she? He couldn't bring himself to tell her. Not the full extent of them anyway, if indeed he could marshal it. To do that would destroy what little faith she had left in him. If only she would curb her spending! But she always had her answers: 'Is it pinched feet you want them to have? Or would you rather see them running barefoot like the Catholic children with no shoes an' socks at all?' Well of course I wouldn't, Henry thought. Nor was he laying the root cause of the debts at his wife's door; both he and she knew why and when the rot had really started! He'd put money on it the Linnakers weren't suffering under the depression! No credit squeeze there! That didn't mean his wife could spend willy-nilly. The new mangle had been the last straw; given time he'd have mended the old one. But she couldn't wait: 'An' how long would that have taken,' she'd said, 'till my back was that bad I couldn't move, I suppose!' Oh, yes, she always had her answers. He did love her though, and knew despite everything he always would. Driving Maggie out of Shandoran had been unforgivable. But he, not Harriet was really to blame for that; he should never have let it happen. It would serve him right if Maggie had put a curse on him and

Shandoran from the grave. She hadn't of course. How could she? – the kindest soul that ever walked God's earth.

Restarting the plough, Henry searched in vain for an exit from his predicament. Diversification was out of the question: he would *never* let go of flax. Gambling wasn't the answer either: Jo Heggerty had made nothing out of it, neither would he. The odd flutter did no harm.

Faced with such an unpromising scenario, Henry's thoughts returned to what Jo had said to him in the pub. He tried shaking it off; it kept coming back. One minute, like the poplar reflections in the Lisanne, it appeared clear-cut; a sure lifeline; the next – not so clear-cut. What if things got out of hand? Or if the inspectors ('They always come round', Jo had said) smelled a rat and, at the end of the day, didn't believe him? Where would he be then?

As the morning came to an end, Henry felt a growing need for his sister, Amy. Just talking to wise Amy might ease his mind; keep him from taking a fatal turn. Wishing for Amy, though, was as pointless as wishing his debts away. He hadn't seen her for four years – yes, almost to the day – and apart from a few words in Christmas cards, hadn't heard from her for nearly as long. In her last card she'd told him she and Phil had over a year to go before their leave. Even then, Henry thought, she might not bother visiting Shandoran as she had two children now, and bringing them and Phil to Cavan might not suit her. Which might, after all, be the best thing: telling Amy the extent of his debts would be too shaming.

At a loss, Henry laid up the plough and horses knowing one of the men would be along shortly to take over; Flemming Young or Paddy Finch most likely as nowadays Matt Doran spent much of his time in the yard. There were always jobs to be done there, Henry's most trusted labourer wasn't getting any younger and Henry's collie, Nancy (also a yard lover) enjoyed Matt's company.

Tracking beside the poplar-lined River Lisanne, Henry was

once again overcome with a pressing need for Amy. A need so great he decided to stick with the mother river, and its tributary the Little Lisanne, and make a wide detour through the wood behind the house to the place where his sister had so often comforted him and where something of her spirit might, despite the distance between them, help him now in his hour of need. Unfortunately Henry, a gut-reaction man, was ill-equipped for picking the right time or place for anything.

On entering the dell he shuddered. To look at, the place had changed little: the half-dead spreading oak beneath which he had so often sat with Amy, still dominated it; wild flowers still carpeted it; the Little Lisanne still meandered through it. But its atmosphere stirred something in Henry's innermost being – something he thought he had buried too deep to be recalled – something he struggled hard to smother as soon as he felt it.

Going over to the stream – the part where it widened into a shallow pool – Henry instinctively counted what remained of his Great Uncle Joshua's phials – mightily blurred now but vaguely indicative of a green, two reds and an orange; there were no stoppers left. Fixing his eyes on the water, he tried to conjure his sister's face. Instead of Amy he saw his mother – bunned, smirking, baleful-eyed – just as she'd been on that fateful night, defying him to do his worst as he'd pointed the gun at Tom. Oh God! Why did it have to happen like it did? And despite Maggie's warning. Dear, kind, Maggie. Why was it surging up now – the baleful eyes were bolted to his – when he so desperately wanted to forget it?

◇

It was the evening of the Linnakers' penultimate day at Shandoran, a day that had earlier seen Amy return to Dublin for the start of another term. As usual, saying good-bye to his sister made Henry a little sad so he spent the afternoon in the yard, meadow-bogs and fields. The previous day's threatened rain had not arrived but it had got very cold and a storm was in the air; some turf needed to be dug, doors, hedges, gates and fences secured; and getting stuck in with the men was second nature to Henry. In the evening he went over to the Vicarage to see Harriet.

Before leaving Shandoran, he carried his cocker, Barney, into the kitchen where he'd rigged up a bed for him by the big, open-hearth fire. Normally he didn't bring him in till last thing at night but because it was so cold and Barney had been snuffling a lot lately, he brought him in early. By day the dog slept on his bed of dry laurel leaves in the street, or in one of the yard's outhouses. Eleanor wouldn't have him in the house, except at night, and then grudgingly. 'Nasty, smelly thing!' she'd say, 'And so bad for the baby!' and chuck his basket outside as soon as Henry left with him in the morning. She had a point: any other animal on the estate in similar straits – old, near blind, half-deaf – would have been put down long ago. Henry could neither bring himself to do the deed nor let anyone else do it for him. 'It'd be a kindness, man,' Matt Doran had said. Flemming Young and Paddy Finch had echoed him, as indeed had Amy. Henry wouldn't, couldn't let go of the dog – his father's last gift to him, his ninth birthday gift.

At the Vicarage, he had an enjoyable few hours with Harriet: singing beside her at the piano, exchanging covert embraces when her Uncle, Reverend Badell, and mother, Mrs Harper, were out of the room discussing wedding plans. He walked home – elated by Harriet's embraces and the prospect that this was the last night he would have to share Shandoran with the Linnakers; quickly, to counter the cold and beat the storm that was already closing in. Half way up the lane he saw a light on the other side of the yard. Assuming it was Matt Doran returned to check something, he called out – 'Is that you, Matt?' When there was no reply, he started walking over to the light, and when still some way off, saw Maggie straightening up beside a lantern on a sill; her shawl had slipped and her give-away white hair had a yellow glow. 'Are you all right, Maggie?' he asked, concernedly going up to her. She turned round. 'Oh, Master Henry...'

'Jesus Christ – Maggie,' Henry burst out, seeing Barney in the maid's arms. 'What's he doing here? Is he alive?'

'He is, Master. But the sooner you get him back in the warmth, the better.' Gingerly she handed the dog to Henry, then adjusting her shawl nervously, picked up her lantern and hurried back to the lane, there being no exit from the yard on the avenue side.

'What happened, Maggie?' Henry pressed, easily keeping pace with her and convinced by her manner there had been foul play.

Reluctantly Maggie told him. 'Oh, Master Henry – Baby Naomie woke up – and was crying something terrible – so the mistress brought her downstairs – but she wouldn't stop crying, and was wheezing too, and the mistress blamed the dog, an…'

'I'll kill her if he dies, Maggie,' Henry broke in menacingly. 'I'll kill both of them.'

'Now don't be talking like that,' Maggie cautioned. 'Whatever would Miss Amy say if she heard it? She told me about the goings on in the parlour yesterday – about the picture an' curtains an' that – and the mistress was getting her own back – on you, Master, not the dog. I tracked him down on my way home, bumbling around on account of the locked doors. Thank God he's all right. Get him in now without more ado and I'll be off home.'

Years of comforting Henry when Amy was not around and of bread-poulticing his boils which his mother could never be bothered to do, allowed Maggie to speak to her Master like this. Scowling he looked at her; he admired her loyalty to Eleanor and knew she would be no less faithful to Harriet. They said good night. Cradling Barney, Henry strode towards the house.

With a massive effort he ignored his mother – still packing, he got a glimpse of the parlour curtains, loyal Maggie had said nothing about that – and his step-father, sitting complacently by the kitchen fire with his pampered pointer, Jess, at his feet. Putting Barney on the floor, Henry went to look for his basket rightly guessing it would be far flung in the street. Returning to the kitchen, he was too late to stop the cocker blundering into Eleanor's feet as she bustled about, annoyed at not having got a rise out of her son over her treatment of the dog, never mind that the dog was still alive; she had hoped a spell in the cold would finish him off. 'Damn and blast,' she said, lashing out with her foot, 'will nobody put that mongrel out of his misery?'

Barney yelped weakly and slunk under the kitchen table. Henry winced. Placing the basket as near the fire as he could, he lifted his dog gently into it and, unable to button his anger any longer, looked pointedly at Tom and muttered audibly – 'Mongrel, indeed! Purer bloody bred than some others around here I could name!'

It was a stupid thing to say given Henry's contempt for his step-father had nothing to do with Tom's breeding. But he'd said it, and it was what Eleanor was waiting for; all she had to do now was goad. 'A fine lot of good your breeding's done you,' she said, moving protectively to her husband's side; the matchbox moustache had begun to twitch. 'If your father, Samuel, could see you now he'd turn in his grave.'

The reference to his father, to the father who had never shown him anything but kindness, incensed Henry. Who did his mother think she was – She, who in marrying Tom had betrayed Samuel's memory; forfeited all right to it? Yet even as his blood boiled, Henry knew he should say nothing more, leave the room: Maggie had warned him, it was what Amy would have counselled, and the insults flying now had all been traded liberally before. But Amy wasn't here, and Henry knew in his heart Barney should be put down. He stayed put, and a not unusual scene in the kitchen quickly got out of his control. 'No more than he would if he knew what you'd married after his death,' he said glowering first at his mother then his step-father.

Eleanor smirked. Unlike Tom – whose edginess had increased despite her proximity – she knew how the evening would end. 'Humph,' she said balefully. 'You're not fit to wipe Tom's shoes. You're a worthless, good for nothing lout; as useless as that mangy mongrel you're too lily-livered to put down. Samuel's son! – My, God!'

Henry wanted to lash out. He couldn't. Because even as he hated his mother, he knew – always had known – he could never physically harm her. He just wanted her out of his life. Right now though, emotion was driving him on and, unable to face her down on his own, he gave emotion its head. Not his father's son, indeed! Lily-livered! Well, he'd show her.

Muscles taut, eyes flashing, cheeks pumping, Henry made for the gun rack.

His stepfather got to his feet. Laughing, Henry lifted the gun off the rack and pointed it at him. Tom froze; even the moustache was still. Eleanor saw through her son and, furious, stood fast by her husband's side. Then, smirking again, she put her hands on her hips (how Henry hated the pose, the ramrod straight back, the sharp-featured prematurely wrinkled face, the stretched back bunned hair!) and defied Henry to do his worst. He gave another laugh; that was the extent of his pleasure...

◇

At this point in his recollections Henry was so sickened by them he just had to get out of the dell. With an immense effort, he unbolted his eyes from the baleful ones in the Little Lisanne and dragged himself away from the water's edge. Before leaving the dell he cast sadly about it. I'll never come here again, he said to himself; Amy can't help me now.

On his way back to Shandoran, Henry's debts bore down on him once more, reminding him about his conversation with Jo and the lifeline it offered. Uncomfortable as before with the lifeline, he decided, as he skirted first the apple trees then the herb and vegetable patch that together separated the wood from the house, to bring home to Harriet the full extent of his debts; it was the only way; come what may, she must be made to understand.

'Was the plough all right, Daddy?' Lottie asked after Henry had greeted his wife and children in the kitchen where they were having their midday meal and where, with considerable difficulty, Harriet got up to get his food.

The reaction of his wife and daughter – so typical, he thought – to his arrival home made Henry smile. 'Yes thank you, darlin'', he said to Lottie, then inquired about Harriet's back – something that necessitated him, not infrequently, driving her into Kilbeg to see Dr McPhearson (senior or junior) rather than drag the doctor over to the estate, yet again.

'It's not been too bad this morning,' Harriet replied, much to Henry's relief. 'All that wringing before I got the new mangle did it no good at all, mind. But as long as I don't overdo things now – and I kept Lottie at home from school today to help me – it should be all right.'

Time and the birth of two more children – a toddler daughter and baby daughter – had led to some slippage in Harriet's figure and some roughening of her beautiful hands. Recurrent backache troubled her, oedema was thickening her legs, old-fashioned had become a bit dowdy. Nothing, though, was so bad it excused her laziness. That she loved her children and husband was not in doubt. Housework continued to be a trial to her and with maids coming and going – mostly going – and scapegoats hard to find, Henry bore the brunt of her moans. His gambling (in reality it didn't amount to much) and perceived thoughtlessness (memory lapses – no more – with so much else on his mind) were useful weapons; having a stick – figuratively speaking of course – to beat him with was important to Harriet.

Harriet's reference to the mangle did not go unnoticed by Henry or the older children. (The toddler and baby were napping thanks largely to Lottie having been at home; Henry would have preferred her at school but he appreciated the peace and tidiness when she wasn't.) Henry ignored the reference to the mangle; using it to highlight the severity of his debts would have been counter-productive. Luke and Billy – nearly eight and six respectively and at school mornings only – started pinchpunching each other under the table; it was the first of the month. Lottie prayed her mother wouldn't mention a purchase she'd made the previous day but not yet told Henry about; Sunday would be time enough to tell him; he might even like it then.

Not yet eleven, and more like Henry than ever in looks and her affinity with the land and animals (already she had a reputation as the best little horsewoman in the County) – Lottie loved both her parents; she just wished her mother would be less critical of her father; tut less. To the best of her ability Lottie helped them both and now, seeing Luke and Billy becoming so excited, she asked what they'd learned at school to calm them down and get away from the subject of the mangle.

'Hymns,' Billy said, prompting Harriet to turn to him and smile, and aver that she really must have a word with her mother about him singing in the Church choir. So far, Billy was the only one of her children to show any musical talent. 'He has such a lovely voice,' she went on, 'and Easter'd be a good time for him to start. Lottie can wear her new coat. I picked it up yesterday in Ballymun. Her old one's so shabby.'

A forkful of food en route to Henry's mouth checked. 'You don't understand, do you?' he burst out, putting it and his knife down with a clatter and purpling like a turkey's wattle. 'The money isn't there, Harriet.'

'Money enough for you to fritter away,' his wife said derisively. 'At least what I spend it on is necessary.' Immune to her husband's outbursts – she really had no idea about the dire state of Shandoran's finances – Harriet had sprung her latest purchase on Henry for no other reason than to provoke him: upsetting him like this made him more passionate in bed, she thought. She reckoned she'd got the mix between riling and loving him just right – as perfect as her soda cake mix – and that she could play her Henry as easily as she played her piano. 'As I was saying,' she went on, deliberately sidelining money matters, 'Easter'd be a good time for Billy to start in the choir. Would you like that, son?'

Billy said he would, and Luke – peeved by all the attention his younger brother was getting, piped up with – 'Who was Painzie, Mummy?'

'Who?' Harriet questioned.

'Painzie,' Luke repeated.

'What is he talking about, Lottie?' their mother asked, bewildered, and only too happy to leave Henry champing at the bit; annoy him a bit more.

Lottie thought for a minute – not to annoy her father, but because she too was mystified and welcomed the diversion from spending. 'He might be in one of the hymns we're learning for Easter, Mummy?' she said, at last. 'Is he, Luke? Billy said you were singing them again today.' Luke nodded, and as no one in the room could remember a Painzie in any hymn, Lottie asked her brother to sing the one with him in it.

'Luke can't sing,' Billy said scathingly.

'Yes I can.'

'Well sing it then.'

As Luke – the only blonde and straight-haired head in a family of unmitigated curly, red ones – collected his thoughts, Henry had another go. By now, though, with his wife and children concentrating on Luke, and himself as puzzled as the rest about Painzie, his words were weightless; the right time and place had eluded him again. 'Maybe we should both curb our spending, Harriet,' he said. 'If we go on the way we're going it'll be the debtor's jail for me and the workhouse for you and the children.'

Harriet laughed. 'Now you're being ridiculous,' she said, shaking back her shiny copper hair; she still found time to brush it. 'An' if you think you can frighten me and the children like that you've another think coming. Look to your own spending, Henry, and keep away from that good for nothing Jo Heggerty.'

Before Henry could say any more, Luke started singing – hesitantly, and off key. '"There is a green hill far away…"'

'There's no Painzie in that,' Lottie put in quickly, as much to spare her brother's embarrassment as from conviction that he was wrong.

'Yes there is,' he insisted, 'he comes later on.'

'Well sing the verse with him in it then,' Harriet said.

'I can't.'

'I told you he couldn't sing.'

'Yes I can. I just don't remember how the verse starts.'

'Why don't you sing the hymn, Harriet?' suggested Henry, convinced by now that nothing he said to his wife about her spending would have any effect. Asking her to sing would please her, and he was as anxious as the rest to get to the root of the current mystery.

Melodiously, Harriet sang.

> ""There is a green hill far away,
> Without a city wall,
> Where the dear Lord was crucified,
> Who died to save us all.
>
> We may not know, we cannot tell
> What pains He had to bear,
> But we believe it was for us
> He hung and suffered there.
>
> He died that we might be forgiven,
> He died to make us good,"'

'There,' Luke put in belatedly, carried away like the others by his mother's singing.

'Where?' chorused his parents and siblings.

'There. "What" Painzie "had to bear..."'

The laughter that followed almost reduced Luke to tears. But Lottie's excuse for the mistake – 'Sure anyone could think that, Luke,' – soon had her oldest brother laughing too.

In the midst of the hilarity, Henry's collie, Nancy, began barking outside and the postman went past the window. Lottie made for the hall, hoping the letter or letters would not be bills. There was one letter – from her Aunt Amy, she recognised the airmail envelope – and Harriet read it out loud as Henry found it hard to decipher Amy's writing.

◇

When Henry returned to the fields that afternoon, he was in an even bigger quandary than when he'd left them. Amy was coming home – earlier than expected: Phil had not been well and the Colonial Office had brought forward his leave on account of his having spent over two years in Siam, and been acutely ill there, before starting his job in Malaya. The family would be leaving Perlemban in a couple of weeks. Amy and the two children would go straight to Knockmore from Kingstown, spend a few days there, then come on to Shandoran for another few days before rejoining Phil in Dublin for the rest of the leave.

How wonderful to see Amy again! Henry thought as he relieved Paddy Finch at the plough. Then he remembered his debts, and his mother who he believed was at the root of them. Try as he would, he couldn't stop his ugliest memory of Eleanor surging up, even without her reflection in the Little Lisanne to fuel it: the memory of what had happened after he'd pointed his gun at Tom.

◇

Trapped in the kitchen with his mother and step-father – emotion driven he could not go back – Henry hung his gun over his arm and conscious of his mother's smirk and malignant eye, mustered as brave an air as he could before whistling to Barney and leaving the room. The cocker, confused though he was by the contradictory signals he'd been getting all evening, climbed clumsily out of his basket and followed his master outside. In the street the wind was strengthening and the atmosphere growing stormier. Picking Barney up, Henry collected a spade from the yard and angrily headed for the dell where he had long ago planned to bury him. On the other side of the kitchen-garden and orchard the storm broke; the rain held off, making its forked flashes and thunderbolts starkly menacing. Holding his quivering dog close, Henry strode on, conscious only that his detestable mother was making him do this detestable thing.

On reaching the dell he propped his spade and gun against the old oak. Crouching with Barney, he stroked his head and floppy ears. 'You'll not feel a thing,' he said, his rage and hatred overridden now with sorrow. Slowly then, he laid the dog on the ground, and stroked his head again before reluctantly and a little awkwardly retrieving his gun and backing away to take aim. The cocker lifted a heavy eyelid; Henry's guts churned; tightening his grip on the trigger he fired the gun.

Dazed by what he had done – putting an animal down, though never easy, had never been so agonising – he went straight into the burial. Moving away from the oak, he started digging, driving his spade hard into the ground and levering out the earth. With every thrust of the blade, he felt as if he was slicing through his mother's heart: more than anything in the world he loathed her; wanted her to feel his pain. Fortified thus, raging again, he dug like a man possessed, and would probably have gone on digging, even when the hole was big enough to accommodate a horse, if the rain had not started: fat, isolated drops presaged a downpour and Henry did not want to bury Barney with his fur wet.

Physically and mentally exhausted, he stopped digging. He secured the spade, and going over to the oak picked up his bloodied dog and carried him to the graveside. Gently and tidily, he laid the corpse in the grave. 'So long me old buddy,' he murmured – broken-hearted... tears welling... blurring Barney whose head he stroked for the last time. With difficulty then he stood up, and had no sooner covered the dog with earth than the Heavens opened. Torrents of rain bounced on the ground, and on Henry's head and broad back, and ran in rivulets down his wavy hair and coarse, reddish-brown stubble. Down the grooves on his scarred hands, to mingle with the fresh bloodstains on his coat, and with his tears as he mourned, not just for his dog, but for his father, Samuel, in the new Churchyard in Kilbeg and the childhood he'd shared with his father. For to Henry at that moment it seemed as if the loveliest part of his childhood was being erased; wiped away for good. By some bizarre sleight of mind he blamed his mother for his lost childhood as well as Barney's death.

◇

Big and muscular though he was, Henry wiped away a tear with his sleeve as he recalled his cocker's burial. Recalling it solved nothing – just as looking for Amy in the dell had solved nothing. That she was coming home was indeed wonderful. But what would she make of the debts? Thank goodness, Henry thought, as the light began to fade at the end of the afternoon's batch of drills – the plough had held up – thank goodness I'm seeing Jo Heggerty tonight.

Chapter Twenty-two

'Keep away from the sides or the big fishes will get you!'

This, Phil's refrain to his son, Robbie, on the voyage home from Perlemban became as familiar to passengers and crew as 'This is your Captain speaking.' For no matter how many times Phil cautioned, Robbie, a nimble two-year-old with a terrifying disregard for his own safety, would be darting back towards danger as soon as his father's back was turned. Fortunately that wasn't often, as minding the children – a baby daughter, Ruth, as well as Robbie – had become a major preoccupation with a reconciled Phil and Amy since the start of their six months leave. The absence of amahs necessitated it, and the pleasure it was providing (unexpected in Phil's case) helped to explain it. But only the unspoken need of both parents to dilute the memory of what had happened (doubly significant in the light of their reconciliation) on the eve of their departure from Perlemban provided a full explanation of it.

✧

That reconciliation had taken place at all between Phil and Amy was little short of miraculous. Ugly exchanges dogged it; Perlemban's sultry insularity and Phil's fondness for Helen Castle repeatedly threatened to stifle it; while its trigger, an ill advised visit by Amy to Hamish McNaughton's home in the jungle, might just as easily have scotched it for good as sparked it off. In retrospect, Amy could not believe she had done such a stupid thing – a madness too far almost.

✧

It was a Saturday, and Phil, chuffed to have been chosen for the job, had gone off at the behest of the Schools' Inspector to check out a new native primary in the jungle. 'Chalk and talk mostly, Handy,' the Inspector had said, 'but useful springboard for the spread of British values' – Phil's sentiments exactly.

After he'd gone, Amy drooled around, wondering how to fill another long, weary day – a day made wearier by the sight of her husband's industry. There seemed no limit to this, including most recently the presidency of a new school employment committee. The Malays in particular were finding it hard to get work, their preferred option – the softest, the Civil Service – having gone in for retrenchment in a big way. 'Take what you can get.' 'Don't be afraid to dirty your hands' – the committee and school magazine exhorted them, and the magazine put its money where its mouth was by printing advertisements (till now regarded as 'unliterary') to keep solvent. The whole of John Street eventually availed of this latter initiative first off the block being Sime Darby and Co Ltd with its 'India tyres – 100% British; Safe and Reliable.' In hot pursuit came: The Federal Dispensary Ltd ('latest in hair cream – gum free NUFIX'); Miss Elsie Tatt ('elocution and dancing lessons'); Kodak ('Brownies – so simple a child can use them'); the Eastern Wireless Company ('electric gramophones – no batteries. Just plug in your lighting socket'). From beyond Perlemban – Singapore and KL mainly – Stanley and Co's sportswear, Peter Chong and Co's stationery, Robinson and Co Ltd's cups and medals were also advertised.

Bored with drooling, Amy decided on a visit to the library where, if nothing else, she could have a chat with Helen, whom she still found better company than any other woman in the Kampong. It was only when Helen was with Phil that her presence really got on Amy's nerves, and even then, Phil, not Helen, irritated her most; more and more she was getting the impression Helen's responses to Phil were arm's length.

Half way along John Street, Hamish McNaughton – the upstate Scottish planter she twirled with at the Club – pulled up in his truck. 'Fancy a run out to the plantation?' he said, aware of Phil's absence for the day. 'I don't bite,' he went on in the friendliest fashion when Amy hesitated (Hamish was still a suspected quota-buster) 'hop in and I'll show you how we planters survive in the sticks.'

Unable to resist the chance to escape from Perlemban, if only for a few hours, Amy threw caution to the sultry air and climbed into Hamish's truck in full view of Major Martin coming out of the library, and Geoffrey and Sonya Pincher on their way to play tennis. The Pinchers' relationship – Sonya's dreams of a roughneck were still dreams – did not preclude an occasional game with each other.

Long before Amy got back to Perlemban, she wished she'd never left it. For months to come recalls of the sordid trip haunted and sickened her. Looking back on it she wondered why she hadn't smelt a rat sooner. Like, for example, when Hamish clamped his hand on her thigh during their ride through the jungle, to reassure her when he diced – deliberately she guessed – with the mangrove where it encroached on their trail. Or when his ramshackle home on stilts came into view in a rough clearing, and his spooky, native manservant – a deaf mute, who eerily anticipated his commands – showed up; or when Hamish left her with her Pimm's on his rickety veranda overlooking a muddy creek on the edge of the mangrove, while he went off to change into 'something suitable.' But he had never so much as laid an inappropriate finger on her before and behaviour like this was in keeping with his ruggedness.

Out of keeping – was his reappearance on the veranda, not in different western clothes but in full native attire: a crimson sarong that clashed horribly with his carroty hair and beard, and a black, open-chested baju that put Amy in mind of the tar brush. Leering lecherously, he plonked his whisky on the table, and himself beside her in his bamboo two-seater – the only seat on the veranda – and without any preliminaries, tried to kiss her. When she pulled away he blocked her in with his body, saying,

'You're not a prick tease, are you?'

Uncertain what to do – she couldn't believe the Scot would force himself on her – Amy said sternly, 'For God's sake, Hamish, I'm a married woman! You *know* I didn't come here for this!' Hamish ignored her. And Amy, unable still to believe he had anything sinister in mind, though suddenly aware of her precarious situation if he had – wedged in the corner of the two-seater, physically no match for him, beyond the veranda lay jungle, mangrove and muddy creek, the deaf mute was unlikely to help – continued to reason with him. Matter-of-factly she ordered him to stop, told him she shouldn't have come, and to take her home – 'Now! Please! Hamish!' He wasn't listening. Clumsily he groped at her blouse and tore a button off it. She panicked – like a freshly caught fly in a cobweb. Mustering her strength, she kicked, punched, scratched to get out of his grip. 'You little vixen,' he said, pinning her hard against the bamboo and hurting her. Ferociously she lashed out. Her half-full glass of Pimm's crashed on the floor. Hamish's whisky followed. 'I'll scream,' Amy shouted, frantic now to escape – anywhere. 'Go on!' the planter mocked.

Then, as suddenly as he had begun his assault, he fell back – red- and shame-faced: a wet patch had appeared on his sarong and was spreading outwards like an inkblot. He slunk off.

On the way back to Perlemban he apologised repeatedly, saying he'd got carried away. Despite her anger Amy believed him, but didn't tell him so.

As soon as she got in she bathed and changed, thankful Phil was still out. She intended only to tell him where she'd been, as if she hadn't done that someone else would have. But she was so badly shaken by the episode, and so relieved to have got out of it in one piece, she told him everything. His reaction infuriated her. 'So the bastard went off at half-cock!' he said, horrified she had done such a stupid thing. 'Well maybe you'll think twice before tangling with him again, Amy! I did warn you!' 'Thanks for your sympathy', Amy said, and, feeling thimble-small left the room to pick up the threads of her weary life, only followed now by a bad smell.

◇

Ironically, the same trip that had evoked such derision from Phil brought home to him something of the depth of his wife's unhappiness: for Amy to have gone off with Hamish like that she must have been really up against it. Even so, Phil felt no overriding compunction to go to her aid; her inner resource would see her through; he had done nothing wrong. When he did go to it, he did so without apologies. Without further recriminations about the foolhardy outing either, though; without grandiose gestures or patronizing. Casually almost, Amy found herself with meaningful things to do.

A pupil at King's – one of the Chinese boys, naturally hard-working and ambitious, and current editor of the school magazine (Phil had been particularly impressed with an article he'd written on Fowl Sickness, a recurrent problem for traders in Perlemban and the East generally) – needed extra tuition in Latin to get into Medical School in Singapore. 'Do you think you could help him, Amy?' Phil said. 'I've spoken to Dyson. He has no objection.' Amy jumped at the offer, brushed up her Latin (a subject, unlike French, she had done well in at Little-go and enjoyed teaching at Glenarkle) and took on the job. Before setting out for another inspection of a jungle school, Phil expressed a desire for Amy's company. 'I'd value your opinion on this one,' he said to her, not expecting her to go. She did go, and had no regrets. Finally, the pact on pregnancy withered away.

Slowly, Amy's perception of the East changed; her papaya regained its savour. By the time her and Phil's long leave came round, they were pedalling in a kind of unison again and she was glad – even her sex life had waxed – she had not run away from her husband or the East.

◇

Nothing in the run up to the Handys' leave, however, prepared them for the revelations on its eve when, in keeping with tradition, the DA and his wife – Chester and Mable Caldwell – threw a farewell party for them.

'We almost made it a valedictory double – Handys and Martins!' the DA told his guests on their arrival. 'But you know Mable! any excuse for a party!'

Prompted by the recent promotion of the handsome, ambitious, incorruptible Head of Police, Major Clive Martin, to the top job in Kuala Lumpur (the Major and his smug wife, Miriam, would be repairing to KL within a month) the DA's remark got everything off to a good start. The cork-popping, glass-clinking evening went with a bang… till the closing stages, when it went horribly wrong for the Handys.

Standing at one end of the lower of the Caldwells two verandas, Phil and Amy were having a few quiet words about their leave, the arrangements for which had been finalised: a week or two with their families – Amy visiting Knockmore first, from courtesy and because of the grandchildren – the rest of the time in a rented cottage in Howth. Phil was depressed – though not without good cause.

Just over a year ago, Dyson had gone on long leave leaving Phil as Acting Headmaster – a position upgraded to full blown Head when the poodle-faker was subsequently posted to a different state in Malaya. Phil revelled in the promotion – another Headship! – and in the continued success of the Cambridge classes for which he retained full responsibility; also, in presiding at Prize Day when he read out the Cambridge results, and in meeting and entertaining visiting dignitaries (Residents, Commissioners etc., or their Assistants) on this and other important occasions like Sports and Scout Jamboree Days. Wisely he relinquished his presidency of the employment committee and had already seriously reduced his input to the school magazine – a biannual by now to further cut costs. Despite the pull-backs and job satisfaction his work had become onerous. And six years in the east (it was late 1934) without a break in the West – four or five years was the norm – was enough to upset the hardiest constitution; Phil's was anything but hardy. His health began to deteriorate (non-specific not helped by drinking) and before he could do anything about it grave news arrived from Fermanagh about his sister, June – the sibling Amy had long suspected and now knew was his favourite. 'I love her more than the rest put together' he'd owned on receipt of one of his letters from home, before adding wistfully – 'Do you think it's because we both have weak

238

chests?' June's current plight had been sparked off by a bout of bronchitis – something that had afflicted her on and off throughout her life – and she'd returned home to Fermanagh from London to recover. Then pneumonia had set in, followed by tuberculosis. The doctors were doing everything they could but consumption was winning the day and the prospect now that his beloved sister might die before he got home was very real to Phil. Amy's heart went out to him; she knew all about sibling love. She played down her own happiness for his sake. Not only had she missed a period and suspected she was pregnant again; she couldn't wait to get back to Ireland to see everyone.

At the other end of the veranda, within earshot of the Handys, the DA, Chester, was smoking a cheroot and congratulating Major Martin on, not just one count (the promotion to KL), but two. 'You did well nailing McNaughton, Clive,' he said, referring to the Major's recent arrest of Hamish for quota-busting. 'We've all suspected him for a long time, I know, but catching his henchmen red-handed was smart work. They had a clever set up in the creek, with the nearby mangrove for cover. Had no idea you were on to them! You could tell that from McNaughton's face when you picked him up a few hours later...'

Listening to Chester made Amy feel quite sick: she too remembered Hamish's face when the Major, in front of everyone at the Club, had clapped handcuffs on him and marched him off to the police station. Amy had not forgotten the Scot's assault on her, but she had long ago forgiven him. Sensing her unease, Phil said – 'The law's the law, Amy! Hamish knew the score.' 'I know,' she replied, 'but the thought of a big, outdoor bloke like that penned up in some God-awful prison is horrible.'

Meantime, Chester had moved on to Major Martin's promotion. 'No one deserves it more than you, Clive, and I'm sure you're as pleased as I am your successor here is not your deputy, Pincher.' Clive nodded, and with deuced fine gallantry, praised the man who had just been appointed to replace him but whose name had not yet been publicised in Perlemban. 'Splendid fellow, Crotchley,' he said. 'Has had two years experience in Singapore and many more in Hong Kong before that.' Then, glancing over his shoulder, the Major added – 'From your neck of the woods, Phil and Amy, I gather.'

'Small world,' Amy said, as casually as she could over her shoulder. The news shocked her; for though Catherine had intimated something like it might happen, Amy had forgotten all about it as their correspondence tailed off.

Phil was struck dumb by the news; rocked to his innermost core. Like Macbeth at the sight of Banquo's ghost, he quaked visibly. His legs – already wobbly from illness and drink – threatened to give way. He sat down. He and Amy looked at each other in silence, grateful for the subdued lighting.

Minutes later, much to their relief, the DA and Major Martin split up. Chester went inside; Clive, down the garden.

On the point of offering some words of comfort to Phil – on top of his sister's suffering, the news about Neil's brother would take some absorbing – Amy was beset by an overriding urge to spend a penny (further proof she was pregnant) and went hurrying off to the lavatory. When she got back Phil was gone.

Assuming he'd taken flight, knowing she would make his apologies, Amy decided to go home too; a number of the other guests were leaving anyway. Annoyingly, she could not find Helen Castle whom she particularly wanted to see to thank her for the warm costume she'd sent over with the boy that morning. Helen kept the costume for Yorkshire and thought it would save Amy having to buy one in Ireland if it was cold there. Amy had forgotten to thank her earlier, and as she and Phil were leaving Perlemban at sun up, it was now or never.

As Amy headed down the garden in a last look for Helen, it occurred to her Phil might not have gone home at all but sought comfort from Helen instead.

The thought sickened her. Dodging among the shadows, she eyed the remaining guests with deep suspicion. At the bottom of the garden a big clump of yellow and white jasmine, lit up by a lantern, took on an especially ominous appearance as, so often on these occasions, Helen was wearing a yellow dress. Amy slowed, too afraid almost to look behind the bush. When she did look, she saw Helen, locked in the arms, not of Phil, but of Perlemban's incorruptible Head of Police, Major Clive Martin.

Overwhelming relief surged through Amy. The library! she thought, beating a hasty retreat. So *this* was why Helen had got the job there! The Major was a known frequenter of the place and Amy didn't doubt Helen had instigated the affair.

Before leaving the party, Amy asked Dr Castle to thank his wife for the tweed costume. As she walked home, feeling guilty now as well as relieved, she wondered whether or not to tell Phil what she had seen. If she told him, he would probably take it the wrong way; think she was trying to put one over on him when all she wanted was to prevent him making a further ass of himself. Who was the *ingénue* now!

He was asleep when she got in, and she didn't wake him. Going out on the veranda, she leant on its rail and stared at the clear night sky, and at the black jungle whose cacophony had long ceased to bother her. Behind her, the Malay boy was fixing a jalousie that had come loose.

Amy breathed deeply, savouring the scented nightfall, and her and Phil's leave. The long vacation in the West would do them both good – further their reconciliation, and help Phil adjust to whatever befell June, to the reappearance of a Crotchley in his life and to the news about Helen and Major Martin which Amy now decided she would tell him. The East was disorientating. In Ireland, they could get things back into perspective. There would be so much to do in their three months there; people and places to visit, not least Shandoran and Henry. Oh how wonderful to see Henry agai...

Amy jumped. A prolonged, penetrating shriek – like a handful of chalk dragged slowly across a wide blackboard – was slicing through the air. Shrill and eerie, it put Amy in mind of a banshee. Quaking, she gripped the veranda rail. 'What is it?' she asked the Malay boy, still struggling with the jalousie. '*Itu burong hantu*,' he replied. Amy shuddered: her Malay, though well below Phil's standard, was good enough for this – 'it's a ghost bird.' Then with a wide sweep of his arm, the boy added hurriedly – '*Tidapu, mem. Itu sina! Itu sana!*' ('Don't worry, Mam. It could be here, there, anywhere!') But somewhere, Amy thought, as a deathly picture of Phil's sister, June, cast a dark shadow over her coming holiday. Forcing a smile for the boy's benefit, she went indoors where Phil, still sleeping soundly, had heard nothing.

The following morning, the Handys went on leave and busied themselves with their children on the six week voyage home – Phil with his copious cautions to Robbie about the big fishes.

◇

On reaching Southampton they wired their impending arrivals at Fermanagh and Knockmore then pressed straight on without a break.

Chapter Twenty-three

It was gone four o'clock at Knockmore and Vincent Linnaker, a strapping lad in his mid teens, home for the weekend from school, had just set off in the pony and trap for Bridgeways – the Linnakers local market town – to meet Amy, Robbie and Ruth; he would be back within the hour. Before leaving, he had brought the cows in and already his parents, Eleanor and Tom, were at work in the dairy and byre. Their mood was sombre – and getting more so by the minute.

Spring had come in with its usual flurry of activity at Knockmore and by now, the end of April – the farm's hundred acre mix of arable and pasture was looking good. Wheat, barley and oats were sprouting in the fields, calves and lambs were suckling. There wasn't too much of anything but wherever the eye fell or the ear harkened prosperity rang out. An orchard flush betokened a bumper crop of russets and crabs not a single one of which would go to waste; freshly white-washed stone walls and the clean clink of metal from the dairy denoted a family on top of its workload. Fat fowl guaranteed full platters, strutting roosters early alarms; there were no sluggards at Knockmore. No arrears either, and credit, if required – though it seldom was – was not a problem; Henry Allen had been right about that. Equipment here was replaced when necessary, new labour-saving materials and gadgets purchased as and when – a new harrow last year, lino on the bedroom floors and a wireless for the kitchen this year. In just over a decade the embattled ex-mistress of Shandoran, and her husband – the ex-struggling pig farmer from Ballymun – had established themselves firmly in County Louth. It was something of a re-run for Eleanor but without the fear of dispossession at the end: this time round, in the event of widowhood her home would be hers.

With so many positives, a sombre mood on the farm was something of a rarity, especially given the impending visit by Amy – a daughter Eleanor loved very much despite her 'I told you sos.' Yet it was just this visit that accounted for the steadily darkening umbra at Knockmore.

Just over a month ago an event had occurred to upset the Linnakers. Unable to do anything about it they had swept it under their freshly purchased lino; never so much as referred to it – in public or private. Now though, they were going to have to talk about it, and it was that – the having to talk about it – that was so blackening for them.

Sixty minutes in the dairy and byre passed quickly – Eleanor attending to separating and churning, Tom to draining udders: work that left little time for chit chat. Yet despite their near silence, each knew what the other was thinking.

'When will you tell her?' Tom asked on delivering his final bucket of steaming milk to the dairy and a faint clip-clop from the direction of Bridgeways came into earshot.

The years had not been unkind to Tom. Since leaving Shandoran he had got a little older looking and a little rounder. His matchbox moustache was still intact; his face, as might be expected, less clean-shaven. Seeing Eleanor upset grieved him. It always had, for despite what people in Kilbeg had said about him (an upstart sowman who'd wheedled his way into Eleanor's affections for his own ends) he loved his wife dearly – for herself as well as her standing. From the outset though he'd grasped – her hatred of Henry would eventually drive her off the estate she loved. His preparations for that time had been meticulous. As Shandoran's chief tallier – in what was once Dr Joshua Allen's surgery over the coach house but had been converted into an office by Samuel Allen for his steward, John Fisher – Tom had salted away small sums: the odd guinea, pound, crown or half-crown; florin, shilling or sixpence; threepenny bit, penny, ha'penny or farthing. Small though they were they'd mounted up and, added to the already ring-fenced proceeds from the sale of his pig farm (he'd hated the pigs) had made a tidy sum, enough in fact to purchase Knockmore. Though not privy to the embezzlement, Eleanor had given it her blessing when Tom told her about it, deeming the moment right when she'd agreed to leave Shandoran. 'Nothing criminal, Ellie,' he'd said to win her round, 'and no more than you deserve,' words that had not only chimed with her thinking at the time but led her in the same instant, he knew, to forgive all his years of idleness (accounting aside) on the estate – something that had rankled with her. Tom had known the move to Knockmore (notwithstanding Harriet's summation of it – 'Uncommonly large for a sowman, Henry!') was a downward step for Eleanor, just as marrying him had been. So what, he had thought. Eleanor would recoup her losses. Tom had heard it said it took two generations to make a gentleman. In his son, Vincent's case – given Eleanor's background and his ambitions (he would work hard on his own place) he was sure it would take only one. Everything had been going splendidly till suddenly – and out of his and Eleanor's control – the unmentionable had happened – unmentionable that is till now. Eleanor of course would do the talking: she wouldn't want to embarrass her husband any more than was already done and knew he would prefer to leave the telling to her anyway. In reply to his question she said – 'After you've gone to bed, Tom. I'd like to be alone with her.'

'Just as you wish, Ellie,' he replied.

As the trap pulled into the yard, Tom sighed heavily. 'How could he do such a thing,' he said. Truly he felt sorry for his wife.

'He was always rotten,' she rejoined disgustedly. With a definite edge to her voice, she added – 'She'll have no choice but to admit it now!'

Lily came to a halt – at Knockmore the pony was always called Lily – and Tom waved at Amy and the children and went back to the byre. Smiling, Eleanor approached the trap. To Amy, the smile was forced. She wondered why; and why Vincent, not Eleanor had come to meet her – something she had wondered about earlier given the length of time that had elapsed since she and her mother had met and given also that she had stressed Robbie and Ruth would be with her.

Grateful the ground wasn't muddy Amy handed Ruth to her mother then climbed out of the trap and lifted Robbie down. Mother and daughter embraced. Straightway Amy *knew* something bad had happened. It wasn't that she expected any great show of emotion on Eleanor's part; that too would have seemed odd; but she knew the norm for occasions like this and the norm was distinctly lacking. Instead, she felt as if she was at the receiving end of a tennis ball that had lost its bounce.

'Is anything the matter, Mama?' she asked, tentatively.

'Sh. Not now,' Eleanor said brusquely.

Vincent backed Lily up to the coach-house, which, unlike Shandoran's was single-storey and an integral part of the yard. Eleanor, Robbie, and a by now extremely worried Amy picked their steps to the back door through freshly spattered cowpats. Pecking and shovelling fowl scattered untidily.

Indoors, where Eleanor was no more forthcoming than outside, questions mounted in Amy's mind; her answers pointed in one direction – Shandoran. For if, as was becoming increasingly obvious to her (the wireless and lino did not escape her eye for long), the changes here were all for the better, whatever trouble was afoot *must* lie at Shandoran. But what could have happened there to upset Eleanor?

Normally setbacks at Shandoran put a smile on Linnaker faces!

Mystified and deflated – some welcome home! she thought – Amy unpacked while Eleanor got the tea, and Tom and Vincent finished off in the dairy. Amy was tired: a second period missed on the voyage home as well as a marked tightening in her bias cut evening dress – her most recent mail-order purchase from Messrs White, Whitely and Co. Ltd. in KL – had confirmed her suspicions about pregnancy; Phil was neither pleased nor displeased by the news – as good a response as could be expected in the circumstances, Amy thought. The journey from Southampton had been exhausting, and would have been more so if Ruth, a placid child, hadn't napped most of the way and Robbie been preoccupied by novelty: the colourful preparations for King George V and Queen Mary's Silver Jubilee on the way to Holyhead; Lily's swaying haunches on the ride from Bridgeways. Currently he was 'heping Ganny' in the kitchen – more interesting than watching his tired mother unpack or baby Ruth napping.

At tea time, Tom and Vincent came in. Tom had never made Amy feel unwelcome at Knockmore. Everyone listened to the six o'clock BBC news – a ritual by now in the house. In England, the Jubilee was temporarily eclipsing weightier matters – fascist and anti-fascist parades; peace movements and calls for rearmament; cabinet wrangles, hunger marches, and dole queues. Further afield, the Stresa Pact was being hailed – just as Munich would be in three years time – as living proof that appeasement worked.

What talk that followed was mostly about the Linnaker children – about how well they were doing. Amy had already gleaned much of it from Vincent in the trap. Iris and Lydia were nursing in Dublin, and Naomie – still at boarding-school – was expected to follow suit. Vincent was lined up for Agricultural College when he left school, a piece of information that reminded Amy of Eleanor's stock reply to Master Gamble's suggestions regarding secondary education for Henry: 'A waste of money, Master,' she used to say, 'hasn't he enough already with the land!' Tom was taking no chances, especially not in the light of the recent bleak occurrence at Shandoran; his plans for gentleman status for Vincent – he made no secret of them – were still on course, give or take.

After the meal, father and son returned to the yard. By the time they finished there, Ruth and Robbie were asleep – in the girls' room with the big feather-bolstered bed where Amy would later join them. Vincent – still in the 'bit' where the apples used to be stored off his parents' room – went upstairs soon afterwards, followed by his father when the clock in the kitchen niche struck nine.

As the clock struck, Amy looked at it, and at the fluted-stemmed goblet on the shelf above it. Both items had come from Shandoran, and both were beautiful – the goblet especially so. A product of the late eighteenth century 'buy Irish' campaign, acme of Anglo-Irish nationalism, it was delicately engraved with a spinning-wheel, flax leaves, and the words 'May The Irish Linen Industry Thrive For Ever.' Why, wondered Amy, sitting opposite her mother by the turf fire, had Eleanor taken it? – For old times sake, or to spite Henry? Either way, it seemed out of place here. What, she wondered next, switching her gaze to her mother, lay behind Eleanor's tightly compressed lips, and eyes fixed on the fire?

'What is it, Mama?' she asked, at length, leaning forward concernedly and conceding that, despite everything (fifty-six years, eight pregnancies, still bunned but greying hair, slings and arrows, and more lines on her face than Crewe Junction) Eleanor had worn well.

'Brace yourself, Amy!' Eleanor replied tersely, her eyes still glued to the fire.

'You aren't going to like it!'

The unfolding that followed was delivered with a repugnance and flint-heartedness that sickened Amy; and with such reluctance, that repeated promptings – promptings best described as insistent bouts of pressure to express a huge and excruciatingly painful boil – were needed to keep it going. 'To what for God's sake?' was the impatient first. 'Was anyone hurt?' the disbelieving second. 'Is the house fit to live in?' the despairing third.

As Eleanor's replies oozed out, Amy slumped brokenly back in her chair. 'My God!' was all she could say. Put bluntly – Henry had set fire to Shandoran to get the insurance to pay off his debts. Immediately, the authorities were on to him. He was in gaol. His family (mercifully none had been harmed) were living in Shandoran's coach-house.

Looking up from the fire, Eleanor found Amy gazing into it. Now will you admit what a no-good man he is, the mother thought – the only thought that had provided her with any comfort in the whole repellent affair. Amy's persistent refusal to take sides against Henry was and always had been insufferable.

For Amy though, the situation at Shandoran was producing quite the opposite effect. Amy felt as if she was being eviscerated; turned inside out like an umbrella in a squall. What she was hearing – her lovely home in ruins; her brother in gaol, his family shamefully reduced – was too *awful* for words. She remembered Hamish and the burung hantu, and heaved; June had completely slipped her mind. How ever would Henry survive behind bars! and how would his family survive without him? What can I do to help? How soon can I visit them? – Tomorrow, the day after? I could bring Robbie and Ruth with me. No – leave them here with Mama. She won't like it, but… Leave them here too while I go and see Henry. Poor, poor Henry!

Barely audibly, she inquired where her brother was confined.

'Dublin,' Eleanor replied disgustedly.

'And who's looking after the land?' Amy asked.

'Matt.' Eleanor's voice was flat; no scrap of comfort must be given to her daughter till she came round to her way of thinking. 'Flemming and Paddy left,' she added, 'no money I suppose to pay them. Matt said he'd stay till he got out.'

'Well thank God for that,' Amy said looking at her mother while picking up on the grain of comfort she didn't want her to have. 'Was anything spared?' she added, desperate for another and livid at Eleanor's callousness. The last thing she wanted now though, was a row. She must keep her sense of balance – the thing that had always tempered her wrath with Eleanor in the past.

'No,' Eleanor said contemptuously, 'nothing but the few sticks of furniture.' In the same demeaning way she pressed on: 'Ah now, Amy, what he did is unpardonable. She wasn't much help to him, I know. But he chose her.' (Always the same disparaging 'he' and 'she', Amy thought) 'Well he's got what's been coming to him for a long time, Amy. Maybe being locked up will teach him a lesson – I doubt it. He's rotten to the core. Sure we always knew it.' (How dare her mother use the word 'we' in such a context, how dare she! She, the cause of so much unhappiness in Henry's life) 'And now he's disgraced us all. Luckily not many – maybe no one – round here knows about it. Your cousin George came over from The Mill in the Bullnose and told us everything. George is a real credit to the family. Not like that other scoundrel. My God, Amy! To think he's in gaol, and the family in the coach-house, Stella's quarters. How will we ever live it dow…?'

'That's all you can think of, Mama, isn't it?' Amy broke in furiously, 'yourself. Even now you can't find it in your heart to feel anything but hatred for Henry. You're a malicious, vindictive woman and I hope you answer for it one day. You never gave Henry a chance, Mama; never tried to see the good in him. Hammered whatever good was in him out of him…No, don't interrupt. I should have spoken out years ago. Nothing you can say now will alter the truth. And what did Henry ever do to harm you?'

'Didn't he drive me out of my home…'

'No, Mama. Shandoran was his home, as you very well know. If anyone drove you out of it, it was Harriet, not Henry. Henry couldn't hurt a fly…'

'Humph, not hurt a fly, you say. I suppose you've forgotten about Maggie! But even if you discount her – and I for one could never do that! – hasn't he damn near killed his children and brought shame on all of us! Tell me you don't feel the shame, Amy. Look me in the eye and tell me you don't feel it.'

Amy looked away, and back at the fire. She felt her mother's eyes on her and heard her say triumphally – 'You can't, can you?'

No, Amy thought, I can't.

In the glow of the embers Amy saw much more than her brother in prison, his children and their mother in the coach-house, and the remains of her once-lovely home. These things were difficult enough for her to take on-board, particularly given the weight she had attached to Shandoran and her heritage – consciously and subconsciously – throughout her life; in her darkest moments in the East, *Flaxfields* alone had sustained her. But bear them she would, she told herself, and give succour where she could. Less easy to accommodate was the even bigger picture in the embers; the picture dominated by her husband, Phil Handy. For Phil, a stickler like his father for legality, having a brother-in-law in prison would be utterly shaming, and doubly hard to stomach in the light of his other travails including, possibly, his sister June's death. Thinking about June reminded Amy of the story about the Mackintoshes toffees. As she recalled it, and remembered June as a delicate wisp of a girl in Ballymun – 'Fine for scrambling' had stuck in Amy's mind – and imagined something of the weight of Phil's grief in the event of her death, and of his horror on hearing about Henry – already his parents would have told him everything, unless of course they hadn't heard, in which case she, Amy, would have to do the telling – she flinched; in her head and in the embers, images kaleidoscoped. 'Dear, Lord!' she lamented silently, 'and just when things were looking up between us.'

The clock in the niche struck eleven. Once again, Amy looked at it, and at the beautiful goblet above it. Ironically she thought – they, at least, have been spared.

Eleanor got up and banked down the fire. 'What will you do?' she asked. 'Will you go over?'

It was a minute or two before Amy answered – 'I don't know, Mama.'

◇

Meantime in Fermanagh, Phil was endeavouring to come to terms with not just the news about Henry's imprisonment – about which his parents had heard – but about June's death too. And in the same way as hearing of Henry's fate initially overrode every other thought in Amy's mind so, hearing about June's death completely overwhelmed Phil: his beautiful, darling sister was dead, and he had not even said good-bye to her. There were memories of her of course. Of the extra special hug she gave him when he came home for his holidays. The extra feeling she put into *Home Sweet Home* when she played and sang it for him at her piano, with her long, blonde hair trailing down her back, the evening before he returned to work. Of her contrite expression when she looked up at him to make her confession about the Mackintoshes toffees. Of her and Rose driving him mad when they practised the latest dance-hall steps to Bye Bye Blackbird. But the memories only seemed to magnify her absence, as did the graphic image Phil conjured of her painful, protracted death. The marasmus, he reckoned, must have been harrowing. 'She just lay in my arms, Phil', his mother told him, 'limp as a withered stalk and never taking her eyes off mine. At the last, her lids flickered – then closed for good, gently as a cabbage white's wings.'

Next to such grief, everything else appeared irrelevant to Phil…as irrelevant as the Good Book to an unbeliever, or someone else's tears in the rain.

By the time he got back to Dublin, though, the news about Henry was impacting strongly on him and the more he thought about it the angrier it made him and the less inclined to mince his words with Amy when he saw her. On top not only of June's death, but of the revelations about Neil Crotchley's brother, and about Helen Castle – he could not believe he had let Helen make such a patsy out of him; just like Neil had – it seemed too much for him to bear. Why shouldn't Amy, she was after all Henry's sister, carry her share of the burden? – ineluctable pitfalls of pride. Hiding his feelings for her benefit was pointless. Better to let her know where he stood. Maybe it would make her less critical of him in future.

Reinforcing the above was Phil's mother's non-stop denigration of Amy and her Allen relatives. Mrs Handy had only met Amy once – drenched to the skin with her basket of charity – but that and hearsay was sufficient for her to have built up a little inventory of grievances against her daughter-in-law. Some of the grievances – 'Families like hers aren't like ours, Phil,' 'The father was terrible wild, you know' – had often made Phil and Amy laugh in the past. Now, accompanied by, 'Your brother-in-law's in prison, Phil,' they did anything but amuse him.

◇

In the dark as to Phil's feelings, not absolutely certain yet if he'd heard about Henry, Amy returned to the capital in a state of fevered anxiety. What if Henry's actions should blight for ever the chance of real reconciliation with Phil?

He met her at the Quays, where he'd seen her off on a bus two weeks earlier for Bridgeways, and seemed so pleased to see her and the children she assumed he'd heard nothing. Robbie ran to him, shouting, 'Daddy! Daddy!' He picked him up and carried him. A porter dealt with the luggage and they took a taxi to the Pillar to catch a tram to Howth. In a very few words Amy commiserated again over June's death. Phil had written to her at Knockmore to tell her his sister had died and she'd written back, making no mention of Henry. He wasn't mentioned now either. Set against June's death, he and his crime seemed somehow out of place, and Phil had made up his mind to let Amy broach the subject. It was only fair, he thought, curious also to see how she would go about it.

A week went by, the last but one in May, during which they settled into the cottage in Howth, each tiptoeing round the other.

By the start of the next month, Amy had had enough.

'I suppose you heard about Henry,' she volunteered, gauging the moment as good as she was likely to get. Robbie and Ruth were having their midday nap, and she and Phil had repaired (the siesta habit was hard to break) with a packet of cigarettes to a wooden seat, weathered white with age, in the most sheltered corner of their tiny, walled-in back garden; out of the wind the

253

sun was warm. On one side of the seat, a manky gooseberry bush promised no more than a wish. A near-dead apple tree on the other side would probably have been chopped down long ago for firewood had it not been for the wild, richly-budded rose threaded through it. Every so often a gust of wind came over the wall and threatened to snag Amy's hair on the rose. Phil noticed that, along with the anguished confusion on his wife's face as she'd spoken. He took his time before replying.

'I did,' he said, 'it was a terrible thing to do.' His tone, sombre but not judgemental, went some way to easing Amy's concern. That he knew was a relief to her. 'It was', she agreed, after which each of them smoked their cigarettes quietly. Amy wondered what Phil was thinking, and everything she thought of saying sounded hollow. She stayed silent, half expecting Phil to let fly at any moment.

'I heard it went up like a tinder-box', he said, casually almost, and after what seemed like an eternity to her, 'with flames and sparks visible the length and breadth of Kilbeg.' A mildly cynical glance in Amy's direction accompanied the last part of the comment. Sensing he was trying to play down the seriousness of the thing for her sake, Amy went along with him; anything, she thought, to lighten the shame. Compressing her lips downwards and with a little upward jerk of her eyes and head, she said, resignedly, 'Aye, Phil, it's all gone – the whole shootin' gallery.' The familiar mannerism (and so adaptable! he thought) and Amy's choice of words made Phil smile. 'Well I'll be damned', he said, flicking his ash on the ground as much as to say – What's done is done. When it came to the crunch, he couldn't find it in his heart to rub Amy's nose in her predicament. He knew what Shandoran had meant to her; what its survival during the Troubles had meant. What the memory of it (fantastical though that was) had meant in the East, and what the prospect of seeing it and Henry again had meant on her way home. Also, Amy had never judged anyone, especially not him – not about the really important things anyway – in her life. She always looked for the redeeming feature; there but for the grace of God… Why should he judge her? For Amy, Phil's smile, his words, his whole demeanour brought an immense feeling of relief. Gratitude and love overwhelmed her. What could have been an explosively embarrassing moment for her – the prelude to a married life of recrimination more than bearing out Phil's ideas on wedlock – was defused.

From here, Amy described further the tragedy unfolding at Shandoran, keeping the emphasis on the estate rather than Henry to make it less unpalatable. 'It must be terrible for Harriet,' she concluded. 'She's lucky to have a daughter like Lottie. I can't imagine they have a maid now, or ever will agai…'

'You didn't go over, then,' Phil said, unable to hide his astonishment.

Amy shuffled on the wooden seat. 'No,' she replied. 'I…I couldn't have left the children with Mama. It would have been too much for her. An', and too much for Harriet if I'd taken them with me.' Her words lacked conviction – she knew it, Phil knew it. 'Maybe', she added, limply, 'I'll go and see Mama again before we go back to Perlemban and visit Cavan then.'

'And Henry?' Phil said.

Amy shook her head, but made no attempt this time to justify her actions – or Henry's. Phil knew all about the debts and mismanagement at Shandoran, and something about the raw deal Henry had had from his mother; making further excuses for him now would not have impressed. As for herself – Amy felt desperately sorry for Henry. What kind of despair had driven him to act as he had? And how much greater must his torment be now! But he shouldn't have done what he'd done, and even before she'd left Knockmore, Amy knew she would not go to see her brother in prison. Phil wouldn't like it. She couldn't face it; it would be hard enough for her to visit Shandoran. She wasn't proud of herself.

Phil didn't press her; the thought of his wife visiting *anyone* in prison was indeed abhorrent to him. 'Well we've each got a cupboard skeleton now, Amy,' he said, wondering how his wife would react in future when people admired *Flaxfields*; not with her usual 'It's just like that on the estate', he'd warrant. 'My, what a wagging of tongues there'd be in the Kampong if ever they got out!' The comment made them both smile, nervously.

At that exact moment, a gust of wind caught the lower branches of the wild rose and drove them sideways into Amy's hair. She pulled at the tangled strands, to no avail.

'Let me do it,' Phil said, getting up and going round behind the seat, from which angle he could best get at her hair. Gently he untangled it, saying, 'Do you remember the time it got snagged on the hedge in Kilbeg's old Churchyard?'

'I do.'

'Right down to your waist it was then, Amy! And a lovely sight to behold!'

Having freed the hair, he caressed Amy's neck and throat. She sat quite still – enjoying the sensation, bewildered mentally. In the churchyard she'd been so proud of her ancestry. Now, it seemed, the single most important thing she had to do on returning to Perlemban was take down *Flaxfields*. As long as the picture hung where it was, it would invite comment; comment to which she could never hope to respond without arousing suspicion. How, come to think of it, could she ever look at the thing again without a deep sense of shame? She felt bereft, and could cheerfully have wrung her brother's neck.

That night, she and Phil made love with a passion they had not experienced in years. It was June the first, but might more fittingly have been the first of April.

Chapter Twenty-four

The peninsula was at its best – an explosion of blisteringly bright gorse, and delicately shaded rhododendrons, heather and thrift. The Dublin Bay air was a real treat – fresh, and full of happy memories. Yet hard as they tried, Phil and Amy were unable to recapture the old magic. The cottage – cramped and rather dreary – fell short of expectation, and the weather – wet and chilly a lot of the time – quickly made them yearn for Malaya's heat. They missed their servants... Amy more so than Phil, who showed little inclination to help out with domestic chores. Amy had not really expected him to, and was grateful enough when he took charge of Robbie; babies baffled him. But as her pregnancy advanced, she would have appreciated a hand with the heavier jobs. Long before they were half way through their leave, not just Phil, but Amy too, empathised wholeheartedly with dyed-in-the-wool colonials.

For Amy though, the biggest worry was not the cottage or the weather or the lack of servants, or even her brother, Henry, the thought of whom in prison was too grim to dwell on. Guiltily, and for Phil's sake, she pushed Henry and Shandoran to the back of her mind, just as her mother had been doing for years, without guilt. Nor was Amy worried about Phil's love for her: she no longer doubted his love and regretted ever having doubted it. No, her biggest worry was Phil himself, and her inability to help him. Indeterminate pains would afflict him, or his appetite would suddenly disappear. The smallest things – being out of cigarettes, Robbie or Ruth crying – precipitated despair. Sometimes he wandered off on the headland by himself or clammed up in the cottage for long periods. As often as not he took refuge in drink – his '*soma*', he said, jokingly. Short term, the drink lifted his spirits; long term, it left him morose. In Siam or Perlemban, his symptoms would have been a clear indication of 'having a liver', a euphemism east of Suez for anything from mild melancholia to serious hepatic disease. Here, they were not so easily explained. One minute he'd be on top of the world, joking with Amy and loving her like in the old days; bounding over the headland with Robbie on his shoulders; playing 'Peep O' with him among the gorse bushes, or chasing after him when he darted about like a little doe with Phil's caveat from the voyage home ringing in his ears – 'Keep away from the sides or the big fishes will get you.' The next minute, he'd be in an abyss…sunk into himself like a snail in its shell, not wanting to be disturbed. It was so unlike him, Amy thought; whatever the reversals, he loved to put up a good show.

Some things of course were harder than others to get over. Amy conceded this, and was in heartfelt sympathy with Phil about June. But if he was working himself into a stew about the posting of Neil Crotchley's brother to Perlemban, or about Henry's imprisonment, there really was very little she could do. Already he knew how she felt about his past, and if he could help her adjust to Henry's crime why could he not help himself to do the same. Everyone in the East had skeletons. Pride was not precious; punctured, it could be patched.

Making it harder for Amy to help Phil was his reluctance to discuss his problems with her except in an airy-fairy way that solved nothing. One such occasion occurred about half way through the leave.

Phil and Robbie had spent the morning on the headland, and everything had gone swimmingly till Robbie tripped over the front doorstep on the way in and cut his knee. He started yelling. Phil got angry. 'A morning spoilt,' he snapped at Amy, as if it was *her* fault, 'Why can't he pick his feet up?' Amy, normally quick to pick up the pieces, but not so quick today – Ruth had been restless, the dinner was late – snapped back, 'I suppose you have him run off them. He is only two!' Phil stormed out, leaving Amy to patch the knee and soothe Robbie, but soon returned – a cigarette had calmed him down – to pour himself a whisky and eat his dinner in silence. Afterwards, Amy washed up, then, still miffed, Phil could at least have dried the dishes, joined him beside the fire in their cramped, chintzy sitting room. No sooner had she sat down, than Phil looked at her and said, straight out, without any preliminaries – 'Would you ever marry again, Amy, if anything happened to me?'

'Nothing's going to happen to you,' she replied irritably. She was tired, and got the impression he was trying to make amends but being rather stupid about it.

'But would you if it did?' he persisted.

A peacemaker at heart, Amy relented. 'No,' she said, honestly enough (she'd had her fill of second marriages) 'I wouldn't.'

'I'm glad,' Phil said, and in an odd sort of way Amy found his words comforting. Then, sensing he wanted to talk, she groaned silently (she really was very tired) and took the cigarette he offered her; the least she could do was listen and there was always a chance something would come out of it.

As he lit her cigarette, Phil asked – 'Do you ever wonder, Amy, why we're here and where we're going?'

'I take it you mean on this earth?' Amy replied, knowing exactly how she would respond if that was so; she had often posed the same question to herself and always come up with the same answer. Noting Phil's affirmative expression, she carried on – 'Well as I see it – we're here to make the most of our God-given talents and to help others do the same with theirs. Does that sound too simplistic?'

Phil smiled; Amy's answer was so typical of her. Then, less smilingly, and with a hint of cynicism he said – 'No, it doesn't. But if it's true – my sister, June, may well have died because she wasted her God-given talents.'

'Don't talk such nonsense,' Amy said, annoyed her words were being construed in such a way, as well as by Phil's tone. 'Your sister died because she had TB…for no other reason.'

'But if she'd stuck to her music and not gone to London she might not have got the TB,' Phil insisted more irritatingly than before.

'Now you're being ridiculous,' Amy said. 'That's like saying –

if we'd never been born we wouldn't ever have to die. Or are you trying to imply that June was somehow punished for not continuing with her music?'

'Well?'

'And just who or what do you imagine punished her? The God you don't believe in?'

'Or the God you do believe in?'

'No, Phil. My God is all forgiving. He gives us the will to do what we do, no strings attached; punishment's man made. June wasn't punished…she was unlucky. There's no punishment in the next world.'

'You really believe there's a next, Amy?'

'I do.' Detecting now a wistful note in Phil's voice, Amy continued in lighter tone. 'It's not one you can easily describe, of course… You can't touch it or see it… It's just there. I suppose it's all down to faith.'

'You and your faith; doesn't anything ever shake it?'

'Oh, yes! Not to the point of extinguishing it, though. Not yet, anyway! It's like the roots of an old oak…stuck fast.

It must be, Phil thought, for surely to God the heritage isn't sustaining her now. The thought amused him.

'You're laughing at me,' Amy said, unaware of what lay behind his smile.

'But I don't expect you to think the way I do, Phil. We're different. You get by with your facts, figures and reasoning. I need more than that for my salvation.

That is, if I'm worth saving!'

'Well if you're not, Amy, God help the rest of us.'

'Oh you do have a God then!'

Phil smiled. 'I asked for that, didn't I,' he said. 'No, Amy, I can't lay claim to any God. Would yours forgive me if you petitioned him on my behalf?'

'I'm sure he would,' Amy said comfortingly. 'It might be better, though,' she teased, 'if you asked Him yourself.'

'You mean borrow him?'

Amy laughed. Little things like this reminded her of the old Phil.

They left it there, and Amy dropped off. Phil looked at her enviously. The surety he had admired from the outset, and wondered if anything could shake, had surely taken a battering. Yet she could still sleep. Some faith! He thought, unable to relax.

◇

Phil's trouble was – he had got it into his grief-stricken mind he would never be able to hold his head up in Perlemban again. The prospect of a double disgrace there – himself portrayed as a man of violence (Neil's brother was bound to exaggerate the staff-room incident), his brother-in-law in prison (it was bound to come out) – was too much for him to bear. He imagined everyone looking at him and Amy, whispering about them behind their backs, laughing at them…maybe even, in time, laughing at Robbie and Ruth. As Head of Police, Neil's brother would be more than well placed to do his worst; and if he had gone to all the trouble of being posted to Perlemban, his worst didn't bear thinking about. So-called friends would melt away, the Castles probably among them. With Major Martin gone, Helen might even take up with the new Head of Police!

Faced with such a scenario, the thought of returning to Perlemban terrified Phil. Blue skies or grey, biting east wind or soft westerly, it tightened its grip on him like a boa. Assumed ever greater magnitude in his mind; haunted him round the clock, thrummed in his head day in day out, beat into his brain incessantly…like a jammed record on a turntable, or Chopin's A flat raindrops. He balked at it.

If the thought of returning to Perlemban was a nightmare, the thought of remaining in Ireland was as bad; another loss of face too great to bear. In Ireland too, people would be pointing the finger, whispering he'd failed at home, failed abroad and come back to Dublin like a whipped dog, and with his brother-in-law in gaol.

Trapped in a vice… on the horns of a dilemma, between Scylla and Charybdis… a rock and a hard place; unable to stand back and view his situation dispassionately; with no God to turn to (sometimes he wished he had but he had spent so long rubbishing other people's he couldn't find one of his own) – Phil turned in on himself. What he saw disgusted him and, no stranger to self-doubt, he gave self-laceration its head. He had wasted his God-given gifts (if that's what they were) in a big way, achieved nothing, let everyone down – his parents, his children, Amy. He prided himself on his honesty, but had been as dishonest as the rest; not been straight with his parents, not been straight with Amy. Whatever which way he viewed himself, the picture reflected the inadequacy of his past, the pointlessness of his future. He was an all time fucker-upper; and if the pains he'd been feeling in his chest of late indicated something more serious than indigestion, so be it. What was the point of going on?

Standing one evening on his own on the cliff tops near the end of the headland, he looked across the Bay at the sun setting behind the Dublin Mountains. About three weeks of his leave remained; he had been drinking, but not to excess. I'll end it here and now, he thought – go down with the sun, only never rise again. Drowning, he'd heard, was not the worst of deaths; if Maggie Scott could face it, so could he. What was it anyway! A lifetime flashing before ones eyes, then nothing. Every dawn and sunset he had known, the high hopes and glittering prizes of his youth, salad days in Dublin with Amy, the romance and glamour of the East, the onset of disillusionment, disgrace. Thirty-six years of under-achievement or, put another way, four out of seven stages.

For a few moments the number seven preoccupied Phil. What was it, he wondered, that made it so special? The Seven – eight, if you included Amy's! – Gifts of the Holy Ghost:

Wisdom, Understanding, Counsel, Fortitude – he knew them all! – Knowledge, Righteousness, Fear of the Lord. Not bad, he thought, for an unbeliever! The Seven Virtues (he knew those too...Christian and Platonic, and each as good as the rest) – Faith, Hope, Charity, Justice, Fortitude, Prudence and Temperance. Away from the Bible, there were the Seven Hills of Rome, the Seven Weeks War, the Seven Years War, the Seven Seas, the Dance of the Seven Veils, Seventh Heaven. Hard on the heels of that lot, bringing Phil back to the Bible and the here and now, came the Seven Deadly Sins. Itemising those would have been a waste of time, he reckoned; for even if he was not guilty of them all, he had sinned enough to forfeit his life. Why should he, a sinner, live, when his darling sister, June – good, beautiful June – was dead. What kind of God allowed that sort of injustice to happen? It was time somebody showed Him.

The setting sun sank almost out of sight.

What's the point of going on? Phil asked himself, stepping forward and teetering uncaringly on a loose stone. The happiness I've known has been real enough but even as I experienced it, seeds of unhappiness were being sown. Reaping them has been painful, and will be more so in the years ahead. I can't face it. Amy and the children will be better off without me. As a husband, I'm useless; as a father, a bad example. And four out of seven stages is not a bad tally. Who wants to be lumbered with pot belly or 'shrunk shank' anyway? Still less, be 'sans everything'? It's my life.

Looking down into the water, Phil teetered again. Some lines from Tennyson ran through his mind – 'Sunset and evening star And one clear call for me! And may there be no moaning at the bar, When I put out to sea.' The loose stone under his foot gave way, and threw him towards the edge of the cliff. 'Jesus,' he exclaimed, struggling to regain his balance. He did regain it; then returned home slowly, more disgusted with himself than ever; I am a funk, he thought.

◇

Faced with Phil's moods, Amy found herself, as her pregnancy advanced, losing patience with him. 'If you drank less, Phil, you might feel better,' she'd snap on this or that occasion. Other times, when concern for his health – his chest pains, his loss of weight he could ill afford to lose, his sunken, grey eyes – overrode her impatience, she'd suggest a visit to a doctor: 'You're not right, Phil. Why not let an expert help you?' He ignored her advice and, unable to influence him, she got on with each day the only way she could, practically.

Getting out and about might have made things easier for both of them. But visiting wasn't easy with the children, and Phil kept finding reasons to stay at home. '"The wretched have no friends", Amy,' he once said, to which she retorted impatiently, 'For God's sake, Phil, catch yourself on.' She did manage a get-together in Dublin with Catherine who, like herself, was expecting her third child. (A terrace house in Rathmines had replaced the flat.) With Catherine's help, and no little hilarity – four children in tow could be fun as well as frustrating – Amy managed to buy a suitable evening dress – a roomy nacreous one – for the voyage home. On another occasion, she took Robbie and Ruth into St. Hilda's where the nuns made a great fuss of them, leading Robbie to refer to them for some time thereafter as 'nice b'ack 'adies, Mummy, wi' tocit bixits.' She would have taken the children into Glenarkle too, only Phil was ill on the day she'd arranged to go, forcing her to phone Mr Appleby and cancel. The Headmaster wished her well and promised to pass on her good wishes to his wife and staff. There were no new faces, he said, among the staff apart from the master who had taken her place.

On balance though, Amy's forays beyond Howth were less rewarding than she'd anticipated. Nothing was quite the same as before despite Dublin having changed little during her absence – or since her return except for the removal of the Union Jack from Trinity's West Front in the wake of the Jubilee. She wondered what Max Stone was making of that! For the rest, conversing with old friends and acquaintances was somehow stilted; the penny took longer to drop; everyone had moved on. Tucked away at the back of Amy's mind, the thought of Henry's imprisonment was, despite what Phil may or may not have thought, a constant embarrassment to her, even though no-one in Dublin knew about it.

Early in August, the Handys said good-bye to their cottage in Howth and headed for Southampton. Before leaving the peninsula, Phil visited Fermanagh briefly to bid farewell to his parents and stand for a few moments beside June's grave.

Amy neither revisited Knockmore nor went to Shandoran or to see Henry.

En route to Southampton, tattered remains of the Jubilee drew a cynical 'yesterday's confetti' from Phil. Amy ignored him.

In the port, they boarded the 'Batavia'.

For Phil, it was a strange kind of embarkation. He felt as though he was doing things like an automaton. His chest pains worsened, and a kind of fatalism possessed him, prompting him to do his duty by day – take care of Robbie – and drink to his hearts content at night. Most nights he went to bed blotto.

Amy was not sorry to be underway. Ireland was doing Phil no good at all, just reawakening his restless rootlessness of old. In Malaya, his work would sober him up, help him to get over June's death and, hopefully, come to terms with whatever cupboard-skeletons got out. For herself, she was pleased she would be well clear of the seas before her baby arrived. She would definitely take down *Flaxfields* when she got back to Perlemban. If it was missed she would think of something to say. As things stood, the thought of her brother's crime getting out in the East was less troublesome to her than living with it, out or otherwise, in Ireland. More than ever now, she understood Phil's original decision to go East.

As always on board, they jogged along from one day and deck party to the next.

Sashaying out of the ballroom after a particularly jolly evening, they took off along a passageway singing and swaying to the receding strains of *The Road To Mandalay*. Half way down a companion ladder Phil missed his footing and, grimly clutching his half-full whisky glass in one hand and half-smoked cigarette in the other, slithered awkwardly into Amy's arms at the bottom. She just managed to keep her balance but couldn't prevent some of his drink spilling on to her new frock – the only maternity one of its kind she had. Annoyed, she abandoned him to his unsteady legs and gave the wet part of her dress a shake.

'I'm sorry,' Phil said, struggling to keep upright and extricate his handkerchief from his breast pocket without spilling any more of his drink or burning his jacket. 'It will wash out, won't it?'

'Of course it will,' Amy replied crossly. In the same tone, she added – 'I'm telling you now, Phil, if you don't stop this drinking, you won't be able to hold down your job in Malaya.' The prospect of this – she'd been thinking about it increasingly, it vied with the one that his job would sober him up – terrified her.

Steadying himself with deliberation, and maladroitly dabbing at her frock with his hankie, Phil smiled sardonically. 'Come off it, Amy. We both know I'll never see Malaya again.'

'Don't talk such nonsense!' Amy retorted, satisfied her dress wasn't ruined and offering to take his weight. He put an arm round her. 'I do adore you, Amy,' he said. 'Come on,' she replied, more irritated than flattered: he only said things like that when he was well and truly tanked up. She took his weight, and they staggered along to their cabin, to the slurred accompaniment from Phil, and Amy's further annoyance, of – '"Twilight and evening bell, And after that the dark! And may there be no sadness of farewell, When I embark".'

Within an hour, he had a massive heart attack. The ship's doctor told Amy it was fatal. Appalled, she sat down on the nearest chair. The idea that he was gravely ill, never mind fatally, had never entered her head.

On the cusp of consciousness, Phil barely survived the night.

Amy sat with him throughout it – regretting having snapped at him earlier on; determined to remain strong for him; not to cry. For a long time, he seemed indifferent to her presence. She held his hand. It was cold, which surprised her as she'd imagined that sort of thing only set in after death; she had never witnessed, never mind touched, a dying person before. Why didn't you listen to me, she thought, haplessly? 'I love you so much,' she said hopelessly, willing him to make one last sign of recognition, one last sign of love. There was nothing. No smile; no word; no squeeze; no glimmer. Motionless – his face and eyes ashen – he stared resignedly, if a little bewildered by what was happening. Amy kept quite still too – not wanting to intrude on his privacy. After what seemed like forever to her, he uttered the words – 'Like a cabbage white's wings.' They meant nothing to her. His next words meant everything. Turning his head slowly, he looked at her sorrowfully and murmured, 'My own, darling Amy.' It was the end and she knew it. Her eyes filled with tears. They spilled over. She thought her heart would burst. Seconds later, he died.

Amy kissed him good-bye on the lips. Then she rested her head on his chest and prayed for his soul, knowing God would take care of it. There was nothing else she could do.

⬦

The burial took place at dawn, half way across the Indian Ocean.

The Captain suggested Amy remain in her cabin with Robbie and Ruth during the Service, but she said she'd rather attend and took her place on deck, where the whole ship's company, dazzlingly white in the early morning haze, was assembled; another passenger took care of the children. Not a ripple on the sea or ruckle in the dress disturbed the air as someone, somewhere, monotoned the prayers. "'I am the resurrection and the life, saith the Lord: he that believeth in me, though he were dead, yet shall he live: and whosoever liveth and believeth in me shall never die…'" The entombment – the long, lonely, drop to the deep – was as chilling for Amy as a Cavan lake, frozen beneath a heavy veil of mist.

Chapter Twenty-five

Somehow Amy got through the next few years. It was a wretched time for her; a time when all too often her life seemed to mirror the creeping disintegration in the world at large.

◇

In Europe, the term *status quo* acquired an empty ring, as fascism and the long drawn-out depression continued to undermine old certainties, and the 'twenties roar' to be replaced by the heavy thud of jackboots. Appeasement cleared a path for the goosesteppers, and by the time the world woke up it was too late. In turn, Germany picked off the Rhineland, Austria and the Sudetenland then trained her sights on Poland. Ireland was not immune to the depression or fascism, but it was the push to republicanism by the South's new leader, DeValera, that grabbed his country's headlines. Not everyone liked the changes. One abolished dual nationality; another renamed the Free State – Eire. Few considered them worth fighting over: in the South, talk had replaced arms, and Protestants grown used to being ruled by Catholics.

For Amy, peace at any price was welcome when she returned to Dublin from the East. Physically, mentally, and emotionally washed up, she felt empty as a drained glass, or a spent Christmas cracker.

Most crushing of all for her on the way back was – not knowing. Not knowing where she would live, Shandoran being out of the question, and throwing herself on her mother, Eleanor's charity unthinkable; the 'I told you sos' would be unbearable. Not knowing how she would manage financially: what money there was – not much, she reckoned (spending, not saving, had continued to be the order of the day in the East) – was in Phil's name; her small colonial pension would not go far; and work, with two small children and a baby on the way would not be easy. Not knowing where her baby would be born, and if it would be all right, or malformed in some way because of the trauma she and it were going through.

Incognizance made her feel helpless and induced headaches, something she'd rarely suffered from, not even in her slough of despond in the East but knew all about from Mrs Appleby's indispositions. Helplessness and headaches made her fume in turn against Phil and Henry; filled her with mawkish self-pity; reduced her to tears; caused her to snap at Robbie, be impatient with placid Ruth, and despair of God. How could Phil have thrown his life away without a thought for her and the children? How could Henry have destroyed the Cavan home she cherished? Whatever will I do now? What will become of me?

These and others like them were the questions plaguing Amy – During the five days she spent in Bombay, a steamy, teaming city where she said good-bye to the Batavia, posted Helen's warm suit – she'd quickly outgrown it – to Perlemban, listened to Robbie's interminable, 'Where Daddy, Mummy?' 'When Daddy coming back?' and eventually boarded a westward-bound liner; during the weary (despite the kindness of passengers and crew) four week voyage home. During her fruitless wait on Southampton's dank, foggy dockside where – seven months pregnant, inadequately clothed (October had arrived), gripping Robbie in a vice, listening to Ruth whingeing (unusual for her) in her Silver Cross pram, piled high with belongings – she wondered if anyone would come to meet her. During the final minutes of her Mail Boat crossing when things that had always lifted her spirits in the past – Kingstown's tickertape escort of frenzied seagulls, its stout granite piers, beckoning spires and banked terraces of pastel-shaded hotels – failed to do so now. Instead, the port's screaming gulls jarred, its granite piers were hard and cheerless, its acuminate skyline, cold and distantly sombre. As Amy made her way cumbersomely down the mail-boat's gangplank – her legs felt like jelly, her stomach griped (a rough crossing had made her vomit repeatedly), her head ached.

Then just when she thought she could take no more, she saw two 'displaced penguins' at the end of Kingstown's wharf. Close to, Sisters Martha and Cecilia's rosy-cheeked, beatific smiles had never seemed more welcoming to Amy; their cassock-laden embraces, pungent of incense, camphor and artichoke soup, never smelled so good. Eleanor had written to St. Hilda's asking for someone to meet her daughter. Straightway, the nuns took Amy and the children to the Convent, offered her a job in its school and the two small rooms at the end of its top-floor corridor.

Unbounded relief and joy – emotions that would reach new heights when she held her baby, Angela, in her arms for the first time – swept Amy up and carried her forward like a fair wind steadying a sailing ship after a storm. Fair winds, though, could presage further storms.

◇

At St Hilda's, teaching (more dogsbodying at the outset) was hard, and despite Ruth's placidity and considerable help from the nuns, Amy found her children demanding. For a long time Robbie fretted over Phil; their closeness made it inevitable. Amy did what she could, which never seemed to be enough. Once – he was still three at the time – he woke up after a bad dream. 'Why Daddy go to big fishes, Mummy?' he asked, tearfully wide-eyed. The question took Amy by surprise, and she was angry with whoever (a Batavia crewmember, she supposed) had described Phil's burial to the child in that way; telling him, as she herself had done, that his Daddy had gone to Heaven where Jesus and the angels were taking care of him, was kinder. Holding her son close, she stroked his silky, fair hair, and reaffirmed the bit about Heaven and the angels. Soothed, he asked her for a 'tocit bixit.' She gave him one (she kept some handy) and after another cuddle, snuggled him into her own bed. She was just dropping off when she heard his little voice again – 'When Daddy coming back, Mummy?'

When he was four, Robbie joined Sister Cecilia's charges

in the smallest of the school's dorms; Ruth and Angela did likewise when they were four. Up to now, Catherine Townley had been St Hilda's youngest new pupil, so adapting to babies was no easy matter for the nuns. They did splendidly, Amy thought.

Others helped too – Eleanor especially. She came up trumps at holiday times and took a great fancy to Ruth not just because of her placid nature but because of her looks: the child's dark hair and eyes, and sallow skin were obvious Daker traits. It was just a great 'pity', Eleanor said, pointedly, Amy hadn't given the child a decent name. Amy became resigned to that, as well as the 'I told you sos'; she became resigned to a lot of things. She never took back or apologised for her outburst at Knockmore, but took comfort from the knowledge that Eleanor's shame over Henry's imprisonment was already waning and that Tom's hopes for gentleman status for Vincent were firmly on course.

Overall it was a slog, and unquestionably the busiest time in Amy's life so far; never before had she had so much to do. Yet never before had peace of mind proved so elusive for her.

This had nothing to do with her bereavement, painful though that was; or with day-to-day uncertainties – meeting deadlines, worrying about her children when they fell ill, and about who would look after them if she was ill; nor had it anything to do with uncertainties in the world at large. Her unease was the result of guilt.

For throughout these early years of widowhood not a day passed when, no matter how busy, Amy did not think about Henry, bleed a little for him and wince at not going to see him. Pushing him to the back of her mind had been possible when Phil was alive; widowhood made it impossible. Her brother needed her. Steadfastly she stayed away from him. Why?

◇

In the aftermath of Phil's death, Amy told herself it would be a betrayal of his memory to visit her brother in prison; such a visit would have been abhorrent to Phil in life; it didn't seem right to go against his wishes now. Nor would her mother have liked it – her mother who was currently being so helpful about holidays. There was also the very real possibility that someone might see her going into or out of the gaol. To the best of her knowledge, no one she knew in Dublin was aware of Henry's situation except Mother Superior whom she'd told on returning to the Convent. A wall of silence had been erected round it at Shandoran, and loyalty to Henry in Kilbeg had much the same effect there; Linnakers and Handys never mentioned it. Amy wanted to keep it that way, for her own and her children's sake. Finally, her children and job left little time for anything else.

But these were only excuses, she knew. Just as she knew what she was doing was unforgivable. She was taking everything; giving nothing in return; abandoning her brother in his hour of need. She prayed for him – something she had found hard to do with any degree of sincerity when Phil was alive; but her prayers only magnified her guilt. She was a hypocrite; a person who mouthed the words of her faith while refusing to act her faith out. Her God had not forgotten her; she was letting Him down badly; she didn't deserve Him. Her behaviour was mean and cowardly; something no amount of tears and sympathy could compensate for.

And there was no shortage of tears and sympathy on her part. One moment in particular was very poignant.

Alone in her room at St Hilda's, she was thinking about making a frock for Ruth. Vespers was underway; Robbie, Ruth and Angela were in bed. The summer holidays were round the corner so she could use her mother's Singer sewing-machine – one of the more recently acquired gadgets at Knockmore and one of the latest hand-operated variety of the machine which Amy much preferred to the old treadle. She had just the remnant for the job in her trunk – a piece of pink, floral cotton that would look lovely with Ruth's colouring.

Even before she opened the trunk, she knew – it always happened – she would get sidetracked. Packed and returned to her from Perlemban by Helen Castle, it smelled of camphor and was stuffed with things that were seldom if ever used but which she couldn't bear to part with. En route to the remnant she went through them one by one, fingering some lovingly, laying others aside quickly. A photograph of Phil with his arm draped round Helen at Port Dickson fell out of a bulging brown packet; Amy, an accessory on the edge of the snap, gave it short shrift, conscience alone prevented her tearing it up. Similarly, though from sentiment not conscience, her white, Shantung silk wedding-dress – without sleeves it would make a nice slip, she thought – and a pair of Phil's white, silk pyjamas – also earmarked for the scissors though to what end she wasn't sure – were still intact. Less likely to be aired – ever – was the contents of a large, flat parcel at the bottom of the trunk. Those of a medium-sized, satin-lined basket tied up with ribbon were dipped into occasionally for bits of lace but otherwise kept under wraps too.

Having unearthed the piece of print cotton she set it aside and randomly selected an old poetry book of Phil's and started flicking through it. *The Ballad of Reading Gaol* caught her eye. She began reading it, and before long, had surrendered herself to the deceptive power of Wilde's lyrical imagery. She felt the pain of incarceration, and the sorrow of being beyond the pale. Tears streamed down her cheeks, forcing her to get up and get a handkerchief to read on. But the tears kept coming, blinding and choking her, so that in the end she didn't know whether she was crying for Henry or Wilde or their fellow prisoners; or for herself or Phil, or for all the sad, forgotten people in the world. It was not the first time she had read the poem; there was a time, indeed, when she could have recited it off pat, like *The Ancient Mariner* and one or two others she could think of. But never before had its impact on her been so intense…so completely overwhelming. And then the moment passed, and she felt silly for having let herself go, and wiped her eyes, and repacked everything except the remnant in the trunk.

Yet traumatic though this experience was, it was not sufficiently strong to overcome her reservations about visiting

Henry. Nor were her recurrent nightmares; nightmares so awful she'd come to regard them as punishment for her callousness. Most featured snakes – a species she had only encountered once in the wild and hoped never to encounter again. In the final stages of pregnancy with Robbie at the time, and bored with Club and Kampong, she'd gone for a walk on her own on a forbidden track bounded by jungle on one side and a river on the other. About a hundred yards down it, and no more than a few paces away, she'd seen the snake – a huge one – winding its way up from the river and crossing the path in front of her. She'd stopped, as suddenly as if she'd hit a brick wall, and, petrified, waited for the ghastly thing to slither out of sight. Then, heedless of her condition, tripping and stumbling, she'd torn back to the Kampong. Phil – he had just arrived home from work – nearly blew a gasket. 'How could you have been so stupid, Amy!' he'd shouted at her. 'It must 'a' bin a python. You *know* you shouldn't go anywhere near the jungle on your own!' Later, when her labour started, he'd been full of apologies and shown nothing but concern for her on the way to hospital in KL.

Tears and nightmares notwithstanding, Amy stayed away from her brother and, stalked by guilt, continued to do so even after Lucy told her he was out of prison.

What good can a visit do now? she asked herself. Serve no useful purpose and maybe make things worse. Another excuse, she knew. Knowing made her wonder how she could live with herself.

The truth was, she had invested so much love and pride in Shandoran, she feared seeing it or Henry as they were now might totally undermine her belief in herself. So much of what had given her life meaning in the past – Phil, Shandoran and her Allen heritage, her relationship with God – was either gone or hopelessly impaired. By staying away, she could cling to what remained of her sullied heritage. So she stayed away – guiltily, and increasingly of the opinion she could never look Henry in the eye again. She could live with – exist might have been a better word, for how could an incomplete person feel truly alive – his crime and suffering from afar. It had become like a bunion or rheumatic joint…a dull ache that flared up from time to time, deluging her in shame but never sufficiently for her to do something about it.

Not, that was, till Harriet's letter arrived. Its timing was telling.

◇

The Second World War had started, and DeValera opted to keep Eire out of it. His decision disgusted many of his countrymen but did not seriously damage relations between Protestants and Catholics. This was because opponents of neutrality came from both sides of the religious divide, and anyone who wanted to could enlist as a Volunteer. Many did. The rest talked. At St Hilda's, the nuns spoke with one voice on the matter: neutrality was wrong, but with God's help – and with or without DeValera's, England would triumph. At Glenarkle – where Amy had resumed her old habit of taking Sunday tea with the Applebys, and sometimes dropped into the staffroom to renew old acquaintances and share in the banter – opinions differed. Max Stone (Classics) took a world view. 'Democracy itself is at stake,' he'd say, 'and past differences should be put aside to defend it.' Peter Pagley (History) begged to differ. 'In an ideal world – yes, Stone; but not this one. Sure how could you expect DeValera's Eire, a country bathed in the blood of martyrs, to turn round and help its former oppressors! The man wouldn't survive a day in power if he took us into war.' William Dodson (English) mollified. 'Now you've both got a point,' he'd say. 'In practice, though, DeValera's way is the only one. Smyllie, here, has the right idea.' With that, Dodson would tap his *Irish Times* on his knee and someone would come up with an example of the said Smyllie's journalistic dexterity in the matter of praising, while not praising, the heroics of the Volunteers. Paying tribute to them openly was forbidden, and Smyllie – a broad-minded man, who had replaced the Anglophile, Healy, as editor of the paper in the thirties – knew exactly how to get round the ruling. Avoiding the word 'Volunteer', he would record the death of one from bullet or shrapnel wounds as death by 'lead poisoning'. If a Volunteer went down with his battleship, the phrase 'boating accident' was used. Everyone knew what he was talking about and his simple terminology struck home with Catholics and Protestants alike. It was the first time they had taken up arms together since the Treaty of 1921.

Listening to the arguments in Glenarkle's staffroom, Amy couldn't but think – *This* was where Phil belonged; not in some God forsaken outpost in the East. On the issue of neutrality, he would doubtless have sided with Stone. She herself went with Dodson, knowing Pagley and the Classics master took no offence. For if cracks were appearing in Glenarkle's Englishness, its gentlemanliness was as strong as ever. So strong, it made Amy wish (St Hilda's could be stifling) she could have been more positive in her response to Mr Appleby when he'd said once over tea that if her old job came up at his school, she could have first refusal on it. At the time, she'd stalled, saying she was in no position then, and might never be able to rejoin his staff. Secretly, the thought of telling him about Henry – something she would have to do if he reengaged her – had not appealed. She'd kept her options open though, on the grounds that she might feel differently about her brother in the future.

When the moment of truth arrived, however, she turned her back on it. And this, despite the tempting nature of Mr Appleby's offer, coupled as it was with the offer of a place for Robbie, who would be eight on his next birthday (too old for St Hilda's) at Glenarkle. 'Let him try for a scholarship, Mrs Handy,' he said at her latest tea party with him and his wife, 'Ways and means!' This – 'Ways and means' – was another of Mr A's favourite expressions; for him, defeatism was no more tolerable than were bad manners.

Despairingly, Amy returned to St Hilda's, wondering if she could ever shake off the ignominy of Henry's crime. Wash away the black spot that blighted her life in the same way as it and Phil's past had blighted his. Now, more than ever, she understood Phil's predicament.

The next day, Harriet's letter arrived.

Dated fifteenth October, 1940, penned childishly, and by a person Amy had never really warmed to, especially in the light of her treatment of Maggie – the letter threw her into a flat spin; catapulted her into action.

'Things aren't as bad as you probably imagine,' she read, after some preliminary comments about the war, and about how well Britain – 'No thanks to DeValera!' – had stood up to German bombing. The reference to DeValera made Amy smile. She read on. 'Henry is home again and trying hard to adjust. He often talks about you. There's another baby on the way and it would be wonderful if you could visit us some time. We both feel very sorry for the hard times you've had and wish we could have helped you more. The flax fields are wasted. We have pigs now! It was Matt's idea – to keep some money coming in. Matt left soon after Henry came home. He took Nancy with him. It was what Henry wanted. Luke and Billy help Henry with the pigs. Lottie is sixteen. I don't know how I'd manage without her. She keeps asking me if you are coming down. I tell her you are snowed under. Come if you can, Amy. Please. Love, Harriet.'

Disgusted with herself, Amy put the letter down. Can it really be that long! she thought, glancing again at the date. How *could* I have been so callous! A quick visit, that's all it would have taken, to show I cared. Now, I'm being shamed into it.

Frightened into it, she might have added. For there were things about the letter – the genuine concern for her; the touch of humour in adversity; the simple plea at the end; above all, the absence of self-pity and recrimination – that impelled Amy to act where conscience alone might not have done.

Immediately she wrote to Harriet to the effect that she would be at Knockmore with the children for half-term and would visit Shandoran from there. Then she wrote to her sister, Lucy, asking if Jo could run her over to the estate from Ballymun and collect her when she left it; up to now she had steered clear of Ballymun as well as Shandoran for fear of bumping into anyone from the estate there.

Then she relaxed a little, told herself she was reading things into Harriet's letter that weren't there at all and that the visit, if nothing else, would help her to understand why Henry had acted as he had; by now she was convinced insurance alone was not the cause of his crime.

Chapter Twenty-six

The night before Amy left Knockmore for Shandoran, she had the mother and father of nightmares. She woke screaming, drenched in sweat.

'Not the snakes again, Amy!' said a worried Naomie on the other side of the bed. Naomie, Amy's youngest half-sister, home for a few days from her secretarial course in Dublin (she'd decided against nursing despite her older sisters loving it), knew all about the snakes. Her ambition was to see the world, something that appalled her mother. 'Do you want to end up like Amy,' Eleanor would say to her, sometimes in Amy's presence, 'homeless, husbandless and penniless?' Undaunted, Naomie kept her sights on the world, a first stop towards which, when her secretarial course and the war were over, would be London. In London she could go and see pictures like *Gone With The Wind* as soon as they came out, not when they were 'old hat'. Pending London, she whetted her appetite for global adventure by listening *ad nauseam* to Amy's stories about the East.

Fretfully, Amy confirmed Naomie's suspicions and, with difficulty, sat up – taking care not to disturb Ruth and Angela, asleep between them in the big feather-bolstered bed; Robbie was in a put-up job in Vincent's room, where the apples used to be stored. Pushing back the bedclothes, Amy rested her feet on the cold lino. Naomie, feeling guilty for having persuaded her half-sister to tell her not only about the python but the *burung hantu* as well before going to bed, came round and sat beside her, and put her arm round her, and listened – raptly – as Amy told her the dream.

An uncannily lifelike Phil – smart, smiling and debonair – had appeared in the bedroom doorway. As he moved forward, Amy felt blissfully happy. She wanted to touch him – to wrap her arms round him, feel his arms around her would be wonderful – but was riveted to the bed. She tried to speak; no words came, just gagging. Anguished, she watched the spectre transmute into a tramp. Dressed in a long, straggly raincoat, with a rope tied round the waist, he came wading through a bright blue flax field. From nowhere, the field filled up with children, skipping higgledy-piggledy through the flowers, waving hurricanes and laughing merrily. Henry, Amy, Lucy and Benjie were among them. Then the flax field gave way to hills and lanes, the children to revellers of all ages, and the tramp – to a grotesque mixture of bandmaster and Pied Piper of Hamelin. Sprouting horns, and a long, scrawny tail (his baton) this weird master of ceremonies high stepped out at the head of a motley crew of sashed Orangemen, bandsmen and standard bearers – many buckling at the knees, all jostling to take up their positions for a parade. Drums rolled; an eerie hush descended. Then with a swish of his scrawny-tailed baton, and a flamboyant leap in the air, the hybrid set the parade in motion. Pipes, flutes and piccolos trilled out familiar tunes – *The Sash*, and *The Green Grassy Banks of the Boyne* – as the marchers got underway, banners aloft, blazoned reminders of Unionist triumphs (the Boyne, Enniskillen, Derry, and Aughrim), of their debt to King Billy, and their loyalty to the British Crown. All along the route, a neverending stream of cheering, flag-waving supporters swelled the clamorous ranks. It was like a great loyalist wave, rolling round Kilbeg; a macabre wave. For the hybrid was everywhere, uglily strutting and prancing as the wild jubilation in colour, wind and timpani, rose and fell up hill and down dale, twisted and turned round lakes, ponds and rivers, woods and marshmeadow lands, fields and bogs, big houses and tied cottages. Then as suddenly as they had appeared, the revellers, musicians, hills, lanes and hybrid vanished. The flax field was back – only blighted now, and traversed by a tortured Henry. He was wearing the tramp's coat, but a knotted snake, with sloughy skin, and gaping, limp-fanged mouth, had replaced the rope. Writhing hideously, the snake was choking itself and Henry to death. Henry's arms flailed; his face contorted painfully; his tangled hair dripped perspiration. Frantic to help him – Amy couldn't; the reptile mesmerised her; like it and

Henry, she choked and gasped for air. I'm suffocating, she thought, powerless to move while every part of her strained to be free. Unleashed at last, she wrenched her gaze from the repulsive waist cord only to find herself staring into the spectre's face – no longer her brother's, nor any recognisable person's, but a terrifyingly nondescript, blanched image whose only discernable features were pitch black holes for eyes. She screamed.

'Oh, Naomie, it was awful', she said, 'I thought I was going to suffocate. I wanted Phil to come back but he didn't... and Henry... my God, Naomie! Do you think it's a sign? Maybe something terrible's happened at Shandoran. Maybe I shouldn't go at all. It's too late...'

'Hush, Amy, dear, hush', Naomie said. 'Don't upset yourself so. I'm sure it's not a sign of anything bad. You'll feel better in the morning. You'll see. Now let's go back to sleep.' Naomie spoke soothingly, and Amy, not wanting to keep her half-sister up any longer, allowed herself to be coaxed back to bed. She slept fitfully – reliving her dream, trying to force a happy ending to it, to make sense out of Phil's death, of her own life, of Henry's crime. Happiness and sense eluded her; everything was painfully blurred.

◇

It was early afternoon when Amy set out with her brother-in-law, Jo, from Aikens' in Ballymun for Shandoran. Lucy had protested at the brevity of her sister's visit but was mollified when Amy told her she would only be spending one night at Shandoran and the next with her before returning to Knockmore.

The winding, bumpy road to Shandoran was so filled with memories for Amy she could concentrate her mind on nothing. On the seat beside her lay a discarded newspaper from the previous day. Its headlines – 'Italy attacks Greece'; 'DeValera stands firm on neutrality' – made little impact on her. The world was adrift; anchorless like her thoughts. Thoughts that swelled and died like wind gusts, and swelled again as pictures from her past zoomed in and fell away. Henry dominated them; Henry and his emotion-charged eyes. Whatever the guise – cowed by his mother's raised arm, exultant in his heritage, exuberant in love, desperate in frustration – his vulnerability was stark. What would he be like now? Amy wondered sadly as she recalled a line from Wilde's Ballad – 'Each narrow cell in which we dwell Is a foul and dark latrine' – and tried once more in vain to make sense of what her brother had done.

But no matter what the reason for his crime, she was not on her way to Shandoran to censure him. Who was she to censure anyone? If anything, she should be asking forgiveness of Henry. She would do that, then offer what help she could. She had been unable to help Phil; hopefully, she could help her brother.

The thought of helping calmed her. For the first time in a long time she began to feel in control; she was *doing* something at last. Instead of dreading seeing Henry, she started looking forward to it. He had a way of bouncing back – like a trampled daisy she used to think in the past when she helped him get over a beating. She knew now what needed saying: words of consolation, encouragement and hope. Her presence would do the rest. It would be like the old days – she, the wise sister, he, the incorrigible brother. Enough tears had been shed. It was time to look to the future…to put the past behind…

'Here we are,' said Jo, a happy go lucky, jovial fellow who had known better than to engage in idle chatter on the short run to Shandoran, 'I'll drop you by the front gate and pick you up here again at noon tomorrow. Will that be all right now for you?' Amy said it would. Thanking Jo, she waved him off.

Left alone, Amy stood outside the entrance to her old home wondering momentarily if Jo had made a mistake. For the once broad, sweeping avenue resembled a cart-track, and not till Amy's eye fell on the elm whose beautiful fissured bark was slowly being strangled by creepers, could she be sure of her whereabouts. Half-open, the gate sagged on its hinges.

Amy went through it, tucking a projecting briar (a habit of hers) that nearly caught her in the face back into the hedge. With enormous effort, she dragged herself forward. Tangled bushes, and dense, overarching branches cut out the light and hemmed her in. Tufts of grass sprouted under her feet. The sharpest eye could not have discerned the avenue's well. Even the beech had lost its prominence.

Rusted and lopsided like the outer, the inner avenue gate was closed. Amy pushed it open, too afraid almost to look ahead. When she did look, everything was much worse than she'd imagined. Neglect and squalor she could have understood. But total dereliction! *That* was something she had not bargained for. The street had shrunk, like a much-loved cuddly toy in the wash; and the little things that used to cry out welcomingly – 'Home again, Amy!' were all defaced. No smiling faces greeted her, no business as usual, no men, no Maggie. In their place were unchecked weeds and scrawny fowl; sprawling, lustreless laurels plastered in hen mess; straggly nasturtiums, the only bit of colour, and that faded, in sight, whose sole hope of survival was to creep further and further into the street. No matter which way Amy looked, the picture was the same: collapsed stone walls; fields, hills and every other vista obliterated by ragged uncut hedges; and in the midst of it all, the ruin of her old home – an ignoble pile of charred masonry and amok ivy.

Unnerved by the lack of life – clucking and grunting were all she could hear – and feeling a lot less confident now about the outcome of her visit than when Jo had dropped her off, Amy walked across to the coach-house from whose chimney smoke was rising. The wide opening into the coach-house from the back lane had been bricked up, as had her Great Uncle Joshua's surgery entrance at the top of the well-worn, stone steps leading up to it from the street. In their place, a new door had been installed giving access to the house from the street on the ground floor.

Amy knocked on the door.

A guarded Lottie opened it.

'Hello,' Amy said, instantly recognising her niece. Lottie had changed. In keeping with her sixteen years, her figure had matured; and her face was so serious and grown-up looking, it could have come out of a medieval painting. But nothing could hide her resemblance to Henry; her eyes, colouring and build were still his, as was her smile when, satisfied by Amy's tone her Aunt had not come to judge, she let down her guard.

'Hello,' she said, at once shyly and eagerly. 'You're Auntie Amy, aren't you?'

'And who else would I be?' Amy replied, a little concerned about her own appearance less than ten years on from when she'd last seen her niece. 'I've not changed that much, have I?' she added, reassured by Lottie's smile and manner that nothing else terrible had happened at Shandoran.

Lottie blushed, and Amy gave her a big hug and smiled at Luke and Billy who had appeared behind her. Both were barefoot.

'Come on in, Auntie,' Lottie said, not the least embarrassed by her surroundings, 'and I'll tell Mummy you're here. She's not feeling well today. It's her legs again. They're very swollen. An' her head's bad too.'

'I'm sorry', Amy said, following her niece inside. Legs, headaches, backaches, she thought – though not unkindly. No change there!

As Lottie made for the fire to put the kettle on, Amy adjusted to the gloom. Through it she deciphered: a small, deep-set, curtainless window; bare stone walls and stone-flagged floor; scraps of furniture; shadowy figures near the fire; bannisterless stairs which must have been hastily installed as there had been no internal link between the coach-house's two floors before the fire. Overall, she got the impression the heart had been ripped out of Shandoran, and its inhabitants were either unable or unwilling to do anything about it.

There was no sign of Henry, and Amy was just about to ask where he was when Harriet called out sharply from above –

'Who's that? Is that you, Amy? Bring her up, Lottie, and make us a cup of tea.' No change there either, Amy mused.

Lottie and Amy climbed the bannisterless stairs. 'Go carefully, Auntie', Lottie cautioned, 'Some of the boards are loose.' Amy found her niece's lack of shame, humbling.

Upstairs, thanks largely to Joshua who liked to see who was approaching his surgery, it was brighter than below. What had been a single room – Joshua's surgery first, John Fisher and Tom Linnaker's office next – had been crudely partitioned into two rooms, each with its own window; Henry and Harriet's overlooked the street; their children's, the lane. Apart from a bed and small cupboard, the master bedroom was bare; the stairs led straight into it.

Lottie returned to the kitchen, and Amy and Harriet greeted each other.

Though desperate to inquire about Henry, Amy refrained from doing so not wanting to give the impression she was more concerned about her brother than her sister-in-law. Also, Harriet's appearance, or what Amy could see of it, was genuinely shocking: care and hardship were disfiguring her more brutally than were the elements the avenue gates. Most noticeably altered were Harriet's hair and hands. The former had lost its sheen and was entirely grey. The latter, roughened and red raw, were unlikely – even if Joshua's piano had not been in ashes – ever to make music again. For the rest, despair had replaced the allure in Harriet's hooded eyes; humiliation seen off her youthful mien. Amy felt truly sorry for her.

At the same time, Henry's absence, coupled with his wife's alteration for the worse revived the anxieties Amy's nightmare at Knockmore, and Harriet's letter had produced in her. In the oncoming minutes, far from being assuaged by what Harriet said, Amy's anxieties mounted steadily.

When she expressed concern about Harriet's health, Harriet made light of her indisposition. 'It's only a turn, Amy, it'll pass. The headache's gone now and the rest'll soon settle. I suppose it's the pregnancy upsetting me. We just wanted the one more, you see, for the fresh start an' that…'

Equally dismissive was Harriet when Amy pointed out the dangers of the loose boards and railless stairs down which Lottie, after she'd delivered two cracked mugs of tea, scuttled to resolve a suddenly erupted commotion among her siblings. 'Don't worry, Amy,' Harriet said, 'we're all used to them.' In the past, Henry would have been castigated for not doing something about them.

Finally, when Amy enquired directly after Henry, Harriet's concern was manifest. Clasping her unsightly hands tightly round her mug, she said, anxiously, 'He's not good, Amy; not good at all; I wish I could say what *was* the matter with him. He won't talk about it, you see. Not about his crime, or prison, or what's troubling him now. Maybe he'll talk to you. I hope so, Amy, I really do. Prison has taken its toll…I know that… and expected it. But I never imagined it could change a man so. I'm not saying Henry didn't deserve to be punished…of course he did. He must have known he couldn't get away with it. Men like him – he's not a bad man, Amy – never do. But men like him don't get over imprisonment easily either…not the way real criminals do. Physically he's fine…I'm certain of that. It's…'

'Is he about?' Amy asked, suddenly gripped with panic and hurriedly getting to her feet, her confidence in Henry's ability to bounce back from adversity fast receding.

Harriet shook her head. 'No,' she said hopelessly, 'an' I dunno where he is. He went out as soon as he heard the car, saying he couldn't face you in this place…' with a tired movement of her arm, Harriet indicated the surrounding squalor, her only reference to it so far '…and that you'd know where to find him.'

'I suppose he means the dell,' Amy muttered from the top of the stairs, trying not to sound alarmist. 'I'd best get over there. You stay where you are, Harriet. I'll give Lottie a hand with the tea when I get back.' Harriet didn't protest and Amy retreated as speedily as she safely could down the stairs. 'And put on the old boots by the door,' commanded her sister-in-law before she reached the bottom. Too worried to give that the smile it deserved, Amy took the boots that Lottie was already holding out in the kitchen and changed into them.

Chapter Twenty-seven

Once outside, Amy walked quickly across the street and round the ruined pile of her old home to the once-flourishing kitchen-garden and orchard behind it. Like everything else in the place, the kitchen-garden had shrunk, but someone – Lottie, Amy supposed – had planted a few cabbages and potatoes in it. In the orchard, most of the apples were going to waste, or fattening starlings.

By the time Amy reached the wood, not a dense one, she was half-running, half-walking. She pressed on, telling herself repeatedly not to be so silly, to calm down. Relentlessly her pace quickened as graphic images of her brother – pushed to the brink of despair, 'And by all forgot, we rot and rot' – forced their way into her mind. It's Phil all over, she thought – only different. Phil had thrown his life away with a wilfulness that defied reason. Henry would act out of desperation. Desperation had driven him to set fire to Shandoran. (Amy was certain of that now even if she still could not fathom what, other than insurance had really lain behind the deed.) Desperation would be driving him on at this very moment. By the time she reached him... Oh, God! Don't let him do it, she prayed, remembering the availability of rope at Shandoran for rescue work in the bogs; and the availability of a firearm.

Frantic to get to the dell, reproaching herself for not having come to Shandoran sooner, and off her own bat – you stupid, stupid woman, she thought – Amy speeded up some more. In her haste – the boots didn't help – she tripped over an exposed root, fell flat on her face and swore out loud. Picking herself up – clutching her bag, ignoring her hat, it had fallen off – she rushed on, with earth and leaves clinging to her coat. Don't let me be too late! Don't let me be too late! she prayed, over and over, in time to her pounding heart.

While still some way off, she saw Henry through the trees.

He was standing on the banks of the Little Lisanne – hunched, tousled, his hands buried in his pockets. The same old Henry,

Amy thought, slowing to a walk, relieved beyond words to see her brother alive. Yet not quite the same – for appearances, she knew, could be deceptive: 'And all but lust is turned to dust in Humanity's machine…'

The twigs snapped loudly under her feet; Henry didn't turn round to greet her.

Closing the gap between them, taking what comfort she could from her surroundings, from the old oak that dominated the dell in particular, Amy stood beside her brother – fearful now of rejection, embarrassed by her panting, unable to articulate anything, not even hello. Henry was struck dumb too, and so quiet was it in the intervals of birdsong the stream's tiniest ripples were audible. In the shallows, a single remaining phial, its colour so blurred it was impossible to say what its original shade had been, was rocking to and fro on the end of a bit of weed, as though clinging on and trying to break free.

'I'm so, so, sorry, Henry,' Amy said, at last.

A long silence followed. And as brother and sister stood there side by side – so close, so sad – Henry knew his sister's 'sorry' was as much for not having come to see him sooner as for his suffering; it struck him as odd that *she* was apologising to him. He wanted to say sorry too, only emotion choked his words. In the stream, the reflection of a small patch of blue sky reminded Amy of another of Wilde's lines: 'Upon that little tent of blue…' Holding back a tear, she glanced at her brother. His tautness and a question in her mind – However did he survive it? – released the tear and loosened her tongue. Tenderly she asked – 'Was it very bad inside?'

'Terri…' It was too much for Henry. Amy lost her voice again too. The pair of them stared at the stream, and at the lone, indeterminately coloured phial in its shallows.

Then Henry tried again to speak. He broke down, shaking and sobbing uncontrollably. Deeply moved, Amy took his arm. 'Come on over here and sit down,' she said. Gently she guided him to the oak, and when they were both seated under it – she in the ill-fitting boots, he with his hands idle – waited till he'd calmed a little, just like in the old days after a beating, before slowly drawing him into conversation. In his own way and time he would tell her everything; she could sense that he wanted to, and would be patient and wait for her cue if he needed a prompt.

'Do you remember the day we discovered this place with Doxey?' she said, talking more to herself than her brother, and handing him a cigarette from the depths of her bag. As she lit it, she noticed Henry's face had got thinner, making his cheekbones more prominent. 'My how she fussed when we found the stream and the coloured bottles!' she went on. 'And told us the bottles had been Great Uncle Joshua's, and not to get our clothes dirty. It must 'a' bin a Sunday. Yes. And the evening before would have been bath-night... with her never ending threats to cut out our bedtime story if we misbehaved. Mind you! She only had two stories...'

'Aye,' Henry put in, 'but didn't she vary them wondrously in the telling!'

'You remember them!' Amy said, astonished her brother could recall a thing like that after all he'd been through.

'I do,' he rejoined.

Encouraged, if still mystified, Amy expanded on her theme. 'Lucy and I liked *Us and Our Donkey* best – didn't we! It was about a poor clergyman's children who gave rides on their donkey to supplement the father's income. Now what was the other one called...?'

'*What Happened To Ted?*' – Henry said, straight off. 'Don't you remember it? Ted was the little boy stolen by the gypsies. An' he had a different adventure every time we heard it. Do you think he was ever found?' A half-smile accompanied this.

Amy laughed. 'I'm amazed you remember them,' she said.

'God, Amy, I remembered everything in that hell-hole!' Henry paused reflectively, much calmer now than at the outset. 'I was lucky with my cell mate,' he resumed at last. 'An old fella called Jed, he was, who couldn't stop thieving. He liked me from the start, I think, and could see I was a bit fiery. One of the first things he said to me was – "Keep your nose clean in here, man, and get out as soon as you can. The turnkeys don't take kindly to disobedience." The last thing he said to me was – "I'll miss you, man."'

For a minute or two Henry fell silent. Amy stayed quiet as a mouse.

'I often think about Jed,' her brother went on. 'For without him God alone knows how I'd have ended up. He used to talk to me at night when I couldn't sleep for worry about what I'd done. We talked about our childhood; his father died when he was young too. About things I thought had been buried forever the night I buried Barney. Jed brought it all back – the good times with my father I mean. Fishing with him in Shandoran Lake, our gallops across the estate; the day he came home with Barney. It made the nights bearable, Amy; stopped me thinking about Harriet and the children. Thinking about *them*, nearly drove me mad.'

Once again, Henry fell silent. Dredging his butt, he stubbed it on the ground. Then, turning to Amy, he looked at her with moist eyes and said ruefully – 'There's no getting away from them now sis, is there! I've ruined everything. Haven't I!'

Taking that as her cue, Amy asked quietly. 'Why did you do it, Henry? It wasn't just the insurance, was it?'

Henry shuffled, reluctant even now to spell it out but desperately wanting to. 'I don't know what got into me,' he said awkwardly. 'Yes I do,' he reneged guiltily. Staring at the ground, he focussed on one of many acorns – flicking them in the air no longer appealed – and struggled to collect his thoughts. Putting the latter in order did not come easily to him at the best of times, and he had never verbalised this particular set before – not even to Jed; in prison he'd stuck to the insurance line. Amy waited.

'What set me off – no two ways about it,' her brother

continued at last, 'was the promise of insurance. I'm not blaming Jo, mind! He gave me the idea but warned me about the inspectors; I was the one who did it. A small conflagration was all I planned, of course; to shake off the debts before you came home on leave; start over with a clean slate; make you, Harriet and the children proud of me. Sure there was no pleasing her, Amy! Whatever I did was wrong in her eyes. Not that I'm blaming her either. I'm to blame. Everything comes back to me. I know that now. I must have been mad to think I could get away with it. I was certainly drunk. And very angry! Angry with everyone, except...'

A discernible crack choked Henry's words. Steadying his voice, he went on. 'Mostly I was angry with myself and Harriet. She never gave me a moment's peace – not a word of encouragement. Sometimes I thought she was turning into my mother. God, how I loathed that woman! – and the thought of him and her prospering at Knockmore was killing me. I saw her again you see, on the way home from the pub – her and her smirking face, just as it was the night I put Barney down. I never told you about that, did I? I never told any one. How I longed to wipe the smirk away. To put shame in its place, the kind of shame – may God forgive me, Amy – that landing myself in gaol would bring. I was mad to even think about it. But I did. Then suddenly I saw Maggie – God's truth – walking towards me on the road, smiling her sweet smile. I'd been thinking about her earlier in the day in Kilbeg when I took Harriet into McPhearson with her bad back. I often thought about Maggie in Kilbeg – I suppose you did too – and about her lonely end in the Lake there; it must 'a' bin terrible. I saw her as clear as I see you now, Amy. Seeing her so clearly, so kind and uncritical, nearly broke my heart. How could I have let her down? Such treachery needed punishing.'

'Come on now, Henry,' Amy broke in – her brother was becoming distraught again – 'we were all to blame for Maggie's death.'

'No, Amy. I let it happen. I should have never have given

in to Harriet. Maggie trusted me; I betrayed her trust. By the time I got back to Shandoran I was so riddled with guilt I scarcely knew what I was doing. My head was swirling. My thoughts pulling me this way and that; my guilt driving me on, driving me to douse the wood chippings in the scullery with petrol – Lottie kept them topped up; God, what a wonderful girl she is – to strike the match, Amy, the cursed match…'

'It's all right, Henry,' Amy said, anxious now to end her brother's agony; she'd heard enough. His explanation of events had been truly enlightening – especially regarding the extent to which Maggie's death – and Barney's – had affected his life; the latter had blighted his childhood; the former, his manhood. In the final analysis though, Henry's motivation had been just as she'd thought: half-crazed, he'd acted on impulse.

'And don't lecture me about it,' he said to her. 'I've had time enough and more to repent my sins. Jesus, Amy, it was Hell on earth in there.'

'I know,' his sister put in quickly, resting her hand on his arm. 'And I wasn't going to lecture you, Henry; I didn't come here to do that. If you must know, I was so pleased to see you, lecturing was the *last* thing on my mind. I..I thought…'

'I know what you thought,' Henry said, giving his sister a sideways glance that made her ashamed of her thought. 'But you needn't have feared,' her brother went on, 'I've learned my lesson and will *never* let Harriet and the children down again.'

Thankful for that and much more, Amy looked at the fading light. She was about to stand up, when Henry said – 'He's buried here, you know!'

At first, she didn't know what he was talking about. Then it came to her. So this was where her brother had spent his last moments with his cocker, Barney! She should have guessed.

Taking hold of Henry's hand, Amy squeezed it and, still holding it, listened while he told her – without tears, too much tragedy had intervened – what had happened all those years ago. It was the first time, he said, he'd told anyone about it.

'And I'll tell you something else for free!' he tagged on at the end. 'I don't hate her any more.' 'I'm glad,' Amy said, squeezing her brother's hand again.

On the way back to the house she self-consciously retrieved her hat. Henry laughed, put his arm round her, and pulled her close. 'You came, sis,' he said. To Amy, that on its own made her visit worth while. A little later, she tentatively suggested her brother sell Shandoran and buy another place – something smaller and more diverse. 'Sugar beet's good,' she said, aware of how much money the Linnakers were making out of that crop, the latest addition to their mixed farm. Henry wouldn't hear of it. 'Me and the boys are doing just fine,' he said. 'We'll have the flax fields back under the plough in no time.'

'That's the spirit,' his sister said, reluctant to pour cold water on his plans, as they emerged from the wood. At thirty-nine, Henry had plenty going for him – his age, his family, and the land, some of which had been sold to clear the debts but most of which remained.

Half way across the orchard, Amy spotted a big, rosy apple. She slowed to pick it up. 'How's the old faggot anyway?' Henry said, booting it to oblivion. 'Henry!' Amy exploded – nearly as much for the loss of the apple as for the unkind allusion to their mother. But her indignation was half-hearted: that Henry had asked after Eleanor was proof enough his hatred of their mother was gone. In seeking to punish her, he had acted spontaneously, not from a desire for revenge; he didn't harbour grudges; wasn't a vindictive man. Amy told him the Linnakers were well. Henry's next words took her completely by surprise. 'She doesn't care, does she?' he said. 'She does,' Amy said, 'and about my visiting you now too. But she'll get over it.' Henry grunted – 'Ah sure maybe it's just as well, sis.'

In the tangle of her mind a single thought held Amy's attention above the rest. Henry had come through his ordeal thanks, in no small measure, to a thief called Jed – a man who had kept Henry on the straight and narrow in prison; made the long nights there bearable for him and, above all, made his childhood memorable again. Who was it, she wondered who wrote (Phil would have known!) that 'even if only one good memory is left in our hearts, it may also be the instrument of our salvation one day'?

◇

In the coach-house, Harriet was up and about, and a meal prepared – cold pork, apple sauce, and soda bread. Not all the apples were going to waste then! Amy thought, as everyone tucked in. She commented on the soda bread, which was particularly tasty. Harriet said Lottie had made it. 'She's done everything, Amy,' she added, indicating all the food on the table. Lottie smiled shyly and pointed out the careful way she'd cut her cross over the sides of the soda cake to prevent it cracking.

Shyly too, Lottie admired Amy's frock. Stylish and made of jersey, one of the newer materials – it was warm and comfortable, 'And *very* hard-wearing!' Amy said, making everyone smile. Harriet's smile brought home to her the true extent of her sister-in-law's suffering, something the removal of the bedcovers had already magnified: aside from her hair, hands and mien, oedema had thickened Harriet's once lovely legs; humiliation seen off her youthful gait. Her smile was lustreless. Less than three years older than Henry, she could have been his mother; with a shawl, an old shawleen.

'I suppose your mother helps out where she can,' Amy said, more worried about Harriet now than Henry.

'No,' Harriet replied, 'my mother's ashamed of us. Everyone's ashamed of us, Amy. And who could blame them!'

Two things struck Amy. She remembered Maggie, and thought – the wheel has come full circle; Harriet's the embarrassment at Shandoran now. She noticed the sarcasm in Harriet's voice – the first she'd heard since her arrival – and the sheepish look on Henry's face, and hurt in Lottie's eyes. A lingering puzzle was solved for her. To the extent Henry was all Harriet had (she needed him as never before), her concern for him was genuine;

but she was not about to let him forget what he had done – now that he appeared so much better. Harriet had her stick.

That night, Amy slept on the old, walnut scroll settee – one of a very few items to have survived both the Linnakers' departure from Shandoran and the fire. It was a long time before she fell asleep, and not just because bits of horsehair stuffing were sticking into her. She thought of what had been and of how it might have been…if ifs an' ans… of Henry and Harriet's misfortunes; and of her own, which were as nothing to theirs: a common cold to pneumonia, a cough to whooping-cough.

Looking around, Amy picked out the meagre bits of furniture in the room; moonlight through the curtainless window and an occasional flicker from the banked-down fire threw them into relief. She imagined what had been there before: traps, ropes, harnessing, spares; even, on occasion, Stella; rusty nails and hooks were still stuck in the walls. My God! Amy thought. To have sunk so low! Individuals, families, whole generations worked their way to the top; then, slap, bang – it was gone. What, she wondered, had it all been for?

She looked at the moon, a full one, and, glad it wasn't new (that would have been unlucky), thought how pure and serene it was compared with the wretched state of things around her and the continuing uncertainty inside her. Her visit, she knew, had not been wasted. Without her, Henry was already getting to grips with what he'd done; already moving on; and that – moving on – was what mattered. Her presence was helping the process along. There was a question mark in her mind about Harriet; she wasn't well. That aside, the family had a home, and the coach-house, mean though it was, was every bit, and more, as roomy as any of the tied cottages scattered across the estate… cottages in which families twice the size of theirs had been surviving – without land – for centuries. In the greater scheme of things, tragedy was cut down to size.

Once again, Amy picked out the room's contents. They seemed clearer now than before. She looked at the moon again, and as she gazed at it, wondering how she could have stayed away from her brother and Shandoran for so long, and where the equanimity and purpose that had once pervaded her life had gone, it seemed to grow bigger. Bigger and bigger, till, like an unburstable balloon, it filled the whole window space, spilled over into the coach-house and her soul. Its luminosity, tranquillity and purity took over her being; she *felt* them, intensely.

Inexplicably, Amy felt whole again; at one with herself, her God, and her battered heritage. Never again would she be ashamed of her past; of anything in her black tin trunk. Perfection was an illusion; she had always known it; just allowed herself to deny it. Nothing and no one were quite what they seemed. The best and worst were all mixed up, and while nothing was lost for good, nothing remained the same either. You had to see and face up to things as they were…to yourself as you were. Running away or amok were not options. Starting over was an illusion; we weren't machines. For too long Phil, Henry and she had been trying to escape from themselves and their world – Phil, by going East, and with the aid of drink; she, by hankering for a mythical past, and refusing to face up to the reality of Henry's crime. And Henry, by allowing emotion to cloud not just the best part of his childhood – the part that can steady us when the ground beneath our feet gives way – but also what little reason he had, and blaming others for his predicament. She and Phil had done their share of blame-transposal too. In a way, they had all been living a lie, refusing to see straight. It was important to remember the past – the totality of our experiences made us what we were – but not to be enslaved by it; letting go was as important as holding on. To acknowledge the truth, and live with it deep inside, in the place that made you you, where ultimate healing lay. Exclusivism, Amy concluded, was a kind of darkness. It stunted growth.

Bathed in moonlight, Amy wanted to cry out, 'Thank you, God,' then realised 'Forgive me, God,' might be more appropriate. She asked for forgiveness then gave thanks for already feeling forgiven. After that she went to sleep.

◇

Before the year was out, Amy got a telegram from Lottie to say Harriet had died. Apart from the date of the funeral, there were no details.

To her extreme annoyance, Amy was unable to go to the funeral: Robbie and Ruth had measles, and Angela was sickening for it; it simply wasn't possible to leave them all with the nuns. As soon as she could, she made a flying visit to Shandoran.

The evening before she left St Hilda's, she was packing, and putting things away in her room, when a knock on the door heralded the arrival of her children: Sister Martha had said they could spend some time with her as she was going away the next day. She read them *The Selfish Giant* – a story they loved – from a bumper book, and left them looking at the pictures while she resumed her sorting. Kneeling down, she reached into her trunk, and was overcome by an urge to dig out the flat package at the bottom. Opening it for the first time, she experienced a huge wave of emotion – love, pride and sadness rolled into one – as *Flaxfields* was revealed. Sitting back on her heels, she held it up to the light and let the beauty of her once-lovely home seep through her – without shame. She saw and imbibed the whole picture.

'Is that what your hair was like, Mummy, when you were a little girl?' a small voice behind her asked. It was Ruth's. She and Angela – both of whom had short manageable hair – had crept up on their mother, and though they had never seen the picture before, Amy had told them a lot about her childhood.

'Yes, darling,' she replied, 'only less biddable.'

The girls laughed, as did Robbie who now joined them. Biddable was a word they all understood: it was what Angela wasn't.

'Are those bluebells?' Robbie asked then, indicating the picture's lush blue foreground.

'No, silly,' Amy said, thinking what townies her children were despite their holidays at Knockmore. 'It's flax. You remember I told you we grew flax on the estate. The picture reminds me of it. Like that little poem I taught you – "I remember, I remember…"'

Robbie took up the verse, and went right to the end, with one or two prompts from Amy. He had Phil's love of words, and she was glad she'd changed her mind about sending him to Glenarkle, and written to Mr Appleby.

Then Angela asked what the two boys in the picture were doing, and when Amy told her, said – 'I don't like fish,' which was no news to any of them; in vain, Sister Martha as well as Amy had tried to impart to the child the brain enhancing powers of her Friday fish portion.

'It must have been lovely,' Ruth said, her big, brown eyes still glued to *Flaxfields*.

'It was,' Amy affirmed, 'truly beautiful.' Then putting the picture down, she put her arms round her children and drew them close to her. 'But this is only a picture, my darlings,' she went on. 'You know as well as I do, we had black skies, thunderous ones sometimes…,' a little squeeze accompanied this, 'at Shandoran too. One day I'll tell you the whole story.'

The children wanted to hear it then, but Amy said no: it was past their bedtime and it wouldn't do to make Sister Martha angry after she'd been so kind to them. Angela protested. Amy was firm.

After the children had gone, she had an idea. She mulled it over, then finished packing. Later, she went to bed, wondering how her sister-in-law had met her end.

At Shandoran, next day, no one knew for sure what had happened to Harriet; it was assumed she'd lost her footing on the stairs and collapsed at the bottom.

('Loose boards' and 'railless stairs' were not referred to.)

When Henry found her, she was dead, with their premature baby a lifeless heap between her legs. The funeral had been low key. Only Reverend Badell, Henry, Harriet's mother, and Lottie and her four brothers and sisters were at the graveside. It drizzled non-stop.

'I never saw Daddy so sad as on that day,' Lottie told Amy in a quiet moment together. 'But he'll get over it, Auntie,' she added. 'I'll look after him; and after my brothers and sisters too. We'll be all right. And you'll come back and see us again soon, won't you?'

Amy said she would, and meant it. Lottie's courage in adversity was awesome, she thought. As for her lack of shame in adversity – Lottie did naturally what Amy had taken the thirty-seven years of her life to date to do.

Tentatively, then, Amy went to her case, and took *Flaxfields* out of it. 'Would you like it?' she asked, handing it to her niece. As Lottie took it, and moved to the window to examine it, Amy told her how she'd come by it and about having nowhere of her own to hang it; and about her children being such awful townies. 'It's beautiful, Auntie,' Lottie said, 'I'll treasure it always. Thank you.' With that, she selected a nail from the many on the walls and hung the picture up. Her accompanying words – 'I'll find a brighter wall for it in our next home, Auntie,' astonished Amy.

'Has your Daddy decided to sell, then?' Amy asked, deliberately not having mentioned the subject earlier on account of Harriet's death being so recent.

'No,' Lottie replied. Then – trustingly, and with a hint of mischief and world of wisdom in her lovely chestnut eyes – she added, 'But he will! And it's horses I really like, Auntie, not flax!'

Amy smiled. Amen, to that, she thought.

Lightning Source UK Ltd.
Milton Keynes UK
UKOW050021110412

190466UK00001B/4/P